LIVING HALF FREE

Haley Whitehall

Expanding Horizons Press

Expanding
Horizons
Press

Published by Expanding Horizons Press
1250 N. Wenatchee Ave., Suite H #322
Wenatchee, WA 98801

Living Half Free

Manufactured in the United States of America

First Edition

ISBN: 978-0-985-18281-6
E-ISBN: 978-0-985-18280-9
LCCN: 2012934037

Dedicated to my parents:
Pete and Patti Whitehall
For their belief, support, and love

ACKNOWLEDGMENTS

I did not do this alone. Many people helped me. It takes a whole team to bring a book to life. Thank you to my manuscript readers for patient guidance: Molly Steere, Nancy Trucano, Morgan Frasier, Anita Van Stralen, and Dan Gemeinhart. Thank you to my editors Sandra Bell Kirchman, Ashley McConnell, and Yvette Davis. You brought clarity to my story and taught me along the way. Thank you to my proofreader Cathy Pike for putting on the polish and to my friend Angie Pike for unflagging support. Finally, thanks, again, to my parents who always encouraged my love of writing and love for books. You've nurtured my dream all these years. This book would not be possible without you.

Author's Note

Great care was taken to write a historically accurate novel set in the antebellum South. Language that was acceptable during that era was used to convey attitudes of that time. If you will think you will be offended by these words, please do not read.

Chapter 1

Strasburg, Virginia
July 13, 1838

ZACHARIAH LAID IN the grass behind the restaurant, his flesh quivering. A copper-haired man stood over him, cowhide whip in hand.

Zachariah wished he could have been staked down or tied from a tree like a normal nigger. Master Norton got delight at watching his slaves jump every time the strap hit.

"You know better than to spill a tray. And in a customer's lap, no less," Master Norton said, low and harsh.

"Yes, Massa," Zachariah choked out.

The whip dug sharply into his back. "Do Massa," he moaned over and over and over. His muscles spasmed in jerky motions.

"Jump rope, nigger," Norton said, plying the whip over Zachariah's shoulders. With a steady hand, he raised the cowhide, generated strength and then the lash descended upon Zachariah's shuddering flesh.

The whip raised large welts and cut the skin, forcing warm blood to trickle down Zachariah's back, dyeing the grass with red dew. Salty tears blurred his vision, and burned his dry, flushed cheeks. His hands clawed the dirt, grasping for something to hold onto, something to hold back the pain.

Finally, Norton stopped. "Get up and fetch firewood to keep the stove hot," he said in a rugged rumble. "I will have Rachel clean up your mess."

"Yes, Massa." Zachariah chewed the inside of his cheek to keep from voicing pain. He picked up his white shirt and black frock coat with frayed elbows but did not put them on. He didn't dare stain his restaurant attire. He set them on a boulder.

The ax stuck in the stump in the middle of the lawn stared at him. Bending over, thrusting the ax into wood, brought agony. Pain shot from his shoulders all the way down to his waist. His fresh welts burned as if smoldering coals were pressed to his skin. He bit his tongue to keep from shouting with each swing. Self-respecting slaves endured pain silently. He had made enough noise already—more than a woman, Ma would say.

Zachariah examined his pale arms as he had done countless times before. His skin was called yellow, though it looked white to him. Most of his flesh wasn't even tan; just his hands, neck and face, since they were exposed to the sun when he worked outside.

"Damn my skin," he muttered. "Wish I's all black, black as boot polish." None of Master Norton's slaves mentioned it, but he knew he was an oddity. How many slaves had yellow skin, golden hair and blue eyes? The fact his hair was waved meant nothing to him. To everyone else it was the only sign of his negro blood.

When he'd finished with the required armload, Ma walked out to him carrying a small jar, her jaw firmly set, fire in her normally kind gray eyes. Without a word, she cleaned and dressed his wounds.

Zachariah grimaced and pulled forward. Her hand followed him, tracing every cut on his back, sealing in the permanent shame and humiliation which would last till his death.

He wanted her touch, but hers was the touch of a nurse, not a caring mother.

"Massa doan like me," Zachariah said.

"Massa doan care 'bout you none atall," Ma said, clear, sharp. "You's a nigger. God made you to serve white people."

"I is a white person," he whispered, insistent.

"No you ain't. You's imitation white. You got de curse of Ham in you."

Zachariah's ears burned and the fiery sensation spread down his neck. There was no way to get rid of the curse of Ham. That's what Preacher Simon said.

"You should feel blessed you's indoors most de time an working for a good Christian massa."

"Just cause Massa lets you go to de colored church you think he's powerful nice."

Ma boxed his right ear.

"Dat's right. In some ways you's a man, Zachariah, but in so many others, you's still a boy. You's fifteen years old and dat's de first severe whipping you's ever got. We doan huv to be up at de crack of dawn to work in de fields wid an overseer standing over us. We get beans wid our meals. You know how lucky we is to get beans?"

Zachariah nodded, to keep from getting his ears boxed. He didn't feel lucky. He felt like the dregs in a cup of black coffee.

*   *   *

The next day, Zachariah returned to serving customers. Walking into the restaurant, he felt the prickle of self-consciousness. His backside, sore from his whipping, made his gait awkward stiff. He knew everyone would notice his ungainly tread and realize the reason for it. He walked to the first occupied table. A middle-aged man and a younger one with hostile eyes watched each step as he approached.

"Took you long enough," the younger man said. "I am hungry."

"Sorry, suh. We just open. What would you like to order?"

"A fried pork chop, two fried eggs and a biscuit with butter, not gravy," the man said.

"And you?"

The older man smiled. "The same."

"Would you like coffee, suh?"

Both men nodded.

Zachariah returned to the kitchen. He walked over to the corner and batted his little sister's braids.

Rachel scowled, gripping her sewing sampler. "Stop dat."

Zachariah allowed himself a gentle laugh. "You huv it easy. All you huv to do is practice yo' sewing and fetch water."

Rachel shrugged and heaved a loud sigh. She stared longingly out the small window. "I's rather be playing outside."

Ma stepped back from the stove and boxed Zachariah's right ear. "Keep focused on yo' work. What did dey order?"

Zachariah's mouth parted. "Both of dem wanted a pork chop, two eggs and a biscuit with butter, and coffee," he said, trying to massage the ringing out of his ear.

Ma cracked two brown eggs into a frying pan and turned the pork chops, already cooking, in another.

Once the food was cooked, Zachariah carried out their plates and then waited on the elderly couple finding their seats.

Zachariah returned to the kitchen, told Ma the orders, and quickly downed a cup of coffee. He gulped it so fast he barely tasted it, though a lingering bitterness stayed in his mouth. Ma said they were lucky to be given coffee. Since it was a privilege, he had to accept it.

The yeasty biscuits, spicy white gravy and greasy pork tempted him to steal a bite. He didn't. At eleven o'clock, Ma would have hot cornbread for all of Norton's slaves. It wasn't fair. Zachariah covered his mouth to hold in the complaints. Thinking like that caused trouble.

Later, Zachariah crowded into the kitchen with Rachel, Ma, Michael, the other waiter, and Ellen, Master Norton's maid. Ma handed each of them an iron spoon and tin plate, with the usual brick of cornbread and beans. They stood and ate. The only place to sit in the kitchen was Rachel's stool and out of respect for the others she never used it for meals.

Zachariah sighed. Some day they'd have a table and chairs, even if he had to make them himself. Even twenty minutes off his feet would be a blessing.

Michael and Ellen carried on a conversation in low voices. The walls always had ears, Ma often said, reminding Zachariah and Rachel to watch their tongues. Slaves rarely had privacy and a stray word overheard by a customer or a passerby could cause a heap of trouble.

Zachariah hated to eat in silence. He wanted to add to the conversation. Should he tell them the dream he had had the night before—the very strange dream? A giant eagle had picked him up by his arms and carried him to a strange land where most of the people were a reddish color.

The most beautiful woman he had ever seen, with piercing green eyes, welcomed him. She dressed like the rich ladies who came to the restaurant in a long gown with a sloping neckline that showed off her shoulders. With one finger, she beckoned him to come nearer. He took a step forward. Instant attraction pulled him closer. Soon he was in her arms kissing her lips and cheeks and neck.

Zachariah touched his tongue to his bottom lip. He'd better keep the pleasant thought to himself. They'd probably scoff at his secret desires.

Zachariah rested his cheek in the palm of his hand and watched Rachel. She looked younger than nine in her blue-and-white-checkered, Osnaburg dress, her dark brown pigtails slightly lopsided. Disregarding manners, she devoured her beans.

"I's sick of cornbread," Rachel complained.

Ma reached down and took it off her plate. "Den you doan huv to eat it," she said.

Rachel's bottom lip stuck out and quivered. Zachariah wanted to give her his cornbread, but if he did, she would not learn her lesson. Instead, he put a caring hand on his sister's shoulder.

*　　*　　*

"Zachariah," Master Norton called loudly.

Zachariah set down his empty plate and headed into the restaurant. His master was talking to the middle-aged man he had waited on first that morning. Zachariah's forehead wrinkled and he cocked his head to the left. Why would he be back so soon? He couldn't be hungry.

"Yes, Massa?" Zachariah asked, standing a step behind him.

Norton opened his mouth but no words came. "I need money," he said at last. "I've sold you to Alexander Galloway."

Zachariah's eyes shifted from Galloway to Norton. "Sold me? Did you sell my ma and sistah too?"

Norton shook his head. "I would not do it if I didn't need the money, Zachariah."

Zachariah lowered his gaze. "I understand," he mumbled. His new master, a slender man with a neatly trimmed beard and mustache, had a revolver bulging in the gun belt around his waist. Zachariah repeatedly licked his lips. Norton never carried a gun. He hoped Galloway never used it.

"Do my ma know?" Zachariah asked.

Norton looked away sheepishly, his face flushed. "No. I figured you could tell her."

Galloway waved at Zachariah. "Go on and do it, boy. I don't have all day."

"Yessuh."

"What did he want?" Ma asked, as soon as Zachariah entered the kitchen.

Zachariah didn't say a word. Tears flooded his eyes, rolled down his cheeks, dripped off his chin.

Ma set down her spoon. She touched his shoulder lightly. "What did he say?"

"He done sell me to one of the customers."

His announcement cracked in the air with the snap of an angry whip. Stunned, Ma gasped and blinked. Rachel started bawling, worrying the sleeve of her dress between her fingers. Ellen reached out and gripped Michael's hand. They'd all been together as a makeshift family since Rachel was born.

"Doan you cry now," Ma said. "You growed, Zachariah. Growed men doan cry. Self-pity ain't goin' to get you nowheres. De good Lawd say it's time for us to be split up, we's goin' to be split up."

"Yes'm."

Ma had faith in the Lord stronger than anyone he knew.

"You do what you's told and do it politely," Ma continued.

"I's be a good boy," Zachariah promised.

Ma boxed his right ear. "You's be a good man," Ma corrected. "You's a man now, Zachariah. You remember dat. You might got to put in a man's day's work. You can do it now. You's got muscles in dose arms."

"I work hard," he said, trying to massage the ringing out of his ear.

He always hated how cold his ma could be, though he had to admire her strength. She was always hard on him and Rachel. Often, a smile or a touch on the shoulder was all the affection that either of them received. After this terrible surprise, he needed love. He longed to hear that she cared for him.

"I's a good waiter. I—"

"Not no more you ain't," Ma interrupted. "You goin' to do what yo' new massa tells you to. You might be planting tobacco or picking cotton."

Zachariah swallowed fighting a surge of nausea. "Oh," he whispered.

Rachel ran over and gave him a tight hug, squeezing his ribs.

Zachariah grimaced. He endured the loving pain and caressed her head. "You's not goin' to forget yo' bruddah, is you, Rach?"

"No, I ain't goin' to forget you," she said, resting her head against his chest.

"Some day, I's goin' to come lookin' for you," Zachariah promised.

He thought about the glass jar buried in the ground under Ma's blanket in their cabin. Ma worked every Sunday washing clothes and moonlighted at night at times to earn money for the family. To earn money to get them all free. Despite its intended purpose, most of the time it went to an extra blanket or something. Easing their suffering seemed best. Freedom cost so much money it was impossible to figure.

Trying to forget the present, Zachariah gazed at the wall. He fingered her oily, dark brown hair.

His eyes flicked back to Ma. Grim lines on either side of her mouth exposed a woman for whom smiling was rare. "I's a man now and a man ought to know dis. Ma, will you finally tell me something?"

The corners of Ma's mouth stretched up ever so slightly, the effort making her shoulders hunch. Her gray eyes remained sad but sincere. "If I can."

"Who's my pa?"

Her cheeks turned fiery red.

"Is it Massa Norton?"

"No," Ma said. After a long moment of silence, she looked him in the eye. "Yo' pa is po' white trash. Yo' pa is de dirt under Massa Norton's feet. You needn't know a darn thing 'bout yo' pa."

7

Zachariah hung his head, disappointed. He had always wanted to know his pa; to have a father, be part of his family.

Ma's voice cracked as she spoke, "When you gets lonesome, you just look at de night sky. De same stars dat's above you is above Rachel and me. God's watchin' over us, just as he's watchin' over you."

"I will not forget, Ma."

The door to the kitchen opened and Mr. Galloway stood there. He eyed all the slaves in the kitchen before settling on Zachariah. "It is time to go."

"Yes, Massa." Zachariah took a deep breath. He had to be a man, a brave man.

Zachariah gave Rachel a peck on the cheek. Then he touched Ma's shoulder. "I love you," he said to both of them.

"I love you, too," Rachel replied with youthful quickness.

Ma nodded to him. A single tear glistened as it fell from her eye. Even if she didn't say it, he knew she loved him.

He lifted his head and walked out.

"I love you, son," Ma said soft, her voice unnaturally sweet.

Zachariah forced a tight smile, though his heart tore into a million pieces. He continued walking, his eyes straight ahead. He hoped Ma would somehow know how happy hearing those words made him.

Rachel's sniffling grew louder. His throat constricted, causing hot tears to nearly choke him. He quickened his step, fearing he couldn't hold in his emotions.

*　　*　　*

Zachariah's fake smile vanished when he saw the coffle waiting for him outside the jail. The fourteen men and seven women were handcuffed two and two and fastened to a long chain running between the two ranks. They were being guarded by a young, white man on a black stallion. This man, who only appeared to be a few years older than Zachariah, watched them with menacing green eyes, fingering the handle of a whip.

An old negro man, wearing a gray suit, drove a wagon that was stopped behind the coffle. Galloway looked Zachariah over with discerning hazel eyes before leading his newly acquired chattel to his place. "You complete the line," he said, as if that was a privilege.

Zachariah hung his head, bit his lip, felt the cold iron clamped around his left wrist. Ma's words echoed in his mind about being a man, and he was the lucky one shackled next to a woman; he didn't want to cry in front of her. She was pretty, though nearly old enough to be his ma. Her black skin looked velvety and her pale pink dress showed off all the curves of her body.

Galloway mounted his bay horse. "All right, let's go." He clicked his teeth, and his horse and the coffle started at once.

Zachariah raised his head, looked down the road then up at the sky. What would happen to him now?

Chapter 2

Strasburg, Virginia
July 14, 1838

DWELLING ON HIS uncertain future muddled Zachariah's mind. His aching heart made him numb to the present. Numb to the chains. Numb to being sold away from his family.

He had heard stories of slaves, not yet fully grown, being torn from their mother's breasts. He didn't figure he'd be one of them. Master Norton liked him. But being liked didn't pay the bills.

His skin and muscle did.

He didn't know why, but walking beside this woman eased the misery of leaving behind his family and friends. He kept glancing at her. She seemed to be ignoring him, until finally she lowered her head, offered a shy smile, and blushed. Zachariah's heart rate increased along with his breathing. He didn't even know her name. He opened his mouth to speak, but instead pretended to yawn.

He examined his other companions. They reeked of sweat, piss and fear. Most had sorrowful expressions. Those who didn't caught Zachariah's eye.

He was relieved he wasn't at the front of the column handcuffed to the stout, fleshy fellow who looked like he could break a man's neck with one hand. The tall, thin man chained to the large fellow seemed listless, resigned to his life of servitude.

Zachariah was pleased he wasn't the only yellow man in the coffle. The other yellow slave, in his late twenties, wore a fancy black suit and he held his head high, giving the air he felt superior to his fellow slaves. Zachariah wondered if he could read and write. Of course, if the man could, Zachariah doubted he'd admit to it since it was illegal.

He had difficulty judging the man chained to the fancily dressed slave. The youth wasn't much older than himself, his head completely shaved. Zachariah searched for the right word to describe him. He examined the man's sober face and slouched posture. He wasn't indifferent or ill or melancholy. Finally, Zachariah realized the young man had a broken spirit.

There was a slender woman with long, straight black hair. Zachariah felt the hateful fire burning in her brown eyes. The dark girl next to her stared at the ground. Zachariah wondered if Master Galloway intended to put the dangerous, intelligent slaves next to those he didn't think would pose a threat. Zachariah stole a glance at the beautiful woman next to him. Did Master Galloway consider her a threat? She didn't look like she'd cause trouble.

The silence of the coffle magnified the bleakness of the afternoon. Amidst the tread of feet and clank of chains came the caw of crows. The noise sent a shiver through Zachariah like a bitter wind. He wondered if it was an omen that he was headed for disaster.

After hours and hours and hours of watching the silent coffle, Master Galloway grew agitated. "Sing," he commanded. Everyone remained mute. "Sing," he repeated in a gruff roar. Zachariah began singing "Amazing Grace."

> *Amazing grace! How sweet de sound,*
> *Dat save a wretch like me!*
> *I once was lost but now I's found*
> *Was blind, but now I see.*

Zachariah completed the first verse and none of the other slaves had joined him. He found comfort in the words of the familiar hymn.

Beginning the second verse, he sang loudly. He wanted to spread his comfort.

Twas grace dat taught my heart to fear,
And grace my fears relieved;
How precious did dat grace appear
De hour I first believe!

The woman beside Zachariah joined him first. He admired her soprano voice, heavenly like from an angel. He admired more than her singing, he longed to feel her touch, see if it was as strong and tender as her voice. Her singing stirred such feeling, a longing he'd never felt before except in his dreams.

The entire coffle sang the last verse. The words uplifted Zachariah's spirit. He thought they sounded lovelier than when the whole congregation sang at Preacher Simon's church.

They finished, and again fell in to silence. Galloway rode his white horse to the back of the line. "Thank you for the hymn, Zachariah. You've earned yourself a double helping at supper."

Zachariah felt his lips start to twitch into a cautious smile barely showing his teeth. "Thank you, Massa."

"I do like that song," the young white man called back.

Galloway grunted. "I wish the words meant something to you."

Zachariah's feet ached, his ill-fitting shoes rubbing his heels raw. He grew tired of the seemingly endless walk. His stomach pained him. Would he ever get the double helping of supper he'd been promised?

Just when Zachariah thought his legs would give out, they halted on a road across from a plantation. In the distance stretched a beautiful sprawling lawn. What would rich people want with him? Zachariah wondered.

"We'll camp here," Galloway said.

"Yes, Pa," the young white man said.

"Do dat mean you's take our chains off?" Zachariah asked.

The young, white man's voice snapped. "You are sleeping in those chains."

Those words stripped Zachariah's face of vitality. "I doan mind sleeping in chains, young Massa," he replied.

"My name's Henry. You can call me that."

"Yes, Massa Henry."

*   *   *

Galloway unchained three of the women. They set to work making camp in the clearing alongside the road.

The old man in the wagon, following the coffle, handed each of the women some corn, a grinder, tin plates and utensils.

Soon, Zachariah smelled coffee and grits and smoke. He felt like a caged cougar whose handlers were holding a juicy deer just out of reach. The taunting, the hunger, the misery were unbearable.

He watched every move the woman with the velvety black skin made. When she bent down to stir the grits, Zachariah's flesh goose pimpled. His pulse sped by a fraction just enough for his gut to tighten with excitement. The woman scooped two ladles of grits onto a plate. She handed it to the gray-haired negro man with the lived-in face, named Joe, who drove the wagon. A frown creased Zachariah's face and his stomach moaned. It felt like hours before the woman returned to her pot of grits. She scooped two more ladles of grits onto a plate, carried it over and handed it to Zachariah.

"What's yo' name, miss?" Zachariah asked.

"Miranda."

Zachariah's urge to eat overcame his desire to talk with her. He shoveled the coarse hominy into his mouth. The two ladlefuls of grits disappeared too quickly. A regular helping would never satisfy his stomach. He doubted he could sing for extra food every night.

He sighed, wishing for his ration of beans. What Ma had been trying to teach him all these years was true. He had been lucky; he had been treated well by Master Norton.

Once all the slaves had food, Miranda began cooking ham for her masters. Smelling the salty ham warmed over the fire, further flavored by smoke, was torture. Of course Zachariah knew he wouldn't be allowed a bite.

Grateful. He had to be grateful for what he had. After Zachariah ate, he got down on his knees and prayed. He opened his eyes and saw both of his masters looking at him. He swallowed to clear the knot of anxiety in his throat.

"He's been eyeing Miranda all day. They should not be chained together," Master Henry said, his voice low, malicious.

Master Galloway ran his fingers through his shaggy, dusty-colored hair. "It won't be my worry if they have a pickaninny," he said. He stood up and re-chained the women for the night. Miranda stared at Zachariah, horror-stricken.

"I heared dem, but you worry none, miss," Zachariah said. "We huv to be married first."

"If you want to marry her I can easily hunt you up a broomstick to jump over, Zach," Henry said in a mocking tone. "We'll all be guests at the wedding."

Zachariah took a deep breath. He realized that Master Henry was going to make his life unpleasant. "My name's Zachariah, Massa, but if you wish to shorten it, I's get use to it. De broomstick's not necessary, but thank you for yo' offer."

Master Galloway's shoulders bounced with the force of his laughter. "Son, that slave has more manners than you ever will!"

Henry blew out air making wisps of his light brown hair jump. He turned scarlet, the veins on his neck pulsating. Scowling at Zachariah, he walked towards him with infuriated steps.

Knowing he could do nothing to protect himself, Zachariah hung his head respectfully and held his breath.

Henry grabbed him by the collar of his shirt, in a guttural whisper he spoke into his ear. "No slave is better than me. I will make sure you know that."

Chapter 3

Murfreesboro, Tennessee
August 17, 1838

BUY ME, ZACHARIAH thought hard. *Please buy me.* With intense interest he watched Master Galloway talk to the owner of the Shady Pine Plantation, Mr. Mercer. He was a handsome man in his mid-thirties, his chestnut brown suit the same shade as his hair. Zachariah wondered how the tailor managed to match the colors.

The man pointed to him. Zachariah's forehead beaded with sweat. Perhaps this was his lucky day. He leaned forward, straining his ears to listen.

The two men walked over to the coffle.

All the slaves got to their feet and tried to look pleasant strong, and healthy, eager to be bought before they reached the cotton and sugar cane plantations.

Being taken to the Deep South meant a quick death. If one didn't die from the lash, disease, or snake bites, they were worked into the ground.

Mercer didn't pay any of the bucks much mind, but leered longingly at the woman standing next to Miranda.

The mulatto woman, in her early twenties, smiled and curtsied. "Name's Laura, sir. I's been a maid and a cook. I's a real good cook, too."

Mercer turned to Galloway. "How much for the wench?"

"Eight hundred."

Mercer walked behind her and felt her shoulders, ran his fingers down her back for signs of whip scars. Then he worked his hands around her waist to her front until he was fondling her breasts.

The woman closed her eyes, but didn't shy away.

"I will take her," he said.

Galloway unchained Laura. He pushed the woman towards Mercer, and asked, "Do you have any slaves you want to sell?"

"If you have the money, you can have several. They are working in the tobacco field now."

Master Galloway nodded. "That is fine. Can I hire my slaves out to you for the day? I would think you could always use extra hands topping, suckering and taking off tobacco worms."

"I can put them to work for sure, but I cannot pay you much."

Galloway rubbed his chin. "Something is better than nothing."

*   *   *

Henry unlocked all of the coffle's chains then mounted his black stallion. Three white men on horseback herded the slaves to the field.

As Zachariah jogged closer to the tobacco crop, he did not hear singing. In all the other fields he'd been to, the slaves sang to help them forget their misery. He heard the overseer threatening a man to work faster and whippoorwills chirping. That was all. The corners of his lips and his spirit sagged thinking of the labor. It would be a long day if a song couldn't escape his mouth and gladden his heart.

Zachariah had spent numerous days on other plantations, cutting the long, slender pinkish-white flower tops of the chest-high tobacco plants. The flowers were prettier than wild roses and they had a sweet sugary scent. Too bad he couldn't give a bouquet to Ma and Rachel.

Joe said the flowers should be cursed not complimented. Once they were removed, the plants produced rank suckers where each leaf was attached to the stalk.

The youth arched his back and twisted right and left to loosen up. He had already experienced the backbreaking work of pulling hundreds of suckers from the stalks. Turning the wrong way brought a dull ache. He had gotten to the point he wanted to cuss those flowers. Zachariah didn't know if he preferred sucker detail or worm patrol.

His rough hands were red and raw from scrubbing off the tobacco tar. Why did he bother? A sticky film soon coated them again.

Zachariah stopped and checked to see if Nelly was lagging again. She was. The woman with silky black hair and dusky amber skin seldom complied with her master's requests.

Master Galloway turned his horse around and galloped towards her. Zachariah held his breath, afraid Master Galloway would knock her to the ground. Instead, he brushed past her, turned his horse around and charged.

Unfazed, the woman defiantly maintained her original pace.

Galloway dismounted and advanced towards her, his pistol drawn.

"I've had enough of you, Nelly," he said in a rumbling roar. "It's time I settle with you."

Nelly spat at Master Galloway's feet.

Galloway cocked his pistol. "You do that again and I will shoot you dead," his voice sharp, earnest. "You only cost three hundred dollars. I can stand to take the loss."

Nelly glared at her master, every muscle tense, mutinous.

Galloway tied her wrists together with rope and made her walk beside his horse.

"You have a paddle, Mr. Mercer?"

The man nodded. "You are welcome to it, Mr. Galloway. It is in the barn."

"Watch the coffle close, Henry. I don't want any of them running off," Galloway said.

"Yes, Pa."

Zachariah swallowed, unable to quell the fear paining his stomach. While hiring out his slaves, Master Galloway left his son to alone guard them. This afforded the perfect opportunity for his young master to bully him.

At the last plantation, two days ago, Zachariah was assigned the task of pulling off the tobacco worms which ate the young, tender plants. Halfway through one of his rows, Master Henry walked up behind him, glared at him, and pointed to a worm he had missed.

Master Henry picked up the fat, two-inch long caterpillar and waved it in front of Zachariah's face.

"Eat it," he ordered.

The many legs on the fat squirming creature made it repulsive. Just the thought of eating it made Zachariah's stomach turn.

"No. I won't, suh."

Henry ran to his horse, got his whip, and gave Zachariah fifteen lashes for disobeying him. He worried what Henry would do to him today.

"Zachariah, stop," Master Galloway commanded.

The boy froze, bent over, about to pull his first sucker.

"You are coming back with me."

Zachariah's eyes widened. A mixture of worry and relief flooded his body. "Yes, Massa."

"That leaves seventeen in the field," Mercer said.

"Eighteen," Master Galloway corrected. "Joe, my wagon driver, is going to pick off worms."

Master Galloway glared at Nelly, tying the other end of the rope around his saddle horn. "You are finally going to get what you deserve."

He dug his heels into his horse's flanks. Nelly ran to stay on her feet, but eventually stumbled and fell. Pulled over rocks on the way back to the house, she screamed.

Her screams made Zachariah's skin goose pimple and his hands folded into fists. He hated the fact he could do nothing to help her. He ran, but wasn't able to keep up with Master Galloway's horse.

Master Galloway dismounted and dragged Nelly into the barn.

"Take care of my horse, Zachariah," he called back.

"Yessuh."

"Then go up to the house and ask for a kettle of hot water. Bring it to the barn."

Zachariah nodded. He took the reins and led the white stallion to the water trough, then tied him to the hitching post and took the saddle off. He dug into the saddlebag and gave the horse a quick brushing. He walked around the house to the side entrance and knocked on the door.

A plump negress answered, her hands on her hips. "What you want?" she asked sharply.

"Massa Galloway, he wants a kettle of hot water."

She made a clicking noise. "I reckon he ain't goin' to shave neider." She left and returned a few minutes later with a steaming iron kettle. "Careful, boy. Doan spill none on yo' toes."

"Yes'm."

Zachariah slowly headed towards the barn. He held the kettle out at arm's length. The water sloshed over the side but safely landed in the grass. He heard Master Galloway cussing Nelly and telling her to strip or he'd tear off her clothes.

Zachariah's heart faltered. He didn't want to hear more. He didn't want to see Nelly naked. He didn't want to witness her beating.

He inched closer. The door was propped open. He froze and bit his tongue. Nelly, naked, stood in stocks cursing Master Galloway like Zachariah had heard the Tennessee mountain folk do when they came to the restaurant.

"Bring it to me, boy," Master Galloway said.

Zachariah set the kettle beside him. Galloway picked up a hickory paddle full of holes, dipped it into the kettle of water, and beat Nelly's backside. The first blow hit the middle of her back.

Nelly screamed. "I's kill yuh."

"Kill me?" Galloway said, then laughed. "You'll be singing a different tune when I'm done or you'll be dead," his words slow and forceful.

Galloway paddled Nelly from her shoulders all the way down. Nelly's screams were deafening. Zachariah took several steps back.

Blisters formed on her flesh and blood gushed through the holes with each infliction. The blood dripped down her backside, trickling down her legs, coating her heels. Before each infliction Galloway dipped the paddle in the hot water to soften the wood. Welts covered Nelly's back as if she had contracted some strange disease.

Zachariah shut his eyes tightly and willed the beating to stop, but when he opened his eyes it continued. He gritted his teeth, his stomach churning at the sight of the helpless woman—shaking, bloody. Her flesh trembled under the force of the paddle. The muscles flexed on Master Galloway's arm. He showed no restraint, laying it on hard.

Nelly's threats for revenge melted in to screams which melted in to soft cries. Galloway continued until Nelly endured the paddling silently.

Galloway turned around, blinked at Zachariah and took many deep breaths.

"Is I next?" Zachariah choked out a whisper, tears flooding his eyes.

Galloway's expression was hard to discern, but he spoke in a calm tone. "Go sit on the porch."

"Yessuh."

Zachariah sat on the bottom step trying to get Nelly's bloody body out of his mind. Why had he been spared from the field? Master Galloway wanted all the money he could get his hands on.

Galloway walked past him and into the house without saying a word.

An hour later, a wrinkled, old negress stepped out of the house. "Bare yo' back, chile."

"What for?" Zachariah asked, his voice thin and weary.

The old woman smiled a comforting smile that could lull a baby to sleep. "Yo' massa wants me to tend to yo' cuts."

Zachariah's took a deep breath, then peeled off his sweaty coat and shirt. With skilled, gentle hands she rubbed salve all over his back. He closed his eyes, enjoying the kind-hearted care. The salve soothed his wounds, her fingers barely touching, seeming more like a light breeze than a person's hands. His nurse smelled of lye soap, like Ma.

"Thank you, ma'am."

The youth dwelled on his helplessness. He had never before witnessed anything like Nelly's beating. He had heard of other slaves being subjected to harsh forms of punishment, but what had happened in the barn was almost beyond his comprehension. He could only pray that he would never have to endure such wrath at his new masters' hands.

The front door slammed shut. Startled, Zachariah jumped to his feet. He turned around to see Master Galloway standing behind him.

Galloway started walking and motioned for him to follow.

The strong silence squeezed Zachariah's heart like a snake suffocating prey. His pulse pounded harder to circulate blood.

Fate is a fine thread, Zachariah realized. He must not break it. He must not push his luck with Master Galloway.

"Why ain't I in the field, Massa?" he asked.

"Property is worth more undamaged."

Zachariah's forehead wrinkled. "What do you mean?"

"I cannot sell you for very much if your back is turned to jelly. I did not think you wanted to eat a tobacco worm for supper."

"You know 'bout dat?" Zachariah said slowly, his voice rising in pitch.

"I know everything that concerns my coffle. My son does not cotton to you. I do not know why. You have never back talked or tangled your chains. You are always polite." He paused. "Maybe that's why. He needs to degrade you because you have so many of the good qualities he's lacking."

"I appreciate yo' good opinion of me." Master Galloway didn't respond, so Zachariah continued, "Fore my beating, I begged Massa Henry to let me pray first, but he just lit into me. Does you think you could get him to let me pray next time?"

Galloway gave him a funny look.

Zachariah hung his head. "Forgive me, Massa." His voice low, sorrowful, "I shan't be askin' favors."

"I will grant your request. I am surprised you asked for the right to pray, instead of keeping my son away from you. You are a very pious young man."

"Pious?"

"Religious."

Zachariah nodded. "Ma, she believes powerfully in de Bible."

"I wish I could get my son some religion," Master Galloway muttered. "Fear of God would do him good. The older he gets, the less he listens to me. His Ma was the only one who could get through to him and she turned idiot after our eldest daughter Diana died during an Indian attack. Our youngest, Bethany, was carried off by the painted savages."

Zachariah's jaw dropped, shocked that such intimate information had been shared with him.

Galloway blushed, clearly realizing his error. He cleared his throat and loosened the collar of his white shirt with two fingers and barely smiled. Zachariah wondered if the smile was involuntary.

"For the benefit of my pocket, I will try to keep my son away from you. I'll have you wait on me instead of being hired out."

Zachariah grinned like a child given the whole cookie jar. "I's be de best waiting man ever."

Master Galloway chuckled.

* * *

Mercer joined them. "I have all the paperwork done. Shall we go to the field?"

Galloway nodded. He pulled several pairs of handcuffs out of his saddlebags and handed them to Zachariah to carry.

Zachariah followed a step behind Galloway and Mercer out to the tobacco field. The two white men weaved their way through the rows of men, women and children working. None of the hands dared stop their task or even look up.

Zachariah's mouth parted and he sucked in his breath. The men working this section wore nothing but a cloth tied round their waist or holey pantaloons. The women wore nothing but a petticoat and a cloth tied around their breasts.

Zachariah felt the flush rising from his neck to his cheeks. Some women had their breasts bare. He bowed his head, averting his eyes. Many of the young children working beside the women and old men did not have a stitch of clothing on their bodies. Zachariah's nose wrinkled at the rank smell of sweaty, dirty flesh. It overpowered even the sweet scent of tobacco.

Mercer stepped behind a small-framed man in his thirties and slapped cuffs on him. The man turned around and looked at Mr.

Mercer and then Master Galloway. He didn't say a word, somehow managing to remain stoic. However, his nostrils flared and his mouth barely tightened.

"This is Thomas," Mr. Mercer said. He took another pair of handcuffs from the pile Zachariah was carrying, and clamped them on a slender negress in her mid-twenties.

The woman crumpled to the ground and burst into tears. She wailed in a high-pitch. "No, Lawd! No!"

Mercer slapped her across the face. "Shut up, Ann, and get up!"

Zachariah helped Ann to her feet. She hung her head and walked over to stand beside the man being sold with her.

Next Mercer handcuffed a tall man with hair more gray than black.

The man's mouth parted with shock. He looked Mr. Mercer full in the face. "I's done live here all my life, Massa. I serve yo' faddah faithfully and now you. Why is I bein' sold down de river?"

Mercer didn't respond. He grabbed the man's arm and directed him to join the others.

The last unfortunate soul was a plump woman working beside a bunch of children.

The pickaninnies' eyes filled with terror. "Mama, Mama," the three girls and two boys cried, clinging to her petticoat and legs.

Mercer jerked them all off gruffly. "Get back to work or I'll take the cowhide to you!"

Tears in their eyes and pale with fright, the children went back to picking off tobacco worms.

"Buy my chillun, Massa," the woman's voice, a shaky plea. "Let me keep at least one of my babies."

"I do not buy children. They are too much trouble," Galloway said.

The woman bawled all the way to the slave quarters—a line of ramshackle cabins. Master Galloway escorted them into their cabins, one at a time, where they were allowed to put on the rest of their clothing.

Both women put on a loose blouse. The men each donned a short sailor-jacket, and the old man was lucky to have a pair of coarse gray trousers as well. Once dressed, they were again handcuffed and led out.

The plump woman continued to sob after Master Galloway chained her to the coffle.

"You'll have to watch her," Mercer warned.

"If they are not working, they are in chains." He paused a beat before saying, "Zachariah, I need to chain you now."

Zachariah walked to his usual spot.

Galloway shook his head. "I am moving you behind Violet," he said, pointing to the distraught mother.

Obediently, Zachariah moved to his new place in line.

"Maybe you can preach to her, Zachariah. I will not stand any more crying."

*   *   *

Zachariah put a caring hand on Violet's back. Her whole body shook with each sob. He didn't know how to console her.

Galloway walked back towards the big house leaving them alone.

Zachariah ran his tongue across his teeth. The three strangers chained with him seemed lost in their own troubles. The young woman was praying and the two men looked to be in a daze, silently staring off in the distance. They weren't offering to help him care for Violet.

Her words came in a rushed burst. "I can't leave my babies." She continued to wail.

"I left my Ma and sister, Rachel," Zachariah said. "All of us is separated from our families. Yo' chillun still huv deir pa to take care of dem."

Violet shook her head. "Massa sold him last year. Dey's all alone." Her voice increased in volume and urgency. "De nurse dat'll care for dem now will starve my lil ones!"

"Starve dem?" Zachariah said, his mouth agape.

Violet nodded. "None of us gets enough to eat. She eats de food she's meant to fix for de lil ones. She always has a full belly and de babies cry from hunger."

How could anyone starve children? "Mr. Mercer won't let dem starve. Doan worry. God'll take care of dem," Zachariah said. The only thing he could think to say. "Our Faddah cares for all de lil ones."

"You believe in dat?"

"Believe in what?"

"De Lawd."

"Of course I do. Doan you?"

She shook her head. "When I's a girl, I heard 'bout Jesus. I believed in Him den; it's just dat so much done happen to me since."

"Believe in Him again," Zachariah said with as much sincerity as he could muster. But he was too distraught for the words to be persuasive.

He started again, this time appealing to reason, like Preacher Simon preaching to a drunk to give up his bottle. "He will give you strength. He will protect you and yo' chillun."

"Protect us." Violet's voice was gratingly harsh. "How? He hasn't ever helped me."

Zachariah fell silent, his lips rolled in. Likely she was too distraught to listen to reason. "Singin' helps me get through de thirty miles," he said under his breath. "By de time we stop for de night, I doan know what's worse … de hunger pain or de achin' feet."

Violet burst into tears again and dropped to her knees.

Zachariah realized she'd heard him. He closed his eyes and rubbed his forehead with his right hand. "It really ain't dat bad, Violet. We's both sing and de time will pass by quickly."

Violet continued to wail loudly.

Zachariah heard the sound of people walking and chattering. He looked over his shoulder. Master Henry and Master Galloway rode beside the exhausted slaves making their way back to camp. Nelly hobbled slowly, her face sunken with pain. She winced with each step, staggering far behind the rest of the slaves. Galloway rode near her, a sharp eye on her blood soaked dress.

Zachariah watched Nelly's every step, willing her forward, willing her strength. Then he returned his attention to the other woman he wished to comfort.

He helped Violet to her feet. "I know you be in powerful sorrow," he said patting her on the back, "but you huv to be quiet. Bite yo' tongue, Violet. Massa Galloway has a temper today. You huv to stop cryin'."

Violet bit her tongue, silent tears streaming down her face.

Galloway and Henry chained the men and the women not tasked with cooking supper.

Violet took deep breaths until she finally calmed.

"Get in the wagon, Nelly," Galloway ordered. "You cannot keep up with the coffle." He gritted his teeth. "Damn half Indian. I shouldn't have bought you. I never will buy another savage."

*   *   *

Zachariah bowed his head and prayed aloud for the first time since he changed masters. "Lawd, may dis food give us strength. Give us po' slaves comfort. Help us bear our sufferings. Huv mercy on Massa Galloway and Massa Henry. Amen."

"You prayed for me," Master Henry said and gave a scornful laugh.

He set down his plate of food and advanced towards the youth. The man's glare made Zachariah shrink back. "You do not need to pray for me, nigger," he said, striking Zachariah with the back of his hand.

"Yessuh." Zachariah shielded his face with his left arm to protect himself from any additional blows.

"Henry, one of these days I just might take the whip to *your* hide," Master Galloway threatened. "The slaves belong to *me*. I will not let you torture any of them just because it pleases you."

Zachariah took a deep breath.

Miranda came over and sat next to him to eat. She didn't say anything, her face blank, unreadable, except for the tears glistening in her eyes. She ate slow and mechanical, one bite after the other. The tar on her fingers made the iron spoon stick to her hand.

"Too tired to talk?"

Miranda kept looking at her pale pink dress which now had black spots and streaks. "You think I's purdy?" she asked, one eye on him.

"Yes, I do. You's bery purdy."

Miranda frowned, childish, sorrowful. She straightened out the bottom of her dress. "I doan think so. People say I's fat and huv an evil cast to de eye. Laura was bought today cause Mistah Mercer thought she was purdy. I's doomed for de cotton field."

"Dose horrible things 'bout you is all lies. You's a good cook. Someone will want you."

Miranda smiled so faintly that Zachariah decided he'd imagined it.

"Thank you."

"You's welcome."

Miranda had dampened his spirit. He glanced around camp for something more interesting, more entertaining, more cheerful. The wagon driver, Joe, was soaking his feet in a bucket of water. Zachariah blinked. Henry sat in the wagon massaging the old man's back and shoulders.

That bastard doing for a slave?

Zachariah shook his head. It made his appraisal of Henry all twisted and hazy.

*   *   *

Borrumb! Zachariah jumped, alarmed, heart racing. Thunder disrupted the stillness, like a ghostly boar barreling its way through the field.

"Everyone on your feet," Master Galloway ordered. "We're breaking camp."

Five miles down the road Galloway found a decent spot to rest for the night. A wooded area full of old growth Virginia pine and hickory trees.

It began raining, the coffle bunched together under the canopy of leaves and branches. Water still dripped through, but at least they weren't completely exposed to the weather.

Nelly climbed gingerly out of the wagon bed. She took a few steps and collapsed. They left her there and didn't bother with the chains.

Zachariah pressed his lips together. His masters would sleep comfortably under the canvas cover. Joe kept dry sleeping in his usual place under the wagon.

Zachariah closed his eyes, but couldn't sleep with raindrops steadily falling on him, soaking his clothes. His companions were all asleep, but he hadn't put in a full day's work in the field like they had. Guilt clawed his stomach.

One of his masters climbed out of the wagon. In the darkness, Zachariah couldn't tell the identity of the shadow. He dreaded that Master Henry planned to finish reckoning with him.

His heart beat faster and faster and faster. Sweat coated his palms. Perhaps Henry was just going to relieve himself.

Zachariah exhaled and his pulse returned to a normal pace. In a quick patch of moonlight, he saw that the man was Master Galloway.

*   *   *

Expression hidden by shadow, Galloway walked over to Zachariah.

The youth sat up, alert with piqued curiosity.

Galloway flashed a disarming smile which melted the worry from Zachariah's bones. He bent down and unlocked Zachariah's chains.

"Is dere something you want me to do, Massa?"

Galloway pulled a small black book out of his coat pocket. "I know you cannot read, but do you know what this is?"

Zachariah looked at the familiar shiny letters on the front. "De Bible."

"If you put your right hand on the Bible and swear to God you won't try to escape, I will let you sleep under the wagon."

Zachariah's eyes widened like a dog about to be handed a soup bone. Just then another shadow emerged out of the wagon.

"You have never favored a slave like this before, Pa," Henry said. "What has gotten into you?"

"He's honest."

Henry scoffed. "You cannot trust any nigger."

"You trust Joe," Galloway fired back.

"Joe's proven himself. He's earned the right. Zach hasn't done a damn thing."

"He pleases me," Galloway said with an edge in his voice.

Henry didn't reply. Those words seemed to take the wind out of him.

"Go back to sleep," Galloway ordered his son. "This does not concern you." He looked at Zachariah. "Come on, boy. Promise like I told you."

Zachariah placed his hand on the Bible. "Lawd, I promise not to run away," he said quick, genuine.

Galloway nodded. "Go on then. Tell Joe to move over."

"Thank you Massa," Zachariah said, a grin stretching across his face, revealing all his teeth.

"If you break your word to God, you're going to hell," Master Galloway warned. "And I'll hunt you down and by the time I'm through, you'll beg to be there."

The words made Zachariah suck in air, like a vicious kick by a mule. "I know Massa. I's keep my word."

His chest seized sending his pulse soaring. His steps rigid, he walked towards the wagon, slowly approaching Henry. His young master's crossed arms showed off his flexed muscles and his scowl increased in intensity.

Zachariah scurried past him and kneeled down beside the wagon. He shook Joe's shoulder, eager for a place to hide. The old man opened his eyes and yawned. Wordlessly, he scooted over.

Zachariah lay down beside him. "Will Massa Henry try to kill me in my sleep?"

Joe rolled his eyes. "No, youngen. He'd huv to answer to his pa."

Zachariah watched Joe close his eyes again, grasping at sleep. He didn't believe the old man. Henry was out to get him. If only he hadn't made that promise. But he had to make the promise to stay dry. Running now would be a sin. He tensed, his lips thin and hard, contemplating whether to act. Adrenaline made it impossible to lay still, his nerves on edge.

The cracks of thunder seemed to shout freedom.

Zachariah's mouth parted. A few minutes passed before he spoke. "Joe," he said in a coarse whisper. "You awake?"

Joe nodded, his eyes still closed.

"Does I have any chance runnin'?"

Joe's eyes shot open, panic flooding his face like a man buried alive. He questioned in a small voice, "Run?"

Zachariah blinked. "I can't stand bein' a slave. Runnin' to Canada has to be a bedda life."

"You knows how far Canada is, boy?"

"Nossuh. Just dat it's far."

"Bery far. You be cold an' hungry and likely get lost. Dat is if you ain't caught by Massa or de patrollers or some bounty hunta. You can't run. All of society's again' you."

Zachariah heaved a dramatic sigh. "I know."

He looked down at his white hands. Why didn't the color of his skin matter to society? He looked white and society saw him as a slave, an object to be owned. But being owned didn't keep dogs from running away. Most days, he was a little smarter than a dog.

Chapter 4

Leesdale, Mississippi
September 6, 1838

ZACHARIAH WENT TO sleep to sounds he had grown accustomed to—the rustle of chains and sobs and whispers.

Galloway's shouting woke him. The lad bolted upright, his heart pounding at a run.

"Thomas and Violet escaped." Galloway said, holding the empty handcuffs in his hand.

The dove and red-winged blackbird morning serenade ceased. Silence lasted a mere second, but it felt like years.

Zachariah bit his lip to quell the excitement bubbling in the pit of his stomach. Every fiber of his being tingled with the hope that the pair made it to freedom.

"They must have been wearing out the links ever since we left Tennessee." Galloway's voice, a gruff grumble, grew louder, sharper. "I bet my right hand that Violet is heading back to Shady Pines to be with her children. Henry, track them down. They couldn't have gotten too far in the night. Run them all the way back!"

Henry quickly saddled his horse, his lips wearing a crooked smile. Henry spurred his horse hard and took off at a gallop.

The fact his young master was so eager for the hunt tightened Zachariah's chest.

"How do you know they went that way?" a negress asked.

Galloway grabbed her by the front of her dress. "Did you see where they went?"

Trembling, the woman struggled to speak, "N-n-no s-suh."

"Did any of you see where Thomas went?" No one answered. Galloway continued, "If Henry doesn't find them and bring them back, all of you are going to suffer for it."

Zachariah swallowed hard.

"Get on your feet," Galloway bellowed, his face red, veins in his forehead protruding. "We're moving out. *Now*."

What about breakfast? Miles and miles of walking down a dusty road answered Zachariah's question. Lice and biting flies plagued them. Each piercing bite swelled ten times worse than the stings of mosquitoes. Zachariah longed for a bath and food. His stomach gurgled and groaned. The sharp hunger pains stabbed his gut relentlessly, like a knife tearing into his vitals.

Sweat trickled down his forehead, burning his eyes. He licked his lips and tasted the salt. He needed a drink, but did not have the courage to ask for water. Not with Master Galloway's anger still spilling from every pore.

The coffle had grown considerably with the new slaves Galloway had purchased. Looking in both directions, Zachariah couldn't see them all. The coffle had more than doubled in size since leaving Strasburg, now numbering thirty men and fourteen women. Because of its large size, the length of chain and handcuffs had run out. Most of the women were bound by rope. Zachariah, the youngest, was the only man given that privilege. The rope rubbed his already chafed wrist where the manacle had dug. He winced whenever he moved his arm.

The soles of Zachariah's feet also burned. Several days earlier his shoes had fallen apart. The bottoms of his bruised feet had yet to callous. After ten miles on the hot, dusty road, he felt like he was walking on smoldering coals. He tried to step gingerly, but it made no difference.

Two slaves towards the front of the line had tangled their chains. After traveling for so long, Zachariah recognized the clinking sound.

Galloway held up his hand. The coffle stopped so that he could untangle them.

Zachariah pulled the worn leather and shoestrings out of his coat pocket. He placed a strip of leather under each foot and tied it in place by wrapping a shoestring around his toes and another around his heel.

They continued forward. Dust coated his sticky arms, neck and face, and stuck in his dry throat. He could taste the grit. He swallowed. The grit felt like it was building up, making it harder for him to breathe. He shook his head trying to rid his mind of such childish paranoia.

A carriage approached, a young white couple talking in the backseat. Galloway held up his hand again. "Look presentable," he ordered.

Zachariah ran fingers through his oily hair and stood up straight. How was he to look presentable when he hadn't had a bath since leaving Virginia? His shirt was permanently stained by sweat, with dirt ground in under his fingernails and toenails.

A negro driver in the customary black suit, top hat and white gloves stopped the carriage. Zachariah had seen many of them since joining the coffle. Fine clothes, easy job. He wanted that position … except all the drivers he had seen were coal black.

The driver got down and opened the door. A young man stepped out and offered his wife his hand. Her skin was snowy white in sharp contrast to her auburn hair tucked under her pale yellow bonnet.

Zachariah's mouth parted. She was stunning … like a diamond, her dress dark blue with tight-fitting sleeves and her waist the tiniest he had ever seen. Ma had told him once that white women wore boned bodices. How could she breathe?

Galloway took off his hat. "Your servant."

The gentleman surveyed the coffle his gray-green eyes going from one slave to the next. "You have a fine lot here."

"Thank you. I've been herding most of them from Virginia. Are you in the market to buy?"

The man shifted his weight and rubbed his gloved hands on his pants. "Actually I was looking to sell."

Galloway pointed at the driver. "You don't mean him, do you?"

The slave did not move a muscle.

The white man barely laughed. "No. My maid and her baby."

"I don't buy babies."

"You can have the baby for free. If it lives you will make a dandy profit."

Galloway nodded. "Then that would have to depend on the maid and the price. Is the maid mulatto?"

"Yes, and..." The woman shot her husband a sharp look, stilling his tongue. He sheepishly swung his head sideways. "Um," he continued, clearing his throat. "The whelp is yellow. Don't worry, the price will be cheap, I assure you. I'm happy to get them off my hands."

Zachariah chewed his cheek. He had a feeling the baby was going to be as pale as him. This baby would never know his father either. He'd live with the same questions and the pain and the abandonment. Zachariah seethed with hatred. Didn't his father care about him? Did he even think about him?

A genteel smile crossed Galloway's lips. "I will call on you then."

"We are headed home, if you would like to follow us."

More walking. Zachariah yawned, and bit his tongue. Master Galloway had rebuked him harshly for stumbling the day before. He had to think of something to keep himself strong. His legs threatened to cramp.

He pictured the red-skinned woman with long, raven black hair that he dreamt of again last night. The nightly occurrence provided him a reprieve from suffering and despair. She invited him into her arms. This time he inhaled her sweet breath. His animal lust gave way to passion. They had kissed hot and hard, sending a tingle all the way to his toes. He wanted to feel close to someone.

Zachariah sucked his bottom lip. On the big plantations, many bucks his age had already laid with a woman. Her image, her ghostly touch, her desire for him made Zachariah smile contentedly like a cat basking in the sun.

He didn't know if this woman was an angel or the devil.

He didn't care. He longed to dream again, to feel her body. He knew he would only feel this happiness in his dreams.

*   *   *

The maid Galloway bought turned out to be around Zachariah's age. She walked with good posture, her dark features soft. She cradled the naked baby in her arms trying to keep him quiet. She wasn't chained, just walked beside the other women.

Zachariah's gasped when she unbuttoned her blouse, revealing her breasts to nurse her child.

The woman caught Zachariah's eye, and he blushed. She knew he was watching. She didn't seem to mind. Taking her time, she nursed the child, her breasts exposed to the sun.

Master Henry leered at her taking in her swollen bosom.

She tried her best to ignore him, focusing on her suckling child. The only time the yellow-skinned baby didn't cry was when he was nursing. The minute she buttoned her blouse, he wailed at the top of his lungs. She rocked him, shushing him—at first calmly, then desperately.

Galloway's eyes drilled into her, saying *shut up that baby or else.*

"Why did I even take the whelp in the first place?" he muttered.

Zachariah caught the fear in the maid's face. He began to sing a lullaby Ma used to sing to him. It worked and the baby went to sleep. Hours later cries announced the pickaninny's displeasure. The cries grew in intensity and no matter what the woman did he wouldn't stop.

"Damn pickaninny. Keep that baby quiet or I will," Galloway threatened.

"Yes, sir," the woman said. She put a hand over her baby's mouth. Muffled whines continued. Her eyes darted from others in the coffle to the baby to Master Galloway, nervousness pleating wrinkles in her face.

Galloway rode back on his horse until he was pacing right beside her. The panic in her eyes increased. She bit her lip and continued to rock her child. Galloway continued to ride beside her, fingering his whip.

Zachariah resumed singing. He felt that the baby's life rested on his voice. Galloway outstretched his arm as if pondering whether to grab the child. The mother moved her hand up covering the baby's mouth and nose. A tight quiet captured the coffle like a net.

Galloway drew a deep breath, eyes closed, as if savoring the moment. He spurred his horse and rode to the head of the column.

The mother exhaled. She removed her hand and kissed the baby's forehead. Whenever Galloway shot her a stern look, she protected her child in this manner. Zachariah feared that one time she would pull her hand away and the baby would be dead.

*   *   *

Henry had not returned with Thomas and Violet. Zachariah pushed that from his mind. He had enough to be concerned about, like whether or not he'd be sold on the way to the market. He always smiled, respectfully lowered his eyes, and intelligently answered questions when buyers crossed their path. His high price had to be the only thing that kept him in the coffle.

Back in North Carolina, an elderly woman had bought Emily. Later, in Knoxville, Tennessee, a wealthy planter had bought several of Master Galloway's slaves, including two women. Each time a woman was bought, Miranda became sullen.

Zachariah heard her more than once cursing the evil cast in her eye. Sometimes, a slave Galloway acquired was with them only a few days before they would be sold in the next town. It wasn't fair.

Zachariah had given up trying to console Miranda. It was all he could do to console himself.

With each step, the coffle got closer to the slave market in Natchez, Mississippi. Zachariah shivered at the thought. The auction block frightened him; frightened him almost as much as hell.

Ma had said growed men don't cry but, since leaving Virginia, Zachariah had seen growed men cry aplenty. Still, he had to be strong for Ma and Rachel.

The sun sank lower on the horizon, painting the sky crimson, the slanted rays stained as red as Nelly's blood.

Galloway rode towards the back of the line. "Sing us a song."

Zachariah licked his cracked, parched lips slow and gentle. "I's sing bedda wid some water, Massa."

Galloway handed Zachariah a canteen.

He unscrewed the cap and took a long pull. The cool water ran down his throat but did little to revive him. He stared longingly at the canteen and finally took another short drink. He had learned any more than that would bring on a terrible stomach ache.

"Pass it around. It looks like I need to water my stock."

Stock? Zachariah jaw tightened. Inside, his chest bunched.

Zachariah handed the canteen to Miranda. He took a deep breath, hoping his anger wouldn't sour his voice.

"Go down, Moses, way down in Egyptland," Zachariah sang loudly. "Tell ol' Pharaoh to let my people go."

Many of the bowed heads around him rose, roused by the powerful words. Some of the slaves looked at the sky as if they expected the Lord to come down, break their chains, and let them go any minute.

> *When Israel was in Egypt's Land,*
> *Let my people go.*
> *Oppressed so hard dey could not stand,*
> *Let my people go.*

The voices of the coffle sang their heartfelt plea.

"Massa Galloway," Zachariah said tentatively, after the song had ended, "may I ride a spell wid Joe in de wagon? My legs hurt awful bad."

Galloway studied him a long time before nodding reluctantly. He dismounted and untied his rope binding. "I shouldn't spoil you so, especially after Thomas and Violet ran, but you haven't caused any trouble."

Zachariah scrambled into the wagon seat beside Joe before his master changed his mind.

"Youngun," Joe said.

Zachariah wanted to ask why the man's gray suit wasn't stained black with tobacco tar, but he didn't.

Joe seldom talked, and his leathery wrinkled face looked stern. Zachariah figured the man didn't like him.

"Joe, how long till we's to Natchez?"

"A day or so."

Zachariah's heart leaped into his Adam's apple. They were close.

Joe patted Zachariah's thigh with a bony hand and let it rest there. Zachariah soaked up the fatherly kindness, the calm strength. He viewed Joe differently now. The old man was quiet, withdrawn, but behind his wall were warmth and wisdom.

The roll of the wagon over the rutted road lulled Zachariah's nerves like a lullaby.

"You need worry none, boy. I think Massa Galloway's keepin' you," Joe said.

Zachariah sucked in his breath. "He done say dat?"

"No, but I know him. He's keepin' you right enough. He's turn down some good offers for you. You's going to be a waiter for sure. He doan even huv to learn you how."

"A waiter?" Zachariah repeated. "I like dat."

Joe shrugged. "It's a bedda life dan many slaves get, worse dan some."

"Where's his restaurant?"

Joe batted a mosquito buzzing around his ear. "Louisville, Kentucky."

Zachariah let out a shrill whistle. "Dat's close to de free states."

"Doan get no wild ideas, boy." Joe's voice was a sharp ax that sliced his dream. "Louisville's a big city in de middle of de state. I's been stuck dere since I's younga den you."

After that, they rode along in silence. Zachariah looked at his lap, silently praying Thomas and Violet would get clean away. Make it back to their loved ones. Like he wanted to do.

Zachariah exhaled softly. If Joe was right, and he was going to be a waiter, then he'd surely have a better life than those in the fields. He couldn't live in the Deep South. He couldn't last in the fields.

He just couldn't.

Chapter 5

Near Natchez, Mississippi
September 7, 1838

"HENRY'S BRINGING THOMAS back," one of the slaves said. The news rippled through the coffle.

"Damnit, Thomas. Can't you run any faster?" Henry said. "You made me chase you down you son of a bitch!"

Henry ran Thomas hard, his hands bound behind his back, a rope around his middle tied to Henry's saddle horn. Violet was not with him.

Zachariah shivered in his seat, excitement causing a fluttery feeling to settle in his stomach. Violet was safe. He bit his tongue to prevent a smile from escaping. She still had a chance to get to her children.

They halted. Sweat poured off Thomas' naked, sunburned body—his skin glistening like polished ebony. Pesky flies and hungry mosquitoes, attracted to the scent, added to his misery. Thomas could barely make his legs keep up. His hairy chest collapsed with each breath. Zachariah knew if he stumbled, Henry would drag the slave the rest of the way.

"You goin' to whip me, Massa?" Thomas gasped, his eyes wide and rolling.

"No," Galloway said. "We're almost to the market and I'm not going to do anything that would fetch a lower price for you."

Thomas tried to catch his breath. "I done learn, suh. I ain't goin' to cause you no more trouble."

Galloway's eyes narrowed, a snarl spreading across his lips. "Oh I am going to punish you, Thomas. I cannot look the other way once a slave runs. Otherwise my whole coffle would take off."

Panic crossed Thomas' face, his hands quivering, his eyes jerking from one person to another, begging for help.

"Where is Violet? You tell me where she is and I will take it easier on you," Galloway said, his voice smoother than usual.

Thomas shook his head. "We done go diff'rent ways. I doan know where she be."

Galloway shook Thomas' shoulders. "You are lying. Where is she?"

"I doan know. Honest."

Galloway gritted his teeth, letting Thomas go with a gruff push. "I will advertise for her in the papers. I know she is headed back to Tennessee. Henry, you know what to do."

Henry laughed hearty and wicked. He dismounted, took the rope off the saddle horn and used it to tie Thomas' legs together.

Thomas tried to take a step forward and landed face first on the ground.

Henry laughed again, louder. He rolled Thomas onto his back, then left and built a fire.

A sour taste rose in Zachariah's throat. He didn't want to know what was about to happen.

Galloway handed Henry a Bowie knife. The long blade shimmered in the sun. Henry kneeled down, holding it over the hot coals, first one side and then the other. Henry approached Thomas, a wild gleam in his eye, brandishing the knife, slashing it through the air.

Thomas dragged himself backward with his arms, but Henry's boot crushing his chest stopped him. Henry ground his boot heel into the man's ribs, Thomas' face withered with pain, but he did not make a sound.

Zachariah tensed, anticipation squelching his breath.

Henry pressed the blade to Thomas' throat.

Zachariah's heartbeat faltered. They weren't going to hang Thomas. Henry would kill him with his knife.

Like watching a house burn, Zachariah didn't want to see the horrible scene but fascination pinned back his lids.

"I'm making damn sure you don't run again," Henry's voice cold, cruel, callous. "Most would cut off your toes or fingers but that would diminish your value considerably. You cannot work as good if you don't have all your digits. There is one thing you don't need though." He picked up Thomas' cock in his left hand and squeezed hard, so hard his knuckles turned white.

"No! No! No!" Thomas said, beads of tears and sweat running down his cheeks.

In one swift motion, Henry sliced off the man's testicles... severing Thomas' manhood, severing his spirit.

Thomas' screams echoed through the air. Echoed through Zachariah's bones.

Joe's hands folded into fists and anger blazed in the old man's eyes.

It made Zachariah feel subjected, shackled, subdued. Thomas' cries and moans were unrelenting. Zachariah shuddered, his chest aching, his mind muddled. He turned hopeless eyes to Joe. He couldn't believe the cruelty inflicted upon Thomas; couldn't believe he had been clipped like a bull.

Joe did not provide any answer or comfort.

"Let dat be a lesson to you, boy," Joe said to Zachariah, soft but harsh. "Doan run. Nosuh."

Henry returned to the fire, blood dripping off his hand and blade. He heated the knife until it glowed then he pressed the blade against the wound. The faint smell of burnt flesh seared Zachariah's nostrils.

Thomas' screams made Zachariah's heart stumble. The screams continued as Galloway and Henry carried Thomas to the back of the wagon.

Zachariah clamped his hands over his ears. It did not block out the cries of agony.

The coffle shuffled forward silently. Joe slapped the reins and the wagon rolled forward slowly. No one said a word for miles—the bleak horror stilling everyone's tongues.

After an hour's travel, Thomas' cries stopped. Zachariah's gut clenched and his heart froze. He took a quick look inside the wagon to see if he was still alive. The man's chest rose and fell. Relief sent a tingly flutter to Zachariah's stomach and restarted his pulse.

"Don't wake him," Joe said. "Best let him sleep."

The sky darkened with each turn of the wagon wheel. The gloom matched the despair resting in Zachariah's chest. Without warning, Joe pulled back on the reins. The horses tossed their heads back and the wagon came to an abrupt stop, throwing Zachariah forward.

"What's wrong?" Zachariah said, loud, alarmed.

"We's heah."

Sucking in his breath, Zachariah looked around, bewildered. Here?

Men on horseback, couples in buggies and families in wagons drove past him in both directions. Whimsical music drifted towards him. At the side of the road, not far up ahead, stood a white boy, a little younger than him, playing his fife and dancing. The boy's hat was turned upside down on the ground, and some of the travelers stopped to throw pennies into it. In the distance, many large buildings loomed.

"Really, we is outside de city," Joe corrected. "Dey won't let us in de city."

Master Henry rode back to the wagon. "Joe, you've been hired out to Mrs. Wilson again until we're ready to leave. Take the wagon there."

"Yes, Massa. How long you be gone?"

Henry surveyed the buildings and the people nearby. His wandering eyes settled on an establishment called the Pink Palace. A busty woman in a revealing burgundy dress stood at the railing, a lacy see-through shawl around her shoulders. "Don't know. Pa isn't keeping me from the sights this year."

"Take yo' time sinnin'," Joe said under his breath.

Henry shot the old man a dirty look and Joe lowered his eyes.

"Zach, help Joe with Thomas," Henry said.

"Yes, Massa."

Galloway walked down the line and freed all of the slaves from their restraints. "You don't have any chance to escape and return to your families now," he said. "So don't bother trying. If you don't want to be in a world of hurt, you will all walk peacefully to the slave pen."

In the midst of the speech, Joe crawled into the back of the wagon and picked up Thomas' arms. Zachariah grabbed Thomas' feet, locking eyes with Joe to avoid seeing the slave's burnt shaft. They carried the man out of the wagon. Joe strained as he helped lift Thomas over the side of Henry's horse. Thomas wailed.

Galloway turned to his son. "Ride to the head of the column. Lead the way there."

Henry nodded. He pulled his pistol out of his belt and waved it at the men. "Stay in formation," he snarled.

Zachariah pressed his lips together, his forehead a torture of grooves. Thomas' screams caused Zachariah's head to throb and his own cock burned.

*   *   *

Joe dragged the chain over to the wagon and slowly fed it into the bed. He looked at all the slaves and shook his head. With a depressed sigh, he climbed into the wagon seat and drove off.

Master Galloway rode alongside the female slaves. Along the way, he tossed a penny into the fifer's hat.

The slaves walked along in silence, until a slender girl asked, "When we be sold, Massa?"

"You will know."

Zachariah's stomach turned with the smell of sweat, tar, and rotting fish. He could taste the burning acid in his throat. He wrinkled his nose and willed his food back down.

The Mississippi River lapped softly at the docks while white men talked business and smoked. They accentuated their points with a wave of their cigars. Slaves pulled barges or unloaded bales of cotton or unloaded cargo wagons. They lifted boxes of tobacco from wagons and hauled them up ramps onto the two steamboats. A few lucky slaves relaxed over a game of cards or caught a few minutes of sleep listening to the waves. Zachariah struggled to catch a glimpse of the vast muddy water, to see the smartly painted ships.

He followed the barge slaves with his eyes, overcome by a deep yearning to join them. It looked like hard work, the sweat pouring off their brows, their drenched shirts, but he desperately wanted to take a ride on one of those big boats. Most slaves spent all their lives on land. He wanted to see more of the country, wanted to know what it felt like to be on big water, to travel with ease.

The coffle shambled uphill to a cluster of rough wooden buildings, in the angle of two roads. Zachariah wondered what all the buildings were for. He soon found out when they were ushered inside one. He surveyed his new surroundings. Dirt floor. One small unglazed window—the lack of glass allowing more light. Already the body heat caused by so many people in cramped quarters reminded him he was a caged animal.

The thick, hot air threatened to suffocate him. He pushed his way through his companions to the window and inhaled the fresh air. No breeze came through. His view showed nothing but fifteen-foot-high pilings which surrounded the slave pen. The pilings were driven into the ground with the posts facing outside to prevent escape.

Turning away from the window, he searched the crowd for Miranda. She sat in the corner, looking at her toes.

Zachariah walked over and silently sank to the floor beside her. She didn't move. The expression on her face revealed her deep sorrow.

"Miranda, I—"

"You done bein' a pet. You won't get favors no mo'," a slave named Gabe said, interrupting his thoughts.

Zachariah stared at the slave. "I's blessed by de Lawd to be treated well till now."

"You won' think de Lawd's blessing you first time de sharp, prickly cotton bolls done tear open yo' hands," Gabe said.

"I believe in de Lawd and dat's all I got to say," Zachariah said sullenly.

He clamped his eyes shut. Why had Joe gotten his hopes up? He wasn't going to be a waiter. He wasn't going to be a house servant. He was going to be a field hand like the rest.

"Zachariah," a familiar voice said.

"Yes, Massa Galloway?" Zachariah asked, his eyes still closed.

"You that tired you cannot look at me?" Galloway said with some degree of agitation in his voice.

Zachariah opened his eyes. He saw Master Galloway standing a couple steps outside the pen door. He pushed himself to his feet and walked over to him. "Forgive me, Massa."

Galloway brushed a finger under his nose. "Would you rather spend the night in here or with me?"

"Wid you," Zachariah said quickly. Then he looked back at Miranda still sitting silently in the corner. Guilt squeezed his heart, but the others would take care of her.

Zachariah followed Master Galloway the mile into Natchez, wondering what the rest of the evening would bring. Yawning wearily he hoped he wouldn't be put to work. He was so tired his feet felt as heavy as stones. Remembering that he'd ridden half the day's journey in the wagon with Joe, pangs of guilt stabbed his gut. Others hadn't been so lucky. Some, like Thomas, hadn't been lucky at all.

Once inside the city limits, Zachariah exhaled, his muscles relaxing. It seemed clear to him that Master Henry was staying at the slave pen. He had to. There was no jailer.

Zachariah's pulse quickened at the sound of a horse galloping behind them. He continued walking alongside Master Galloway's horse trusting the rider wouldn't plow into him. The hoofbeats behind him slowed to a trot and Zachariah felt menacing eyes burning holes in the back of his head. He didn't have to look to know who was following him. The hairs on the back of his neck told him.

Trouble.

*

Galloway stopped his horse in front of the hotel and dismounted. "Son, did you get to the newspaper office before they closed?"

Henry nodded, handing his father a piece of newsprint.

Galloway barely nodded as he read the advertisement, smiling tired but pleased. For once, his son had done something right that didn't involve violence. It would be a miracle if Henry lived another ten years with his reckless ways. If he died, he'd make do with Zachariah.

SLAVES! SLAVES! SLAVES!

FORKS OF THE ROAD, NATCHEZ.

The subscribers have just arrived in Natchez, and are now stopping at my old stand, Forks of the Road, with a choice selection of slaves consisting of:

FIELD HANDS, COACHMEN, COOKS, MAIDS, and GENERAL HOUSE SERVANTS.

Slaves will be sold at reasonable prices according to the market. The Louisiana guarantee will be given on all purchases. Planters and others interested in buying slaves are requested to call and see this new lot before purchasing elsewhere. Alexander Galloway.

"That will bring business," Galloway said. He folded the paper and put it in his pocket, then handed his son the reins to his horse. "Take my horse to the livery."

"Have Zach do it."

Galloway scowled. What had he done to deserve a son like Henry, a lazy troublemaker, who had a knack for finding mischief?

"When I was your age," Galloway said, "I was up at the crack of dawn to plow the fields with my pa and brother."

Henry rolled his eyes. "Or to hoe the field or bring in the harvest or take it to market."

Galloway shot his son a look that could leave a bruise. "Just because I have slaves does not mean that you do not have to work. You will take my horse to the livery. I figured you would be heading in that direction anyway. To get your whore." Galloway spat out the last word.

"That's right." Henry inched his mount closer to Zachariah, leering down at him. "What did you think of the market?"

Zachariah shrugged. "I did not get much of a look, Massa."

"You'll get a good look tomorrow when you're standing up to be sold."

46

Even in the stifling heat, Zachariah's skin paled as if he was cold. "Yessuh."

"And everyone else will get a good look at you. Men are going to feel your hands, arms, and body, turn you about, have you bend over and touch your toes, make you walk to and fro across the room, make you open your mouth, and show your teeth." Henry grinned malicious, baiting.

Galloway's voice carried a bite, "Quit badgering the boy. You know that I am keeping him."

"Keeping him, huh?"

Galloway rubbed his forehead. He wasn't in the mood for Henry's usual power struggle. "I could use some young blood in the restaurant."

Zachariah's eyes brightened and his lips twitched as if not knowing whether to smile. "Thank you, Massa. I's goin' to serve you faithful."

"You better," Galloway said, his voice casual.

Henry grunted and wheeled his horse and left them.

Galloway shook his head, disgust in every line of his face. "Come with me." He entered the hotel and climbed the stairs to his room, fumbled with his key, and finally pushed the door open.

Moonlight streamed through the window, but he still lit the lamp on the small table by the bed. There was a single bed with white covers and two pillows, the small table, washstand and the door on the far wall that looked to be the wardrobe.

"Where's Massa Henry goin'?"

"A place to sin," Galloway replied with a don't-ask-any-more-questions look. "You may sleep there," he said, pointing to the blue rug beside the bed.

Zachariah sat down and beamed, the soft fibers caressing his skin. He ran his hands up and down the rug a long time before lying down. "Thank you for dis favor, Massa."

Galloway washed his face. "You still going to keep your word to God about not escaping?"

"Yessuh."

Galloway pulled a package out from under his bed and tossed it to Zachariah. "I hired you out. You'll be working in Lucky's Tavern. You needed to look respectable for the job."

*

Zachariah's forehead creased. Look respectable? His pulse sped as he tore open the package. His eyes bulged. Inside lay a clean white shirt of coarse cotton, brown pants and a matching frock coat. At the bottom of the box was a pair of stockings and a new pair of brogans. He rubbed his hands across the rough, russet leather and turned them over to look at the wooden soles. He couldn't believe it. Master Norton gave him a pair of new shoes once a year without stockings. The shoes chafed his feet. If they fell apart, or he outgrew them, he walked around barefoot.

He put on his new outfit then sat on the ground and pulled on his stockings and shoes. The shoes felt stiff and sturdy on his feet not the usual shoddy construction. He examined his new outfit with pride, then stood and continued admiring how his new clothes fit him.

Zachariah grinned like he had been handed a pot of gold. He didn't know what to say. Thank you didn't seem enough.

Galloway chuckled softly. "Now you look worthy to be hired out." He wrinkled his nose. "You still stink though. In the morning take a dunk in the horse trough. I ain't buying you a bath."

"Yessuh."

"Oh. I almost forgot." He opened the wardrobe and handed Zachariah a dove-colored felt hat, high-crowned with a black band.

Zachariah's mouth parted. His first hat! His fingers explored the felt, excited to have such a treasure. A hat meant he was moving up. A hat meant he was a man.

Before daybreak, a gentle kick in the side made Zachariah sit up. "Please Mr. Burch or I'll sell you." Galloway said, his words clipped, without much feeling.

"Yes, Massa," Zachariah said, in the midst of a yawn.

He sprang to his feet and headed towards the door.

Galloway grabbed his shoulder and spun him a round. "I mean it, boy. If you cannot make it as a swamper, I do not want you to work for me."

The gait of Zachariah's heart increased and his chest collapsed. The words took the breath out of his lungs. "Massa, I wuk hard. I's please him."

He headed down the stairs and outside. The early morning sun tickled on his cheeks. Luckily, at this hour not many people were on the streets. A bath in a horse trough. In all his young years, Zachariah had never heard of such a thing. He stripped and quickly climbed in, not wanting everyone on the street to see his nakedness. The slimy horse drool at the bottom of the trough coated his feet. He splashed in the water and rubbed energetically at his arms and legs. Without soap, of course. He scrubbed hard to get rid of all filth. The dust and dirt clung to his skin.

With slight amusement he noticed the sun had darkened his hands to a deep tan.

A black horse walked up to the trough and smelled Zachariah's hair. A smile cracked the boy's lips. He reached up and pushed the horse's nose away.

A pot-bellied white man dismounted and shot Zachariah a cold stare. The black coat he wore could barely button. Obviously he had slaves to work for him. He didn't look like he had worked a day in his life.

"Stop polluting the water," the man said, his voice abrupt. "The likes of you will make my horse ill."

"Yessuh," Zachariah said, climbing out.

The overweight man stood there and took in all his manhood with a scrutinizing eye. "Are you Zachariah?"

"Yessuh." A burning sensation spread through Zachariah's body. The need to clothe himself was almost as powerful as the need to breathe.

Hoping he wouldn't be chastised for being rude, he quickly dried himself off with his old clothes. Over the long journey they had been reduced to rags. He dressed in his new suit.

The man brushed his mustache. "Mr. Galloway put a couple years and a few pounds on your description, but I guess you'll do. Go inside and take down the chairs."

"Yessuh, Massa Burch."

Zachariah entered the tavern. A wave of liquor and tobacco juice hit him—a manly scent of strength and power. His insides tangled, apprehension tightening his face.

Plain wooden chairs were stacked four or five to a table. He grabbed the closest chair while scanning the rest of the establishment. The bar, made of solid oak, long and tall, it was the size of three tables.

Back in Strasburg, Ma and Rachel always said good morning to him before he went to work. He hadn't realized how much he'd miss little things like that. He lifted down the next chair while trying to remember his sister's high-pitched voice and Ma's richer one.

He swallowed to force down the sadness rising in his throat.

Were they trying to remember him?

He didn't get a moment to rest. Sweep the floor. Carry in more kegs. Wipe the tables. He breathed heavily, a thin line of sweat forming on his forehead. The tavern was as hot as a smithy. Being a swamper took much more energy than he expected. Still, it offered its own brand of enjoyment.

The boisterous men talking at the bar made Zachariah smile, though he locked his laughter deep inside. He shook his head. White men could sure make fools of themselves. Telling stories about their women, playing cards, swapping the worst jokes Zachariah had ever heard.

May, a negress perhaps in her thirties, served beer to the tables and from time to time made and served plates of food. She bustled around making sure the guests were content. The men grabbed her by the arm and pulled her into their laps, or reached out and slapped her butt. It didn't seem to bother her.

* * *

Massa Henry's loud footsteps announced his presence. He walked to the counter. "Bartender, give me a beer."

Zachariah, bent over cleaning out the bar's spittoons, kept his attention on his work, silently praying Henry would overlook him. Henry put a coin on the counter. The bartender poured the beer. Seconds later, the cold, sticky liquid ran down the back of his neck.

"Sorry, Zach. My mistake."

Zachariah took several deep breaths before straightening up. He looked way off to the right to be as respectful as possible. "I understand, Massa. De apology ain't necessary."

Henry smirked. "Bartender, I need another beer."

Fearing it would be spilled on him too, Zachariah asked, "Massa Burch, may I relieve myself?"

"Yes."

Zachariah hurried outside. He took his time behind the large holly bushes. He preferred risking Mr. Burch's temper to being tormented by Henry.

When he returned, Master Galloway stood at the bar talking with his son. Neither of them paid him any attention. He squatted down and resumed scrubbing the spittoons.

"I only have a few left to sell," Galloway said. "If I can get anyone to buy that half-breed, Nelly, it will be a miracle."

"Can we stay another week, Pa?"

Galloway's chest rose and fell as if pondering the question took great effort. "Well … you have been on your best behavior. I guess … another week won't make much difference. With Joe and Zachariah working, it does not cost us."

Galloway rubbed his chin and flicked a quick glance at the ceiling. "I am heading back out to the slave pen. You coming, son?"

"As soon as I finish my beer. I will just be a few minutes."

Master Galloway left leaving Zachariah unprotected.

Malice flashed in Henry's eyes. He scowled at Zachariah, grabbed him by his collar, and pulled him close. Zachariah looked down to avoid his young master's gaze.

"Pa's restaurant won't be your home for long, Zach," Henry whispered in his ear, his words short, pressured. "I cannot stand the sight of you."

Zachariah's nose wrinkled at the stench of the man's hot, liquored breath. Zachariah's pulse and breathing sped up, as if racing for a finish line. Henry let him go with a shove. Zachariah reeled backward, unable to keep his balance, and fell to the ground. His young master's mocking laughter taunted him. He pushed himself to his feet, his stomach cramping. Teeth gritted, he watched Henry leave the bar.

Burch watched Henry leave, too, then, shook his head. "Zachariah you need to wash your clothes."

"Yessuh." He headed into the small kitchen and slumped down on an overturned barrel.

"Lawdy chile," May said, turning over the catfish in the frying pan. "You smell like a drunk."

She took a wet rag and started scrubbing Zachariah's neck. Zachariah bit his cheek. He didn't want to seem ungrateful but she was putting as much muscle into cleaning him as she did cleaning the floor.

"Massa Burch be none happy if he took a whiff of you. People might get the idea he's selling spirits to a nigger. Take off yo' coat and shirt. I's wash dem soon's I can."

"Yes'm." Zachariah blushed. He did not like sitting there only half-clothed. She tried to hide it but Zachariah caught the woman sneaking glances at the whip scars on his back.

A little while later, he was wearing drenching wet clothes. "Hurry outside 'fore you make puddles on dis whole floor," May said. "Stay dere till you's dry."

Zachariah leaned against the side of the building. The wood touched his raw neck. He winced and closed his eyes. Drops of water tickled his back. The sun, hot for the middle of September, warmed him and melted the tension. His muscles relaxed. His anxiety relaxed. His thoughts relaxed.

The gentle breeze fingered his hair and brushed his cheek, like Ma's caress when he was little. He envisioned Ma standing outside over a big pot of boiling water using a long stick to stir the clothes she was washing for the Milton brothers...moonlighting for them to earn extra money. Zachariah took a deep breath and could almost smell the lye soap on her hands.

His mind wandered down the main road in Strasburg back to Master Norton's restaurant. He pictured Rachel sitting on a stool practicing her sewing. Even in the dead of winter she stayed warm by the kitchen stove.

"Wake up, chile," May said, shaking him. "Massa Burch is callin' you."

Zachariah jumped to his feet, his heart racing. He hurried into the tavern. "You want me, suh?"

Mr. Burch pointed to the spittoons. "Finish cleaning them. I do not pay for you to sleep."

"Yessuh."

Zachariah got down on his knees and resumed the degrading labor. Working in the tavern was better than spending all day with Master Henry, but then again, most anything would be. Still, he was kneeling before a white man. He clenched his teeth and looked into the foul-smelling spittoon. He wouldn't spend the rest of his life being belittled.

He'd get his chance. The chance to redeem himself.

Chapter 6

Joy, Kentucky
December 5, 1838

GALLOWAY QUIVERED WITH rage, his horse ill at ease. A large vein on his neck pulsated. His eyes, narrow slits, could run the devil competition.

Henry's rebellious air remained strong as if fed on his pa's loathing, unfazed he ate every spoonful his pa dished out. He looked straight ahead avoiding his pa's stare, ignoring him. Henry had been sullen since leaving Natchez. He hadn't exchanged a handful of words with his pa. Neither man was about to break, about to step down.

Zachariah chewed his right cheek until it was raw and sore, then changed to the left. Would his masters murder each other before they got home? The heavy air invaded Zachariah's lungs, causing him to cough, sweat, his chest to constrict.

Galloway gritted his teeth, but it actually seemed to make it worse. His voice thundered, "My son is a convict."

Zachariah sat in the wagon seat beside Joe, a hand over his heart, trying to will it to beat at a normal pace. Master Galloway had been repeating that ever since they left Natchez.

"Relax, boy," Joe said. "Henry can't do nothin' wid his Pa around."

Zachariah nodded.

He had worked hard to promote himself in Galloway's eyes. It had helped that Henry had gotten himself thrown in jail for two months for getting drunk and disorderly, and drawing a knife on a crowd. Zachariah shuddered at the thought. Good thing he didn't have his gun. Guess guns weren't allowed at the Pink Palace.

Mr. Burch's tavern and the bustling city had long faded into the distance. Each day they ventured closer to Louisville, closer to Galloway's restaurant. Closer to his new life.

Closer to daily being at Henry's mercy.

After a stay in jail, Henry was meaner than ever, his face carved into a permanent scowl. Zachariah reckoned Master Henry was really mad at the world, with he himself as the main target. The youth endured every ounce of his young master's wrath.

Zachariah cupped his hands over his mouth and blew on his red, aching fingers. It failed to offer much warmth. He put his hands down into the pockets of his frock coat, wishing the wool was thicker. He wiggled his toes, which were warm inside his brogans. The corners of his mouth turned upward slightly. Galloway had bought him another pair of stockings before they left Natchez. He wore both pair and his feet were comfortable. Perhaps if he continued to please his master, he could get a pair of wool gloves and a thick gray coat like Joe's.

Zachariah's masters were both bundled in heavy wool coats. To expel his envy he sighed.

His coat not doing the trick, Zachariah sat on his hands to warm them. His bony rump dug into his palms. At least he wasn't walking to Kentucky.

Galloway rode to the wagon. "How about a song, Zachariah?"

Zachariah nodded inwardly laughing. His master made it sound like he had a choice whether or not to sing, though the youth knew he didn't. With a slightly quivery voice he began a bawdy song he learned while working in the tavern.

Henry slapped his thigh to keep time.

When Zachariah finished, Galloway nodded and rode back to his son.

Henry was so cross at his pa he hadn't paid Zachariah much attention today. The lad didn't mind staying invisible, Joe's quiet passenger.

"Berry's Ferry's up ahead," Joe said.

"Is we goin' on de ferry?" Zachariah asked eagerly.

Joe shook his head. "Dat ferry takes you cross de boarda to Illinois."

Disappointment pulled the corners of his mouth down, weighing heavy on every line of his face.

Joe chuckled. "You young, boy. Might get to de ferry later."

*　　*　　*

Zachariah raised his head and his eyes bulged. In the distance hundreds of Indian men, women, and children huddled in groups. Others walked around under the watchful eye of cavalrymen. The wagon rolled closer. Zachariah heard crying and made out bits of their conversations, some in a tongue he couldn't understand. Most of the Indians were dressed like lower and middle-class white folks in modest suits and dresses. However, some of the people, especially the elderly and young children, wore beads and feathers and leather clothing.

"Damn savages," Galloway said.

"Filthy bastards," Henry muttered. They neared close enough to smell the sweat of the Indians and the leathery scent of the hides some of the frail wore draped over their shoulders.

A sergeant rode out to greet them. "Where you headed?"

"Louisville," Galloway replied.

The brown-haired soldier nodded. "Good, cause we haven't been able to use the ferry for days on account of there being too much ice in the river."

Galloway pointed to the Indians. "What are you doing with all of them?" Galloway asked.

"Escorting the Cherokees to the reservation."

"Good," Henry chimed in. "They don't deserve that gold and rich farmland."

"Cannot help but feel sorry for them though," the sergeant said, scanning the poorly clad natives. He took a deep breath. "Well, I have just come to tell you that we have taken all the muskets away from the Indians. They are peaceable. We want you to pass on without causing any trouble."

Galloway rubbed his hand across his mouth taking in the sight of all the Indians and negroes mixed in with the crowd, many in their own segregated groups. His eyes glowed as if struck by an idea. "Can we talk with them?"

"Yes. Many of the younger ones speak English."

Galloway dismounted, handed the reins of his horse to his son and walked over to talk to a young man who looked like he had white blood mixed with the Cherokee in his veins. He had short black hair and was wearing a stylish brown pin-striped suit.

Zachariah quickly realized that some of the Indians had slaves. He gritted his teeth. In society, negroes were even below Indians. What would it be like to be an Indian's slave? He didn't know much about them, but he had heard from a peddler that they had strange ways. They even ate dogs.

His eyes fell on a young, slender Indian woman with deep amber skin, her skirts so full she resembled a bell. Her straight black hair rested on her shoulders; while the style was unfashionable, he realized it kept her warmer. She wore a white dress with green polka dots that matched the color of her eyes. Her white bonnet stood in contrast with her black hair accentuating her nativeness.

With a graceful motion she turned her head and looked at him. Their eyes locked.

His heart stopped for a second, he held his breath and blinked. Her every curve seemed familiar—all too familiar. He licked his bottom lip, slow, hungry.

She was the woman from his dreams—the woman calling to him. The woman whose warm embrace he imagined at night. The woman was happiness in the flesh.

She did not return his smile, but her soft features seemed to invite him over, her eyes calling to him.

"Massa Henry," Zachariah said in a timid whisper, "may I go talk wid de Indians? I ain't saw an Indian 'fore."

Henry grunted. "No."

"Yessuh."

Zachariah searched the crowd to find the Indian woman again. She was now talking to a lady who appeared a little older than herself.

Both women rubbed their arms vigorously over their tightly wrapped dark brown, crocheted shawls. Her every shiver sent a knife into his tender soul.

"Massa Henry."

"What?"

"Can I go talk to them? Just for a minute. I's stay in sight, right close. Please, Massa," Zachariah said, whining, childish.

Henry turned his head away, his eyes upward, and sighed with annoyance. "Go on."

Zachariah jumped out of the wagon. His gaze locked with the Indian woman as he approached. He held his breath watching her brush a strand of hair behind her left ear. She fingered her cross necklace like she was bored. He stopped and bowed to the two ladies.

"Ma'am, may I talk wid you?"

The older lady laughed mockingly. "Sister, this man must be serious if he bows before speaking."

Zachariah sucked in his breath. He hadn't realized he had done something wrong.

"Leave us be, Bessie."

"Ma would not approve. You need a chaperone."

The young woman rolled her eyes. With an exaggerated turn of her neck she looked at all the soldiers around them. "There are plenty of people watching us."

The joking in Bessie's eyes vanished. She pressed her lips together and walked away.

"Don't mind my sister," the young woman said, shaking her head. "My name is Lillian Hildebrand. What is your name, sir?"

Zachariah blinked, momentarily speechless at being called sir. "Zachariah," he said, careful not to look her in the eye.

"You have not had much practice being around girls, have you, Zachariah?" Lillian smiled; her eyes had a laughing gleam. She took a deep breath and the hint of ridicule disappeared. "I do not mind. Most of our men are too bold. I like that you are shy."

Zachariah blushed. "You huv a pretty name, ma'am. Like lily flowers. You's beautiful like a lily."

"Thank you, Zachariah." She watched Master Galloway, who had already purchased two male slaves. "You with him?"

"Yes, ma'am."

"Where you headed?"

"Kentucky. He has a restaurant in Louisville."

"We are headed to Indian Territory." Her voice faded. She took a deep breath before continuing. "We were going to leave in the summer but the heat was unbearable and we turned back. Now we're freezing. But the army is still escorting us there anyway."

Zachariah took off his coat and held it out to her and spoke soft and genuine. "Please, Miss Lillian take my coat."

Lillian shook her head. "I am sure you are freezing too. You are in need of winter clothes as bad as we are."

"It will warm my heart knowin' dat you's not shivering. I huv a thick blanket to wrap up in, Miss. Please put it on."

Lillian took off her shawl and handed it to Zachariah. He felt the heat from her body in the fibers, inhaled her smoky scent. She put on his brown coat. It fell nearly perfectly on her petite frame. She outstretched her hand for the shawl and wrapped it over her shoulders.

"Thank you. You are very kind." She sighed. "Sometimes I wonder what it would be like to be a white woman. I wouldn't have been forced to leave my home." She glanced over at Mr. Galloway. The distant tone in her voice vanished. "You have a good life with your pa, Zachariah?"

His eyes widened and filled with worry. He took a step back as if to warn her that she wouldn't want to be near him once she knew what he was. "I ain't his son, ma'am. I's his slave."

Lillian covered her mouth with her hand. "But you're white."

Zachariah looked down at his shoes to hide his conscious blush. "I's yellow, ma'am, not white. If you doan want to wear a slave's coat, I understand."

Lillian reached over and gently pushed up his chin. Zachariah's heartbeats tumbled headlong into one another. Her emerald eyes seemed to search his soul. What would she discover?

"Don't be ashamed, Zachariah," she said, strong yet soothing. "Your heart is pure. My skin is colored too."

He offered a tight smile, trying to hide his fear and panic. He failed. "Thank you, ma'am." He took a step back and looked over his shoulder. Henry waited, drumming his fingers on his horse's neck. "I should go."

*   *   *

Zachariah climbed into the seat beside Joe. He felt like grinning, but the mixture of thoughts swirling around his head confused his lips.

Joe sighed, a wise, aged sigh like a floorboard that had seen the tread of too many feet. "I hope it was worth it, boy. You's not gettin' another coat till summer."

Zachariah raised up and pulled the thick blanket out from under him. About to wrap up in it, Massa Galloway's voice stopped him.

"Get down here," Galloway ordered in an obey-me-now tone. He stood by the wagon, his face red, eyes scowling, fists folded.

Zachariah stepped to the ground. He looked past his master to the four men and two negresses he had acquired.

"Where is your coat?" Master Galloway's words were more of an accusation than a demand.

Henry flashed a you're-caught-now look. "He gave it to an Indian squaw, Pa."

Galloway bared his teeth like a vicious dog. "I bought that coat for you, not an Indian!"

Zachariah swallowed to calm the acid churning in his stomach. Massa Galloway's disapproval hurt worse than all of Henry's cross words. He knew better than to justify his actions. In a squeaky voice he said, "Yessuh."

"Henry, get the rope and bind them. We do not have far to go but I don't want to chance losing one of them."

Henry nodded, walked to the back of the wagon and returned with the rope wrapped around his left shoulder.

Galloway gave Zachariah a razor sharp look. "You are walking too, boy. You are lucky I let you off at that."

Zachariah frowned, hanging his head like a scolded pup. As he expected, Henry made him the last in line so he wasn't standing beside anyone. The two women were at the head of the little column, and

Zachariah could barely see them with two taller men in front blocking his view.

No one spoke until the Cherokees were out of sight. Then the slaves began a conversation in hushed whispers. Zachariah felt shunned. No one spoke to him for the longest time.

Being forced to walk did not seem much of a punishment at first. His felt hat kept his head warm. He could endure a little exercise, though he hated being unable to talk to Joe. Glancing over his shoulder, he saw the old man's downcast face. His chest bunched and he darted his eyes back ahead. The old man had a lonely journey on his wagon, often exchanging nothing but a word with the team for miles.

Small, soft, powdery snowflakes tickled Zachariah's nose and eyelashes. Then the snowflakes doubled in size soaking his thin shirt. The wind kicked up with a shrill shriek as it blew through nearby evergreens. Zachariah's teeth chattered, and his arms and trunk felt painfully cold. He closed his eyes and prayed to be numb. Just as he was starting to lose feeling, the snow stopped.

Joe built several fires, and Zachariah huddled over one trying to dry himself. With all the cooks sold, the old man made everyone their evening meal. Then he saw to the team and his masters' mounts.

Staring at his plate, Zachariah groaned. His ration had been cut back to one ladleful of grits. White men were so fickle and quick to hold a grudge. He had hoped Galloway's favor couldn't be snapped so easily. He held the hot cup of coffee to his lips to thaw them, and his hands.

"I don't know what I am going to do with you, Zachariah," Galloway said, between puffs on a cigar. "I know you are smart, but you keep doing foolish things." He paused and breathed in more tobacco. "I cannot have you waiting on my customers half dressed," he continued, blowing out the smoke in Zachariah's direction. "Guess I will have to find another job for you."

Chapter 7

Louisville, Kentucky
December 15, 1838

ZACHARIAH PEERED AT the red sign hanging on a pole sticking out from the building's second story. Three inches of snow rested on top and several icicles extended below. He studied the bold black letters bouncing off the red background, his hands folded across his chest, shivering with each breath.

They seemed to spell his undoing.

"Hickory Rail Inn," Galloway said, untying the rope around Zachariah's wrist. The man looked back at Joe. "Show them to their cabin, take care of the horses, and you can spend the rest of the night with your wife. I will write you a pass."

Weary lines creased around Joe's eyes and the sides of his mouth. "Yessuh. Thank you." He shook his head at the seven half-frozen slaves. "Follow me."

Zachariah rubbed his sore wrist. He was the first to follow the old man. Walking at the back of the line, he had missed spending time with Joe. In Zachariah's mind, Joe meant comfort and wisdom. The youth knew he could learn from him how to survive.

They weaved their way through a wall of white ash, oak and hickory trees, stepping sideways through the gaps in the thick line. Three rickety shacks stood in the clearing, looking as if a vigorous gust of wind might blow them away. The inn was spared the sight of the ugly buildings by the shaggy stand of trees between them. Only a few patches of dilapidated wood were visible between the trunks and through the branches and blended in well with the surrounding grove.

The barn next to the shacks was much larger and of stout, solid construction. Zachariah took a deep breath and pressed his lips together. Of course. Horses were more valued than negroes.

Joe held open the cabin door while the group filed in.

"Dere's wood in de corner," Joe pointed, "and blankets and matches in dat wooden crate."

The two women built a fire while the oldest man handed out blankets. Lacking the energy to stand, Zachariah lay with his feet towards the fire. The threadbare blanket did little more than decorate his tired limbs.

Hours later, a loud knock woke him. He rubbed his eyes. His body longed for more rest. Without windows to let light in, he had no idea how to estimate the time. The knocking continued until one of the women opened the door.

Joe stood outside with an armful of clothes. "Good mornin'," he said. The cheerfulness in his eyes matched his voice.

Zachariah groaned, his head throbbing, muscles sore.

"If you smile, life doan look so dreary," Joe said.

The women laughed as if he was crazy.

Joe's smile did not diminish. "Brought you new clothes." He looked at Zachariah. "Not you. For dose dat needs new clothes." He motioned with his head towards the house. "De door down the path and straight ahead from de quarters leads to de back of de kitchen. You can start workin' dere."

Yawning, Zachariah stepped outside. The winter air snatched his breath and roused him with a rude slap. He was back to working in a kitchen, in a restaurant. Would it be the same as being a waiter for Massa Norton?

His stomach tightening, he jogged towards the kitchen door, feeling like an orphaned pup. Would the rest of the pack accept him?

When he burst inside, four colored faces turned towards him—two middle-aged men, one in a brown suit, the other in a gray one, and two younger women. The negresses stood over the large cast iron stove, their hair pulled back under red bandannas.

The thinner woman gave him a hard look. "Goodness, chile, is de devil chasin' you?"

"No'm."

The four strangers erupted in laughter. "My name's Virginia," the thinner woman said, when she could speak, "and dis here's my sistah Robin."

"Pleased to meet yuhall." He turned to the man in the gray suit who was stacking plates. "What's yo' name?"

The man flicked a cautious glance in his direction but did not respond.

"Mark," Robin said. "He doan talk much."

"My name's Zachariah."

The tall, copper-skinned man in the brown suit nodded. "You's wearing brown troussas. So you's de new waiter. Name's August. I's working wid you."

Zachariah looked down at his pants. Since when did brown have a meaning? Did that apply to other colors? "What do gray mean?"

"We's not to be saw by de people," Robin said.

"Den Joe's not to be saw neider," Zachariah said.

"Dose his travelin' clothes," Virginia explained. "He wears what he wants. He do what he wants most de time," she said, then started laughing.

"I does, does I?" Joe said.

Virginia hushed, her face serious.

Joe lingered just inside the back door. Soon two women and a wiry man from the coffle crowded the kitchen. Both women wore brown dresses with white aprons. The man was in a gray suit.

"Alice and Eliza. You's goin' to be maids in de hotel," Joe said. "Dis place gets dirty fast. You's stay busy. Out de door is de restaurant.

Through de restaurant is de inn. I's shore dis place already needs cleanin'. But none of yuhs go into de last room at de top of de stairs."

Without a word, the two women walked into the restaurant attached to the kitchen.

"Got you some help, Mark," Joe said.

"But Joe, Massa say he bring me back help," August said with an angry undertone. "And Zachariah's in brown."

"When the boy gets a new coat, he will help you," Joe said. "Till den, Mark washes de dishes and Zachariah dries dem."

August crossed his arms and scowled at the floor.

Drying dishes. Sadness weighed down the corners of Zachariah's lips. He was back to being the shaft of the wheat: unwanted but necessary. It had taken him three years to become a waiter for Massa Norton. How long would it take to regain that position?

He walked over to Mark and sat down in a chair across from the stove. A bucket of soapy water lay at his feet.

*   *   *

Joe shot stern eyes at the small-framed man beside him. "William, you's de errand boy. You's in charge of keepin' de kitchen stocked wid wood and water. De ax is restin' against de side of de kitchen if you didn't see it on yo' way here."

Robin looked at William. "We use de last of de wood dis mornin'."

Sober and silent, William went out into the cold again.

A few minutes later, Zachariah heard the rhythmic sound of the ax biting into a log.

"Joe, what does you do?" Zachariah asked.

"Besides taking care of Massa Galloway and Massa Henry, I sit at de inn's front desk half asleep and hand out keys to de people wantin' rooms."

Zachariah's eyes widened with a mixture of excitement and fear. Knowing letters equally terrified and excited him. "Doan you need to read for dat?"

Joe shook his head. "I knows a few words like 'name' and 'room'. Dat's all. But I can count money good."

"Joe," Galloway called.

The old man shot Virginia a I'm-watching-you stare. "I does what I wants, does I?" he muttered and left.

Once Joe was gone, Mark asked, "You ever work in de fields, Zachariah?"

"No."

"In de field you huv a white overseer and of'en a black driva making sure de hands do dere wuk. Joe's our driva. You does what he says widout question."

Zachariah touched his lips. Wasn't answering to two masters enough? Now he had to do what Joe said?

He wanted to ask Mark about working in the fields but didn't. He was relieved he wasn't there.

William walked in with an armload of wood and set it in the rack next to the stove. With no other place to sit, he walked back and leaned against the wall close to Zachariah. In a tired voice he asked, "How'd you manage widout us?"

"Hired slaves," Virginia said.

She cracked four eggs into her pan. Robin started frying squirrel meat. The sizzle and gamey smell made Zachariah's mouth water.

August handed Zachariah and William each a cup of coffee, drank the last of his own, picked up his tray, and headed into the restaurant. "Back to takin' orders," he said. "Takin' orders and followin' orders. Dat's all I does."

"William, where's de others?" Zachariah asked.

"Gone. Dey's hired out to Massa's bruddah to wuk in his rope factory. Dey left soon as dey got clothes on. Massa's bruddah's not happy huvin' to stay here so long and run de place."

"I doan mind it," Virginia said, then pursed her lips together and turned the eggs over.

Soon August returned to the kitchen with the first orders of the day.

Zachariah sat on an overturned wooden box next to Mark, and dried the plates from his masters' breakfast. Many of the customers didn't finish their morning meal. Zachariah ate a chunk of tangy squirrel meat and the crumbled leftovers of a biscuit.

He licked his lips to clean off the bit of butter. "William, what's it like livin' wid Indians?"

William shrugged. "Dey keep slaves same as whites. I wuk alongside my Massa."

What would it be like to work with his master as well as for him? "The Indians nice to you?"

William half-shrugged. "Even if you doin' de same work as yo' massa, you knows yo' place."

Zachariah nodded.

He couldn't imagine Lillian hurting a spider, let alone a slave.

He disguised his soft sigh with a yawn. Hopefully, Lillian was warm in his coat. And safe. Remembering her gentle beauty would help him get through his daily drudgery.

*   *   *

In the middle of the midday rush, Joe entered the kitchen. A knowing look passed between him and Mark.

Mark set down the bowl he was washing and walked outside.

Joe took the man's place next to Zachariah, finished washing the bowl, and whistled a tune. He handed Zachariah the bowl.

"Joe," Virginia said, "how come you's so happy today?"

The man's face glowed with pride. "I learns last night from Caroline my grandchile not born yet."

The mood in the room instantly lightened. "You wan' a boy?" Robin asked.

"Yes'm. You knows I huv three doddahs and two grandoddahs."

Zachariah smiled like the rest though bitterness surged up his throat. He clamped his teeth to hold it in. Joe had been a slave all his life and he still got to be with his wife, daughters and granddaughters. He got to be a pa.

But Zachariah was denied a relationship with his pa, denied being with his ma and sister too.

"Is Mark in trouble?" Zachariah asked.

Joe shook his head. "No. He just takin' care of Missus."

"Massa Galloway's wife? I didn't know she is—"

"She spend de day confine in a large room upstairs," Joe interrupted.

"Why?"

The whole kitchen fell silent except for the crackle of meat frying. Zachariah's stomach twisted. He had said something wrong.

Virginia and Joe exchanged a concerned look. Joe exhaled as if the weight of the truth rested on his shoulders. "She sees things and talks to people who ain't dere," Joe said finally. He added in a softer tone, "And sometimes she gets violent."

The back door to the kitchen banged. A heavyset white man held it open with his left foot. He stared at them with dull brown eyes, his right hand folded into a fist.

Virginia, Joe, and Robin hurried back to their work.

Zachariah looked at them and knew to do the same.

August walked into the kitchen carrying a tray of dirty dishes. When he saw the white man, August put his fingers on his lips and took a deep breath. "I's get Massa Henry, Mistah Price," he said.

*　　*　　*

Mr. Price shut the door and met Henry outside. Zachariah strained to listen to their conversation.

"You owe me three hundred dollars."

"Pa only gave me two hundred for the trip. You'll have to wait a little longer for the rest."

"I've waited six months for this money. I expect to have it all *now*."

There was a moment of silence. Then Henry asked, "What if I bet you that one of my slaves would choose a beating over denouncing Jesus? If I win, you forget the other hundred."

"If you lose, you will owe me two hundred more. Haven't you gambled enough?"

"I will win. You remember what you said about slaves and religion?"

"Sure."

"I think I have found a slave who will prove you wrong."

Mr. Price laughed. "This I must see. Remember, I get to do the asking."

The back door opened again. "Zach, come out here," Henry ordered.

Somber and guarded, Zachariah lowered his head respectfully and walked outside. Without thought, the expected response, "Yes, Massa," escaped his lips. His heart clenched, his muscles tensed, anxiety making each step painful as if tiptoeing around rattlesnakes in the sugar cane.

Mr. Price shut the door with a boom.

Zachariah flinched. He squeaked out, "You want me to do somethin', Massa?"

Henry's beady green eyes flared with wrath. He took a step towards him. Zachariah smelled the pungent tobacco on Henry's breath.

Zachariah's throat dried like sunburned cotton. He tried but couldn't get enough saliva to swallow.

A smug smile crossed Henry's calculating face like a cat that had cornered a mouse. "I want you to do something for Mr. Price." He folded his arms and waited.

Zachariah's mouth parted. "What can I do for you, suh?"

Mr. Price towered over him, his hands folded into fists. "I want you to deny that Jesus is your Lord," he said in a cruel, demanding growl.

Zachariah's cheeks flushed. He pressed his lips together, his face taunt, and blinked.

Mr. Price socked him in the stomach. "Say the words or I will whip you till I spill every ounce of your blood."

Zachariah gasped. As soon as he recovered he shook his head, afraid to speak. Ma had dragged him to too many sermons. Preacher Simon had said denying God was a ticket to an eternity in a pit of fire.

Mr. Price punched him again, knocking him on his back. The breath left his body in a grunt.

Taking advantage of the prone position, Mr. Price switched to using his feet. His boots felt like rocks being slammed into his sides and chest and stomach.

He curled up in a ball and sobbed. "Please no. No. Please doan make me say it."

Henry's butcher dog smile widened, the mouth ends pulled down, stretched with enjoyment. Zachariah closed his eyes against the blinding sun. "Why is you allowin' dis, Massa Henry?" his voice a quivering moan.

Price's fists answered instead. Relentless and well placed, they landed with punishing power again and again on their target.

Zachariah's flesh screamed for mercy, but he refused to cry out. Blood dripped off his chin. Evil chilled his bones. He closed his eyes, his pulse sounded in his ears as loud as thunder.

"You ignorant nigger, you miserable wretch," Mr. Price said in a slow growl.

Zachariah opened his eyes and saw the whip in Mr. Price's hand. Bile rose in his throat. It burned.

"If you don't take off your clothes I will whip them into shreds," Mr. Price said.

Paralyzed by terror and indecision, Zachariah finally bared his back.

Mr. Price didn't wait for him to lie down. With eager malice, he cut into Zachariah's flesh—thwak after thwak after thwak.

Raw tears stained Zachariah's face.

"Say it," Mr. Price ordered. "I'll stop as soon as you say the words."

The whip was snake venom infecting his blood and soul. His back burned like the fires of hell. Mama was wrong—he didn't need to die to be in hell.

God was a white man, wasn't he? Violet had been right. God didn't do anything for negroes. God didn't care about slaves. He didn't mind that Mr. Price tortured him.

Heaven didn't exist for slaves. Slaves died like animals, their flesh and bones left to rot in the ground with their souls.

If he was crippled, he'd never get him and his family free. Running to freedom wasn't going to happen. He had to find another way to escape.

Zachariah's voice rammed through his locked lips. "Jesus is not my Lawd."

Mr. Price stopped, threw his head back, and laughed loud and deep, the noise ringing through the afternoon stillness. "He didn't even last through the first round of scourging. You must have already tanned his hide good. You owe me another two hundred dollars." Mr. Price made a fist and gently struck his outstretched palm. I will give you a week, Henry, to avoid broken bones. One week."

Henry struck Zachariah with both fists. "You fool nigger! You turncoat! And you call yourself religious."

Zachariah covered his bruised face with his hands. He rolled away from Henry, his tender ribs creaking. "I done what you say, Massa," he cried, his insides knotted with fear. "I mean what I say too. Dere ain't a Lord for de black man."

Henry flashed his teeth at Zachariah.

Mr. Price laughed again like a crowing rooster.

Henry walked to the barn and returned carrying a bucket.

Zachariah felt his master's hands on his back and the burning sting of saltwater being applied to his cuts. Raspy cries of pain escaped Zachariah's sore throat. He couldn't see through his torrent of tears.

"Stop Massa, please stop," he begged. He bit his lip. Henry pushed the salt deeper into his wounds. He tasted bitter blood in his mouth. "No more. Please."

Zachariah's voice gave out. His cries became silent pleas. Pleas left unheeded.

Henry finally stopped and stomped back into the kitchen. "Pa!" he called. "I need to talk to you."

Dazed, it took Zachariah several minutes to pick himself up. He stumbled back into the kitchen.

Virginia made a clicking noise and shook her head. She took a pot of heated water off the stove, dipped a rag into it and began to gently clean his wounds.

Zachariah stewed as she nursed him and made a promise. A promise he intended to keep no matter the costs.

Some day I's be my own boss, make my own money, get my family free. I'm going to protect and provide for de women in my life like white men do. I's be the man of the family. Some day.

He needed to get out of the inn. He needed to find a friend. He needed to find help.

Chapter 8

Louisville, Kentucky
December 16, 1838

HENRY WALKED INTO the kitchen. Zachariah's heart faltered, his terror left him mute. The man toyed with him the way a dog toyed with a fox.

Zachariah took quick shallow breaths trying to prevent another flood of tears. He couldn't give Massa Henry that satisfaction. He angled his upper-body away from him and glanced at the door.

Virginia shook her head. She glanced at Henry then back at Zachariah. "Po' chile," she whispered.

Zachariah sat down, grimacing, biting his tongue to keep from voicing pain. He resumed drying dishes. A hollow, empty feeling settled in his chest. A piece of himself was gone. Henry had robbed him of his self-respect, robbed him of his faith in the Lord.

Faith—the only thing he had left from his mother. Now gone. She'd understand, he consoled himself. He did it for his family. Ma and Rachel would want him in once piece.

A moment later, Galloway appeared in the kitchen.

Zachariah looked at him with one eye. Did he know what Henry had done to him? Surely, he'd heard the whip, or at least his cries for mercy. Did Galloway care?

Perhaps. He sensed the man's irritation.

Galloway put his hands on his hips and stared down his son, his eyes as sharp as knives.

"Henry, why can't you come and find me instead of yelling for me at the top of your lungs?"

Henry shrugged, a light flush darkening his cheeks. He shifted towards the door. "Sorry. Can we step outside?"

Galloway glanced at the slaves focusing on their work. He seemed satisfied that everyone was doing their jobs. He gave his son a quick nod.

*

Henry shut the back door behind them. "Pa, I am in trouble again."

"Blast you, Henry. How much this time?"

"Five hundred."

Galloway shouted, "What? Are you trying to bankrupt me? I do not have that kind of money to give you." His words grew louder, harsher.

"Yes, you do. We just got back from New Orleans. All the slaves sold for—"

"For money to pay off my taxes and my bill at the mercantile and the blacksmith and the people in town who let me hire their slaves. Take a look at the books some time. We do not have money to throw around."

"But…" Panic flashed in Henry's eyes, his voice pleading, "If you do not give me the five hundred, Price will break every bone in my body."

"That is what you deserve. I have bailed you out too many times already. You have not learned a damn thing."

"Sorry, Pa."

Galloway shook his head, his breaths coming fast, angered. "Sorry does not help, Son. I keep trying to find your redeeming qualities. I do not think any exist. But after losing Bethany and Diana, you are all I have left."

"Does that mean you will give me the money?" Henry's voice came out squeaky and thin.

Galloway rubbed his chin, thinking.

*

Zachariah leaned his head towards the door. He wanted to catch every juicy detail of Massa Galloway chewing out his son.

Without warning, a middle-aged woman walked in the kitchen. A single blonde braid fell to the middle of her back. She wore a pink dress, a paisley shawl wrapped around her shoulders.

Joe jumped up and walked over to her. "Missus Galloway."

Mark strode after her, panting. "I had de door open for one minute and she done walk out."

"What are Alexander and Henry yelling about?" Mrs. Galloway asked.

"Just business, ma'am. Nothin' you should worry over," Joe said.

Mrs. Galloway cocked her head and gave Joe a funny look.

Henry and his pa continued to fight over money. Surely, Missus Galloway could hear it too.

If Galloway didn't have the money, would one of the slaves end up in the fields? Zachariah's head throbbed and he rubbed his eyes. That was something he didn't want to consider. Henry would put him there if he could—at the first opportunity.

Taking off the target Henry had placed on his back was a priority. It was a matter of survival.

"Joe, the inn isn't making enough money, is it?" Mrs. Galloway asked, agitated. "I told Alexander years ago that we should open a store instead of a restaurant and hotel. A fancy place to sleep and eat is a luxury. Buying flour and coffee is not."

Joe did not respond.

Mrs. Galloway passed him with determined strides.

The old man reached out to stop her. His arm brushed her dress as she strode past.

She flung the door open and stepped outside, her words as sharp as her narrowed eyes. "If you need money for the business, Alexander, ask your brother for a loan."

Henry regained some of his vitality, a grin sweetening his sinister face. "Thank you, Ma."

Galloway grumbled, the lines around his eyes deepening. "If you keep spoiling him, Lola, you will ruin him."

Mrs. Galloway headed back into the kitchen, smiling. Mark held the door to the restaurant open for her. "We should finish our game of checkers," she said.

"Yes'm."

*   *   *

Zachariah wondered how often Missus experienced a fit. What were they like? Lost in thought, the next wet plate slipped out of his hand and landed on the floor with a loud crash. The sound seemed to echo between the walls. For a moment, all the slaves stopped and stared at the white pottery strewn throughout the kitchen.

Zachariah's legs turned to rubber, his hands turned clammy, he swallowed hard. Lightheaded, he sank to his hands and knees to pick up the mess.

William joined him.

Joe reached down and gathered the chunks close to his seat.

Master Henry burst into the kitchen. He spoke rough, demanding. "Who dropped it?"

Zachariah's heart raced, his breathing accelerated, making his vision fuzzy. His voice stuck safely in his throat.

No one said a word.

Henry's gaze raked them over hot coals. "Who was it, damnit?"

Frozen with fear, Zachariah held his breath. He shot a pleading glance at Joe.

"I did, Massa," Joe said.

Henry's face softened and he left without a word.

Zachariah blinked at Joe. "Why did you say dat?"

The right side of Joe's mouth curled upward. "I's protectin' you. You done take enough guff from Massa Henry."

"Ain't you goin' to get in trouble?"

Joe shrugged. "Yes, but Henry won't touch me."

Zachariah wanted to ask why, but figured it was none of his business.

Many buckets of bowls and cups and plates later, Mark returned to the kitchen and resumed washing dishes. Joe walked back out to the front desk.

"What you do when you gone?" Zachariah asked.

Mark looked at Virginia and Robin.

Robin nodded.

Mark's mouth opened, but it took a second for the words to come. "Missus gets bored. Massa Galloway and Massa Henry see her durin' de day but dey huv business. She doan like bein' alone long. Me and Joe spell dem and stay wid her."

* * *

"Alice and Eliza is sweepin' up. Restaurant's empty and closed," August announced. He leaned backward and twisted from side to side.

Zachariah nodded, anxious to return to his cabin. He stood up but sat down again when Joe walked into the kitchen.

Yawning, Joe said, "Coffee."

Virginia poured a fresh cup and handed it to him. "It goin' to be a long night," he mumbled.

"You goin' to sleep?" William asked.

Joe laughed wearily as if he didn't laugh he'd cry. He sighed into the coffee. "Half de time I sleep at de hotel desk. Someone got to be dere at all times. I always get a few hours lyin' down."

Master Galloway opened up the back door and gave Joe a hard come-with-me look.

The old man set down his cup of coffee and walked outside.

Zachariah bit his lip when he heard the first lash and Joe cry out in pain. Silently, he counted each stripe. His heart beat in unison with the whip. Tears rolled down his face.

"Massa, no more. Please," Joe begged in a choked voice.

Galloway stopped after twenty licks.

Joe walked into the kitchen, eyes downcast and picked up his cup of coffee again.

Zachariah couldn't look at him. He tugged on his bottom lip and stared at the stove.

After a moment of tense silence, Robin said, "Joe, show de boy yo' back. His guilt is eatin' him somethin' awful."

Joe sighed again and set down his coffee. He pulled off his coat and shirt.

Zachariah's eyes widened as he saw the drops of blood. It looked like Joe's back had been pricked by a pin twenty times. He took a deep breath, inhaling awkward relief.

"But you was hollerin—"

"Relax, boy," Joe interrupted. "We's just playin'." Joe winked. Then his playful demeanor changed into grim seriousness. He looked around the room at everyone and whispered, "I already got my visit for dis week so Massa say I ain't allowed to see my family next week. Some night if my wife shows up in a buggy and I disappears, yuhall keep yo' mouths shut or I done make yo' lives miserable."

"How can you make our lives miserable?" William asked.

Joe advanced towards him stopping inches from his chest. He poked him in the ribs with a long, bony finger. "Do not test me," he said, slow, strong, threatening. He kept poking. "I have more power dan you ever know. Power wid Massa Henry and Massa Galloway. I can take away yo' food, yo'—"

"I doan say," William said, cutting him off.

Robin looked at Mark and Virginia. "We ain't saying a word," she said.

Joe growled into Zachariah's ear. "What 'bout you?"

"I doan tell," he promised.

Joe clapped him on the shoulder with his big strong hand. "Good."

*   *   *

Zachariah wrestled with his blanket all night, his dreams filled with Henry. He was the first slave to enter the kitchen in the morning. Mrs. Galloway stood at the stove in a navy blue dress. He turned his open-mouthed surprise into a yawn and asked, "May I help you, ma'am?"

"Bethany's old enough, she needs to learn to cook."

Zachariah stared at her, his mouth partly open. Then he remembered Galloway said that his youngest daughter, Bethany, had been carried away by Indians. He wondered whether he should tell the woman her little girl was gone. After what Joe had said, she might attack him with a frying pan or butcher knife.

"Yes, Missus," he said finally. "My name's Zachariah. Can I do somethin' for you?"

Mrs. Galloway looked at the stove and then down at the empty wood rack. "I need kindling to start the stove."

"Yes'm."

He walked outside and began chopping wood. The exertion warmed his cold body quicker than a hot cup of coffee. His cheeks stung from the cold when he walked back into the kitchen and replenished the wood rack.

Mrs. Galloway put a couple logs into the stove. "Now I need hot embers to start the fire."

Zachariah nodded. Where would he get embers? He headed out the back door towards his cabin, hoping one of the fires hadn't burned out. Along the way, he saw all the other slaves either heading into the hotel or the kitchen.

"What is you doin', chile?" Virginia asked.

"Missus is in de kitchen. She wants to start a fire in de stove."

Virginia and Mark ran towards the kitchen.

"What's wrong?" Zachariah said, chasing after them.

"She done set fire to de house once," Mark called back.

Zachariah pictured the whole establishment engulfed in hungry flames. Charred wood. Reduced to a pile of smoldering ashes.

And all his fault.

Chapter 9

Hickory Rail Inn
December 21, 1838

FIVE NIGHTS LATER, half asleep in his cabin, Zachariah pondered Ma, Rachel and Lillian's fate. Hoofbeats in the distance jolted him alert. He sat up and yawned, wondering if he'd imagined it. It continued, horse hoofs again softly striking the dirt at a slow pace.

He walked outside and saw a negress dressed in a black dress and cape, driving a one-horse buggy. She pulled up in front of the hotel. Joe walked outside, stepped into the buggy and she drove away.

Zachariah went back to bed. He hugged his blanket close, fighting pricking concern. Joe knew what he was doing.

He woke to a piercing scream and ran outside. Yellow and orange hues mixed on the horizon beneath the dark ocean of night. The screaming continued. It was clearly the high-pitched wail of a woman. Soon all the slaves had joined him.

Virginia put a hand on Zachariah's shoulder. "Joe will help Massa calm her down."

"Joe ain't here," Zachariah said. "He rode away in a buggy."

Virginia put a hand over her mouth. "Massa will find out for shore," she said through her fingers. She turned to Mark. "Come on. Dey's goin' to need our help. Rest of you go back to bed."

Zachariah knew he couldn't sleep any more. "May I come too? Missus done listen to me 'fore."

Mark half-shrugged. "If you want."

The three slaves ran through the kitchen door, through the restaurant into the hotel and up the stairs to Master Galloway's room.

"Joe's de only one wid a key," Virginia said out of breath.

"Won't Massa just open de door?" Zachariah asked.

Mark and Virginia looked at him like he had grown a second head. "You doan understand," Mark said.

Virginia reached down, took a pin out of the hem of her dress and began picking the lock. After what seemed like forever, she opened the door.

Zachariah was speechless. Mrs. Galloway was lying on her back on the bed, trying with every ounce of strength she had to break free from the grasp of her son and husband. Master Henry held down her arms and Master Galloway her legs. The woman's face was tense, strained, a light shade of purple.

"Let me go," she shrieked, loud, urgent. "The Indians are going to kill us all! They are yelling loud and constant and hideous. We have to go before they surround this place!"

"There are no Indians, Ma. You are in our hotel. You are safe," Henry said, soft, soothing.

"Where is Joe?" Galloway's voice was rough and deep.

"He's not feeling well," Virginia said.

"Damnit."

"Calm down, Ma. There are no Indians," Henry said, pleading, a tear running down each cheek.

"Mark, take over for me," Galloway instructed.

Mark walked over and held down Mrs. Galloway's legs.

"I will be right back, Lola," Galloway said.

"Alexander, wake up Diana and Bethany," Mrs. Galloway said, panic in her voice. "Get them out of the house. We all need to get to the cellar."

"I will get the girls, Lola," he said, and walked out of the room.

Virginia quickly shut the door behind him and locked it.

"Last time it wuked bedda to give in to her visions," Zachariah said.

Henry glared at him, his words harsh, rushed together. "You want me to tell everyone in the hotel we are being attacked by Indians?"

"N-n-no."

"Lord God, keep those savages away from me!" Mrs. Galloway shouted in a high-pitched screech. "Smoke. I smell smoke. Fire! Fire! Fire!" She shrieked like a pig stuck with a meat hook. Virginia ran and put a hand over the woman's mouth.

*　　*　　*

Henry's face withered with grief. "I do not care if Joe is ill, he needs to be here," he said loud, irritated. His eyes darted to Zachariah. "Go get him."

"B-b-but he can hardly walk."

Henry's eyes narrowed into angry slits. "Then help him up the stairs," he said slowly, like Zachariah was touched in the head.

Virginia nodded to him. With a heavy pounding heart Zachariah headed for the door.

Henry unlocked it. "And be quick about it."

The snap in Henry's voice caused Zachariah's chest to bunch. Holding his breath, he checked the hotel desk. No Joe.

Zachariah licked his bottom lip. What was he going to do now?

He trudged back up the stairs with his head bowed.

The door was locked. He swayed sideways. Henry would have to open the door for him. He raised his hand to knock when Galloway appeared behind him. Zachariah took a step back. Galloway and opened the door carrying a small bottle and a spoon.

"Lola, you need to relax." His voice calm, measured, reassuring. "You are going to frighten all our guests." He pulled up a chair close to the bed, sat down, and gently touched her waxy, white hand. "This will help you." He poured liquid out of the bottle onto the spoon. "Hold her nose, Virginia."

Mrs. Galloway turned from pink to a deep shade of red. Finally, she opened her mouth, gasping for air.

Her husband made her swallow the spoonful of medicine.

"Zach, come hold her arms. I need a break," Henry said.

Zachariah flashed a small, helpless smile at Mrs. Galloway. It took all his strength to hold her still. Her green eyes filled with fear from memories that plagued her, the demons that haunted her, the past that stalked her. Sweat ran down her forehead, wetting her hair and nightgown and sheets.

"Sing her a song, Zachariah," Master Galloway said, his voice paltry, thin.

Zachariah took a deep breath, softly he began singing. "Let's go a-huntin', says Risky Rob."

Mrs. Galloway shrieked, wild, animal-like. "Hunting. They are hunting me."

Master Galloway shot Zachariah a stern fix-this-or-I'll-fix-you look.

"Um," Zachariah said. He struggled to think of another song. "Um." He began humming a tune then sang.

> *Cherry-ripe, ripe, ripe, I cry,*
> *Full and fair ones; come and buy.*
> *If so be you ask me where*
> *They do grow, I answer: There,*
> *Where my Julia's lips do smile;*
> *There's the land, or cherry-isle,*
> *Whose plantations fully show*
> *All the year where cherries grow.*

Mrs. Galloway quit struggling. With Virginia standing in front of the door, in case she decided to run, Zachariah let go of the woman's arms and Mark let go of her legs. Zachariah kept singing

By the time he had finished it for the fourth time, Mrs. Galloway was resting peacefully, her eyes closed.

Zachariah studied her. She looked to be several years older than Master Galloway with deep wrinkles on her forehead.

"You did it, Zachariah," Master Galloway said worn, weary. "You calmed her down."

"I thought it was de medicine."

Galloway shook his head. "No. It takes a lot longer for that to work."

Henry's eyes widened like he had remembered something. Zachariah's Adam apple jumped.

"Zach."

Zachariah raised his head and spoke soft, airy. "Yessuh?"

"Zach, where is Joe?"

No one said a word. Galloway glared at Virginia. "You said he is ill. Where is he? Do I need to send for a doctor?" Again no one replied. "He is not ill, is he?"

Henry shot Zachariah an accusing look.

The hair on the back of the boy's neck stood at attention.

"Zach, where is Joe?"

Zachariah shifted upon the balls of his feet. He swallowed hard. His voice stretched paper thin, "He rode away in a buggy right after dark."

"Thank you, Zachariah," Galloway said. "For everything." He paused and watched his sleeping wife thoughtfully. Without turning his head he said, "Leave now."

The three slaves headed down the stairs. Virginia shook her head. "Joe's really goin' to get it," she said. "It not been so bad if Missus ain't gone into a fit."

"Why?" Zachariah asked. "Joe say he play a game wid Massa Galloway."

"Dat game only go so far," Mark said.

Zachariah swallowed hard. He hated breaking his promise to Joe, hated knowing he got the old man in trouble.

Hated the beating that awaited his friend.

*   *   *

The clouds shone tulip pink, with specks of bright orange. They moved slowly, puffy flowers in a vast garden. Zachariah stood in the kitchen watching the sky. Virginia and Robin heated the stove, working silently. Any minute the restaurant would open.

Joe would return.

The creaky sound of an old buggy caught Zachariah's attention before it came into view. He didn't want to, but a feeling deep down told him he was obligated to see what happened. He got to his feet and walked outside.

Master Galloway sat in a chair on the hotel porch, a whip in hand.

Seeing him from a distance, the woman stopped the buggy short. Joe stepped down.

"I don't want to see you around here again, Caroline!" Galloway's voice boomed.

The negress turned the buggy around and raced back down the road.

"You are lucky the patrollers did not catch you, Joe. Why did you leave?"

"I's see my grandson be born," Joe said his voice unsure, shaky. "He done not live but a few hours." Joe looked up at Master Galloway his cheeks stained with tears. "I's real sorry I had to slip out, Massa, but you's doan get many people comin' at night in de middle of winta."

Galloway's face and neck turned dark red. His words dripped with sarcasm and anger. "I am sure you are sorry. Strip."

Joe hung his head and began shedding his clothes.

Zachariah retreated deep inside the kitchen, dropping to his chair. He couldn't bear to watch.

The first time Joe yelled he could tell that the man's pain was real. His guilt grew and grew and grew. With each infliction. With each wrenching cry. With each beg for mercy.

Zachariah counted by drawing lines in the dirt to mark each stripe. Too many lines. He threw the stick against the wall. He slid out of his chair onto the floor, tears stinging his eyes.

He shut them tightly, held his knees and rocked back and fourth waiting for the beating to stop, wishing for it to stop.

Needing it to stop.

Finally, it did.

Galloway stood, bloody cowhide dangling in his hand. "All of you get out here." His voice was one to be obeyed.

Zachariah swallowed hard and stepped outside. The others followed.

"I should give each and every one of you a whipping," Galloway said.

Zachariah's heart raced. How could Galloway's anger not be abated after giving Joe such a severe beating? Or would he really take Joe's actions out on everyone?

"You all had a hand in this. If I had been told of his plans I would have stopped him and not have resorted to such severe measures to maintain discipline. I realize you may think that you answer to him, but you answer to me."

Galloway thrashed the ground with the whip several times. "Is that understood?"

"Yes, Massa," they all said in unison.

"Good. I want you all to file past Joe before returning to work. Get a good look. Maybe you will make a better choice next time."

The old man was left, tied by his wrists, hanging from a bare peach tree in the yard. His shoulders and back were so lacerated that blood pooled at his feet. The second he saw him, Zachariah froze and looked down at his shoes.

"Boy," Joe called, his voice weak and hoarse.

Zachariah did not move.

"Boy, come closa."

Zachariah took a few steps towards Joe, still looking at his shoes. He made a conscious effort not to wrinkle his nose, the bitter, iron-like smell of blood pungent.

"Doan feel bad. I done got myself in trouble. And I do it again."

Zachariah swallowed the guilt crawling up his throat and headed back into the kitchen. He found Master Henry talking to Mark and William right inside the door. Zachariah's terror left him mute.

Henry bit his lip. "Mark, go cut Joe down and take him to your cabin. Help him William."

Mark nodded and William followed him outside.

Zachariah went over to the corner and began stacking the plates so that Virginia and Robin could get to them easily. The women were lighting the stove and moving their pans around. Soon the aroma of strong, bitter coffee filled his nostrils.

"Pour me a cup," Henry ordered.

Robin handed him one.

Henry sipped it and walked outside.

Zachariah rubbed his chin. Why wasn't Henry having breakfast with his pa? Zachariah left his work and followed him at a distance.

Before Henry entered one of the slave cabins, he pulled a small bottle out of his pocket and poured some of the liquid into the coffee.

Zachariah's heart, drumming his ribcage, urged him forward. Adrenaline flooding all reason, he ran towards the cabin and burst through the door, shouting. "Doan drink it, Joe!"

The old man already had the cup to his lips. "Why, boy?" Joe asked, the cup shaking in his hand.

"Its poison."

Joe laughed and then grimaced. "Tastes like coffee and whiskey to me."

Zachariah looked at Joe, lying on his stomach on a blanket, then over at Henry.

Henry's voice dropped to just above a whisper. "It helps with the pain. But Pa does not like it." Henry tapped his lips and seemed to be in deep thought. "Stay with him, Zach. I do not want Joe to be alone. William can dry for you."

Zachariah nodded, too shocked at Henry's action towards Joe to speak.

Henry shook his head. "Some of those cuts look deep. You need to stop the bleeding. Fetch his clothes from the yard. I will have William bring a salve later. If Joe starts getting feverish or anything, come to me. I will write you a pass to get the doctor." Zachariah blinked at Master Henry.

Henry's face hardened. "You do not tell anyone I favor Joe. No one. If I find out that you did, you will answer to me."

Zachariah swallowed. He knew the beast couldn't resist spitting threats. Still, the hint of kindness in Henry's eyes was unmistakable.

Perhaps there was hope.

Perhaps if he took care of Joe, it would soften Henry's hate.

Perhaps if he was on his best behavior, one of the customers would want to buy him so he could leave this miserable place.

Chapter 10

Hickory Rail Inn
December 24, 1838

ZACHARIAH PEEKED OUT the kitchen door to see the Christmas decorations Alice and Eliza were placing in the restaurant. Candles and pine cones lined the fireplace mantel. Evergreen boughs were wrapped along the staircase banister. A tall pine tree decorated with candles and ornaments stood stately in the corner of the restaurant. The strong scent of pine drifted back into the kitchen.

Soon the meaty smell of smoked ham entwined with the spices from the pumpkin pie made Zachariah's stomach grumble. His mouth watered as Virginia pulled gingerbread cookies out of the oven. He tried to reach for one, but the woman slapped his hand.

"Dey for de party tonight," she said.

Robin and Virginia had been cooking nonstop the past three days. Mrs. Galloway had joined them when she was in a good state of mind. She had even taught Bethany how to cook sugar cookies.

Zachariah let out a soft whistle at the memory, the woman's imagination still amazed him. Missus had left to get Diana and Bethany ready for the party, which included dance lessons. He wondered if Master Galloway would allow his wife to attend the celebration.

Christmas carols filled the air from the two fiddlers Galloway had hired. Zachariah began singing along. The lyrics to the hymns came naturally, but he didn't feel the words. How could he? He'd already denounced Jesus as his savior. Now being stuck with Henry was preparation for the buzzards to peck out his eyes.

"Hark! De herald angels sing glory to de newborn king."

"Wid a voice like dat Massa might huv you sing for everyone," Robin said.

Instantly Zachariah stopped singing. He didn't want to give Galloway any ideas. "I wish I could play de fiddle like de slaves out dere."

Robin stirred the apple cider with one hand and the syrup for the popcorn balls with the other, a twinkle in her eyes. "I love Christmas time."

"William, I need mo' water," Virginia called, "and de wood is gettin' low too."

William groaned and walked outside.

"Guests is arriving," August said, walking into the kitchen. "You should see Missus Johnson's red dress. It has more layers dan I done see 'fore."

"Carry de ham out," Virginia said, "and de potatoes."

August rolled his eyes. "I hate Christmas! Joe always helps me except now."

"I wish Joe was here too," Mark said. The kitchen fell silent.

"Docta say he not to do much for two weeks. Zachariah, you can carry him out a plate later," Virginia said. "I need someone to try de punch. I doan know if it need mo sugar."

"I will," Zachariah said, quick and excited. Virginia ladled a little into a cup and handed it to him. He drank a sip and grinned. "Tastes good to me."

Alice and Eliza walked back into the kitchen.

"Decorating's finally done," Alice said, exhaling loudly, her hands dropping limply to her thighs.

"Good," Robin replied. "Take out de cider."

August, Eliza and Alice went in and out of the kitchen so many times Zachariah wondered how the door managed to still be on its hinges.

Every time the door opened he heard the roar of people talking. After a few hours of catering to the guests, Eliza and Alice leaned back against the kitchen wall and closed their eyes.

"Here's another bowl of gravy. Take it out," Virginia said.

"No," Eliza said.

Alice shook her head.

Virginia put her hands on her hips and lit into them with a blade-like tongue. "You good for nothing wenches! Po' August can't do it all on his own."

"We's need to rest," Eliza said.

"De only way you goin' to get to rest is when you stove up like Joe. You want Massa Galloway to tear up yo' hides?"

Alice and Eliza gave Virginia a hard look and reluctantly took the gravy out along with a bowl of sweet potatoes.

*   *   *

All the slaves stopped what they were doing when Master Galloway walked into the kitchen. "This is the busiest Christmas Eve we have ever had," he said. He gave Zachariah a long look. "You have not really earned this, but I need you now."

A puzzled crease edged across Zachariah's brow. He took the package handed him, untied the string, tore open the paper. His fingers tingled when he saw a new brown coat. He put it on quickly, fumbling with the stiff buttons.

"Thank you, Massa."

"Now take your hat off and get out on the floor," Galloway said, his gruff voice clipped.

Zachariah laid his felt hat on his seat. He took a step forward to follow Galloway out the door when Robin tapped him on the shoulder and handed him a plate of gingerbread cookies. "I doan expect you to leave dis kitchen empty handed tonight."

Zachariah nodded. "Yes'm."

Seeing the cookies he licked his lips, but resisted the temptation. He walked into the restaurant and quietly gasped, overwhelmed by the number of people. Men in their best suits, and ladies in their festive dresses, occupied every seat, every table. More people were standing and talking around the bowls of punch and cider.

August walked back to him. "Dere's a dessert table," he said, leading Zachariah through the crowd.

The boy set down his plate of cookies next to the popcorn balls. He looked across the room at the two negro men pulling their bows across the fiddle strings, playing I Saw Three Ships. The sprightly tune had many couples dancing. Zachariah watched Galloway twirl his wife around the open floor on the left side of the room.

"I's glad we doan gotta serve all dese people," he said.

August nodded. "Dey serve demselves at parties and we just keep de food on de table."

The song ended and Mrs. Galloway returned to her table, laughing. Her husband stood behind her chair his head lowered so he could hear what she was saying. He looked up a little disgruntled and motioned towards August and Zachariah.

The two slaves looked at each other. August pointed at his chest. Galloway shook his head.

"He wants you, boy," August said.

Zachariah walked over to his master's table. "Yessuh?"

"Make an announcement that Diana is going to sing a carol," Mrs. Galloway said. "She has a beautiful singing voice."

"Lola," Master Galloway said, "Diana ate too many sweets. She is not feeling well and went to bed."

Mrs. Galloway's bottom lip quivered. Her husband rubbed her shoulder. "What song would you like to hear, my dear?"

"You know that 'Silent Night' is my favorite."

"Do you know it?" he asked Zachariah.

"I knows de song, suh."

Galloway took a deep breath. "Go tell the musicians to play it for you."

Zachariah's heart twisted. He hoped his lack of enthusiasm wouldn't show. "Yessuh."

Galloway clanged a spoon against his glass to get everyone's attention. "Would you all be kind and be silent for a few minutes? One of my slaves is going to sing a carol for us. I hope you enjoy it."

Zachariah walked over to the musicians. "You's to play 'Silent Night' next."

The taller of the two men dipped his chin.

Zachariah stood next to them. Everyone's eyes were on him—like when he had been examined by buyers. Nervous energy shot through his body and he had to force himself to stand still. He rubbed his sweaty palms on his pants. He took a deep breath unable to slow his racing heart. He nodded to the musicians, hoping his voice wouldn't crack.

They began and he sang the first verse in a loud but wavering tone.

> *Silent night, holy night,*
> *All is calm, all is bright*
> *Round yon virgin mother and Child.*
> *Holy Infant, so tender and mild,*
> *Sleep in heavenly peace.*

After surviving the first verse, he proceeded through the rest of the song calmly, the butterflies no longer in his stomach. Finished, he looked over and saw Mrs. Galloway clapping, her eyes twinkling.

Zachariah bowed then walked over and stood next to August again.

"Dat is nice," August said.

"Thank you."

August yawned then said, "Looks like we needs mo' biscuits. I hope dey huv dem made."

"I's get dem," Zachariah said, picking up the empty plate.

On his way to the kitchen, he passed the dessert table and slipped a gingerbread cookie into his coat pocket. When he returned, he stood at the back of the restaurant watching all the guests.

Eliza joined him.

"You look tired."

Eliza nodded. "Best go see if Massa wants anything. You got fresh legs, Zachariah."

He nodded and picked up the empty sugar cookie tray on his way there. "Can I do something for you, Massa?"

Galloway shook his head and resumed talking with his wife.

Across the table, Henry stared at Zachariah, his eyes silently beckoning. Zachariah timidly approached fearing Henry's displeasure. Henry grabbed Zachariah gently by the collar of his shirt, pulled him down and whispered in his ear, "Bring me a glass of punch and take my cider to Joe."

Zachariah nodded.

He left and returned with a glass of punch, put the cider on his tray, along with dirty dishes, and walked back to the kitchen. Mark whistled to the music outside. When he opened the door, he saw the man had guilted William into washing dishes. Zachariah handed William the stack he had brought in then turned to Virginia.

"I's told to make a plate for Joe."

Virginia handed him a plate already made. On it was a flat biscuit, one of the fattier cuts of ham, some mashed potatoes and gravy and a slightly burnt sugar cookie.

Zachariah walked out into the cold holding the plate in one hand and the cider in the other. Snowflakes landed on his cheeks gentle like silken kisses. He breathed hard and watched the air turn white. He reached the cabin and kicked the door.

"Come in," Joe said.

Zachariah pushed the flimsy door open with his right knee. Joe, lay on his stomach on his rug, a wool blanket covered his backside. Only his head was visible.

"How you doin'?"

"My rheumatism is hurtin' me bad as my back. Fever's bedda though."

Zachariah set the cider down in front of Joe then lowered himself to the ground beside him. "Henry told me to give you dat."

Joe took a drink. "Cider and whiskey lots bedda dan coffee and whiskey." His chest sunk in and expanded with each breath. "I's gettin' too old for a whippin' like dat." He fell silent, his eyes settling on the plate. "Dat food looks good. I's mighty hungry."

Zachariah set the plate next to the cider. He got to his feet and headed towards the door.

"You huv to go?" Joe said, sorrowful and soft. "I's awful lonesome."

Zachariah rolled in his lips and looked back at the old man. In the darkness of the room, Joe's gray hair appeared whiter. He sat down next to the old man and watched him eat. He didn't know what to say.

Joe grimaced.

"What's wrong?" Zachariah asked.

"Sharp pain in my legs." Joe moaned. "It's bad in de winta and bein' in dis shabby cabin makes me hurt something fierce."

Zachariah crawled over and began massaging Joe's legs.

Joe closed his eyes. "Bless you, boy." He took another sip of cider.

"Why won't Massa Henry harm you? Why does he like you?"

"Like me?" Joe laughed. "Boy, I's here de day he be borned. I's also here de day his oldah sistah die and de youngen was carried off by de Indians. Henry doan get along wid his pa, never has." Joe's mouth parted and he rubbed his tongue against his bottom gums. "A man needs to huv connections wid others. Henry de same. His sistahs gone, Ma ill, he bonded wid me."

Bonded with you? Zachariah's heart plummeted. He wanted to be close to the old man. He searched for the right words and his voice wavered, "Do dat mean dat Massa Henry see you as family?"

"Family?" Joe laughed again and it turned into a raspy cough. "Mo' like his favorite horse."

Zachariah's shoulders slumped and stared at the cabin wall. He dipped his chin, his voice soft, shy. "I's hope you could help get Henry to like me."

Silence settled on the cabin floor smothering them like a blanket. Zachariah trembled, his cheeks suddenly hot. He shouldn't have asked.

The tip of Joe's tongue stuck out of his mouth. "Boy, Henry's always had a mean streak even as a youngen. Him and his pa dey doan see eye to eye on nothin'."

"At least he huv a pa," Zachariah interrupted.

Another moment of awkward silence followed. Zachariah shifted his weight. Joe put his hand on top of his. Zachariah sucked in his breath wanting the moment to last.

"Henry's mad cause his pa gets along wid you," Joe explained. "You too close to Henry's age. He's jealous."

Zachariah groaned. "I can't change dat."

"Hard for a slave to change much 'bout his life. I's lucky I marry a free woman. My chillun and grandchillun is free. "Joe patted Zachariah's knee. "Some day maybe you huv a family and feel deir love and support. For now, you best get back to work."

"We's awful busy tonight. I's a waiter now."

Joe smiled, accentuating the wrinkles around his eyes and mouth. "I see yo' brown coat. I huv a feeling dat'd happen. You know, boy, Henry can't change dat. Massa Galloway runs de place."

"I know," Zachariah said, not clearly convinced. Being a waiter was something, but it still meant a life with Henry.

And it was far from freedom.

*   *   *

Zachariah took the gingerbread cookie out of his pocket and popped it all in his mouth at once before anyone could catch him. The sweet spiciness slid down his throat. He licked the crumbs off his lips, destroying the evidence. His stomach smiled, but his face remained sober as he walked back to the kitchen. Once inside, he stood for a minute next to the hot stove to warm up. Then he headed out into the restaurant. He saw Mrs. Galloway wagging her finger in the air at the empty seat next to her. He walked over with quick strides.

"Bethany, I told you to bring me a glass of punch," she said to the air.

"Ma, don't you think you've had enough punch?" Henry asked.

"It's Christmas Eve. I should be able to enjoy the occasion."

Galloway stood. "Would you like to dance again, Lola?"

The woman replied with a hint of playfulness in her voice. "You know I can't resist an invitation to dance."

While they were waltzing, Zachariah brought a glass of punch and set it on the table in front of Mrs. Galloway's plate.

"How's Joe?" Henry breathed.

"Good except for de cold."

"I will get him another blanket after the party."

The thought of the party ending brought him boyish delight. He'd get a plate of the leftover food. "Does we work tomorrow, Massa?"

Henry shook his head. "We're closed on Christmas. Ma likes us all to go to church."

Church? The thought of listening to the story of Jesus' birth made him sick to his stomach. It was all lies. The Bible was all lies to make slaves obedient to their masters, to justify their evil actions.

"Can I stay here wid Joe, Massa?"

Henry's eyebrows rose along with the pitch of his voice. "I thought you would be elated at the chance to go to church. I was going to have Mark stay with Joe, but you can."

"Thank you, Massa. You's bery kind."

Master Henry studied him a long time. "You do what I say, Zachariah, and we will get along fine."

Zachariah took a deep breath pushing down the guilt that had taken up residence in his chest.

*   *   *

On December 26, the slaves were summoned to work early. To make up for their day off, the women were put to work mending a pile of clothes, while Zachariah and the other men scrubbed the floors.

On his hands and knees, Zachariah froze when Galloway walked into the room. The hair on his neck prickled. The boy looked up at his master, a lump in his throat.

"You are a waiter from now on, just in case I did not make that clear. The ladies are cooking now. You can finish this later."

"Yessuh," Zachariah said, a cautious smile slowly turning up the corners of his mouth. He got to his feet and walked into the kitchen whistling softly. He wasn't about to mess this up.

Robin handed him a cup of coffee.

He drank it in three gulps and entered the restaurant. Only one customer waited at this early hour. He walked over to the table.

"What would you like to order, suh?" he asked, clear and polite.

The middle-aged man chuckled to himself at the private joke. "So Mr. Galloway finally got another waiter. What is your name, boy?"

"Zachariah, suh."

The man nodded. "Well, Zachariah, I come in here for breakfast every morning. I always order two eggs, a biscuit and whatever meat is being served for the day."

"Yessuh. I will remember, suh. Would you like a cup of coffee?"

"Yes."

"I will bring yo' order soon," Zachariah said, then headed back to the kitchen.

He saw a plate with two eggs, a biscuit and squirrel meat already sitting on the tray on the counter.

"You forgot de coffee," Zachariah said.

"Oh." Virginia poured a cup of coffee and added it to the tray.

Zachariah picked it up carefully. He held his breath, walked to the table, set down the plate. "Can I get you something else?"

"No."

Zachariah nodded. He looked around. Three more people were sitting at the restaurant; a young couple and an elderly lady. August was taking the couple's order.

Zachariah walked over to the elderly lady.

After several trips in and out of the kitchen, August patted him on the back. "You doin' a good job."

"Thank you."

That evening, Zachariah talked to August while Alice and Eliza stacked the chairs. Being a waiter again made him smile, made him feel useful, made him feel important.

Master Galloway walked into the kitchen. "Zachariah, I'd like to talk to you."

Zachariah nodded and followed his master outside.

"I am very pleased with your performance today. I had three customers compliment me on my new waiter."

Zachariah beamed and his chest swelled.

"You are smart, Zachariah. You do what is expected and one of these days you just might end up running this establishment for me. Joe cannot do it much longer."

"Really?" Zachariah had worked as a waiter for Mr. Norton for three years, but had never received such a promise. Galloway surely knew that.

"In time. After you prove yourself as a waiter and prove you are trustworthy."

Zachariah took a deep breath, pride quickening his pulse as Galloway walked away.

From what he'd seen, Joe had the best life of all of Galloway's slaves. If he could get that job, he'd be living high. But could he handle the responsibility that would come with that entrusted position?

Chapter 11

Hickory Rail Inn
March 13, 1842

HE'D COME A long ways, Zachariah thought, as he carried a tray with five plates of country-fried steak up the stairs to Massa Galloway's room. The door remained propped open for him. Mr. and Mrs. Galloway were engaged in a conversation. Henry sat at the table with his parents drinking coffee.

Zachariah handed a plate to each of them. He gave a practiced grin to the two empty seats at the table.

"You wearin' a purdy dress today, Miss Diana. You too, Miss Bethany," the young man said, placing a plate in front of each of the imaginary ladies.

"You have learned a lot in four years, Zachariah," Galloway said.

"Thank you, Massa."

He walked into his and Joe's small adjoining room and shut the door. In it was a desk with a lamp on top and on the floor was two green rugs and two new blankets. He sat down on his rug and waited to be called to carry the plates away. He silently named off the different kinds of fruit on the wallpaper as he had done countless times before.

"Zachariah," Mrs. Galloway called finally.

Zachariah picked up the tray and walked back into his master's room. "Yes'm?"

"We are finished. I am afraid that Diana and Bethany were not very hungry this morning."

Zachariah nodded, stacked the dirty dishes on his tray and then added the two untouched plates. He headed towards the kitchen and Mark brushed past him with empty plates.

"Mornin' guests already in de restaurant," he said. Mark, finally a waiter, grinned constantly. He handed his dirty dishes to William, and Zachariah did the same.

William dipped them into the water and began scrubbing them. Then he handed them to Taylor, the dark youth sitting next to him.

Zachariah shook his head. Things had sure changed. It didn't seem that long ago that his job was drying dishes. He added two cups of coffee to his tray. He saw the newest slave, Dennis, pulling a bucket of water up from the well. Near the slave cabins Joe sat outside in the sun, asleep in his chair again. The old man's chin rested against his chest showing his full head of white hair.

Zachariah walked over to him, set his tray on the ground, and gently shook his shoulder. "I hope yo' hungry."

Joe raised his head slowly as if moving required great effort. "I's always hungry. Good thing Bethany and Diana ain't."

Zachariah's mouth stretched holding back a laugh. "Yessuh." He handed Joe a plate of food and cup of coffee then sat down in the chair next to him to eat.

"Massa Henry gamble again last night?"

Zachariah nodded. "Doan know how he can play good drinking whiskey, but I heared he won."

"Most time he doan. Only reason Galloway doan turn him out cause he needs him to help care for Missus." Joe wiped his mouth with the back of his hand. "Soon you's goin' to Natchez again."

Zachariah pushed around his food with his fork. He hated the city and he hated working in the fields on the way down even more.

"I's be driving yo' wagon. It doan seem right."

"My wagon," Joe said, then grunted. "Doan feel sorry for me, boy. I's got it easy now." He pulled a piece of paper out of his coat pocket.

"You knows you bery old when you get a pass to go anywhere and do anything whenever you please."

"I was thinking it was time I done start a family of my own."

Joe's head bobbed the way old folks do. "Massa Galloway will give you permission to marry. You know Alice has grown to like you."

"I doan feel for her dat way."

Joe patted Zachariah's thigh. "You will find yo' girl soon enough."

Zachariah bit his tongue to keep from saying he already found one; an Indian woman who would remain in his imagination to tease him. "I hope so," he said finally. "You goin' to see you doddahs today?"

Joe pushed on the arms of the chair to stand up and Zachariah handed him his cane, which had fallen on the grass in front of him. "Nice sunny day. I's goin' to do dat if I's can get a ride dere."

Zachariah put the dirty dishes on his tray, carried them into the kitchen and handed them to William. Then he walked into the restaurant. On his way into the hotel, he nodded to August, who was waiting on a young couple.

Master Galloway sat at the front desk. "You want me to take over for you, suh?" Zachariah asked.

Galloway nodded. He looked out one of the big hotel windows at the sun filtering through the leaves in the line of trees, creating dancing shadows on the ground. "It's a nice day to go hunting. That's one thing Henry enjoys doing with me." He rubbed his chin. "That means until we get back, you are running the place, Zachariah."

"Yes, Massa. I's handle it fine."

*   *   *

He could run the hotel, but could he take care of Missus too? Hopefully, she wouldn't have one of her fits with both of them gone. He had yet to handle one alone.

He hummed a tune to ward off loneliness. Running the hotel was less demanding work, but being the new driver, as Mark had put years ago, distanced him from the other slaves. He looked forward to spelling William so he could play chess or checkers with Mrs. Galloway. He wondered if Joe had felt the same way about washing dishes.

An older gentleman walked into the hotel. "I would like a room."

Zachariah nodded while admiring the man's burgundy vest. He reached behind him and pulled a key off the nail. "You can huv room 14. It's upstairs and to de right." He pointed to the registry. "Please sign in, suh, and de room costs fifty cents a day or four dollas a week."

The man signed his name, reached into his pocket then threw four dollars on the table. He took the key and headed up the stairs. Zachariah put the money in the lock box behind the counter.

Minutes ticked by slowly. Zachariah traced pictures on the desk with his finger. There wasn't much else to do. After several hours of pure boredom, Alice brought him a cup of coffee. "Thank you."

Alice licked her bottom lip slowly. "William and Mark and me spend time wid Missus. Eliza's talkin' wid her now, but she wants you mighty bad. You's de best 'sides Joe at playin' long wid her visions."

"I gotta stay at de desk," he said annoyance in his voice.

"I knows dat. Can we let her come downstairs to talk wid you?"

The young man pressed his lips together, pulled her room key out of his pocket and handed it to Alice. A little later, he turned his head when he heard a long skirt brushing the stairs. Mrs. Galloway beamed, walking down the stairs ahead of Alice. The maid grabbed a chair from the restaurant and brought it over so Mrs. Galloway could sit down then handed Zachariah back the key.

"Men get to work and go hunting and such," Mrs. Galloway said, then heaved a sigh. "I do very little. I barely even get to go shopping. I can only sew and read poetry for so long."

"I done wish I can read poetry." Zachariah pressed his lips together, regretting his words. "But I know I's lucky wid my life here."

Mrs. Galloway's eyes focused on nothing in particular, distant. "You sing to me. I will start reading to you."

"Thank you Missus. I's like dat bery much."

"I would like to take a trip. I hate it here. Too many Indians here."

Zachariah sucked in breath, but exhaled when Mrs. Galloway didn't start screaming. "Where would you like to go?"

"New Orleans. My family's from New Orleans. It has been so long, Diana, Henry, and Bethany probably do not remember their grandparents."

"I's shore dey do. Some day I's like to ride one dose big riverboats."

Mrs. Galloway nodded and arranged her skirts. "We could take a steamboat to New Orleans. Likely you would come with us."

Zachariah's chin dropped. Mrs. Galloway kept talking, but Zachariah was lost imagining a steamboat ride. The big boat loaded down with tobacco and cotton and passengers. The loud whistle blew and the boat chugged away from the docks, riding stately through the water to the next port, a big, bustling city.

"Where are you from?" Mrs. Galloway asked.

"Oh. Um. Strasburg, Virginia, ma'am. Last summer when Massa Galloway go to Virginia buyin' slaves I look for my ma and sisstah. I's look again dis year."

"You do not like it here either, do you?"

How should he answer? "I likes it here, Missus," he whispered. "How old's Miss Diana?" he asked hoping to get the conversation off of him.

"Twenty-four." Mrs. Galloway's eyes widened.

Zachariah tipped his head to the side and listened. "I doan hear no Indians, Missus," he said, having realized a long time ago that helped to ward off some of her fits.

"Diana's twenty-four and no one's courted her. She keeps going to dances and she's very pretty. I do not understand why she's not married. She needs to get married. I want grandchildren."

Zachariah blinked at her. "Missus, perhaps Miss Diana doan want to marry."

"Nonsense! She just has not found the right man. There are plenty of guests in the hotel and restaurant each day, but many are too old and others have a hard look about them." She sighed. "I will have to talk to Alexander about that."

Zachariah looked at the hotel door, hoping Massa Galloway would walk in.

"I wore my ma's wedding dress when I married Alexander." Her eyes saddened. Her posture sagged. In a shaky voice she said, "It burned when the Indians set our house on fire."

"I's real sorry. But Miss Diana will huv a real purdy weddin' dress I's shore."

"Yes. Yes, she will."

Zachariah rested his head in his hand listened to Mrs. Galloway plan out every detail of her daughter's wedding. He bit his tongue and forced himself to keep his eyes open.

Time was dwindling as slow as a frozen jar of honey. Slower than any day he could remember.

He sat erect when he heard someone approaching the hotel. Galloway walked through the door, his musket in hand.

*   *   *

Mrs. Galloway ran over to her husband, blocking his path. "Alexander, I'm concerned that no one has been courting Diana," she said, her voice high-pitched, strong.

Master Galloway rubbed his forehead. "Lola, can't we talk about this later?" his said with a degree of agitation in his voice. "I did not shoot a thing. Henry's giving the cooks *four* birds to clean—"

"This is more important than your wounded pride," Mrs. Galloway said, cutting him off. "You want Diana to be a spinster?"

"No. I do not want that. I am tired, Lola."

"Alexander Wes Galloway!"

He groaned numerous times. "Go up to our room. I will join you in a bit."

Mrs. Galloway nodded.

He watched his wife head up the stairs. "Blasted woman," Galloway said as soon as she had shut the door. He gave Zachariah such a hard look the young man felt struck by brick. "How'd she get the idea Diana had to get married?"

"I just ask her how old Miss Diana was, Massa."

"Damnit! Why can't she accept that Diana is dead and Bethany is gone from us forever?"

"If Miss Diana done marry, den she will live here no more."

"Then I would only have one imaginary child," Mr. Galloway said. "But where am I going to get a groom to go along with this ridiculous wedding?" A tricky grin reminiscent of Henry spread across his face. He turned and looked at Zachariah.

Zachariah felt light-headed, strength drained from his body. His hands tingled and a warm sensation spread across his skin. A high-pitched, childish plea squeezed through his throat. "No, Massa. It ain't right." He swallowed then said more calmly, "Doan make me. I can't."

"Sure you can. I just have to get you some fancy clothes, a haircut, shave and teach you how to talk right. The only one you have to fool is my wife."

Zachariah shook his head. "It won't work. Please no."

Galloway's eyes narrowed. "You got yourself into this mess. You are the reason my wife thinks Diana needs to get married. You are going to go along with this act and that's that." Galloway raised his musket, took a step forward and shoved the muzzle into Zachariah's stomach. "Do not make me use any harsher persuasion."

Zachariah swallowed, taking a step back, sweat running down his face. A lead ball through the middle wouldn't be any better from this distance.

Galloway continued to glare at him.

Zachariah's heart tightened. It was his duty to follow his master's wishes even if that meant trickery. "Yessuh. I's do it."

"*I'll*, not I's. Mrs. Galloway imagines things, but if she catches you talking like that, it will be a waste of time."

"Yessuh. I un'erstand."

"Yes, sir. I understand," Galloway said clearly, showing the pause between words and enunciating each letter sound.

"I doan—"

"*Do not.* Do not worry." Galloway patted him on the back. "You are smart. You will figure it out. After I talk with my wife, I am coming back down here to continue working on your speech. I will sit here at this desk with you for months if it takes that long."

Zachariah groaned as his master headed up the stairs. He looked down at his pale hands. "Damn my white skin."

*   *   *

Three days later, slanted rays of the setting sun cast a glow through the open kitchen door. Zachariah watched the ball of light sink lower and lower and lower.

Robin handed him a cup of coffee. "You look worried."

Zachariah sighed. "I hate de-the front desk now."

Mark laughed harsh and scornful. "You can come back to de kitchen, Mistah Zachariah. I's take you's job any day."

"Stop dat! He ain't done nothin' to you," Virginia scolded.

"What if it doan-does not work? So many things could go wrong."

Robin placed a caring hand on his shoulder. They all turned when they heard the door to the restaurant swing open.

Henry walked in.

Instantly, everyone froze.

"Zachariah, come with me," he ordered.

Zachariah set down his coffee and followed Master Henry outside. "Did I do something wrong, sir?"

"Yes," Henry hissed. "You are marrying my sister."

"I ain't," Zachariah stopped and corrected himself. "I am not marrying your sister. Your sister is dead."

Henry slapped him across the face. "I have a mind to tell Pa you tried to run off so this disgraceful wedding doesn't happen."

Zachariah's knees buckled. He dropped to Henry's feet. "Please do not, Master. Dis-this was your pa's idea. I did not want to." For a second, he pictured himself hanging from the peach tree like Joe, his flesh torn from his shoulders to his heels and then the shaking and fever that would follow. He closed his eyes as they welled with tears.

Must please Henry. "Please do not, Master Henry. I know you are upset." He leaned over and kissed Henry's shoes then looked up at him with big, cow eyes.

Henry glared at him, channeling the devil. His teeth gleamed like tiny razors. He crossed his arms. "I tried to get Pa to change his mind. If people in town find out about this disgraceful deception, then I will be the laughing stock of town. We all will be."

Zachariah licked his lips and held his tongue. His mind supplying the response, people whispered about Henry's ma being touched in the head, Henry was just too drunk to notice.

Henry spat a steam of tobacco juice on Zachariah's neck. "A slave pretending to be white is not something to encourage. Pa's asking for trouble." Henry grabbed Zachariah by the back of his shirt and pulled him to his feet. "Don't you go getting any notions of joining the blasted Underground Railroad."

Zachariah shook his head.

Henry smirked, clearing enjoying his power. "Get back to the front desk."

"Yes, Master. Thank you."

Henry gritted his teeth and started walking towards the slave cabins. "Teaching you how to talk," he muttered. "Pa's replacing me, and I will not stand for it. Next, he'll be teaching you how to read."

His voice returned to its usual harshness. Back to its cruel threats. "You forget your place and you will be a dead nigger!"

Chapter 12

Reverend Nelson's House
April 3, 1842

AUGUST STRAIGHTENED ZACHARIAH'S silk tie. He looked over the man's shoulder and saw Mrs. Galloway still in the opposite corner of the room talking to the wall.

"You nervous, Mistah Jackson?" August asked.

Zachariah rubbed his sweaty hands on his black dress pants and looked down at his burgundy vest. "Is it that noticeable?"

August laughed. "Only natural to be nervous. Doan worry. Miss Diana won't back outa de weddin'."

Zachariah glared at August until the man's face became serious.

"Joe shore learn you lots in four years," August said. "You actin' whiter ebery day."

The reverend, with strawberry-blond hair, stood in the middle of the room, Bible in hand, tapping his foot. Was he impatient or irritated by the charade? Would God be displeased by this mock wedding? Zachariah swallowed the jitters and anxiety worming their way up his throat. They all had good intentions and he was damned anyway.

Out of the corner of his eye he saw Mrs. Galloway, in a new yellow dress, her facing glowing.

"Lola, we better not keep Reverend Nelson waiting much longer. Diana is as beautiful as an angel in that blue dress." Mr. Galloway squeezed his wife's hand and nodded to the reverend. "Let's start the ceremony."

Zachariah took a deep breath and walked to his place in front of the reverend.

"Why couldn't we have invited a few friends?" Mrs. Galloway asked.

"Because Edward and Diana wanted a private wedding. It is their day after all."

Galloway brushed a tear out of his left eye. He pretended to hook arms with his daughter and escort her to Zachariah's side. "My dear," he said in a shaky voice, "I can't believe you're all grown up. You are a lovely bride." He leaned over and pretended to kiss his daughter's cheek, then left and stood by his wife. Henry stood on the other side of her, a smile plastered on his face as fake as the nuptials.

Zachariah looked Reverend Nelson in the eye. The man had a friendly stern face.

"Dearly beloved," the reverend began in his usual rich, reverent tone, "we are gathered together here in the sight of God, and in the presence of these witnesses, to join together this man and this woman in holy Matrimony; which is an honorable estate, instituted of God, signifying unto us the union that exists between Christ and his Church and is commended of Saint Paul to be honorable among all men. Into which holy estate these two persons present come now to be joined. Therefore, if any can show just cause why they may not lawfully be joined together, let him now speak, or else hereafter forever hold his peace."

Reverend Nelson looked up, glanced over at Mr. and Mrs. Galloway and then at the slaves present at the back of the room. His lips were so tight and thin they looked painted on, but his eyes were welcoming.

"Wilt thou have this woman to be thy wedded wife, to live together after God's ordinance in the holy estate of matrimony? Wilt thou love her, comfort her, honor and keep her, in sickness and in health: and, forsaking all other, keep thee only unto her so long as ye both shall live?"

"I will," Zachariah squeaked out. His heart pounded so loudly he barely heard the reverend's words.

Reverend Nelson turned and looked at the air beside Zachariah. "Wilt thou have this man to be thy wedded husband, to live together after God's ordinance in the holy estate of matrimony? Wilt thou love, honor, and keep him, in sickness and in health: and, forsaking all other, keep thee only unto him so long as ye both shall live?"

The room was silent for a second. Zachariah's pulse thrummed strong, steady.

"She said I do," Mrs. Galloway said, agitation in her voice. "Get on with the ceremony."

Mr. Galloway patted his wife's arm. "Lola, let the man perform it as he sees fit. I am sorry, Reverend."

Reverend Nelson nodded. He looked at Zachariah again. "Take Diana's right hand and repeat these words."

Zachariah swallowed, but nervousness still tightened his throat. Where was her hand? He reached out and pretended to take Diana's hand, hoping Mrs. Galloway wouldn't think he was doing it wrong.

"I, Edward Jackson, take thee, Diana Galloway, to be my wedded wife, to have and to hold, from this day forward, for better, for worse, for richer, for poorer, in sickness and in health, to love and to cherish, till death us do part, according to God's holy ordinance."

Again, there was silence. Everyone waited for Diana to repeat her portion of the ceremony.

The Reverend cleared his throat. "Forasmuch as Edward and Diana have consented together in holy wedlock, and have witnessed the same before God and this company, and thereto have pledged their faith to each other, and have declared the same by joining of hands; I pronounce that they are husband and wife together, in the name of the Father, and of the Son, and of the Holy Ghost. Amen."

Zachariah let go of Diana's hand, bent over and kissed her.

"On the lips not the cheek, Edward!" Mrs. Galloway said.

Zachariah swallowed. Galloway had showed him where Diana's cheek was, but he had to guess about her lips. He bent over, imagined the Indian woman from his dreams, and kissed Diana again.

He exhaled when Mrs. Galloway clapped. He straightened up and shook Reverend Nelson's hand. He ran his tongue around his mouth to generate saliva when he saw Mr. and Mrs. Galloway and Henry walking towards him.

"Welcome to the family, Edward," Mrs. Galloway said, tears drowning her eyes.

"Thank you, ma'am," Zachariah said.

"Call me Lola."

Mr. Galloway shook Zachariah's hand. "Edward. I know you will make my daughter happy."

"Thank you, sir. I will do my best." Then Zachariah lowered his eyes a little and shook Henry's hand.

Zachariah escorted Diana out of Reverend Nelson's house and into a carriage waiting for him. His smile sagged. He was too weary to carry on this pretense of happiness. William, in the driver's seat, turned and smiled at him. "Mr. and Mrs. Jackson," he said, aware Mrs. Galloway stood outside so she could watch her daughter disappear down the street.

William slapped the reins and got the horses trotting. "Nice day for a weddin," he said.

Zachariah bit his lip and nodded. "Yes." He looked behind him. Mr. and Mrs. Galloway were no longer visible. "I'm glad I could give Missus this special day."

*　　*　　*

William pulled the carriage into the livery stable. The wheels groaned to a halt. He climbed out and Zachariah followed. "Yo' clothes is under de seat," William said.

Zachariah bent over and pulled out his white shirt, brown coat and pants. "I did like dressing up."

Holding onto the side of the carriage, he lifted his feet up one at a time and pulled off his dress shoes. Then he took off his derby hat. He half frowned, half scowled at his plain appearance—his usual attire, depressingly bleak, depressingly slave cotton. He folded his dress pants and shirt nicely and set them under the seat next to his hat and shoes. He held the burgundy vest a long time before laying it on top of the pile along with his silk tie.

"Doan look so sad," William said. "I hear you goin' to get new clothes for pleasin' Missus."

Zachariah nodded. "They won't look like those," he said, unable to take his eyes off the dress clothes.

"No. You ain't never going to be a manservant or a gentleman. But dey mi' not be brown neider," William said. He gently pulled on Zachariah's arm to get him away from the carriage. "Come on. We's huv to walk back to de restaurant."

Zachariah walked, sober, stewing, mute. It was a few miles back to Hickory Rail Inn. A cool spring breeze blew. The sun warmed his face, but not his thoughts towards his lot in life.

"I almost forgot," William said, handing him a piece of paper.

Zachariah blinked at the script he couldn't read. A pass. He wasn't free to walk the city without a reason, because he wasn't free. His ears burned. He kicked a rock as hard as he could across the street.

After a quick taste of being truly white, he craved the fancy clothes. He craved being able to shake Mr. Galloway's hand and look the reverend full in the face. He craved getting married and being able to take care of his family. He craved the right to walk wherever he pleased, whenever he pleased without carrying a piece of paper signed by his master.

Zachariah gritted his teeth. It had been taken away in an instant. The charade was just to tease him, taunt him, torture him.

As if Master Henry didn't do that enough on his own.

Zachariah's eyes narrowed, his jaw tightened.

"You all right?" William asked.

Zachariah covered his face with his hands. "Yes." He focused really hard and made a wish. *Some day I'm going to be free. Some day I will be reunited with Ma and Rachel. Some day I will free them and take care of them.*

"Zachariah, you missed the wedding," Mrs. Galloway said when he walked into the hotel.

"I's real sorry, Missus," Zachariah said, consciously slipping back into dialect. "I's out running errands for Massa. We doan 'spect dey take so long."

Mrs. Galloway nodded. "No matter. Diana's with her husband, and now Alexander and I are going on a trip!"

"Where you goin' to go, ma'am?" William asked.

"Just to Nashville, but I can't wait. We're leaving tonight," she said, then hurried up the stairs.

Zachariah walked over to the front desk and shook Joe awake. A tired, happy smile crossed the old man's face like a child climbing into bed. "Youngen."

"Are you going to work at the front desk while I go with Master and Missus on their trip?"

Joe shook his head. "No. I's going to go on de trip wid dem. Be gone three weeks. My last chance to see my lil bruddah." His dark brown eyes brightened. "Dis trip is more a favor to me dan a favor to Missus," he whispered. "Hard to travel wid her."

Zachariah framed his face with his palms. "So Master's brother coming down to run the inn?"

"No. Henry's staying here and Bethany," he said, then winked.

Zachariah's heart gave one solid thump and then stilled. He grasped his shirt and pressed his lips together.

Joe put his hand on top of Zachariah's hand. "Three weeks will go by fast."

*   *   *

Zachariah dropped off the dirty dishes from his masters' evening meal and walked to the front desk. He rounded the cushioned chair which now had a permanent indention of his butt. At least it was cushioned, for his masters' comfort, not his.

He sat down, his chest heavy, arms heavy, eyelids heavy.

Footsteps on the stairs.

Master Galloway carried their trunks and Joe walked ahead to get the door.

Henry walked up behind Zachariah and watched his parents leave.

Master Galloway stopped when he got to the door. "Wait in the wagon, Lola. I will be right there." He returned to the desk.

"Did you forget something, Pa?"

Galloway nodded.

Zachariah eyes intently followed his master leave the room and return, a brown papered package under his arm. He licked his bottom lip when the package was handed to him. He tore open the paper, his mouth parted. Inside were the dress pants, shirt, coat and burgundy vest he had worn at the wedding.

"I cannot take them back," Master Galloway said, "and they are too small for Henry. I figure you deserved them anyway. You can wear them while we are gone and when my wife is locked in her room. She cannot see you dressed like that."

Zachariah nodded. "I understand, Master. Thank you."

"You are in charge of things now, Zachariah."

"You are leaving a nigger in charge of the place instead of your own son?" Henry's angry words did little to disguise his hurt.

"If you want to sit at the desk for three weeks straight, I will give the honor to you," Galloway said, matching his son's harshness.

Henry bit his lip.

"Thought so." Galloway's eyes narrowed and he glared at Henry as if he was trying to raise welts on his son's flesh. "I am warning you. If you lay one finger on Zachariah while I am gone, I will lay open your hide when I get back. You might be a grown man, but I am still strong enough to overpower you and get the job done. You can bet on that."

Zachariah's eyes bulged. Out of the corner of his sight he saw Henry's face turning red.

His son fuming silently, Master Galloway left and shut the door loudly behind him.

"I won't wear these clothes if you do not want me to, Master Henry," Zachariah said, soft and sad.

"Go ahead and wear them. I do not give a damn!" Henry stormed out.

Zachariah looked down at the fancy clothes lying on the desk. He wanted to wear them. He wanted to look white and rich and respectable. The fabric was soft, caressing his skin like gentle kisses from a handsome woman. Zachariah licked his lips. It was too much to resist.

He disappeared into his room to slip on his new attire. They were *his* clothes after all. Holding his head high, he walked back to the desk. He sat down and brushed his fingers across his burgundy vest.

Zachariah watched Henry walk up to the bar in the empty restaurant. He reached over the counter and pulled out a bottle, opened it and took a long swig.

Thinking of his young master drunk sent dread down Zachariah's back. He figured that Mr. Price and the rest of Henry's gambling friends would show up any minute. With his pa gone, Master Henry could get drunk and whip him for no reason.

He better enjoy the clothes while they were still on his back.

* * *

Zachariah crossed his legs and shifted in his seat. He had been at the front desk all morning, the urge to go was almost painful, but he continued to hold it. Lately, any request for Henry to be at the desk had been answered by blows. He massaged his bruised cheekbone which still hurt from yesterday. Two weeks had gone by painfully slow.

A white gentleman in a fancy black suit walked into the hotel. A beautiful young woman with amber skin and emerald eyes hung on his arm.

"We would like two rooms for four days," the man said.

"Two rooms?" Zachariah repeated.

The woman smiled coyly and brushed a strand of black hair that had fallen out of her bun behind her right ear. "This is my brother-in-law," she said.

"Oh," Zachariah's cheeks flushed. He reached behind him and pulled two consecutive keys off the rack. "You can have rooms 12 and 13. They are upstairs and to the right. That will be four dollars."

The man handed him the money and signed the register.

"Dennis," Zachariah called. The youth hurried to his side. "Carry their trunks up to their rooms."

Zachariah watched the young woman head into the restaurant, a thought plaguing him. She was vaguely familiar. The trim on her brown dress matched her eyes. Most women didn't have piercing green eyes. He stared at the register admiring the loops in the letters. If only he could read her name.

A few minutes later, the white man walked back down to the desk. Zachariah looked at the man, in his mid-twenties. "Is there something wrong, sir?"

"No. Lillian will want to take a bath."

"Five cents. Dennis can take care of that for you."

The man nodded and handed him a half-dime. "You run this place?"

Zachariah hesitated answering. Could the man really think he was white? "At the moment I do," he said carefully.

"I like my room. We are traveling and this is far better than some hotels we have stayed at."

"Thank you, sir."

As soon as the man disappeared up the stairs, Zachariah made sure the money box was locked and hurried into the restaurant to find Henry. Early afternoon streams of light shown through the windows, but did not brighten Henry's demeanor. His master stood at the bar pouring himself a glass of whiskey.

"I need you to stay at the desk for a moment, Master."

Henry drank down the liquor in one swallow then slammed the glass on the counter.

The sound caused Zachariah to flinch.

Henry boxed Zachariah's ears twice, then headed to the front desk without saying a word.

Zachariah saw Lillian eating biscuits and gravy in the back of the restaurant as he ran through the kitchen to the outhouse. Much relieved, he walked leisurely back taking in the fresh air and sunshine.

He kept thinking about the amber-skinned woman. Her emerald eyes and black hair and gentle voice all seemed familiar. He had met her before. Where? The realization hit him and his mouth dropped open.

Lillian was the Indian woman he had given his coat to.

He looked down at his appearance. He was still wearing his dress clothes. Lillian had made no sign she recognized him. He laughed then stopped and glued his lips together. There was no reason to be cheerful.

He could never be with her.

There was no reason to reveal his identity.

The realization amputated the joy from his heart, leaving him slumped and somber.

* * *

Early that evening, Zachariah heard footsteps approaching. Fearing Henry's fists, he bit his tongue forcing himself alert.

"I am sorry I startled you," Lillian said. She stood before him her hair undone.

"That is all right, ma'am," he said, an unconscious smile spreading across his lips. "I do not mind being surprised by you."

Lillian blushed. "I did not want to approach you in front of my brother-in-law. When Dennis brought in my hot water, I asked him your name. Just to be sure."

Zachariah's heartbeat fluttered just enough to cause a tingling sensation in his stomach.

"I still have your brown coat, Zachariah. I look at it and think of you."

Speechless, he looked away.

"What are you ashamed of? It looks like you are doing well."

"For a slave," he said with downcast eyes, "I reckon I am, Miss."

"Out of curiosity, I asked Henry if he was willing to sell you. He said he would do so gladly if it was up to him, but you belong to his pa."

Zachariah nodded. "If Henry could find a way to get rid of me, he would. However, this place could not run without me."

"You should take pride in that."

"I do, Miss, but I dream of getting away from here. Perhaps I could just walk out the door and keep on walking." He put two fingers on his lips. "I look white. I talk white," he said in a muffled mumble, then looked up at Lillian, fear draining the blood from his face. His stomach twisted. "I can't believe I just said that. Please Miss—"

"I can see why you have those thoughts." She curled a strand of hair around her finger. "Henry's in the other room drinking and gambling. Terrible vices. They ruin a man's character."

"That is for sure."

"Many young Cherokee men do the same when they are trying to forget their past."

Zachariah looked up at her alarmed. "Miss, do not tell Henry you are an Indian. He hates Indians."

Lillian nodded. "I have not mentioned it. He was so focused on his cards he did not even look at me."

"If he finds out he might try to hurt you—but I would not allow it."

Lillian's eyes brightened as if a candle burned inside her. "If getting away from Henry meant moving to an Indian reservation, would you want to?"

The tip of Zachariah's tongue escaped his lips. "Master Galloway has his vices too. There have been days when I have thought that the cotton fields would be a better place to live." Zachariah hesitated. He just had to say what was on his mind. He would torment himself if he let his chance go by. "Forgive me for being so bold, but if it meant I would be able to see you I would love to move to an Indian reservation."

Lillian smile widened. "Thank you. That is very kind."

Zachariah swallowed, unable to take his eyes off her. The silent teasing tension between them was a fog invading his thoughts. A fog that carried with it images of her naked. He swallowed again. "Miss, I can see you have money. Please buy me." After the words escaped his mouth, Zachariah wished he could take them back. What was he doing?

*

Lillian turned her head and looked out the window. She couldn't seem eager to comply. The tip of her tongue gracefully touched her bottom lip. "Why would I want to buy you?" she asked in such a casual tone she amazed herself.

When she resumed looking at Zachariah, she saw his hopes fall with his sagged shoulders.

"I can be a good waiting man, drive your carriage, I would even work in your stable." As he said stable, his nose crinkled and his eyes barely squinted.

Lillian held her breath to keep from laughing. Obviously he really didn't want to clean up after horses. "My brother-in-law has graciously paid for my tour of the South. I do not have money to spend on an extra bonnet let alone a slave."

Zachariah rubbed the back of his head, lowered his hand to his lap, and then resumed rubbing the back of his head. His body tense and face tight, something was clearly on his mind. Finally, he divulged his thoughts. "Would you buy me if you could?"

Lillian didn't know what to say. He must really want to get away from Henry. "I suppose. When is Henry's pa supposed to be back?"

"Six days, ma'am, but he won't sell me either."

She nodded and gave him a sly look, the corners of her lips twitching upward. "Is Henry a good gambler?"

Zachariah shrugged. "I don't understand the game, but he seems to lose more than he wins."

"And he drinks a lot."

Zachariah bit his lip and nodded.

"Thank you for the pleasant conversation. Good night, Zachariah."

*

After Lillian headed up the stairs Zachariah said, "Good night, Miss Lillian."

She disappeared around the corner.

He sighed, voicing the deep longing in his heart.

He shook his head. What was he thinking? Those kinds of thoughts would get him in more hot water than Henry could devise.

Still, he hoped tomorrow Lillian would give him another smile. He'd burn it into his memory for the rest of his days.

It seemed he'd be spending them at the inn. Her gentle beauty would likely be the best memory he'd ever have.

Chapter 13

Hickory Rail Inn
April 22, 1842

ZACHARIAH EAGERLY ANTICIPATED Mr. and Mrs. Galloway and Joe's return. He strained listening for wagon wheels. His heart rose and fell each time a customer entered the hotel. He changed back into his brown suit, just in case his master came back early.

Family was important to Joe. He doubted that they'd arrive ahead of schedule unless Mrs. Galloway's imagination changed their plans. Zachariah pressed his tongue to the roof of his mouth, seething with jealousy. At least the old man got to see his family.

Zachariah tried to stay hopeful, but he didn't know if he'd ever see Ma or Rachel again. Rachel was a young woman now and he doubted he'd recognize her if he had to wait a few years longer.

A middle-aged man in a black suit walked into the hotel. He rubbed the dark circles under his eyes and yawned.

"Would you like a room, sir?" Zachariah asked.

"No. I'm here to play poker."

Zachariah motioned towards the restaurant. "The game's in there." He followed the stranger with his eyes, curiosity piqued. The man looked like he was about to fall asleep, walking with slow, heavy steps. It wouldn't be hard for a newcomer to learn about the nightly game played at Hickory Rail Inn. Still, the game was for locals and a stranger had never joined before.

Zachariah leaned back in his chair and looked at the clock above him. The clock struck ten. Slowly his head lowered to the desk. When he awoke, he pushed the registry book back to its place. It had become his pillow. Groggily he looked at the clock again. Midnight. He sighed. Hard to get restful sleep at the desk.

He heard the men still playing cards in the restaurant, their voices muffled by the closed door. Didn't they need to sleep?

Henry hollered. "Zachariah, get in here."

The young man's heart constricted. Fear seeped through his pores into his bloodstream, paralyzing him.

"Zachariah!" Henry's voice was now urgent, almost desperate.

Zachariah's mouth parted slightly, his eyes closed. He took a deep breath. He had to compose himself.

He checked to see that the money box was locked before heading into the restaurant. "Yes, Master?"

"Stand behind my chair."

Zachariah gave him a funny look, but obeyed. He wrinkled his nose. Henry puffed on a strong cigar. He reeked of smoke from his hair to his toes. Zachariah felt a cough coming and clamped his mouth shut.

He had avoided Henry's drunken poker games and his flesh goose pimpled now that he was called in to be a witness.

He glanced nervously towards the front desk, fingering the bottom of his vest. Someone needed to be out there.

Henry smiled slyly, taunting like a snake about to strike, his eyes locked on the stranger. "I call."

The stranger laid his cards face up on the table. "A full house. Three fives and two nines."

Henry stared at the man's cards, the blood draining from his face until he was as pale as a corpse. He meekly turned over his king high flush in hearts.

"When do I get his paper?" the stranger asked, poker chips clinking in his hand.

Henry continued to stare at the man's cards.

"His paper," the stranger repeated.

Henry swallowed. His words came out soft and mechanical. "Tomorrow. My pa comes home tomorrow. He has it."

"That is fine. I have had a lucky night," the stranger said, standing. He proudly wore a I'm-a-better-player-than you smile. "I better leave while I'm ahead."

"May I go back to the desk now, Master Henry?" Zachariah asked.

"Go ahead and get back to work," the stranger said. "I'll come back for you tomorrow." Then he looked at Henry, a gleam in his eyes. "Table stakes. You just made me a very rich man." That said, he strode quickly out of the restaurant. In the silent room everyone heard the door shutting behind him.

"What is he talking about?" Zachariah's voice rose. "What does he mean he'll come back for me tomorrow?"

Henry sighed. "I bet you and lost."

"Bet me," Zachariah said. "But, but, but you can't bet me! I do not belong to you."

"I know." Henry put his right elbow on the table and rested his forehead in his hand. "I do not know what Pa will do." His words slurred into one another. "That man does not want money—he wants you."

Zachariah's face heated, his heart raced. He felt numb as he walked back to the front desk. Surely, Master Galloway wouldn't let him be dragged away, would he? His legs turned weak and wobbly. He grabbed the arm of the chair and sank to his seat.

*   *   *

The next morning, Eliza walked out and handed him a cup of coffee. "Is it true?" Her voice was tentative as if she was afraid of the answer.

Zachariah took a long drink. He hadn't slept much and the hot coffee roused him from his depressed stupor. "It's true."

Eliza bit her lip.

"Go about your work. You cannot help me standing here."

She nodded, eyes filled with worry like a mama fretting over a sick child.

Her expression sent an echo of shivers through him. He didn't need her pity. He wasn't an object to be pitied like a three-legged dog or a blind mule. Zachariah massaged his temples.

The stranger walked into the hotel. Zachariah's stomach knotted. He looked down at the registry book not wanting to see him.

The stranger walked up and put his right hand on the desk. "Is it too early to order breakfast?"

"If the ladies have the chairs on the floor, the restaurant's open," he replied, in a small, squeaky voice.

The stranger walked into the restaurant.

Zachariah raised his head and attempted to take a deep breath, but only a small gasp escaped his terror-gripped lungs. Nausea hit his stomach with a powerful punch and bile burned a path up his throat. He clamped his teeth shut not allowing himself to get ill.

Why had he wanted to get away from Henry so badly that he'd have done anything? Now that it could be happening, the idea made him shudder. He had friends here.

Where he was going could be worse. It could be the fields. The cotton, snake infested, overseer ruled fields.

He ran his clammy hands through his hair repeatedly.

Around noon, Zachariah heard the sound of a wagon driving up in front of the hotel.

Three familiar voices greeted his distraught ears. He couldn't contain his emotion any longer and tears burst forth like a waterfall.

Joe held the door open and Mr. Galloway escorted his wife into the hotel.

"Massa Galloway, please help me!" Zachariah said, running towards him.

Galloway set their trunks on the floor, confusion and alarm whirled in his eyes. "Did my son hurt you? I told Henry if he laid one finger on you I would—"

"He did not hurt me. He lost me!" Zachariah sobbed uncontrollably.

Joe walked over and put an arm around him.

Zachariah cried on Joe's shoulder. He took deep breaths struggling to gain his composure.

"Lost you? What are you talking about?" Galloway said, his voice filled with confusion and agitation.

Zachariah brushed away his tears. He raised his head and looked at Master Galloway. Words tumbled out of his mouth in a shaky rush. "In a poker game, sir. He lost me to a stranger in a poker game last night."

Galloway's face and neck turned scarlet. Both of his hands folded into fists. "HENRY! Get your goddamn, good-for-nothing ass in here this minute!"

Henry sheepishly walked through the restaurant door into the hotel. The stranger followed at his heels.

"I was drunk, Pa. I know that's no excuse, but I never would have done it otherwise."

Galloway approached his son and with one powerful blow knocked Henry flat on his back.

Henry groaned, blood running out his nose. He slowly got to his feet.

Mrs. Galloway screamed.

"Take her to her room, Joe," Master Galloway said, advancing towards his son with strong, unyielding steps.

Joe hurried the woman up the stairs as fast as his old legs would take him.

Galloway grabbed Henry by his shirt collar, pulled him to his feet and struck him again.

Henry wheeled backward, but regained his balance. Next he was socked in the stomach.

Henry gripped his middle. "Pa," he said breathless. "Please, no more."

"No more! I have ignored your drinking and gambling for far too long. After the attack, your ma turned idiot and you turned the devil's son. You need to find a better way to drown your grief. I'm not going to take it any more," he said, striking Henry's jaw.

A shiver of pleasure made Zachariah's fingers tingle. He bit his tongue. Henry was finally getting what he had coming to him. His pa was putting him in his place.

"As much as I am enjoying watching this family quarrel," the stranger said, "I am a businessman. We have business to discuss."

Galloway let Henry go with a gruff push. His expression remained business-like, but his lips threatened to press into an unfriendly line. "My son had no legal right to bet a slave he did not own."

"A man's family can be made to pay his debt. I could take it to court."

"You have no legally binding contract."

"I have several witnesses who were playing poker with us. I believe some of them are well-esteemed in town. A man's reputation can easily be ruined."

Galloway glanced up the stairs towards his wife's room.

"We are both businessmen. Zachariah is worth 1,500 dollars. I will give you that in cash. Then we'll be even."

The stranger shook his head. His sharp gray eyes looked Zachariah over. "That yellow man is young, has a sound body and he's right smart. Over his lifetime he'll make more for me than 1,500 dollars."

Galloway's face grew serious like a doctor about to deliver bad news.

Zachariah held his breath. He realized the man was determined to take Master Galloway for every penny.

"Two thousand dollars," Galloway said.

Zachariah's jaw dropped and his heart beat erratically. He didn't know he meant that much to Master Galloway.

The stranger shook his head again.

Galloway tensed and straightened. "I will give you $2,300. We both know that is expensive for any slave. That will give you quite a profit for one night of poker."

The stranger grunted. "I'll take Zachariah's paper now." He held out his hand.

Galloway glanced at Zachariah, mouth sober, but eyes betraying his sorrow. He turned back to the stranger, sighed and nodded. "I'll write out a paper gifting you his rights," he said, sadness in his voice. "Henry, stay here. You'll have to sign as a witness."

Zachariah's heart sunk, regret weighing it down, making it beat slower and slower and slower. Fate had listened to his plea.

His body felt like stone. With great effort, he bowed his head to hide the sorrow in his eyes. Anxiety dried his mouth.

What kind of work would this man have him do? After turning down so much money for him, he feared it would be difficult.

Galloway returned holding two pieces of paper. "I would like to know what a professional gambler is going to do with a slave," he said, in an irritated grumble.

"Professional," Henry said, anger and disbelief in his voice.

The stranger's lips twitched until a slight smile escaped.

"Henry, you are as dense as a rock," Galloway said. He walked over to the front desk and wrote out some information.

Master Galloway walked over to the front desk and wrote out some information. Galloway and the stranger were talking, but Zachariah couldn't make it out. He couldn't think straight. He saw Henry and the stranger sign the papers. The stranger folded one of the papers and put it in his coat pocket.

"Come on, Zachariah," he said.

Zachariah took a deep breath. He shot Galloway a pleading look then assessed the stranger.

Apparently professional gamblers wore black dress pants, a long black coat and navy vest. Zachariah figured he might be moving up in the world. If his master dressed like that, he could afford to take care of his slaves well. Zachariah pressed his lips together. At least he hoped so.

*   *   *

"Master, may I say goodbye to my friends?"

The stranger pulled a silver watch out of his vest pocket. "If you do not take too long."

"Yes, sir. Thank you."

He walked through the restaurant into the kitchen.

Virginia beamed when she saw him. "I knows you's stay," she said.

Zachariah's mouth curled down, forming a hollow beneath his lip. "I've come to tell you all goodbye."

Virginia and Robin walked over and gave him a hug, their eyes welling with tears.

He walked over to William and extended his hand. The man gave him a wet, soapy handshake.

Zachariah nodded to Taylor and Dennis. He leaned against the wall and waited for August and Mark to enter the kitchen.

"Good afternoon, Zachariah," August said cheerful, a bounce to his syllables. He walked in with a tray full of dirty dishes.

"This isn't a good afternoon," Robin said, "Zachariah's leavin'."

August gaped. "I never figure dat you…" He set his tray down and shook Zachariah's hand heartily. "I hopes you huv a good life. I knows you huv lots of dreams."

It took every ounce of strength for Zachariah to muster a tense, reluctant smile. "Thank you. Likely you will get my job. You deserve it."

Mark hurried into the kitchen and nearly ran into August. "Two bowls of stew, buttered biscuits and coffee," he said to Virginia. "Mornin' Zachariah."

"I am leaving. Master Galloway could not buy me back."

Mark's bottom lip quivered. "You mean Henry really lost you?"

Zachariah nodded.

Mark's lips retreated into a grim, deep frown. He shook Zachariah's hand.

"I best get going," Zachariah said. "Tell Alice and Eliza I wish them well." He headed towards the kitchen door. Before he reached it, he stopped and turned around. "I won't forget any of you."

Zachariah took a deep breath and headed up the stairs to say goodbye to Joe. He didn't know what to say to the old man. After being separated from his ma, and sister, Joe had become his family. Joe had even treated him like a grandson.

Zachariah knocked on the door. "Come in," Mrs. Galloway said.

He pushed the door open. Joe was playing checkers with her.

"Missus, may I speak to Joe for a minute?"

Mrs. Galloway nodded.

Joe followed Zachariah into their small room. They silently looked at each other, tears running down their cheeks. Joe gave him a hug, squeezing him so tight he felt the man's ribs. "I's been blessed to know you, Zachariah."

Zachariah's voice quivered along with his bottom lip. "I don't want to leave you."

Joe choked out a laugh. "Youngen if you doan leave me, I's leave you soon enough. I can't live forever."

Zachariah took a deep breath and pulled away from the man's embrace.

"I hope you get to do all de things I never did. Most of all I hopes you get free, boy. I knows Henry got to you, but you needs to keep thinking 'bout freedom."

Zachariah nodded. "I will."

He picked up his folded dress clothes, re-wrapped them in the brown paper he had saved, tucked the bundle under his arm and headed back into Mrs. Galloway's room.

"Master Galloway signed my paper over to that stranger," he said. "Goodbye Missus. Maybe some day I can get someone else to read poetry to me. I already said goodbye to Miss Bethany."

Mrs. Galloway's eyes moistened. "It isn't right," she said. "I do not want you to go."

Zachariah walked over and patted her hand. "Thank you, Missus, but I have to go. Master Galloway has to pay off Henry's debt."

Anger flashed in the woman's eyes. "I did not even know Henry had a gambling problem. I am going to talk to him." She jumped up.

Zachariah's jaw dropped slightly. Was she that out of her head?

Joe shot him a concerned look.

Zachariah licked his lips. He didn't know what to say or do.

"Please sit down, Missus," Joe said. "Massa Galloway, he's talkin' to him now. You can talk to him later—and we have a game to finish."

Mrs. Galloway sat down and Zachariah exhaled though his nose.

He nodded to her and Joe then headed down the stairs. Henry sat at the front desk. Galloway was standing over him, talking. Zachariah's eyes got bigger and bigger as he listened to the conversation.

"You're going to be working off your debt sitting right here. It is going to take you so long to earn 1,500 dollars that you are going to forget what fresh air smells like and what whiskey tastes like. If I smell it on your breath, I will turn you out without a penny to your name."

Zachariah's smile at Henry's punishment, slipped away as he approached the door. Silent and sullen he followed the stranger out of the hotel. Into his unknown future.

Chapter 14

Hickory Rail Inn
April 23, 1842

ZACHARIAH'S NEW MASTER untied a white horse from the hitching post and mounted. "That bay mare there is yours," he said, pointing.

Zachariah stuffed his bundle of clothes into the horse's saddlebag, untied her and mounted. "My own horse?" he asked, disbelief giving a lift to his words.

"I ride fast. I hope you can keep up." The stranger turned his horse and galloped out of town.

Zachariah kicked the mare's sides and chased after him.

After several hours of fast riding, they stopped beside a lake to water the horses. Zachariah got down on his stomach on the bank and scooped a handful of water to his mouth.

His master tossed two canteens at him. "Fill them up while you're down there."

Zachariah held them under the water. "What's your name, Master?" he asked, standing.

The man took his top hat off and ran his fingers through his black hair. "You do not need to know my name."

Why? Was he wanted? "Yes, sir." Zachariah shifted his weight repeatedly. "Back in town, why weren't you afraid I would run off?"

The stranger laughed. "I read eyes for a living. I read your eyes and knew you were honest. Besides, if you ran off I'd track you down."

"But you don't even have a gun."

The man reached into his right boot, pulled out a long knife and threw it. The knife whizzed as it flew past Zachariah's right ear, landing into the tree trunk an inch away.

Zachariah blinked at the knife. Then he looked back at the man who wouldn't even say his name. He swallowed. In a quivering voice he asked, "What's going to happen to me?"

His master fetched the knife. "I'm going to sell you."

"Then why did you not sell me back to Mr. Galloway?" Zachariah said, not even trying to hide his anger.

"Because I know a buyer who will pay more."

Zachariah bit his tongue. He couldn't imagine anyone paying more than 2,300 dollars for him. He wasn't strong. He didn't have special skills.

Each day he rode with his new master he came up with more questions he never asked. After four days of hard riding, all of Zachariah's muscles ached. Ached so much that at night he couldn't sleep. He lay, miserable, throbbing, moping on the firm, cold dirt. He worried the blanket between his fingers and stared at the stars.

A soft yellow glow brightened the darkness. Slowly the pale yellow rays stretched across the sky. Muscles heavy, eyelids drooping, Zachariah dug into his master's saddlebag and pulled out the sack of coffee. The rich aroma filled the air and his master awoke.

The man sat up and Zachariah handed him a cup of steaming coffee. "You do aim to please." He took a sip. "Today, we will arrive to where we're going." He gave Zachariah a sly smile like a child keeping a secret. "I think you will be pleased with your new life."

Zachariah swallowed. "What is my new life going to be like, sir?"

"That is not for me to decide."

Zachariah's brow creased. He opened his mouth then shut it. Further questions would seem too forward. "Yes, sir."

*   *   *

Zachariah and his master rode through the city and stopped outside a hotel.

They tied their horses to the hitching post out front. Zachariah unbuckled their saddlebags and carried them inside.

"Would you like a room?" the white man at the desk asked.

"Yes. A room for one night," his master said, throwing coins on the counter.

He walked down the hallway and unlocked their room.

Zachariah put the saddlebags on the floor.

His master rubbed his forehead. "I'm tired of my cooking. Come on, we are eating in the restaurant."

Zachariah's eyebrows jumped. He couldn't believe this mysterious man was going to share a table with him.

A negro youth walked over to their table. "What would you gentlemen like to order?"

"I would like a steak and he would too," his master said, "and coffee."

"Yessuh." The waiter disappeared.

Zachariah blinked at his master. "St-st-steak?"

The man shrugged. "I am in a good mood." He glanced over his shoulder at a game of faro being played in the back corner. With shifty eyes, he scanned all the people in the restaurant.

Zachariah heart stopped when the waiter handed him his plate of steak and potatoes. He stared at it.

"You do know how to eat, don't you?" his master asked.

Zachariah licked his lips. "Yes, sir."

He picked up his fork and knife and cut the tender meat.

His master picked a napkin off the table, unfolded it in the air then put it in his lap.

Zachariah stopped and did the same. When he tasted his first bite of steak, his mouth rejoiced. Perhaps his new life wouldn't be that bad.

Or there would be a price to pay for the good food.

He felt the color draining from his face. His stomach bunched. He ate the rest of his meal inwardly cringing.

*   *   *

After finishing his meal, his master handed him the room key. "Go upstairs, change into your dress clothes and stay there. I will be up in a few hours." His eyes returned to the faro game still in progress. "I am going to work for a while."

"Yes, sir."

Zachariah looked at the room key with the etched number four. He climbed the stairs and looked for the room with the same number. He unlocked the door, turned on the lamp, then sat on the bed and pulled off his shoes. Once in his dress clothes he ran his fingers over his burgundy vest.

The lack of sleep weighed him down like a ton of cotton.

Zachariah yawned. He looked down at his clammy hands then over at the door. The worst part about being a slave was not controlling his future. He pulled himself off the soft bed. His master had been kind so far, but he reckoned he'd be punished if he didn't sleep on the rug where he belonged.

After several hours, a loud knock awakened him. He got to his feet and opened the door. Standing outside was his master and Lillian. Zachariah's jaw dropped. It took a second before his mouth closed.

"I hired this man to win you," Lillian explained. "After you practically begged me to get you away from Henry, I knew it would haunt me if I didn't. I want you to have the life you deserve."

Zachariah blinked at her. He didn't know what to say.

Lillian's face grew concerned. "Is something wrong? I hoped you would be happy serving me."

"I am happy, Miss, very happy. Thank you."

"I want to change your name to Zachary. Does that bother you?"

He shook his head. "No, Miss. I like how it sounds when you say it."

Lillian nodded. "Good. Get your things and follow me."

Zachariah picked up his work clothes and followed her down the hallway.

She unlocked a door. "This is your room for the night, Zachary," Lillian said. "I hope you like the horse I picked out for you. I probably should have let you pick out your own horse. If you do not like her, we can trade her in at the livery. It looks like you need a new hat and shoes. After all that traveling, a bath would be good too."

Zachariah stood there, frozen, mouth agape.

Lillian smiled, the corners of her mouth twitching as if trying to hold back a laugh. "Montgomery, my brother-in-law, says I talk too much. We have plenty of time for all that. I will let you rest."

She left and closed the door behind her.

Zachariah heard the click of the lock. Understandable but unnecessary—he wasn't about to leave. He shut the curtains, took off his shoes, pulled back the covers and crawled into bed. The soft mattress eased his aching limbs. The more he thought about serving Miss Lillian, the more his grin widened and widened and widened.

He knew with her, he wouldn't be treated like an animal.

If this was a dream, he did not want to wake up.

Chapter 15

Memphis, Tennessee
May 16, 1842

ZACHARIAH CLIMBED INTO the driver's seat of the carriage. He bit his tongue, watching Lillian's brother-in-law help her into the backseat. He longed to touch her soft amber hand. Longed to feel her skin against his. If only he could help her, wait on her, cater to her every whim. The man had yet to allow Zachariah to do much for Lillian in his presence.

Zachariah rubbed his chin. Strange he had been instructed to call Lillian's brother-in-law by his first name, just his first name—Montgomery.

"Turn left at the end of the street," Montgomery said.

Zachariah wondered what store Lillian would want to go in next.

Montgomery looked at his gold pocket watch. "We better hurry or we are going to miss the boat."

"They are expecting you. They will hold it," Lillian said.

"Yes, but they are trying to keep to a schedule."

Zachariah pressed his lips together. Would he be going on a boat too? He glanced at Lillian, but was afraid to ask. Maybe they'd hire him out in town and travel without him. He looked over his shoulder. His horse was still tied to the back of the carriage. He didn't want to leave her. They had just gotten acquainted.

His sucked in his breath when he realized he was driving down to the steamboat docks. Two steamboats were anchored there, one in the process of unloading. The passengers, already ashore, picked up their trunks. Negro men carried the last of the cargo down the gangplank.

The air felt sticky and heavy. A breeze carried the familiar scent of sweat, tar and rotting fish towards him. It smelled just like the steamboat docks in Natchez. Zachariah wrinkled his nose, glad his stomach was empty.

He stopped the carriage behind a wagon.

Montgomery helped Lillian down.

A colored boy, not more than twelve, and a middle-aged negro man walked towards them.

Zachariah let out a soft whistle. He was one of the fanciest dressed colored men Zachariah had ever seen. He wore a burgundy frock coat, brown paisley vest, black pinstriped pants, a top hat and silk tie. Zachariah blinked when he noticed a gold watch chain draped out of the man's vest pocket. The negro man took their trunks out of the rear of the carriage.

"I will take your carriage, Master Barlow," the colored boy said, climbing into the driver's seat.

"Thank you, Patrick," Montgomery said.

The boy turned the carriage around and drove away.

"But my horse," Zachariah said, arm out wanting to drag him back.

"He is coming with us," Lillian said. "On a barge. Animals are not allowed on the steamboat we are taking."

"I am going on the steamboat?"

Lillian nodded, smiling small, cautious. "I hope you enjoy it."

"Welcome back, Mr. Barlow," the fancy dressed negro man said. "The *Princess* is running a little behind schedule today."

"I am not surprised, Arthur. She never keeps time well."

Zachariah looked over at the slaves in coarse shirts and pantaloons loading the boat. Their clothes were torn and covered in a reddish coat of dusty grime. The muscular giants rolled barrels of molasses up the gangplank. Others carried crates of tobacco on board. The white mates cussed at the men to pick up their pace, but it did little good. They worked at steady pace, exhaustion in their movements, ingrained in their faces. At times, whip in hand, a mate would lay into one of the men.

Montgomery shook his head. "The boys could be working a little faster."

Arthur laughed quietly as if this was a familiar joke. "Yes, sir," he said, starting to head for the largest steamboat at port.

Montgomery escorted Lillian up the plank.

Zachariah followed.

"We have time to make up." Arthur shouted at the slaves on the dock. "Look lively! Master Barlow's here!"

Zachariah's mouth dropped open. "You own all those men?" he asked Montgomery, his words slow, hushed.

"Yes, and the steamboat," Montgomery replied just as if he had said the sky was blue.

"Your room is ready, sir," Arthur said, "and Miss Lillian's stateroom." He handed Montgomery two keys. "I did not know you were bringing a friend, sir. All the other staterooms are occupied."

Montgomery nodded. "That is all right. Zachary is staying with me."

"Yes, sir. Is there anything I can do for you?"

"No. That is all for now."

"I will take your trunks to your rooms then." The wiry man left them and climbed up the stairs to the boiler deck.

Montgomery walked over to a well-dressed white man. "How's business, Mr. Hargus?"

"Good, Mr. Barlow. We're nearly full with passengers and freight each trip."

Montgomery motioned for Zachariah to join him. "Zachary this is Mr. Hargus, my chief clerk."

Mr. Hargus extended his hand.

Zachariah lowered his gaze and did not shake the man's hand.

Mr. Hargus' eyes crossed. "I do not bite. You are as meek as a nigger."

Zachariah felt his face turning hot.

Mr. Hargus gave Mr. Barlow a tight, business-like smile, lowering his hand. He returned his attention to Zachariah, "Pleased to meet you, Zachary. You are one of the lucky ones. Anyone traveling with Mr. Barlow I do not charge fare."

Montgomery walked back over to Lillian. "Shall we dine, my dear?" Lillian nodded.

Zachariah followed the two of them up the stairs. He heard people talking and laughing and smelled thick cigar smoke. They walked into a long parlor constructed of solid maple, hand-carved and inlaid with woods of contrasting colors. He resisted the temptation to bend down and feel the burgundy carpet. He looked around. The rows of high windows let light in. Golden chandeliers, hanging from the ceiling, provided nighttime illumination.

Nearby were several round tables draped with fine white cloth for dining and set with silver. At the other end of the room were gaming tables and a bar, above which was the biggest mirror he had ever seen. A deep-throated noise sounded and the boat pulled away from the dock.

Montgomery chose a table and Zachariah hurried over to pull out Lillian's chair before he could. He wanted to please her, not out of fear, as with Henry, but out of gratitude.

"Thank you," she said.

Zachariah nodded. He put his hands behind his back and remained behind her chair.

"You may sit down. You are dining with us."

"Lillian," Montgomery said, his tone sharp, disapproving.

"You dine with Arthur and his wife," Lillian said, in a barbed whisper, locking eyes with him.

Montgomery's facial muscles tightened. He glanced at the ceiling, exhaled loudly, then motioned to a chair by Lillian. "Have a seat, Zachary."

"Thank you."

Awkward silence engulfed the table. Lillian and Montgomery both focused on him. Zachariah looked down at the tablecloth trying to avoid their attention.

"Have you ever been on a boat, Zachary?" Montgomery asked.

"No, sir," Zachariah said, raising his head.

Montgomery and Lillian exchanged a knowing look.

A bell tolled. The passengers got up from their chairs lining the parlor walls, left the bar, and gaming tables and sat down in the dining area.

A negro waiter in black dress pants and a white coat walked over to them. "Steak, sir?" he asked.

"Steak for Lillian and myself and a bowl of stew for our friend."

The waiter nodded and walked away.

Zachariah puckered his lips, disappointed that all he was getting was stew, but he wasn't about to complain. After the horse, shoes and hat, he knew he was lucky. Very, very, very lucky.

Halfway done with his stew, Zachariah's stomach pitched. He looked down at his bowl, closed his eyes and gripped his middle.

"Can I get anything else for you, Mr. Barlow?" he heard the waiter ask.

"Arthur."

* * *

Before Zachariah knew what was happening, Arthur had helped him down the stairs, led him though the maze of stacked firewood, tobacco crates and other goods, and over to the ship's whitewashed railing. He grabbed Zachariah's top hat before it fell into the Mississippi.

"It takes a while to get used to the roll of the water," Arthur said. "It is best to look out at the horizon. Looking down can make it worse."

Zachariah raised his head. He bit his lip, trying to concentrate on keeping his food down. Nausea hit in relentless waves and he vomited into the water below.

Arthur put a caring hand on his back. "I will help you to your cabin when you think it has passed."

Zachariah continued vomiting for several minutes. Some of the chunks landed on the railing. His stomach empty, he turned away from the rail. He staggered a couple steps and Arthur steadied him.

"That was why I was going to help you, sir. Your legs and your stomach have to get used to being on a steamboat." Arthur looked at one of the Irish deckhands who was on his hands and knees scrubbing the floor. "Clean the railing too."

The deckhand's eyes narrowed. He got to his feet and folded his right hand into a fist.

"Clean the railing," one of the mates instructed.

The Irishman gritted his teeth, his nostrils flared. He walked over to the railing, rag in hand.

"The deckhands don't like it when you tell them what to do," the mate said.

"I know, but sometimes I cannot help it," Arthur replied.

"It would be easier if you remembered you were a nigger," the mate said. "I know you are the steward but that does not give you the right to act like a white man," he muttered, then walked away.

Arthur sighed and aided Zachariah to his room.

"Thank you," Zachariah said. He lay down on the mattress with a groan.

Arthur placed Zachariah's top hat on the dresser then gently pulled off his shoes. He poured water into the washbasin, dipped a cloth into it, rang it out and placed it on Zachariah's forehead.

"Why are you helping me?"

"It is my job to make sure that you are comfortable," Arthur said. He pulled the covers over Zachariah's shoulders. "There is a chamber pot at the foot of the bed if you get ill again. I will check on you later. Try to get some sleep."

*　　*　　*

A knock at the door woke Zachariah. He opened his eyes, his mind groggy. Another knock. He threw back the covers and stood slowly. Another knock. He yawned as he walked to the door.

"Do you think you can eat breakfast?" Lillian asked, concern heavy in her voice. "You slept through the bell."

"I am awful hungry, Miss. I would like to try."

He followed Lillian back to the dining room at a respectful distance, but still within her shadow.

"Where is Mr. Barlow?" he said, once he realized it was just going to be the two of them at the table.

"He is talking with the clerk. Montgomery kicked Arthur and Charlotte out of their room last night. Hopefully, another stateroom will become available today so that they can get their room back tonight."

"What would you like to order?" the waiter asked.

"Biscuits and gravy for both of us," Lillian replied.

Zachariah watched the waiter walk across the room and wait on an older couple. "What is my new job going to be, Miss?" he whispered. "You could hire me out to be a waiter on the boat."

Lillian smiled, sweetly cunning. "You will learn your new job in time, Zachary."

Zachariah ate his meal slowly, hoping that would help his stomach. Lillian was stunning in a violet dress with a white shawl draped over her shoulders. Their eyes met. Goose pimples popped on his wrists and spread up his arms.

Peaceful chords of music emanated from the middle of the room, separating the gaming and dining areas. A slender negress, in a tight-fitting, light blue silk dress, played a piano, her skillful fingers moving gracefully across the keys. She was older, but quite handsome, her dancing eyes as whimsical as her music.

*

Lillian huffed. Why must every man, slave or free, white or colored, gawk at Charlotte? She wanted to give Zachary a piece of her mind, but that would make her goal harder to achieve. She took a deep breath and slowly her chest relaxed.

She touched his shoulder to get his attention and gave him her best distracting smile. "Would you like to see more of the boat?"

"I would like that very much, Miss."

Lillian brushed a stray strand of hair behind her right ear. Zachary was the man she'd been searching for. Brought up to be passive, he wouldn't harm her, take advantage of her, rule over her; the heart of a gentleman in the trappings of a slave.

She wasn't going to give up her identity to please her pa. She wasn't going to give some brute her body even if he was a man of prestige.

Zachary's every action was gentle, uncertain. He must have had a rough life.

Lillian pressed her lips together. That gave her something to mold. She'd take him in her hands and transform him into what she wanted, what she needed.

Her lump of clay would not be recognizable with fine manners and learning.

She'd get him used to everything a little bit at a time.

*

Zachariah followed Lillian across the room to the gaming tables. She stopped, took a step back and hooked arms with him, then continued walking.

He bit his tongue. Her soft touch made him tingle, made him long for more. His heart beat wildly, but it did not divert his nervous thoughts. He held his breath as they approached Montgomery who was talking to a man running a black and red wheel.

"There are more people talking and reading on sofas and in the rocking chairs than there are gambling," Lillian said.

"It is a might early for most people, especially if they had a late night." Montgomery scanned the room. "The black jack table is doing well though."

"We will go watch the players," Lillian said.

Zachariah turned as pale as the white tablecloths. "Miss, I have had enough gambling to last all my life."

Lillian patted his hand. "We are just watching."

They stood behind the black jack table, giving the players distance. His eyes doubled in size and he ran his tongue across the back of his teeth. He recognized the man in the black suit and navy vest. Without warning, a young man across from the professional gambler jumped to his feet.

"You're a cheat!" he said, pointing at the professional gambler.

Zachariah's heartbeat increased by a fraction. He held his breath, his toes curling in his shoes.

"Calm down, sir and take your seat," the gambler said in a monotone, exhaustion engrained in his face. "You are just having a bit of bad luck. It happens to everyone."

Montgomery hurried over to the table. "What is the problem here?"

"Your dealer is cheating!"

Montgomery turned serious. "I run an honest establishment, sir." He pointed to a big sign hanging above the bar counter. "If you can prove the house is cheating, I will refund your money. That is my policy."

"I saw him put a card in his vest pocket."

Montgomery's eyes narrowed and he shot the gambler a what-are-you-up to look.

The gambler put both hands on the table. "Check my vest."

Montgomery searched his vest pockets and pulled out two cards.

Zachariah gasped.

Montgomery threw the cards face up on the table. "I do not know about you," he said, "but there are no jokers used in my black jack game."

The young man's face flushed. He spoke strained and slow. "I am sorry. If you cash me out, I will leave."

The gambler mechanically counted out and handed him some bills.

"The black jack game is closed for a while, men," Montgomery said. "My dealer needs a break. You can play better on a full stomach. I suggest you order something to eat."

All the players got up from the table and walked away, muttering to each other.

Montgomery's eyes drilled the gambler.

"Sorry, Boss," the man said, looking down at the green felt tabletop.

"If I catch you cheating, I will throw you in the Mississippi and you better hope we are close to shore."

"Yes, Mr. Barlow. He was just a sore loser. I have been called a cheat before. Why are you so agitated?"

Montgomery did not respond.

"I am still catching up on sleep," the gambler continued. "A rider brought me your message. I got off the boat and rode to Louisville then back to the boat—"

"I know, Jasper," Montgomery said, cutting him off. "And I really appreciate that. Go take a nap."

"Thank you, sir." The gambler rose. "Miss Hildebrand," he said, nodding to her. "Zachary, it is nice to meet you again."

After Jasper left Zachariah asked, "So I take it he works for you?"

Montgomery tilted his head to one side and then the other. "At times."

*   *   *

Zachariah spent all day with Lillian touring the steamboat. They poked their heads inside nearly every nook and cranny, including the barbershop. Spending time on the main deck made the hair on his arms stand on end. Poor white people and slaves slept there, resting against cotton bales. The tall, muscular roustabouts made him nervous. Though Montgomery and Lillian had introduced him to everyone as a friend he was sure they knew otherwise.

The pitch of the boat was worse on the main deck—a rocking, rolling ride. More than once, Zachariah leaned over the railing. Lillian put her hand on top of his each time he vomited. The comforting yet strong touch soothed him. By evening, his body had adjusted to living on the river and he had adjusted to escorting her places without blushing.

After supper, Lillian dragged him back to the main deck. "I love being close to the water," she said. "Looking through a window or even walking along the railing on the upper decks isn't the same."

Zachariah nodded, though he did not see its special charm. He took a deep breath, inhaling the fishy smelling breeze, balmy for a spring night. He looked at the stars twinkling in the sky. It seemed a long time ago since Ma told him the same stars would shine over him and her and Rachel no matter where he was.

If Ma saw him now, she'd be in shock. He had left Strasburg, Virginia far behind and now he was traveling the country. Still, he had to keep his promise to get his ma and sister free. He was the man of the family. They depended on him for their freedom.

The white deckhands took turns at standing watch. They looked warily at the travelers' body-servants chained to the deck. Seeing none were causing trouble, they glanced over at the roustabouts who had gathered in a circle.

"How come they are here?" Zachariah asked, motioning with his head to a well-dressed negress. "And in chains."

"Only Mr. Barlow's slaves are allowed on the upper decks."

"But what about—"

"You are with me." The end of Lillian's words dropped to a whisper.

Zachariah read her lips and it sent a thrill to the marrow in his bones. He rolled his shoulders and shook his arms slightly to work out some of the adrenaline-charged energy.

Banjo music began. He turned and saw the roustabouts clapping with the beat. One man, with a deep voice, started singing a plantation song. Zachariah's eyes lit up like a candle illuminated his desolate soul. The beat resonated through his body. He opened his mouth, and Lillian squeezed his arm.

"I am getting tired, Zachary. Please escort me to my room."

Zachariah nodded with a pleasant smile though his spirit sagged with disappointment. He escorted Lillian to her stateroom. He stepped inside and paused to take in the plush burgundy curtains and gilded mirror above the washstand before turning to leave.

"I did not tell you to go," Lillian said.

Zachariah's mouth opened. "Forgive me, Miss. I thought you were going to sleep."

Lillian slowly removed her shawl and teased him with her provocative smile, bare shoulders, and arched back. She laid her shawl on the bed, took off her black hair net, and undid her bun.

Zachariah leered as her fine black hair fell down her back.

"You like what you see?" she asked.

Zachariah licked his bottom lip, his cheeks heated, but he didn't answer.

She walked over to the washstand, picked up the silver brush, and handed it to him.

He stared at it as if it would bite.

"Do you know how to use a hair brush?" she asked, sitting in the chair by the bed.

"Yes, ma'am." He walked up behind her. "I brushed my sister's hair till the old brush broke."

Lillian tilted her head and peered into his blue eyes. "Do you know how to count to one hundred?"

"I know how to count to thirty-nine... that's the most I've been whipped."

She lowered her head. "Fine. Count to thirty-nine and keep going until I tell you to stop."

Zachariah tenderly cradled her soft hair with his left hand as he ran the brush through.

"Do you like the boat?" she asked.

"Yes, Miss. It is like a floating city."

"Yes it is. It is so much better than the reservation. My sister, Bessie, was so disappointed she couldn't come. Bessie's in the family way. It will be her and Montgomery's first child. He wants a boy and she wants a girl. In Cherokee society, rights are transferred through the women in the family. So having a girl is important."

Zachariah nodded, though he didn't know what that meant.

He continued brushing her long hair gently. Not wanting to hurt her, he hesitated at every tangle. But she didn't seem to notice.

"What does your family do, Miss?"

"My pa is an elder in the council. He's been elected to that position many times. We have a big house and big apple orchard. We also raise horses."

"I like apples."

"You might be picking them some day."

"That sounds like hard work," he said, before he could stop himself. An awkward anxiety overwhelmed him.

Lillian laughed. "I would only have you pick enough for a pie." She paused before saying, "Tell me about your family."

Zachariah swallowed. "I am from Virginia—Strasburg. My ma's name is Catherine. She's a cook and I have a little sister Rachel. She's going to be a seamstress."

"And your pa?"

Zachariah pressed his lips together and looked at the floor. "I don't have one."

"You mean he died?"

"No'm. I just never knew him."

Lillian tapped two fingers against her lips and seemed to be thinking. The door, cracked a little, allowed the faint sound of piano music to echo through the room. She stood up, turned around, smoothed the front of her dress.

"Do you know how to dance?"

Zachariah turned pale. "Dance? No, ma'am."

*

Lillian placed the palm of her right hand in the palm of his left and stretched out his arm. Then she guided his right hand to her waist and placed her left hand on his right shoulder.

The heat of his body, his tentative touch drew her in. She wanted a deeper connection, a different kind of dance.

Zachary stiffened, stared at her, fear in his eyes.

"Relax," she said. "This does not hurt."

She moved her right foot back gracefully, while looking down at their feet. "Move your left foot forward. Now step forward and to the right with your right foot. Slide your left foot quickly over to your right and stand with your feet together. Step slowly back with your right foot. Quickly step back and to the left with your left foot. Quickly slide your right foot towards your left and bring your feet together." Lillian raised her head and looked into his eyes. "That's it. When the next song starts, we will do it again."

Zachary swallowed. "Miss Lillian, why are you teaching me to dance?"

She tucked a strand of hair behind her right ear. "I believe everyone should know how to dance. Arthur is a great dancer."

Zachary's shock increased the volume of his voice. "You have danced with Arthur?"

"No. Arthur's married. I have watched him."

"What does his wife do?"

"She plays the piano."

The music started again. Zachary tried to remember the steps and in what order to do them. Lillian tried not to laugh while he muddled through, but failed. He bit his lip and on the third song, finally got the hang of it.

"It is called a box step," Lillian explained, "because we are making squares."

*

Her hand felt smooth in his—like silk. He couldn't believe his hand was on her waist. He wanted to keep it there forever. Zachariah took a deep breath, but couldn't calm his racing heart. Each step made him more nervous. They were so close he smelled her rose perfume. It was like being surrounded by the Garden of Eden.

She looked up, her emerald eyes locked with his, her lips spreading into a seductive, sultry smile.

An excited shiver spread up his spine, through his arms to his fingertips. He leaned in, his lips close to hers, inhaled her peppermint breath. What was he doing? He pulled back, his face hot.

They continued dancing and he stiffened. His face became stoic. He had to remember his place. He couldn't kiss her.

After the sixth song, Lillian sat on the edge of the bed, her face glowing with new found freshness.

"Thank you, Zachary. I love dancing."

"Thank you for teaching me to dance, Miss."

Lillian lay down, stretched her arms above her head and yawned.

Zachariah shifted upon the balls of his feet and gnawed on his lip. He felt uncomfortable seeing her in that position, but he couldn't tear his eyes away.

"It is a long boat ride. I will teach you many things," she said. "You may go now. Shut the door behind you."

"Yes, ma'am," Zachariah said.

He walked into the parlor eagerly anticipating what she would teach him next.

Chapter 16

Aboard the Princess
May 18, 1842

ZACHARIAH AND ARTHUR stood looking over the railing of the boiler deck. The boat stopped to take on firewood. The procession of firemen walked ashore, climbed the levee, picked up several logs, almost as tall as they were, and walked back across the narrow plank. They then deposited their loads crossways near the fire pits at mid-boat.

Zachariah raised his eyes to the smokestack which would soon be enveloped by a sooty cloud once the ship had built up a good head of steam.

Arthur waved at the children gathered at the landing.

A thought floated around Zachariah's mind and he finally blurted it out. "Does Mr. Barlow own you?"

Arthur's smile vanished and his face became rigid. "Yes, sir. He does. None of the colored crew's free. Mr. Barlow thinks he avoids trouble that way. I feel free except when he's on the ship. I am the steward—the captain of all the servants."

Arthur paused and his usual smile reappeared. Pride filed his voice. "Even the mates have come to respect me."

Zachariah turned his head to get a good look at him.

"Not hard to read your mind, sir. I get cussed at once in a while or struck by a bag or cane from a disgruntled passenger. That's all. I have a good life on the water and my family's well taken care of. My wife plays the piano and I have two daughters who are cooks, working safely away from the public. My son..." his words died.

"What about your son?"

Arthur sighed so deep, long, and loud Zachariah's eyes moistened. "He was taken off the ship when Mr. Barlow got married," Arthur said. "He works at his house on the reservation. I haven't seen him in two years. Mr. Barlow tells me about him and I get a letter once in a while." As soon as he said that, panic flashed in his eyes.

"You can read?" Zachariah said a little too excitedly, envy and concern swirling together.

"No. Mr. Barlow he w-writes the l-letters an-and I get one of the d-dealers to r-read them to me."

The ship pulled away from the dock with a lurch. Not losing a step, Montgomery walked over to them. He watched the roustabouts playing a game of dice on the deck below.

"Is there something I can do for you, sir?" Arthur asked.

"Lillian would like to see both of you in her room."

Arthur's eyes widened, begging for an explanation, but Montgomery didn't say more. "Yes, sir."

Zachariah followed Arthur into the parlor, where Arthur paused and let Zachariah get ahead of him as they walked down the hallway. Zachariah knocked on her door.

Lillian did not greet them with her typical rosy glow. They stepped inside the room and she quickly shut the door.

"Arthur, I have a big favor to ask," she said.

The man's stiff posture softened. "Anything, Miss."

"I want you to teach Zachary to read and write. Numbers too."

"Teach him to..." He looked at Zachariah, to Lillian, then back at Zachariah. "You mean he's—"

"Yes," Lillian said. "But *no one else* is to know." Arthur opened his mouth as if to protest. "Montgomery knows," she added. "This needs to happen quickly. Zachary is smart. He will learn fast. I don't need to remind you this also needs to be a secret."

Arthur swallowed hard. "Yes, Miss. I will do it."

"Thank you, Arthur. I knew I could count on you. Do you still have the primers you used to teach your children?"

"I do not know what you are talking about, Miss," Arthur said quickly.

Lillian's eyes narrowed and her voice took on a threatening tone. "Don't play games with me. My sister and I know many of your clandestine doings aboard this ship. Montgomery is not good at keeping secrets. Half the letters he sends you are not in his script."

Arthur looked away sheepishly, like a child caught stealing a piece of pie. "Yes, Miss. I still have them," he whispered. "And a slate."

"Wonderful. Get to work then. My room is yours." Lillian handed Arthur a ruler.

"Miss," Arthur said, a little hesitant. "How does Mr. Barlow expect me to see to my duties and teach Zachary as well? I get precious little sleep as it is."

"Montgomery can handle his own slaves for a while and delegate. He knows how to run the ship."

Arthur nodded. "Yes, of course."

She walked into the parlor.

Arthur rubbed his forehead. "She's planning something," he said. "Her sister gets that same look in her eyes. I do not know what it is, but she's planning something." He looked Zachariah over and pointed to the chair at the small desk. "Sit," he ordered.

Wordlessly, Zachariah obeyed.

"I will be right back," Arthur said. He returned carrying a carpetbag. He set it on the floor and pulled out a primer, slate, and piece of chalk. He opened the primer to the first page.

"This is the alphabet," he said in a hushed tone. "There are twenty-six letters. The first letter is A. It makes a sound aaa as in apple." He drew an A on the slate. "Now copy that as many times as you can until the slate is full."

Zachariah studied the large A as he drew it.

*   *   *

Hours later, Zachariah shifted in his seat. He felt like ants were crawling up his legs. He hadn't been given a break all day. Arthur even made him eat his afternoon meal in the room and study at the same time.

Now that he had learned all the letters, Arthur instructed him to write his name—Zachary. He stuck out his tongue a little as he concentrated on making each letter properly.

Arthur stood behind him, ruler in hand.

"Is that correct?" Zachariah said, a nervous twinge in his voice.

"That is correct…" Arthur stopped talking. Soft humming came from outside the door.

Lillian walked in, a bowl of custard in hand, her womanly charms on display. "How is he doing?" she asked, standing beside Arthur.

"He is making progress, ma'am," Arthur replied. "By the time the *Princess* makes her second trip down the river and docks in Arkansas City, he'll be able to read the Bible," he said confidant and boastful.

"I can write my name now, Miss."

"Show me."

Zachariah picked up the chalk and wrote his name on the slate again.

"I think that deserves a celebration," Lillian said. She placed the bowl of custard in front of him.

"Thank you, ma'am."

Lillian bent down close to him and wrote her full name on the slate. "Lillian Hildebrand," she said.

Zachariah swallowed his first bite of custard and beamed. The creamy dessert, like sweet milk, was even better than steak. The smooth, slippery delight slid down his throat. He eagerly devoured another spoonful.

"I will learn to write your name too," he said. Then his face became solemn. "I wish I had a last name."

Lillian ruffled his wavy blond hair. At her gentle touch, the corners of Zachariah's mouth began to turn upward. She continued playing with his hair until he grinned.

"Why do you want me to learn to read and write, Miss?" Zachariah asked, a mixture of anxiety and excitement settling in his gut.

Lillian's eyes glazed over as if she was dreaming. "Your lack of learning is the only thing denoting your slave status. I want you to pass for a gentleman. Would you like that, Zachary?"

Zachariah wanted to grin, but he restrained his lips to a normal smile. If he could walk around town without being asked to show a pass, he might be able to get a job or to just escape and go back to Virginia to rescue his ma and sister. After all, if he could pass as white—he could pass as free.

Zachariah nodded. "Yes, Miss. I'm honored that you want me to be educated."

Lillian retrieved her shawl from her trunk and wrapped it around her shoulders. She flashed him a sweet smile though her eyes had hardened. "I trust you will do your best. Do not fail me, Zachary."

"Yes, ma'am."

It was strange being owned by a woman. Did they whip their slaves too? He wouldn't find out. He wouldn't fail in his studies. He felt something different inside. He felt a yearning to please not out of fear but out of respect.

Letters were something white men held dear. Letters and money.

Zachariah's eyes brightened. He had his own motives for becoming learned.

Chapter 17

Aboard the Princess
May 18, 1842

ZACHARIAH WATCHED LILLIAN leave, his eyes intently following the sway of her hips.

Arthur shook his head and chuckled.

The door shut. Zachariah took a deep breath, returned to the slate, picked up the chalk and carefully copied her name.

"Why does she want me to be a gentleman?" he mumbled to himself.

Arthur shrugged. "An educated negro is worth a lot of money if he is well-mannered. You'd be a good waiting man."

Zachariah grinned. He felt tingling in his chest, the sense that his pulse pounded with enthusiasm. That would be wonderful. "If that is what Miss Lillian wants, I will work hard at it."

Arthur bent down and turned a few pages in the primer. "Now for your beginning words. The word 'in' is spelled I N."

"Why can't you just use the N? It sounds the same."

Arthur shook his head. "Every word needs a vowel. A, E, I, O and U are vowels." He wrote the vowels at the top of Zachariah's slate.

Zachariah nodded and wrote 'in' on his slate.

"How do you think you'd write 'on'? Think about the sound of the word."

Zachariah stared at the slate as he ran through the alphabet in his mind. Finally, he wrote O N.

"Miss Lillian was right. You learn fast."

Zachariah's chest puffed with pride.

*   *   *

By the time they got to four letter words, Zachariah groaned. "Can I take a break?"

"No," Arthur said firmly. He picked up the chalk and wrote a short sentence on the slate. "What does that say?"

Zachariah blinked. The white lines looked blurry. His head throbbed above both eyes, and he couldn't concentrate. "I don't know."

"You did not even try." Arthur took the ruler and rapped it on his pupil's fingers.

Zachariah let out a high-pitched yelp.

The doorknob began turning. Miss Lillian would alert them before entering. With an urgent air, Arthur picked up the primer and slate and shoved them in the desk drawer then handed Zachariah the ruler.

"Stand up and hit my hands," Arthur said, presenting his palms.

Zachariah's brows furrowed and he blinked.

The door started to open. Beads of sweat formed on Arthur's forehead. "Now," he whispered.

Zachariah's training to be obedient made him slam the ruler down on Arthur's hands. The smack echoed through the silent room.

Arthur cried out in pain.

"Miss Hildebrand, are you all right?" a man's voice asked.

"I'm sorry, sir. I will get that for you," Arthur said, backing away from Zachariah.

He turned around and his face flushed when he became nose to nose with a thin white man with graying hair. Arthur bowed his head slightly and tried to brush past the man and out the door.

The man grabbed his shoulder delaying his retreat. "Mr. Barlow's friend put you in your place?" he asked, then chuckled.

"Yes, sir," Arthur said. "I told him I was not a waiter, but then he reminded me that as a steward, I do whatever I'm told to make the passengers comfortable."

The white man grinned, creating a welt on Zachariah's heart. Arthur's humiliation was his fault.

"I am glad he got you to understand that. Mr. Barlow lets you do whatever you want," the man said and walked out.

Arthur returned with a tray bearing a tall glass of lemonade. He shut the door behind him with one hand and then set the tray down on the empty desk. He pulled the slate out of the desk drawer.

"You read that sentence, and you can have the lemonade," Arthur explained. He rubbed his hands on the sides of his pants. "The pilot house is going be roaring with laughter in a minute," he grumbled.

"I thought you said the mates respected you."

Arthur's forehead creased, his lips pinched. "The mates do. He was an officer." Arthur pointed to the slate. "Read that sentence."

Zachariah massaged his eyes then looked at the words. "The do-og ra-an."

Arthur nodded. "You may take a break now."

Zachariah exhaled, picked up the glass and greedily drank down the sweet lemonade. "Can I eat supper in the parlor?"

"Yes. I am getting cabin fever myself." Arthur rolled his shoulders. "We both need to stretch our legs, I have chores to do and I haven't seen Charlotte since this morning."

*   *   *

Zachariah searched the room for Lillian. He found her sitting at a table with Mr. Barlow. He didn't know what he was going to say, but he found himself walking towards them.

Lillian's eyes sparkled when she saw him, like twinkling stars in the night sky. "Montgomery do you mind if—"

"No. I will go." He smiled at Zachariah, tight, shallow, not at all genuine. "I hope you're enjoying your trip on the *Princess*. You can eat my catfish when it comes."

When the song ended, Arthur clapped quietly, bent over and gave his wife a kiss on the cheek. The bell tolled to call the cabin passengers to the dining room.

Montgomery walked towards the bar, but stopped when he saw Arthur escorting his wife to the staircase. "Arthur, let's play a game of cards."

Arthur frowned so low the sides of his lips nearly touched his chin. His wife gave him a long kiss.

"We will have supper later," she said sweetly and headed back to the piano.

Arthur and Montgomery walked out of the parlor. A few minutes later, a woman screamed loud and urgent.

Zachariah's head whipped around. A pudgy man gripped both of Charlotte's arms. Charlotte kicked him in the shins.

"Why you wench! I just wanted a kiss."

Zachariah bolted across the parlor, adrenaline pumping through his blood, pulse roaring in his ears. Without a moment's hesitation he gave the white man a right hook.

The man let go of Charlotte's arms and wheeled backward. "Hey, what was that for?" he said, loud, dragging out his words.

"You were hurting the lady," Zachariah said, his eyes narrowing into threatening slits. The burning sensation in his ears crept down his neck, an outward sign of the anger bubbling in his gut.

"She isn't a lady she's a negress." The man swung at Zachariah.

Zachariah ducked and punched the man again. This time he hit the floor and didn't get up.

By this time, Montgomery and Arthur had heard the commotion and returned to the parlor. Mr. Barlow hurried over to the piano where the white man lay sprawled on the floor.

The fire in Zachariah's blood dimmed as realization sunk in. What had he done? His heart raced like an untamed stallion.

Montgomery gave him an indescribable look, his lips tight, vein on his temple twitching.

Zachariah's lungs bunched and his breathing became short, shallow, rapid. He didn't want to know how he'd be punished for striking a white man.

"He was drunk, sir," Charlotte said. Arthur comforted her with a long embrace.

Montgomery looked at the white man then back at Zachariah as if trying to comprehend it. "I didn't realize you were so good with your fists," he said. "That man's out cold."

"Charlotte screamed and I just acted without thinking. I didn't mean to hurt him."

"You did not hurt him," Montgomery said. "Arthur, get some men to carry him back to his room. I'm going to the pilot house."

"Yes, Mr. Barlow. And, sir, may I dine with my wife?"

Montgomery nodded.

"Charlotte, are you all right?" Zachariah asked.

"Yes, sir." She paused and straightened her dress. "Thank you for coming to my aid. I am used to men looking me over, but I will never get used to them being physical."

"And you never should."

Charlotte blushed. "I know you have been spending a lot of time with my husband, sir. I hope you find your time on the *Princess* pleasurable."

*

"Zachary," Lillian called. She rubbed her tongue across her teeth, her heart fluttered. He acted so heroically. She had made the right choice getting him.

He turned his head and saw her motioning for him to come back. "Please sit down. The food will be here soon."

He took a seat next to her. "You've been treating me very nice, Miss Lillian. I—"

"I like to take care of my friends."

"Friend?" Zachary's voice rose.

"Yes." Lillian reached over and held his hand under the table.

Zachary stiffened.

She studied his tall, thin frame and looked into his kind, blue eyes. Zachary's face showed a mixture of shock and confusion. She smiled inwardly, pleased with his progress. The underlying element of fear was gone. Her plan was working.

She searched for the right words to calm him. "Arthur is my friend too," she said finally.

"Yes, but he—"

"This is not like at the Hickory Rail Inn, Zachary. Do you understand that?"

Zachary looked away to break her gaze. He studied the men lined up at the bar for a moment before looking at Lillian again. "Yes, I understand."

She lowered her voice so it was barely audible. "Montgomery takes care of Arthur and Charlotte, and I want to take care of you."

A waiter appeared with two plates of catfish. "Where did Mr. Barlow go?" he asked.

"Business. Zachary is dining with me."

The waiter set the plates on the table and disappeared.

"But I am supposed to take care of you," Zachary said.

"That is not how it works in Cherokee society, Zachary. We take care of each other."

"But Arthur works," Zachary said. "I don't do anything."

Lillian laughed delicately. She finally let go of his hand so she could start eating. "You provide companionship. I haven't had any luck finding a male companion on the reservation. It became chaotic after we were forced to move and rebuild our lives. There are too many violent, drunk, skirt chasers and gamblers."

"So my job is to be your companion?" Zachary asked.

Lillian could tell by his tone of voice that he was still trying to comprehend it. "Is that agreeable with you?"

Zachary nodded enthusiastically. "Yes, Miss."

"That's another thing I like about you Zachary, you don't argue with me like our men do."

"I want to please you. You're beautiful, graceful and gentle. Cherokee men would be lucky to be your companion."

Lillian felt her cheek heating twenty degrees. "Usually they view it the other way around. Do not be so shy, Zachary," she said, teasing. "I like to see your handsome blue eyes."

*

Zachariah shifted in his seat. Feeling he had been instructed to, he looked up from his plate and into her mysterious green eyes.

"You will get used to it," she said. "What would you like to do after we eat?"

"I ... uh ... you are asking me what I want to do?"

Lillian nodded.

Anticipation made his fingers tingle. He wanted to hold her in his arms, but he couldn't say that. "I would like to dance ... but Charlotte's eating with Arthur."

Lillian flashed him a deep grin making Zachariah wonder if she had been thinking the same thing.

"We can dance," she said. "We don't need music." She leaned closer to him. "Afterward, we have business."

"Business, Miss?"

Lillian's face pinched with irritation. Her eyes danced from table to table, watching the other people dining. Finally, she returned her attention to Zachariah. Her voice was soft as if for his ears only. "I will go over your books."

One of the ship's officers, sitting at a nearby table, shot Lillian an appalled look. "A woman shouldn't be involved in business ventures," he mumbled.

Lillian's lips thinned along with her determined eyes. "Zachary you will soon learn that I care little for properness and tradition."

Chapter 18

New Orleans, Louisiana
May 20, 1842

FROM THE MAIN deck, Zachariah watched the carriage and horses being driven off the barge onto the landing.

Lillian walked up behind him and put a hand on his shoulder.

He turned and smiled, pleasant but tight, trying to disguise the joy he got from being in her company. He had gone from fearing to craving her affectionate touch. Spending most of his time learning to read and write he barely saw her.

This morning, Lillian's black hair was pulled back under a green bonnet adorned with yellow flowers. Zachariah took a deep breath, his mouth slightly parted, so he could drink in her beauty. It would get him through the desert of words and sentences until he saw her again.

"I have a surprise for you, Zachary. I am going to show you some of New Orleans."

A burst of excitement made Zachariah's thoughts spin. He had to kiss her. He leaned over, their lips perilously close. He inhaled her breath. Shivers rippled down his body. He lusted to feel her skin, taste her skin. At the last second he caught himself, pulled back, and kissed her hand.

"Thank you, Miss."

A mixture of shock and pleasure registered in Lillian's eyes. She put her hand on her chest and took a deep breath.

He escorted her down the gangplank and noticed her rosy cheeks, her whole face beaming with vitality. Montgomery was waiting for them, standing by the carriage. Zachariah quickly grabbed and opened the door and helped Lillian into her seat.

"Mr. Barlow, would you like me to go with you?" Arthur asked.

Zachariah looked over his shoulder and saw Arthur and his wife walking off the boat.

"That will not be necessary. I can drive the carriage."

"Yes, sir."

Charlotte stopped and pushed open a cream parasol that matched the trim on her violet dress.

"Where do you want to go, Charlotte?"

"Besides the bath house?" she said, then gave a dainty laugh. "I want to buy piano music."

Arthur rolled his eyes. "You want to spend our allowance on piano music?"

Montgomery chuckled. He reached into his pocket, pulled out a half dollar and pressed it into Charlotte's hand. "The lady should get what she wants. Besides, I would like hearing some new songs."

"Thank you, Mr. Barlow," Charlotte said with a little curtsey.

"Arthur, be sure to bring back some eggs and ham," Montgomery said, climbing into the driver's seat. He slapped the reins and the carriage rolled forward.

"Where are we going?" Lillian asked.

"I have to see someone about a cradle."

Lillian's mouth burst open into a tooth revealing grin. "You are buying Bessie a cradle! She'll be so surprised."

"Well, we will need one for the little man."

"Or lady," Lillian reminded him.

Montgomery shook his head and turned down the street. He stopped the carriage in front of a building with a big green sign hanging in a large window that overlooked the street.

"What does that say, Zachary?" Lillian asked, pointing to the sign.

"G-ree-n-vi-lle fur-nit-ure and w-oo-d-wor-k-ing."

"That's right." Lillian gave him a peck on the cheek.

Zachariah's heart fluttered nervously like a bird learning to fly. He looked at Lillian wide-eyed. His words strained leaving his throat and came out in thin wisps. "You-you k-kissed me."

Lillian nodded. "Please help me down."

Smiling, he climbed out and offered her his hand when they entered the shop he heard hammering and sawing going on in the back. He silently oohed and aahed at the intricately carved dressers, washstands and other furniture.

When they reached the cradles, Lillian sucked in her breath. "They make me want a baby."

"You need to find a man and get married first," Montgomery said.

Lillian looked at Zachariah out of the corner of her eye, a smug smile flickering for a second. "I know."

After much debating with Lillian, Montgomery bought a large walnut cradle that rocked.

The shopkeeper had a man load the cradle into a wagon and drive it down to the docks.

Zachariah offered his hand to help Lillian back into the carriage.

She shook her head. "I thought you and I could take a walk."

"If you want, Miss."

"I'll leave you and conduct the rest of my business then," Montgomery said. He gave Lillian a long stare. "Don't go too far. I do not like leaving you alone."

"I am not alone," Lillian responded, agitation in her voice. She added force to each syllable. "Zachary will take care of me."

Montgomery drew in his lips as if he was about to protest.

"I will not let anything happen to her, sir," Zachariah assured him.

Montgomery stayed there for what seemed like eternity. He drummed his fingers on his thigh, clearly not convinced. He eyed Lillian, but she did not even twitch.

"Women," he muttered at last and drove off.

*   *   *

Lillian took Zachariah's arm. "There's a store I want to take you to." Before he could respond she was dragging him down the street, sweetly humming. Finally, she stopped.

Zachariah's mouth gaped open. In front of him were more books than imaginable.

"Read the sign."

Zachariah tipped his head back to see it. "R-an-d-ol-ph and s-ons b-oo-k-st-ore. You mean all of those books are for sale?"

Lillian laughed. "Yes." She unhooked her arm and walked towards the door.

Zachariah quickened his step so he could open it for her.

"How can I help you?" the short black-haired clerk asked.

"I would like *The Last of the Mohicans*," Lillian said.

The man nodded and pushed his glasses up on his nose. He walked around the counter and up a ladder. He came back down, book in hand. "Is there anything else I can get you?"

Lillian looked at Zachariah who had his head tilted so he could read the book spines. "Do you want to read about anything?"

He straightened up and scanned all the books along the wall. "Is there a book that explains all the words?"

The clerk studied Zachariah for what felt like years.

Zachariah swallowed hard. A terrible feeling soured his gut. He knew he had said something wrong. He should have said no. He didn't want people to realize he was a slave. He didn't want Lillian to get in trouble for having him learn his letters. He didn't want to get Arthur in trouble for being his teacher.

"A dictionary," the clerk said at last. "Do you want the abridged or unabridged one? The unabridged one is two volumes."

Zachariah shrugged.

"We will take the unabridged one," Lillian said.

She paid the man and Zachariah carried the books out of the shop. He walked beside her as they headed down the street.

"Don't go asking any more fool questions." Lillian's voice snapped like the rap from a ruler.

He bowed his head. "Yes'm."

*   *   *

After a couple blocks, Lillian's eyes filled with desire and greed and the sheen of precious metals.

Before she could ask him to, Zachariah read the sign hanging in the window. "Ho-ra-ce Kin-ka-de Jew-el-er."

Zachariah gawked at the jewelry through the window.

"You can look at them better inside," halfway through the door.

He blinked and slowly came out of his daze. He followed her into the store.

A pudgy man in a gray suit greeted them.

Lillian walked over to the glass case on the counter which contained diamond rings.

"Ah," the man said. "You are looking for a wedding ring."

Zachariah's face turned bloodless pale and he shook his head.

The jeweler laughed then looked at Lillian. "These are wedding rings, miss."

"They wouldn't have to be." Lillian pointed to a silver ring with the biggest diamond. "I would like to look at that one."

He pulled it out of the case and handed it to her.

She slipped it on her ring finger then sucked in her breath. "It fits perfectly." She looked coyly at Zachariah. He fingered the gold pocket watches, a dreamy expression on his face. "What do you think?" she asked.

"It is real pretty," he said, barely looking at her.

Lillian rolled her eyes. "Men." She looked back at the jeweler. "I'll take it."

"You'll take a wedding ring?"

"Yes. I have the money. You needn't worry."

The jeweler's eyes flared, his voice jumped higher. "You are carrying that much money with you?"

"No. But my sister and brother-in-law have an account here, sir. Bessie and Montgomery Barlow."

His mouth gaped open. "You are one of the Indian princesses."

Lillian put a hand on her chest. "Heavens, no! Indian princesses are for trashy dime novels. My father is not the chief. He's just an elder in the Cherokee council."

The jeweler nodded, a little bewildered.

"What happened to Mr. Kinkade?"

"I bought him out. He moved to Natchez to care for his aged mother. Mr. Barlow can pick this up before the *Princess* sails."

Lillian nodded. "Thank you, sir."

She turned and smiled at Zachariah, his eyes still glued to the display of watches. She tapped him on the shoulder. "We have more stores to go to."

They hadn't walked far down the street before she stopped. "I forgot something. Stay here. I will only be a minute."

Zachariah stood there holding the books. He opened the first volume of the dictionary, and turned to the first page of words. The words blurred together and the chambers of his heart glued shut. It would take him a lifetime to learn everything.

"We can go now," Lillian said.

Zachariah looked up. Engrossed in the dictionary, he hadn't heard her come back.

Lillian looked around at the line of shops with large window displays and the bustling street with wagons and carriages and men on horseback. "I love New Orleans," she said, then sighed. "But we really should get back to the ship, especially since Montgomery has to come back and pick up my ring."

Zachariah nodded. They were almost to the ship when he saw a clump of dandelions growing on the side of the street. He set the books down and picked them. "For you, Miss Lillian," he said. "I wish they were roses."

With a finger, Lillian touched their soft yellow heads. "They are lovely. Yellow is one of my favorite colors."

*   *   *

Zachariah and Lillian stood at the main deck railing and watched the commotion down below. Two roustabouts were finally loading the baby cradle aboard the ship, under Mr. Barlow's supervision.

Montgomery spoke loud and deep. "If you drop that cradle, it will be the last thing you do."

The hands carefully carried it aboard. All of Mr. Barlow's slaves, who had witnessed it, let out a cheer, Arthur the loudest of all.

He walked over to Lillian. "Mr. Barlow says that is for his son."

Lillian shook her head. "Bessie is having a girl."

Arthur smiled trying to restrain a laugh. "The only way you'll convince him of that is when the good Lord makes it happen."

After eating a ham supper with Lillian and Montgomery, Zachariah waited for Arthur, sitting on the sofa as close as he could to the piano.

Arthur walked into the parlor and announced, "Grub pile's ready." The cabin crew filed out of the parlor eager to eat.

"Sir," Arthur said, standing next to Zachariah. "Is there something I can do for you?"

Zachariah stood, his face sober. "Come with me," he said, "I'm not happy with the linen." He led the way to Lillian's room. His skin stretched tighter each time he had to act to slip out of the parlor with Arthur.

It took a minute for his chest to loosen. He resumed studying with vigor, learning new words with enthusiasm. He wanted to be able to read the book Lillian gave him: *The Last of the Mohicans.*

Arthur handed Zachariah the slate and chalk. "Write down what I say."

"Yes, sir."

"Flowers grew by the white fence. The cat sat nearby. He was watching the birds fly."

Zachariah showed Arthur his slate, "That rhymed," he said.

"You remember everything you're told, don't you?" Arthur yawned. "That is enough for today. We'll get an early start tomorrow to make up for the time we lost." He handed Zachariah a little box. "This is from Miss Lillian."

A present from Lillian? A fluttering feeling migrated from his heart to his stomach. He opened it and gasped at the shiny watch face staring back at him. Carefully, he pulled out the pocket watch and turned it over. 'Zachary' was engraved on the back. He held it up and it twirled around on its gold chain.

Arthur shook his head. "Before long, you will have my job," he said, good-naturedly, but with a hint of worry.

Chapter 19

Aboard the Princess
June 1, 1842

In the parlor, LILLIAN SCOOTED CLOSER to Zachary on the beige sofa. Their legs brushed and a tremor of excitement rippled through her body.

Zachary turned the page in *The Last of the Mohicans*.

Lillian rested her elbow on the low back of the sofa, her cheek in her hand, listening intently. She marveled at how well the words rolled off his tongue. This was the third day that Zachary had read in the parlor. The room was noisy from passengers eating and drinking and gambling and talking and Charlotte's piano music, but she knew a few people could hear him.

Today his face was a light shade of pink, his voice louder, more confident. She smiled softly, lost in the rhythm of his voice—the movement of his lips. He was getting used to his role as a learned man; becoming accustomed to his voice and to the eyes of the public. Her plan was working.

Zachary began the next passage:

As the rights of hospitality were, however, considered sacred among them, this little departure from the dignity of manhood excited no audible comment. Had there been one there sufficiently disengaged to become a close observer, he might have fancied that the services of the young chief were not entirely impartial. That while he tendered to Alice the gourd of sweet water, and the venison in a trencher, neatly carved from the knot of the Pepperidge, with sufficient courtesy, in performing the same offices to her sister, his dark eye lingered on her rich, speaking countenance.

Zachary paused. "You don't mind how they describe the Indians in this book?" he asked.

"Compared to most books I've read, I think Mr. Cooper is respectful. The story is set almost a hundred years ago. I find it entertaining, especially the love story."

Zachary's stomach rumbled. He looked at his gold pocket watch. Soon the bell tolled calling them to the dining room.

*

After a pleasurable meal, just the two of them, Zachariah returned to Lillian's room to continue studying with Arthur. With his reading and writing now sufficient to pass for a white man, though far from polished, he was now learning math skills. This came even faster to him. All the time he spent at the hotel desk taking money came in handy.

Memorization was a skill he didn't know he had. He soaked up the information like dry sand when the Mississippi rose.

"Nine times nine is?" Arthur asked.

"Eighty one," Zachariah responded with no hesitation.

He had spent so much time with the negro man he finally felt comfortable asking a question that had been on his mind a long time. "Arthur, how come you know all this?"

"Mr. Barlow spends most of his time on the reservation or traveling. I help run the ship in his absence."

"You run the ship?" Zachariah's voice stretched into a shrill soprano.

Arthur rolled his shoulders. "Well, sort of … I buy the food, keep track of the expenses used, care for passengers and slaves, and send Mr. Barlow letters informing him of business."

"If you can walk off the ship at any of the major cities, why do you come back? Why don't you just disappear?"

"Well, nearly everyone in those cities knows me and my wife and knows we work on the *Princess*. If I disappeared I would never see my children again. And I'd go from living like a king to…" his voice trailed off.

"Don't you want to be free?"

Arthur stared out the window, his jaw tense. He didn't move for several minutes. "Everyone wants to be free. There are many ways to gain freedom. My whole family will gain freedom in time. Mr. Barlow has said he'll free us and he's a man of his word. I just have to be patient. I have a feeling in my bones that freedom's in your future too."

A charge of excited energy sped to Zachariah's legs. He gripped his seat with both hands to keep sitting.

Arthur smiled, and then the corners of his mouth slowly sagged. "Of course you could have a pleasant life while still in bondage like me."

Zachariah nodded.

Arthur rubbed the back of his neck and proceeded with the lesson, weariness invading his voice, slowing his words. "Nine times ten is?"

"Ninety."

Arthur took his top hat off and ran his fingers through his hair. "Let's take a short break."

Zachariah watched the sun sink lower, illuminating the clouds with a red glow. The room darkened and Arthur lit the lamp on the desk then took a sip of his glass of water.

Zachariah cleared his slate. He bit his lip, tipped his head to one side and then the other, thinking what to write. Finally, he picked up the chalk.

> *Indian maiden, Lillian by name*
> *My loyalty to you, I forever claim.*
> *Hair as black as a raven's wing*
> *As beautiful as the first day of spring.*
> *With a voice like a mockingbird*

Speaking nothing but kind words.
Gentle and full of grace
With a lovely angel's face.

Once again, there was sweet humming outside the door. Zachariah's heart went from ten to a thousand beats per second as he watched the doorknob turn. The anticipation caused his limbs to ache.

Lillian walked into her room twirling around a few times to the last of the piano music. She gave Arthur a quick look and instantly the negro man left.

She stepped closer. Zachariah's breathing increased and his arms goose pimpled. He sensed that something was about to happen, something life changing. His stomach tightened, bracing for the news.

She took his hand, interlocking his pale fingers with her amber ones.

Zachariah swallowed, his voice escaped his lips, timid and nervous. "I wrote this for you, Miss Lillian," he said, looking at the slate.

Lillian's smile blossomed into a grin revealing all her teeth. "Oh Zachary," she said, airy, loud, excited. "I have never read a better poem."

Zachariah looked at his poem again. His racing heart blurred his thoughts. "Words can't rightly express how I feel."

"Do you remember when we first met that December day by the ferry?"

Zachariah nodded. "I had a cold walk into Louisville," he said mostly to himself.

"You have a big heart, Zachary." She paused, her mouth partly open. "I was not able to get you out of my mind these past few years. I knew I had to find you. That is why I went on this trip with Montgomery, to find you. To find the handsome white one held in chains."

"Why me?" he asked, confusion palpable in his voice. "There's nothing special about me."

"That is where you are wrong. You are so thoughtful, so… It is hard for me to find the words to explain." She looked out the window at the beautiful sunset. "You know we will be landing in Arkansas City in a few days. That is where I get off."

"I know, Miss." Zachariah swallowed, tingles running from his neck to his toes. "Am I coming with you?" he asked, a pleading tone in his voice.

She pulled him to his feet and over to her bed. They both sat on the edge of the mattress. "What I have to say might take a while." Lillian patted his hand. "I have thought of you constantly, Zachary. I think unconscious thoughts are very powerful. I believe they often try to direct our future. I believe our ancestors can control our thoughts and dreams. They are trying to help and guide the living."

Lillian paused and scooted closer to him, their thighs touching.

Zachariah tensed briefly, but her inviting smile put him at ease.

"It is because of these plaguing thoughts," Lillian continued, "because I was worrying about your welfare, that Montgomery agreed to help me rescue you from Henry. I knew I would never be at peace, never happy with anyone or happy in general until I knew you were well."

Zachariah hung on every word. He searched her emerald eyes for an explanation to the questions he couldn't ask. He had been dreaming of her before they even met. He wanted to tell her, but he held his tongue.

*

Lillian opened her mouth but no words came. She didn't know how to say this. She took a deep breath. She had to try. Hopefully, he'd understand.

"I have not treated you like a slave. You know that. I do not want to treat you like a slave." She paused. "I know many men make slave women…" she stopped what she was going to say. "Though my heart yearns for companionship, I can't do that to you. You have a choice, Zachary. I am telling this to you now so that you will have a few days to think about it before giving me your answer.

"You can stay on the *Princess* and work as a waiter. It will be a good life. You can get off in the major cities like Arthur. I will give you your own allowance of money. You will have fine clothes, fine food. I promise all your needs will be met and more. Or you can spend the rest of your life with me on the reservation."

She bent over, while gently holding the back of his head, and gave him a long kiss on the lips—warm, wet, sensual. She felt Zachary's racing heart against her chest. The kiss made her whole body quiver with delight.

She pulled away and saw his deep blush. "I do not favor you, Zachary. I love you. If you come to the reservation with me, I want you to marry me. I want you to be my husband."

Zachary blinked at her. "Marry you? How can I?"

Lillian sucked in her breath. It felt like butterflies had hatched in her stomach. "How is not an issue. You're white except for the wave of your hair. I realize that our life together will not be the same as my fanciful dreams, but I do love you. Do you love me? Do you want to marry me?"

*

"Yes," Zachariah breathed, a tingly sensation overtaking his body. He bent over and gave her another kiss. When he pulled away, she grabbed him and made the kiss last longer. "Yes, I will marry you," his words eager, rushed.

"From this day forward you have a new identity. You are a *white* man. You need to pick a last name and a profession. We have to make up your past and the whole way to the reservation you will learn it."

"A profession?"

"Is there anything you're good at or know very well?"

Zachariah looked at the wall, rubbed his hand across his mouth. He shrugged. "All I've done is waitering and running a hotel."

"Those won't do. Can you think of something else?"

"No. A few times Michael, the other waiter at the restaurant I worked at in Virginia, he mocked me saying I had the makings of a preacher."

"Perfect! We have to get you a fancy Bible and some black clothes in Arkansas City. The reservation could use a good preacher."

He spoke slow, soft, words weighted with worry. "You want me preaching to the reservation?"

"Of course. My father would not let me marry a loafer. There's really nothing to it. I can help you write your sermons. Then there are weddings and funerals. We've had a lot of funerals lately with so much violence..." her voice faded.

Zachariah's mouth felt stuffed with cotton. He ran his tongue around his gums and tried to swallow.

"But I am dammed," he said finally. "I turned my back on the Lord a long time ago. I can't preach."

"Nonsense. Don't you believe the Lord brought us together?"

Brought them together? She had a professional gambler win him from Henry. What did God have to do with that?

Zachariah had practically begged to go with her. Sure, it was practically a miracle he was being asked to become a white man and marry a rich, beautiful Indian woman. But he had his doubts that it wasn't just luck.

He looked into Lillian's hopeful eyes. "I guess I'll preach," Zachariah said. "If it means being with you. I will do anything to be with you. I love you something fierce."

Lillian gave him another kiss. "I've wanted to kiss you since Jasper brought you to Knoxville. But I did not want to scare you. Oh, Zachary. I am so happy you said yes."

She let out a giddy laugh. "Usually the man asks the woman to marry him, but my pa said I was born outspoken." She glowed with rosy vitality, her words bounced with excitement. "We have so much to do and there's so much for you to learn. I'll make you the happiest man. I promise."

A deep, wide grin stretched across his face making his jaw ache. Married to her, he'd be something. Married to her, he'd be respected.

Married to her, his dreams would be within reach.

*　*　*

The next afternoon, Lillian took Zachariah up on the hurricane deck. He wondered who occupied that row of rooms, but didn't ask. They walked along the promenade holding hands.

"Looking out at the Mississippi makes me feel so small," he said.

"I felt the same way when I went aboard a steamship the first time." She smiled at him, pleasure and eagerness reaching her eyes. "I want to show you something."

She led him into the pilot house. Montgomery sat on a leather cushioned high-backed bench looking out at the river. He was talking with a handsome brown-haired man sitting on the large sofa across from him. Both men rose when they entered.

"Lillian, you should have let me know you were coming," Montgomery said.

"I didn't know I needed permission to enter the pilot house." She turned to the white man on the sofa and spoke in a cajoling tone. "Or do I, Captain?"

The middle-aged man shook his head. "Of course not, Miss Hildebrand. Your visits are always a pleasant surprise."

The pilot nodded to her, his head barely reaching above the wheel.

Another officer looked out the starboard window. When he turned around, Zachariah realized it was the man who had walked in on him and Arthur weeks before.

"Miss Hildebrand," he said, smiling. "May I be introduced to your friend?"

"Of course. Levi Barnaby this is Zachary Degan."

Zachariah extended his hand. "Nice to meet you."

Degan, his last name. Reverend Degan. He took a deep breath and along with air, pride filled his lungs.

Lillian sat on the bench next to Montgomery and Zachariah joined them. Being welcomed into an exclusive area of the ship, and sitting with the officers sent an eerie feeling up his back, like a spider.

No, it was more than eerie. He knew it was wrong.

The pilot pulled a brass knob attached to a cord, and two long, low notes from the big bell floated into the breeze. Then there was a pause and he rang the bell one more time.

A man's voice followed, from the hurricane deck—"Larboard lead! Starboard lead!"

The cries of the leadsmen began to rise out of the distance, and were repeated in drawn out tones by the Irish deckhands.

"M-a-r-k th-ree! Qu-ar-ter-less th-ree! Half twain! Quarter twain! Mark twain!"

The captain half-smiled at the pilot, a playful sheen in his eye. "Showing off for our guests I see. We knew it was safe running, no need to check the depth."

The pilot didn't respond.

Zachariah looked around at the showy burgundy window-curtains, new oil-cloth on the floor, a big stove for winter decorated with costly inlaid work. Lillian held his hand.

"There's enough room one could dance in here," she said.

The captain spoke with a hint of amusement. "Only a woman would think of that."

A slender, negro man wearing a white apron walked in with a tray of tarts and coffee. All the officers took one of each. "Can I get you something, Miss Hildebrand?" he asked.

Lillian shook her head. She stood up and Zachariah followed. "I just wanted to show Mr. Degan the pilot house. Good day, gentlemen," she said and left. "Are you getting used to your last name?" she whispered.

"Yes. You've been saying it enough." They walked into the parlor.

Lillian smiled like someone about to burst with good news. "I am glad. Because tonight I am going to announce our engagement, or rather you are going to announce our engagement."

Zachariah blushed and nodded meekly.

*   *   *

The clock bonged with each passing hour, but nothing changed. Lillian barely left his side. She even stayed in the room during his math lesson. Was she afraid he'd change his mind? Zachariah took a deep breath. Having her glued to his side was disconcerting.

They sat down to supper, "Are you getting tired of me?" she teased.

"No, ma'am," he responded, holding back a laugh.

When the waiter returned, Lillian ordered two glasses of champagne.

Zachariah took a sip. His mouth burned. His face contorted. He had to make a conscious effort to swallow the sour liquid. It seared his throat on the way down.

Lillian giggled. "I guess reverends don't have to drink. You *do* have to make the announcement."

Zachariah's heart raced so fast, he put his hand on his chest and willed his pulse to slow. Beads of sweat popped on his forehead as he walked over to the piano. "Charlotte, I need to make an announcement. Please get everyone's attention."

Charlotte played a few commanding notes. The room fell silent.

With one finger, Zachariah loosened the collar of his shirt. He held the glass of champagne in the air. "I have some good news to tell everyone. Miss Lillian has just agreed to marry me."

The room was filled with rousing applause. Zachariah walked quickly back to his table. He passed Montgomery who appeared as rattled and confused as a bear woke in winter. Arthur stood beside him, mouth agape.

*

Montgomery waited for Lillian outside her door, his arms folded. "We have to talk now," he said, his voice rough.

Lillian huffed and opened the door. She already knew what he was going to say. She sat on the bed, preparing for the lecture.

"What were you thinking?" His voice low, deep, disgruntled. He shut the door with a bang.

"You don't have any claim to me," Lillian fired back. "You are not my pa."

"You know it is illegal."

Lillian jutted out her chin. "No one will ever know Zachary has African blood."

"Secrets have a way of escaping the tightest lips."

"I will put the fear of God in Zachary. He will keep his mouth shut."

"Is that why you are marrying him?"

Lillian looked off in the distance, remembering her friend Bird Whitmore collapsing at her feet, her dress torn and bloody. Violated by a Cherokee man. Not just any man—the brother of the man she was supposed to marry.

"You know that you are already promised to Bill Harris," Montgomery said. His words were rocks thrown through the glass window of her thoughts.

"I am not a brood mare my pa can pair with a stallion. Bill Harris may be well-respected in the community, but I have no love for him. He abuses his slaves and his dogs and likely he'd abuse me."

"A firm ha—"

"Don't start that Montgomery. You married Bessie out of love. I want that opportunity too."

"Society frowns upon strong-willed women. You will be the butt of many vicious rumors. Your family will be disgraced."

"I cannot sacrifice myself for my family. I love my parents and I love my sister, but I do not love Mr. Harris. If I cannot marry for love, I will throw myself in the river."

Montgomery rolled his eyes at her dramatic words.

Lillian knew he was peeved by her headstrong outspokenness. Her ma had that streak, her sister too. Bessie was the worst, arguing with devious truthfulness. But after marrying Montgomery she had toned down her ways.

Lillian did not plan on changing.

"Your father is going to have something to say about this." Montgomery's harsh tone, ground her plans deeper into her mind, encouraging her rebellion.

Chapter 20

Fort Smith, Arkansas
June 14, 1842

THE SUMMER SUN beat down on the top of the carriage, hot, forceful, relentless. Zachariah wiped the sweat off his forehead with a white handkerchief while holding the horses' reins in the other hand. Lillian used a large flowery fan to cool herself. At least some of the air reached him.

"Do I have to wear these black clothes all the time?" Zachariah asked, unable to hide the worry in his voice.

"No. Just on Sundays."

"Today isn't Sunday."

"I know. After you meet my family, you can change into something more comfortable."

With one eye, Lillian watched Montgomery, driving a wagon alongside them; the other eye remained focused on him.

In the wagon, Montgomery toted their trunks, provisions, and the baby cradle. His lips tightly closed, the corners drooping downward and his eyes hard-set. He had the look of a man whose mind had been firmly made. "You can't go through with this," he said.

Lillian's eyes narrowed, her face flushed. Zachariah wouldn't be surprised if sparks flew from her tongue. "Watch me!"

Montgomery gazed into the distance, seemed to be in heavy thought. The silence made Zachariah uneasy, he shifted in his seat.

"I won't say anything," Montgomery said at last, his voice tired, deep, sorrowful. "I can't. But you know it is illegal. If it gets out that Zachary is a negro, they will whip both of you."

Zachariah's eyes widened like a pig taken to the butcher. "Lillian, I don't—"

"Don't worry," Lillian interrupted. "My brother-in-law is just trying to scare us. The Cherokee council seems to pass a new law every year trying to dictate who a woman can marry though they aren't regulating partners for men. I don't believe they should have any say. We are in love and that's that."

"Yes, but…"

Lillian shot him a sword-wielding gaze that cut what he was going to say short. "It will just give you more of an incentive to be convincing."

Feeling lightheaded, he bit his lip and nodded.

"We're almost to the reservation," Montgomery said. "I cannot wait to see Bessie."

"With all your money, the council was delighted you married Bessie, but I'm sure you would have fought tooth and nail to marry her if you would've been broke. You should know better than try to stand in the way of love, Montgomery Vincent Barlow."

Mr. Barlow cringed at hearing his whole name. "I give you my word, I will keep your secret."

"You remember everything I told you?" Lillian asked Zachariah. He didn't respond. "Who is the president of the United States?"

Zachariah rolled his eyes. "John Tyler."

He ran his tongue around his dry mouth and patted his pants pocket which had the ring Lillian had picked out in New Orleans. "I'm nervous about meeting your family. What if they do not approve our marriage?"

"That would be the best thing for both of you," Montgomery said.

Lillian glared at him, her features hardening. She took a deep breath and returned her attention to Zachariah. Smiling sweet and confident, she patted Zachariah's thigh. "It just takes five dollars to buy a marriage license. You will meet my family and then we will have the ceremony. That is it. As long as I'm happy, my parents won't protest. They want more grandchildren."

Montgomery grunted.

*   *   *

A slim, well-dressed negro galloped towards them on a strawberry roan. He appeared close to Zachariah's age. "Master Barlow, Missus she's having the baby now."

"What?" Montgomery's said in a high-pitched shout. "It is not time yet."

"You tell that to the baby. Doctor's with her."

Montgomery slapped the reins and the wagon sped down the road.

The negro man stayed. He swung his horse around so he rode beside the carriage. "I will escort you the rest of the way."

"Thank you, Isaiah," Lillian said. "Isaiah is Arthur and Charlotte's son."

Zachariah nodded, keeping his eyes on the road.

"Isaiah, this is Reverend Degan. We are engaged."

Isaiah gave Lillian a what-do-you-mean look.

She raised one eyebrow and tapped the side of the carriage with her long tapered fingers as though waiting for him to take it back.

"Where are my manners," Isaiah said, flustered. "Congratulations."

Zachariah did not know what to say.

Isaiah shifted in his saddle. "I belong to Mr. Barlow, but I get shared with the family." His short laugh helped ease the tension. "If there is anything I can do for you, Reverend Degan, let me know."

"Thank you, Isaiah," Zachariah said stiffly. He offered the imitation of a smile. If anything it was too tense and deflated. It had never crossed his mind that he'd be ordering slaves around.

"How are my parents?"

"Just fine. Your sisters too, though I only talked to them for a moment."

"There's going to be plenty of excitement. First, Missus is having a baby and now you are getting married."

They pulled up alongside a two-story white frame house. Montgomery was already pacing outside as he drank repeatedly from a silver flask.

Zachariah helped Lillian down from the carriage.

Bessie cried out in pain. Lillian shot Zachariah a worried look then she looked at Montgomery.

"Caleb!" Isaiah shouted.

A colored boy came running from behind the house.

"Take care of the horses."

"Yessuh," the boy said, unhitching the team.

"They shooed me out of the house," Montgomery explained. He took another drink. "You are turning into your pa more each day, Isaiah. He'd be proud."

Isaiah puffed out his chest. "Thank you, sir. I hope to see him soon."

Montgomery did not reply.

Lillian walked over and put a comforting hand on Isaiah's shoulder. Then she hooked arms with Zachariah, and led him over towards the porch where an older amber-skinned man in a black suit sat, rotating a top hat in his hands. "Pa, I would like you to meet Reverend Degan."

The Indian man stood and extended his hand. "Name's John."

"Zachary Degan. It's a pleasure to finally meet you, Mr. Hildebrand."

John smiled business-like, his gray eyes looking at the reverend curiously. He turned to Lillian, raised eyebrows tightening his forehead, silently waiting an explanation.

"We met on the *Princess*," Lillian explained. "And while traveling the Mississippi," she stopped and looked at Zachariah sweetly, "we fell in love."

"Is that so?" Mr. Hildebrand said, stroking his bare chin.

Gritty spit in his mouth threatened to choke Zachariah. "Yes, sir," he said. "And we want to get married."

Mr. Hildebrand nodded, silently, his face revealing no emotion. "I am afraid, Reverend," his voice carried a warning, "my daughter has not been truthful." He paused and looked at Lillian. "She is a dreamer and does not see the importance of marrying the right man."

Lillian turned scarlet.

"I thought I had taught you better than to lie to a man of God."

Zachariah's forehead wrinkled along with his mouth. "I do not understand, sir."

"Lillian," Mr. Hildebrand said in a firm tone, "has not been honest with you."

Zachariah looked at Lillian and then back to Mr. Hildebrand. Neither of them spoke. "What does that mean?"

"She is engaged to a Cherokee man," Mr. Hildebrand said.

Zachariah's eyes widened. His head jerked around till he was nose to nose with her. "Is that true?"

"Engaged is not the same as wed," she said. "I am not in love with him."

"Love has nothing to do with it," Mr. Hildebrand said. "He is a member of the Cherokee elite. The marriage will benefit the family."

Lillian spat at her pa. "Disown me for all I care." She grabbed Zachariah's hand. "I am marrying Mr. Degan. All he needs is to buy a marriage license. And you can't stop me."

Mr. Hildebrand took a step forward, his hand raised.

Fire burned in Lillian's eyes.

Zachariah swallowed his fear in one gulp. He stepped in front of Lillian. "I will not let you harm her," he said. "Lillian's dishonesty is between her and me."

Lillian stepped out of Zachariah's shadow. "Go ahead. Strike me. Show Reverend Degan what kind of men the Cherokee are." Her voice, loud and rich, carried a bite.

Mr. Hildebrand gritted his teeth and lowered his hand. "You better watch your tongue. Do not speak ill of your own people, lest it come back to haunt you."

Lillian huffed.

"I will only put up with so much, Lillian. But, I guess you could have done worse than a man of God. We will see about this."

* * *

An older negress ran out of the house, the bottom of her pink dress flying up. "It's a girl!"

Lillian flashed Montgomery a smug smile, a rosiness coloring her cheeks and her voice. "I knew it was going to be a girl."

Montgomery stuffed his flask into his coat pocket and hurried into the house.

Mr. Hildebrand and Lillian waited through a few anxious minutes exchanging looks, shifting their weight, and tapping their feet before going into the house.

Zachariah took off his top hat, holding it in his hands in front of his waist, and followed. He hesitated to enter the room with the crying baby.

Lillian grabbed his arm and pulled him in.

Montgomery sat in a chair by the bed holding the swaddled baby. An older Indian woman in a red dress stood behind him. Her dark brown hair done up in a brown hair net. Her eyes kept moving between the baby and Bessie. An old white man had his hand on Bessie's forehead.

"You are very lucky, Mrs. Barlow. For being early, your daughter is healthy." He shook his head. "I do not believe it."

"Why is her skin yellow?" Bessie asked, her words weak, tired.

"Jaundice. It should go away in a few weeks. I will check back and make sure it does. Nurse her as soon as you can. If you excuse me, I have more patients to visit."

Zachariah moved out of the doorway to the let the doctor pass.

"Look at our granddaughter, John," the Indian woman said.

Montgomery handed the baby to her and she walked over to Mr. Hildebrand, Lillian and Zachariah.

Mr. Hildebrand pushed back the white blanket so he could see more of the baby's face. She had green eyes, the same shade as Lillian's.

Zachariah stood in awe, holding his breath.

"Her name is Dinah Louise," Bessie said.

"What a lovely name," Lillian said, taking her turn holding Dinah.

Lillian's ma finally took her eyes off the baby and realized there was a stranger in front of her. Her mouth parted in surprise. "Lillian, are you going to introduce me to this young man?"

"Ma, this is Reverend Zachary Degan. Reverend, this is my ma Ester."

Zachariah nodded to her. "Mrs. Hildebrand."

Lillian did not give her ma a chance to say anything. She passed Dinah to Mrs. Hildebrand then grabbed Zachariah's arm and led him over to Bessie's bed.

The young woman was buried under a mound of covers. He could only see her face. She looked nearly identical to her sister—same green eyes and fine dark hair.

"Bessie, this is Zachary Degan. Reverend this is my sister Bessie."

Zachariah smiled, tight and uncomfortable. "I have heard much about you Mrs. Barlow."

"You have?" Bessie and Mrs. Hildebrand said in unison.

"Reverend Degan courted me on the *Princess*," Lillian explained. "We want to get married."

The only sound in the room was Dinah's cries. Mrs. Hildebrand carried the baby over and nestled her in the crook of Bessie's arm.

"Congratulations," Bessie said, a weary smile on her lips, her eyes partly closed.

"Thank you." Lillian looked at her parents. "I hoped you would be happy for me too."

Mrs. Hildebrand glanced at her husband. The worry in her eyes disappeared after John nodded. She turned her attention to her daughter, the ends of her mouth not even curving up a hair. "We are happy for you, dear. It is just a shock. I do hope we will get to know Reverend Degan before your wedding."

"Certainly, ma'am," Zachariah said.

Lillian beamed. "Well, we all better leave and let Bessie and Dinah rest."

Montgomery watched Dinah kicking her ma's side. A loving smile stretched his lips. He took a couple steps outside the room and motioned with his hand.

Isaiah and Caleb carried the cradle into Bessie's room and set it next to her bed.

"Oh Montgomery," Bessie said. "It is a beautiful cradle." She rose up in bed and looked at everyone in the crowded room. Her pale face flushed slightly. "You can all come back to see Dinah in a few hours, but I would like to nurse."

Lillian nodded.

Zachariah followed her and Mr. and Mrs. Hildebrand out of the room.

Mrs. Hildebrand looked at Zachariah with piercing eyes making his heart stutter and skip. He feared she would see through him, see his ugly secret.

"Reverend Degan, would you accept our invitation to supper tonight?" she asked.

Zachariah scrambled for a smile and finally found it, his heart beat resuming, steady and even. Supper. That's all she wanted. "Yes, ma'am. I would love to."

*   *   *

Zachariah rubbed and rubbed and rubbed his sweaty hands on his pants, walking with Lillian towards the two-story white frame house, identical to Bessie's. He had to do this. He had to do this if he was going to be accepted by the Nation and wield the power of a white man.

Zachariah swallowed hard. His stomach was in so many knots he feared he wouldn't be able to eat. He escorted Lillian inside. His whole body felt hot. He rolled his tongue around his mouth and with two fingers he loosened the collar of his white shirt.

"May I take your hat, sir?" the doorman asked.

Zachariah handed him his hat and followed Lillian into the dining room.

He watched wide-eyed at the negress setting the table. They were going to be eating off fine china.

Wordlessly, he pulled out a chair for Lillian and then sat down next to her. Mr. and Mrs. Hildebrand sat on the opposite side of the small table.

Zachariah looked out the window. He saw the slave cabins in the distance and the horse corral. He bit his tongue to keep from opening his mouth. Mr. and Mrs. Hildebrand had horses of every color. So many horses there didn't seem like room for them to move in the corral. To the left of the corral were rows and rows of tall trees, their branches bending under the load of green apples.

They were rich. Almost as rich as Montgomery.

How could he ever fool them into believing he was white?

The smell of pork caught his attention. He turned his head and saw a negress bringing in plates of pork chops, mashed potatoes and corn. His mouth watered looking at it. Even after his countless delicious meals on the *Princess*, the good food looked like a Christmas feast.

"I am sure you would like to say grace, Reverend," Mr. Hildebrand said.

"Yes, of course." He swallowed, but the lump in his throat remained. He pressed his hands together, closed his eyes and bowed his head, trying to remember what Lillian had told him to say. "Lord, thank you for ensuring Mr. and Mrs. Barlow's daughter Dinah came into this world healthy. Please continue to watch over them and the rest of Lillian's family. Bless this food that we are about to eat so that it may nourish our bodies. Thank you for directing me to go on the *Princess*. It is your divine hand that has brought Lillian and me together. I pray that I may be fully accepted by the Cherokees. I pray for peace and prosperity for the Cherokee Nation. Amen."

Mr. Hildebrand rubbed his chin. "I do not think I have heard a better prayer."

"Thank you, sir." Zachariah remembered to put his napkin in his lap before he began eating.

The silence that followed lasted all of eternity. He shifted in his seat. There was a middle-aged negro man standing behind his chair to hand him condiments and bat the flies away. He bit his tongue. He hated being waited on.

"Tell us about yourself, Reverend," Mr. Hildebrand said.

"I am from Virginia. I'm an only child. When I was away at seminary, my ma and pa died in a house fire."

Mr. Hildebrand gasped. "Oh dear."

Zachariah looked down at his plate. "I do not..." He paused, his frown sinking deeper. "I do not have any family to speak of or any money for that matter." He continued slowly. "My pa was a farmer. He owned one slave. We think he was the one who set the fire. He has not been seen since."

Horror flashed on everyone's faces. "That is awful," Mrs. Hildebrand said, shaking her head. "You cannot trust niggers."

Zachariah bit his lip.

"Why were you on the *Princess*? Where were you going?" Mr. Hildebrand asked.

Zachariah finally raised his head. "I had no ties to Virginia. I wanted to get far away from there. I was looking to start a church in New Orleans." He let out an awkward, nervous laugh. "I do not know why I picked New Orleans. All my life I have heard that New Orleans is a city full of life. And I was in need of life."

His speech over, his tense muscles relaxed. He took a deep breath and smiled at Lillian more out of relief than happiness. "The Lord answered my prayers. Your daughter has given me life. I would like to get married and build a church here."

"Do you want children?" Mrs. Hildebrand asked eagerly.

Zachariah nodded. "As many children as the Lord wishes to bless me with. I love your daughter with all my heart. I'm sorry I don't have much to offer her, but I will take care of her to my dying breath."

"That is all right, Reverend," Mr. Hildebrand said. "All that matters is Lillian's happiness. And I'm sure she has told you about all the lost souls in the Nation. Many believers lost their faith after our forced removal to the reservation. We are still rebuilding. I hope you can help lead our men back to the Lord.

"But, you should know," his voice carried a jagged edge, "Mr. Harris will not be pleased losing Lillian's hand in marriage."

*   *   *

After supper, Lillian led Zachariah outside. "I want to show you around," she said.

He waited as she put on her white bonnet. He licked his lips. He felt everyone watching him and his charade. Lillian had warned him that if he wasn't believable that she'd ship him back to Henry to save her skin from the whip. She might have told her parents that she truly loved him, but he doubted her words.

Why did she want him to go through with this charade? He just knew he couldn't go back to Henry and that restaurant—not after living like a white man on the boat.

Besides, he loved her.

He escorted her outside into the warm evening air. In the dusky sky he saw the glimmer of fireflies dancing. The two of them walked hand in hand out to the horse corral. He wrapped his fingers tighter in hers.

She brushed a strand of hair behind her right ear, her eyes playful. Her beauty made him shiver with pleasure and he smiled back. The sound of horses snorting and stamping their hoofs made him instantly hold his breath. He noticed Lillian didn't seem afraid. She let go of his hand, walked up to the fence and stroked a black stallion's nose.

Zachariah exhaled and joined her. "I've never seen so many horses," he said, shaking his head.

"We will sell many of them. My horse and Rambler are in the barn."

They walked through the orchard. Crickets chirped in the distance. It became louder and louder then stopped. Zachariah pushed several branches out of the way to make sure they didn't hit him or Lillian. Once they made it out of the orchard they arrived to a dirt path.

Lillian pointed down the road. "Chief Ross lives down there a piece."

Zachariah squinted, but he could not see the house from where they stood. "You live that close to the chief?"

Lillian nodded. She turned around and walked down the road in the opposite direction she had just pointed.

Zachariah followed her, a little bewildered. He quickened his stride to catch up with her. When they stopped, they were in pasture land behind the row of slave cabins.

"This is used as grazing land for the horses," Lillian said.

She linked arms with him and they continued walking. Finally, they stopped at a double log cabin. His forehead wrinkled when they arrived at the two one-and-a-half story buildings connected by a single roof.

"Isn't it late for visiting?" Zachariah asked, hoping he wouldn't have to meet anyone till tomorrow.

"No one lives there—at least not yet."

"What do you mean?"

"Pa bought this land before the army made us move. He rode out to Indian Territory with other wealthy Cherokees to get the land ready for us. We couldn't go with him because Ma was ill. Neither Bessie nor I wanted to leave her. Then when Pa returned we decided not to leave until we had to as a show of support for the rest of the Cherokee people.

"Much of my parents' money has gone as loans to help people get farms, orchards, and ranches started again. This was our house for the first few years until Bessie met Montgomery. He said he wouldn't have us living in a log cabin." Lillian laughed. "I don't know if he thought it was too Indian, undignified or... I do not mind living in a log cabin though. This will be our home."

Zachariah's mouth parted in a silent O. He kissed Lillian on the cheek, gentle as the breeze. "This is very close to your parents, but it will be fine. I always dreamed of having my own house. I mean—"

"This is your house. Perhaps it will turn into a white frame house some day." She gazed off in the distance with a peaceful expression and the twinge of a smile. "You can sleep here for the night. Tomorrow we will get married."

Zachariah's heart and stomach flipped. "Won't it take longer than that to get everything ready?"

"Yes, if we were to have a fancy ceremony. Is a private wedding in front of the judge all right with you?"

Zachariah nodded vigorously. "I would be *much* more comfortable with that." He squeezed Lillian's hand. "And I don't want to wait to get married."

She gave him a quick kiss on the lips. Then they walked back to her parents' house.

Mr. Hildebrand sat on the porch smoking a cigar. "It has been a while since I took a lover's stroll." He reached into his vest pocket and pulled out another cigar. "Smoke, Reverend?"

"No, thank you."

Mr. Hildebrand put the cigar back in his pocket.

"Pa, we are going to have the judge marry us tomorrow."

One of his eyebrows rose, the other remained seated. "You do not want to be married by a man of God?"

"Mr. Hildebrand, we are all the Lord's children and therefore men of God. The Lord will bless our marriage."

Inside, he cringed remembering the slave that served him at supper, his denial of the Lord under Henry's fist, and the urgent need not to make a mistake – any mistake – or he and Lillian would suffer for it.

He blinked at his future father-in-law and sincerely hoped God's children included imposters.

Mr. Hildebrand nodded. "True, Reverend. Very true."

*   *   *

The following afternoon, all the Hildebrands waited at Montgomery's house for the judge to arrive. Bessie sat holding Dinah rocking her back and forth. Montgomery stood behind her with his hand on her shoulder.

Zachariah took deep breaths, but they did not ease his heart palpitations. He rubbed his sweaty hands on his pants. He had been nervous for the fake wedding, but saying real nuptials were worse.

He smiled at Lillian, but it didn't stay on his lips long. She seemed as anxious as him. She worried her dark green dress between her fingers. The dress matched her eyes. His favorite color. Her black hair was pulled up in an emerald hair net. She lowered her head and inhaled the sweet scent of her rose bouquet.

Dressed like a wealthy white man, Zachariah wore a fancy new black dress suit and gold vest. He swallowed in a vain attempt to push down the cold, hard lump out of his throat. He rolled her wedding ring around in the palm of his sweaty right hand. To think his beautiful Indian maiden had wanted to marry a slave like him.

He glanced towards the door, eager to get the ceremony over with before anybody could call him out. Finally, the judge entered wearing a somber black suit and Zachariah exhaled.

Zachariah and Lillian stood facing each other as the judge read from a tattered old Bible. Zachariah held his breath and waited for Lillian to repeat her lines.

Each time it was his turn, Zachariah's voice wavered and his gut bunched. Every sentence he uttered brought him closer to the life he wanted, had wanted so badly for so long. Still, he feared it would evaporate in an instant like a dream if he but blinked.

The door to the parlor flung open. Everyone turned to see the disturbance. "What in the world," Montgomery said, strong and harsh.

A thick-set Indian man shouted. "I forbid this wedding!" Even from across the room he reeked of smoke and liquor. He took determined strides towards Lillian. "You were promised to me. I have a claim to you."

Lillian's jaw tightened, her eyes angry lines like a cat sharpening her claws. "You have no claim to me," she spat back, her body shaking. "I am not a horse. You have no bill of sale."

"I had your word and your pa's word. Apparently the Hildebrands are not trustworthy."

"I couldn't stop him, sir," Isaiah said, running into the room.

Mr. Hildebrand broke away from his wife and walked up to the man slow, casual. "You are drunk, Mr. Harris. You are in no condition to have this discussion."

"Lillian drove me to drink," Mr. Harris said loudly, his words slurred. "Marrying up with a white man, betraying her race just like her sister. How can you allow it?"

"Unfortunately, there is no law forcing her to follow my wishes."

"So you wish she would marry me?" Mr. Harris said.

Mr. Hildebrand hesitated. The whole room fell silent recognizing the delicate nature of this lose, lose situation.

"I'll take your lack of complaint as a yes." Mr. Harris pulled a pistol out of his coat.

Zachariah held his breath. Likely he'd be the target.

Lillian stood stone still, regulating her breathing. Her eyes betrayed her fear. They darted from Montgomery to her pa to Mr. Harris.

Isaiah was the only one who dared to move. He gave Mr. Harris a wide birth and walked back towards Zachariah.

"Mr. Harris," the judge said, drawing his attention. "You know it is illegal for anyone other than an officer of the law to carry weapons."

"Hell, Judge, sure it's in the code, but it's not enforced. Everyone and their brother carries weapons."

"I know this was a shock to you, Bill," Mr. Hildebrand said carefully, calmly. "I am sorry."

"Sorry?" The word sparked the anger in his eyes. His voice tripled in volume. "Being sorry is not going to mend my broken heart. No reason to disrupt the ceremony. Everyone is gathered here. All I have to do is wed the bride."

"You will do no such thing," Lillian said, then quickly covered her mouth.

Mr. Harris waved the pistol in her direction.

"Threatening me and my family will not gain you my favor or my daughter's hand," Mr. Hildebrand said. "Please leave."

Mr. Harris stood still. He leered at Lillian. "You will wish you married me."

Lillian huffed.

"Your half-breed children will not fit in anywhere. They will not be Cherokee or white. You are ruining your life by marrying him."

"You are forgetting, Mr. Harris," Lillian hissed, "that I am already a half-breed."

Mr. Harris laughed, but it sounded more like a guttural grunt. "And I was doing you a favor by overlooking that fact. Your half-breed children can go to the devil."

He tucked his pistol back under his coat and walked out with floor-shaking strides. The door behind him slammed shut.

Lillian jumped.

Zachariah reached out, took her hand and felt her thundering pulse. He knew how she felt. His heart hammered his ribs.

The room was silent. Everyone exchanged glances. Zachariah's skin prickled, it felt like ants were treading on his flesh. Would Mr. Harris return and forcefully take Lillian?

A few tense seconds passed and then the room let out a collective breath.

"Isaiah," Montgomery said.

"Yes, sir?"

"Make sure the wagon is ready."

Isaiah nodded and left.

The judge cleared his throat. "Shall we proceed with the ceremony?" he asked.

"Yes. Please do," Mr. Hildebrand said.

Zachariah returned to looking into Lillian's eyes. When the judge ordered him to, he held Lillian's soft hand and gently placed the ring on her finger.

"I pronounce that they are husband and wife together, in the name of the Father, and of the Son, and of the Holy Ghost. Amen."

"Amen," Zachariah said, then kissed Lillian on the lips.

Mr. and Mrs. Hildebrand beamed at the newlyweds. "We'll have to have a reception in a few days," Mrs. Hildebrand said, her voice excited, bouncing, "Once Bessie and Dinah are stronger. It will be a double celebration."

Zachariah helped his bride into the carriage. He drove the short way to their new home. Isaiah drove a wagon filled with Lillian's belongings behind them.

Montgomery rode Rambler with Lillian's horse tied to the saddle horn. As they all rode up, the scent of apple pie wafted through the open windows.

Zachariah reined the horses to a stop at the side of the house.

Caleb walked out the door. "Master Degan, I will take cur of yo' horses," he said.

Zachariah blinked at him. Caleb unharnessed the two horses and led them into the barn.

Montgomery rode Rambler to the barn.

Zachariah looked at the barn, then Lillian, dumbfounded. "What is Caleb doing at our house?"

"He is part of your wedding present," Montgomery explained. "Mr. Hildebrand put a few horses in your corral and two cows in your barn, so I figured you needed a stable boy."

Zachariah's mouth parted in surprise. "Thank you, Mr. Barlow."

Lillian stepped into the house. "Oh my," she said loud, high-pitched.

Zachariah rushed in after her. His eyes widened when he saw a negress with graying hair and a young negro couple with two children, a girl about six and a boy about four waiting for them.

"That is the rest of your wedding present," Montgomery said, stepping into the house. He motioned at the old lady, "Dorothy and her family," he said.

"Her whole family?" Zachariah whispered.

Dorothy walked up and took Lillian's hands. "Congratulations, honey," she said. "I done know afta Miss Bessie get married it not be long and you's be married too."

"Thank you, Dorothy." Lillian grinned at Montgomery and looked like she was about to burst with excitement. "Oh, you spoil me so."

Montgomery laughed. "Perhaps. But I do not believe in separating families. Reverend, this is Martha," he said, gesturing to the young negress.

The woman took a step forward and curtsied.

"Her husband Jake and their children, Ivy and Francis."

Zachariah opened his mouth, but no words came. He couldn't take his eyes off them. A whole slave family. Grandma, ma, pa and children. He clenched his jaw. It wasn't fair that they weren't separated like he had been.

Then he remembered again that he was just a slave himself. How could he be both slave and master? An uncomfortable heaviness sunk to his stomach. He didn't want to own one slave let alone an entire family.

"We hope you will be happy here," Lillian said. "Do I smell an apple pie?"

Dorothy nodded. "I made you an apple pie to celebrate yo' weddin'." She left and returned with plates and silverware.

Lillian, Zachariah and Montgomery sat at the table. Before eating Zachariah bowed his head and prayed, "Lord, bless this pie and bless my family. Thank you for coupling me to a wonderful woman. May you protect us and guide us by your word. Amen."

As they were eating, the slaves helped Isaiah unload the wagon. Zachariah couldn't believe they knew exactly where everything went. Not one question interrupted their meal.

He ate each bite silently, a blank expression on his face. He looked more at his pie than at Lillian or Montgomery troubled by the slaves scurrying about the house.

His brother-in-law finished eating. The fork rested against the plate with a clank. Zachariah felt Montgomery's critical eyes on him. He didn't move. He didn't have any pleasant thoughts.

"I need to be getting back to Bessie and the baby."

"Thank you Montgomery," Lillian said again.

He nodded. "I will see you tomorrow, Mr. and Mrs. Degan."

Zachariah and Lillian stood and followed him to the door.

Dorothy walked over, picked up their dirty dishes and carried them into the kitchen.

Zachariah pressed his lips together. He listened to the creak of the wagon wheels as Isaiah drove away. He glanced around the room at the six black faces watching him.

"Is something wrong, Master Degan?" Martha asked.

Everything was wrong, he wanted to say. "Would you all please go outside for a few minutes?"

Lillian's mouth opened slightly, a question on her lips.

Martha nodded. "Let us know when you want us," she said, walking out the door. The others followed.

"What was that for?" Lillian asked.

"I do not want them to hear us. Where is our bedroom?"

Lillian's eyes brightened. "This way," she said with a wide grin.

Zachariah followed her into the bedroom.

Lillian undid her hair, untangled it with a few strokes of her fingers. His smile disappeared as if it had been slapped off her face. Concern wrinkled her brow, her nose, her eyes. "What is wrong?"

*　　*　　*

"I did not realize that being a slave-owner came with marrying you." His grating words scratched his windpipe.

"Oh," Lillian replied, her mouth slightly open. "You did not expect me to cook and clean, did you?"

Zachariah bit his lip. "I can't own slaves. It's wrong."

"Many free negroes own slaves," Lillian responded quickly.

He did not reply. He wasn't really free because Lillian owed him. Tension hung thick in the air nearly suffocating him.

"You do not own the slaves," Lillian pressed, taking a step towards him. "They are all in my name."

"That doesn't make me feel any better. They will still be calling me master."

"They are a wedding present from Montgomery and my sister. Even if I wanted to, we cannot refuse them."

Zachariah remained silent.

"You do not have to be mean to them. Montgomery doesn't whip his slaves. He usually just gives them a cross word."

He spaced his words to add power. "Owning other people is wrong."

"You are just going to have to get used to being a slave-owner," she said, grating agitation in her voice. "My ma and pa own slaves. Montgomery and Bessie own slaves. Chief Ross owns slaves. It is what the Cherokee elite do, just like white people."

Zachariah's heart alternatively sputtered and raced. His breathing accelerated until he panted. He hadn't considered that owning slaves was part of being white. "I do not want to be put in this position."

Lillian's face flushed. She took another step towards him, invading his space.

Her eyes were furious. Her lips were furious. Her hands were furious. They made him take a step back.

Her voice hit him with the force of Henry's fists. "You do not have a choice."

*

Lillian's heart palpitated. She had expected Zachary to crack. She had expected him to break down. She had expected him to even apologize. Instead, he was holding his ground.

She smiled at him coyly, tracing circles on the sheets. She had to get his mind off slaves, off of the distance between them. Her feminine wiles had always served her well in the past. She took several deep breaths until her face was calm, demeanor relaxed.

"Let's go to bed." She stopped tracing, and beckoned with her finger for him to come closer. "We can talk about this more tomorrow."

"We will talk about it *now*. I do not want to go to bed angry with you on our wedding night."

"We love each other. Don't let the fact you are lucky enough to now have people to take care of you come between us."

"Be lucky to have people to take care of me," he said in a questioning tone, loud and irritated. "I guess I shouldn't have expected better of you. You're just as corrupt as the rest of the rich folks."

Lillian jumped up, her eyes flared. "Don't say that. You do not mean that, do you?"

He looked away, his cheeks turning red.

Lillian turned his face to her and put a hand over his mouth. "Shh calm down. Yes, you are lucky," she said, her voice as smooth and slick as butter. "Lucky to be doing my bidding instead of your former master's. You remember how that was with Henry.

"You have to give this a chance. Remember you told my parents that your pa had one slave. And you will be preaching in favor of slavery in your sermons. That is how it is. Do you understand that?"

*

Zachariah shook, anger quivering every muscle. This was not how he envisioned his life with Lillian. She had deceived him.

"You are my possession," she whispered. "A sweet possession, a valuable possession, but still my possession." Her hands glided around his neck and the warmth of her skin made him tingle and hunger for more.

"Do not be angry with me," she said, her hot breath on his ear. "This is our wedding night."

Her loose, playful smile said she wanted him. Zachariah licked his lips. He should enjoy it. Still, he wanted a voice in their relationship. Not pulled along on a string.

He gently unwound her fingers from his neck and took a step back. "There were not any slave quarters outside. Where is the help going to sleep?"

"The quarters burned down a couple years ago. It's the middle of summer. They can sleep under the dog trot—the covered open section between the two buildings. Tomorrow they can start building their cabin."

"I will not have them sleeping outside. Dorothy is getting older and Ivy and Francis are just children."

Lillian rolled her eyes.

"We have a big house, more rooms than we need. They can sleep in the other section of the cabin, can't they?"

Lillian nodded and heaved a weary whatever-you-want sigh. "I guess that would be best anyway. Less chance of them being stolen."

"Stolen?" Zachariah exclaimed.

"Since moving to the reservation, many white men have taken advantage of our vulnerability and stolen slaves from us, especially women and children." She paused then said, "Now will you come to bed, Zachary?"

He didn't move. "Are you going to whip me if I do not," he said, sharp, rushing his words together.

The two glared at each other. Zachariah hated the fact Lillian's jutted chin and fiery eyes turned him on.

Without lowering her gaze, Lillian slowly peeled off her chemise and revealed her inviting breasts.

Those amber breasts melted the last of his resistance. His heart raced as her seductive body drew him closer until she was in his arms. They lay on the bed and he timidly reached out to touch her nipples.

She exhaled softly and moved his hands down so that he cupped her breasts.

Feeling her tender flesh and the pounding of her heart sent hormones raging through Zachariah's body. He stood up and quickly slid off his pants and then his jacket, vest and shirt. He knew he shouldn't leave them on the floor, but he had to feel her against his body.

Lillian reached up and ran her fingers through his hair and then gave him a long, sensual kiss. "You want me, don't you?"

"Yes," Zachariah said, his physical attraction to her stronger than the warning bell in his head.

He'd pleasure her for now. Likely, it would give him more power in their relationship. But he still wanted to be his own man some day. He just didn't know when that would be.

Chapter 21

Park Hill, Cherokee Reservation
August 19, 1843

ZACHARIAH HELD LILLIAN'S HAND AS THEY walked to the Barlow's house, his heart fluttering. She had a rosy glow in her cheeks and was less bossy lately. Not that she was ever demanding. That was unladylike. It was more of a wouldn't-you-like-to with her eyes hammering home the point he didn't have a choice.

But still he couldn't help loving her.

Zachariah tilted his head closer to her shoulder. "You look beautiful today."

"I am very happy because," she dragged out the word and batted her eyelashes at him with a jaw busting grin. "I am." She glanced at her stomach.

Zachariah's eyes widened. His mind swirled with happiness and concern and disbelief. "You mean I'm going to be a pa?"

Lillian nodded.

Zachariah's heart skipped several beats. He didn't know what to say.

"You're pleased, right?" Lillian asked eager, high-pitched.

"Yes, yes of course I am. It is just a surprise."

Lillian laughed, her eyes bright. "I know. A wonderful surprise!"

When they got to the Barlow's house, Lillian told them the news. Montgomery and Bessie congratulated them and Dinah cooed. Then Lillian told Isaiah and all the other servants in the house, who then passed on their well wishes. Zachariah barely spoke. He was in a daze and he had one thing on his mind—his ma and sister. They should be with him, be a part of his growing family.

He went through the charade of the proud husband again at her parents' house. He was happy to be having a baby, happy to spend time with the woman he had deep feelings for, happy to be respected in the community.

But it wasn't enough.

There remained a hollow hole in his heart which would only be filled by having his family reunited.

*   *   *

The moonlight streaming though the window made Lillian's black hair shimmer as she undressed. She sat on the bed and flashed him a coy smile. "Come on. I know you enjoy this as much as I do."

Zachariah pressed his lips together. It was true, but he didn't want her to know that.

"What's on your mind?" she asked, stretching her arms above her head.

"I want to bring my ma and sister to the reservation to live with us," he whispered. "I want them to be a part of our children's lives."

Lillian's eyes widened. Her arms fell to her sides. "They would recognize you. It is impossible," she said, curt and quick.

Zachariah drummed his fingers on his thigh. "How would you like to be separated from your parents and Bessie? I need to have my ma and sister with me. I need to take care of them." The room fell silent. He added, "I can explain the situation to them. They will gladly go along with it."

More dreadful silence constricted Zachariah's lungs. He shifted his weight repeatedly. His heart screamed that he must get a response. The response he wanted. The response he needed.

"How can we find them?" Lillian said at last.

Zachariah's mouth opened, a cleansing breath reviving and relaxing him. "They are living in Strasburg, Virginia. My ma, Catherine, and sister Rachel. They work at Mr. Norton's restaurant. And if they have been sold it should be possible to track them by talking to Mr. Norton."

"If it will make you happy, we can try to get them. Tomorrow I will talk to a man to start the search. If he can buy them, he will bring them back in a small coffle so as not to raise any questions."

Zachariah grabbed her wrists and pulled her nakedness to him. He kissed her neck and worked his way up to her cheek. "Thank you," he whispered into her ear.

He began massaging her shoulders, his fingers migrating to her breasts. Her breathing came short and rapid, making her voice airy, her volume fluctuating. "Though you will have to treat them like slaves. They have to remember you are Reverend Degan, their *master*. Our future depends on that."

His smile shrunk a little and the happiness he felt did not show in his serious voice. "They will, Lillian. I promise."

*   *   *

Lillian rubbed her swollen stomach feeling the baby kick. Zachariah stood behind her and gave her a kiss on the cheek. Her growing stomach noted that six months had passed. Nothing much had changed. They had settled into a married routine. Now that the baby was almost here, Lillian was in good spirits, laughing and smiling with ease.

Perhaps she was developing genuine feelings for him. He wasn't sure. She was such a good actress.

"Massa Degan!" Caleb shouted.

Zachariah ran outside into the brisk morning air. A white man on horseback directed a coffle of eight slaves towards them. He searched their faces for Ma and Rachel, but they were too far away to recognize. His heart raced in anticipation.

"Lillian," he called, quick and squeaky. "Mr. Akins is here."

Lillian walked outside, hands on her large pregnant stomach. Rachel had altered some of her dresses, but she wore a violet sacque to hide her expanding figure. She grabbed his arm and whispered in his ear, "I will explain things to them. You have to go inside."

Zachariah headed back into the house, excitement quickening his stride. He sat at his desk tapping his feet. He planted his feet firmly on the floor, and began tapping his pen against the desk.

His unfinished sermon stared back at him.

*

The coffle came to a stop in front of their house. Mr. Akins took off his hat. "Mrs. Degan."

Lillian smiled and did a slight curtsey. That was all she could manage in her current condition. "Mr. Akins. I didn't expect you back so soon."

Mr. Akins nodded. "We made good time. The free boat ride helped." He gestured to the group of slaves. "Which of them do you want?"

Lillian walked up to the coffle. She flashed a disarming smile at the youngest, a copper-skinned girl of fourteen. The girl focused on her bare feet.

"What is your name?"

The girl raised her head. "Rachael, ma'am. I's a seamstress. I sew real good."

Lillian nodded. She looked at the older mulatto woman next to Rachael. "What do you do?"

The woman looked sorrowfully at Rachel. "I's a cook, ma'am. I's been a waiting woman too."

Lillian rubbed her stomach. "Have you had experience with children?"

"Just raisin' my own. Rachel's my dottah. Buy both of us, ma'am. I's be a real good mammy. I won't let nothin' happen to yo' chillun, treat dem like royalty."

Lillian didn't respond. She walked further down the line and looked at the four men. "I need a strong laborer. I have horses, and poor Caleb needs help with them and come spring I want a garden."

Mr. Akins pointed to a stocky man. "Andrew is the politest field hand I've ever seen."

"I'll take him, Rachael, and her ma."

Mr. Akins dismounted and untied them. "The rest go to Mr. Barlow?"

"Yes, sir."

The man nodded. "I will come back later with the papers for you to sign." He turned his horse around. "This way," he ordered. The coffle began walking again.

Catherine, Rachel and Andrew stared blankly at Lillian.

Lillian smoothed the front of her dress. A pleasant feeling settled in her stomach like a rotten egg. The kind she got after she did something she knew she'd regret. "Caleb," she called.

"Yes'm?" the stable boy said, walking around the side of the house.

"Take them to their quarters."

Caleb motioned for the three to follow him. There were now two small slave cabins on the property. He opened the door to one of them and the four walked in.

"Rachel, dis is a regular house," Catherine said, tapping her hand against the wood. "No wind will get through de walls. Livin' wid Indians might be good afta all."

Lillian, who had followed at a distance, waited a few minutes then knocked on the door. Andrew answered it. "Go help Caleb with his chores. He's waiting by the corral."

Andrew nodded and left.

Lillian stepped into the cabin and shut the door.

Catherine gave her a puzzled look.

Lillian examined her oldest purchase from head to toe. How should she explain the situation?

*　　*　　*

"You are Catherine?"

Catherine's eyes widened. "How you know dat, ma'am? I doan tell you."

"Your son," Lillian stopped and took a deep breath, "Your son, Zachariah, lives with me."

Rachel gasped. Catherine's jaw dropped. "Praise de Lawd!" Her right hand flew up to cover her open mouth.

"Your son," Lillian continued, "had Mr. Akins search for you. Zachariah is my husband."

Ma's hand moved from her mouth to covering her heart.

"He's yo' husband?" Catherine said, a mixture of confusion and excitement livening her whisper. She looked at Rachel. There was a moment of silence as that sunk in.

"You mean Zachariah owns us?" Rachel asked.

"He's your master," Lillian replied. "And his name is now Zachary Degan. He is a reverend. He has a church on the reservation."

Catherine put a hand on her chest. "My son—a reverend!"

"No one can know that you are related," Lillian explained. "You must all remember your places. You must remember Zachary is your master."

"Yes'm. When can I see Massa Degan?" Rachel asked, fast, high-pitched, eager.

"I doubt he has finished his sermon for tomorrow. Come with me."

She led Catherine and Rachel into the house, down the hallway and into Zachary's office.

The young man beamed when he saw them, his heart swelling with joy. He jumped out of his chair. Lillian smiled at him, a warning in her eyes. She left them alone.

*

"Catherine," Zachariah said, embracing his ma. She stiffened, but he didn't care. Tears streamed down both their faces.

Zachariah's voice cracked and he took a deep breath to restore his composure. "My you've grown Rachel," Zachariah said, looking at his sister. "You're already as tall as your ma." He gave her a hug and the girl laid her head against his chest.

"I missed you something awful," she whispered in his ear.

Zachariah wiped away her tears.

"I always promised that I would buy you and Catherine," Zachariah said. "I missed you too. You have both been good to me," he said, conscious of his words in case one of the other slaves happened to hear him.

Before their arrival, Lillian had coached him carefully. They had practiced for hours what he could say. After living with Dorothy and her family for several months, he was finally used to being called master and telling them what to do, but he still hated it, hated it with every fiber of his being.

"I cannot free you," he explained in a controlled monotone to hold back anger and bitterness. "But at least we are together and Lillian and I will be having a child soon. Tomorrow you can listen to my sermon. I am not as long-winded as Preacher Simon."

Rachel put a hand over her mouth to stifle a laugh.

Ma's eyes settled on the unfinished sermon on Zachariah's desk. "You can read and write," she said.

Zachariah's eyes narrowed. "Of course I can read and write, Catherine."

"Forgive me, Reverend. I wasn't thinkin'." She sighed, smiling. "I's get to take of you again and yo' chillun. Dis is wonderful."

Zachariah sat down at his desk. "Are you hungry?"

"Nosuh," Rachel said, "We ate fine on de boat and got three meals a day when we's walkin'."

Zachariah rubbed his hand across his mouth. He had made sure of that. He didn't want to say the wrong thing. He licked his bottom lip. "You may stay here with me if you wish. I need to finish my sermon."

Rachel and Ma both sat on the floor. "We ain't going to go nowheres," Ma said.

*   *   *

Zachariah was unable to sleep; his body flooded with adrenaline. He couldn't wait to get to church and show his ma and sister who he had become. He wanted to show them his learning and the respect he had garnered in the community.

After the congregation sang a few hymns, Zachariah stepped up to the pulpit. Everyone took their seats. He rubbed his hands on the front of his black pants and looked to the back of the room where Ma, Rachel, and the rest of the negroes sat. Then his eyes moved up the rows of benches to his dark and amber-skinned Cherokee congregation. He took a deep breath and began his sermon.

"At times what man has intended for evil, God intends for good. I know many of you are still suffering from leaving Georgia—a place that many of you refer to lovingly as the center of the world. Forced to move here which feels like the middle of nowhere. If you are patient, I believe you will see the good that God has planned for all of you. I am reminded of one of my favorite Bible stories: Joseph and the coat of many colors."

Ma and Rachel hung on his every word. Unlike when she was little, Rachel's eyes did not start to close. The two of them sat up straight, attentive throughout the whole sermon.

Zachariah finished and took a deep breath. The warm flush in his cheeks began to fade. After preaching for months, his hands no longer trembled. The congregation clapped. Lillian, sitting in the front row next to her family, clapped the loudest.

They still believed him. They were still pleased with his sermons. They were still fooled by his performance.

Did he have himself fooled? He didn't know the nature of his true faith. He read the Bible and spoken verses so often that they came naturally.

It seemed more right that God existed. But did God care about him and the other negroes?

*   *   *

Zachariah walked out of the church. He inhaled the cool winter air and then wiped his forehead. Preaching made him sweaty, even in February. He smiled and nodded to members of the congregation as they left. His lips stretched farther for those he was fond of and shrunk to a business-like curve for those he disliked.

A slender brown-haired man walked stately out the church. He joined Zachariah, held his tall beaver hat in his right hand and smiled at the Cherokees leaving the church. If his black suit hadn't have been so fancy the short, stout man, might have been mistaken for another preacher.

The man's blue eyes brightened. "I think that was your best sermon, Reverend," he said.

"Thank you, Chief Ross."

"You like being Cherokee?"

I'm Cherokee except when Lillian reminds me I'm still a slave. Zachariah told his lips to smile. "If I never return to white society, I will be happy."

Chief Ross focused on the stream of people continuing to file out of the church. "I've heard what happened to your parents, Reverend Degan. I am sorry. I am glad you are happy here.

"We need good preachers. We also need strong Cherokee children. I will be one of the first to congratulate you after the baby is born. Good day." He stepped into his carriage and the coachman drove off.

Zachariah tugged on the bottom of his coat and waited for Lillian to join him. He looked over his shoulder. She walked slowly, the pink dress revealing the growing baby inside her.

"Chief Ross liked the sermon," Zachariah said. "I still cannot believe he's the Cherokee Chief. He does not look like an Indian. He looks white."

Lillian's lips twisted into a smile, her eyes laughing. "He's one-eighth Cherokee. Looks can be deceiving. You should know that."

Zachariah's put a hand on her stomach.

Lillian took a step back. "Not in public."

Zachariah flushed. He didn't understand why, in polite society, being pregnant had to be hidden. Slave women's growing stomachs were on display.

His eyes still brightened. Even with the wraps Lillian was using, some looks couldn't be deceiving. He didn't care if she had a boy or a girl, as long as the baby was healthy. At least his child would be free. His happiness paled and he pressed his lips together.

Freedom. Hollow grief settled in his stomach. Then slowly anger bubbled inside him. He bit his cheek to repress any outward signs of his discontent.

Surely, Lillian would free him too. Hopefully, after the baby was born.

How could she keep him enslaved when he was the father of their child?

Chapter 22

Park Hill, Cherokee Reservation
March 17, 1843

ZACHARIAH, ALREADY DRESSED, rolled over in bed and kissed Lillian on the cheek. "Happy birthday."

Lillian rubbed her stomach. "I wish the baby would want to have a birthday too," she said, her voice a low groan. "Without Catherine's help, I wouldn't get out of this bed."

"You have to get out of bed. Your family is coming over this afternoon for cake. Dorothy and Ivy are busy making it."

Lillian rolled her eyes. "Ivy has a sweet tooth. That little girl will eat half the batter."

"No, she won't. Dorothy's been threatening her with the big wooden spoon."

Lillian laughed.

"I remember when Rachel was Ivy's age. I do not know where the years go."

"When is your birthday?"

Zachariah's brows dipped towards each other. "You know slaves do not mark those occasions. All I kept track of was whether it was Tuesday or Sunday."

Lillian held his hand. "Your ownership paper says you're nineteen."

Zachariah cringed. He hated being reminded he wasn't free. He didn't know how long he could walk the line passing as white in the Cherokee community while being in the unsettling position of both husband and slave to Lillian. She seemed to take evil delight in her power over him.

She reached out and put her hand on his chest. "When do you want to celebrate your birthday? Just pick a month and day."

"I like summer—late summer when it isn't too hot." He tilted his head to the side. "How about August 25."

"I will let everyone know."

Zachariah smiled and kissed Lillian's cheek again, light and gentle. "But right now we have to celebrate your birthday."

He sat up on the bed and put on his shoes. He softly sang part of a hymn about God taking care of children.

Lillian laughed as she tossed back the covers. "You are almost as anxious for this baby to be born as I am."

She grabbed her stomach and grimaced.

Zachariah looked at her, worried. "Are you all right?"

"Yes."

"I will send Catherine in to help you dress."

Later, Catherine held the door open and Lillian walked into the parlor wearing a billowy white dress. Lillian felt the back of her head. Catherine insisted on putting her hair up for the party.

"You look beautiful, Misress," Rachel said as she went about dusting.

"Thank you. Keep telling me that because I do not feel beautiful."

"What would you like to eat, ma'am?" Martha asked.

She wanted to say nothing, but she knew Zachariah and Dorothy wouldn't allow it. "Biscuits and gravy."

Martha nodded.

After breakfast, Lillian stayed at the table. Zachariah brought her *The Last of the Mohicans* and handed it to her. "You can read to pass the time."

She tilted her head back, her eyes smiling more than her mouth. "The book has a black cover and I thought you were bringing me the Bible."

Zachariah laughed. "Well, you can read that instead if you wish. I figured this household has got enough religion."

"True." She opened the book and read the inscription she had written: To Zachary—you have the inner strength of a warrior and the heart of a chief. Your Indian maiden, Lillian.

She began reading the book aloud to Catherine, Rachel and Caleb. Zachariah placed his right hand on her shoulder and listened to the familiar words.

A knock on the door. Rachel left to answer it. Andrew stood outside holding a bouquet of wildflowers. He handed them to Rachel.

"Give dese to Misress for me," he said, "for her birthday."

He returned to plowing a plot of land for the garden.

Rachel put the wildflowers in a clear glass vase, filled it with water and set it on the table. "Dese is from Andrew."

"How nice." She leaned forward and smelled them. "The flowers are out early this year."

The morning hours seemed to push the hands of the clock to turn faster and faster. Every once in a while Lillian would grimace and grab her stomach. Wordlessly, Caleb ran towards the door. Lillian stopped reading and watched him, alarmed. She relaxed when she heard horse hoofs and the roll of carriage wheels.

Lillian waved at her parents, sister, and brother-in-law from the table. Bessie walked over and gave her sister a hug.

"Happy birthday," she said.

Dorothy brought out a large white cake with white icing.

Martha walked behind her carrying a bowl of punch.

Dorothy cut the cake into pieces and Martha passed them out on plates.

"Lord, bless this cake. Thank you for bringing the family together. Amen," Zachariah said quickly.

"Now that is a prayer I like," Montgomery said.

Lillian looked at the punch in front of her and then down at the table. "Jake, get me a glass of water please."

"Yes'm."

Zachariah looked over at the cake. Half of it remained. "Dorothy, you may share the rest amongst yourselves. Make sure Andrew, Caleb and Francis get some. They are outside."

Rachel's eyes widened. She licked her lips.

"Thank you, Master Degan," Dorothy said, carrying the cake back into the kitchen.

Mr. Hildebrand shook his head. "You spoil your slaves, Reverend." His voice had a gruff undertone.

"Masters, give unto your servants that which is just and equal; knowing that you also have a Master in heaven. Colossians 4:1," Zachariah said.

Mr. Hildebrand did not respond. Bessie bit her lip. The table fell into silence.

Zachariah shifted in his seat. The air so thick with tension it threatened to smother him. He shot a Lillian a flicker of desperation, but she did not come to his aid. Zachariah struggled to breathe air into his cramped lungs.

"Presents?" Montgomery asked finally.

Lillian nodded.

Zachariah exhaled through his nose hoping they did not notice his discomfort. He hadn't expected Montgomery to change the subject. Mr. Hildebrand pulled a small bottle out of his coat pocket and handed it to her. "From your Ma and I."

Lillian unscrewed the cap and inhaled the perfume. "Lilacs. Like the trees we had in Georgia."

Mrs. Hildebrand patted her daughter's hand. "I hope we can grow lilacs here too. When you were little, you and Bessie used to sit under those trees and read for hours..." her soft voice trailed off.

Bessie handed Lillian a small box wrapped in brown paper. Lillian carefully unwrapped it. Her mouth parted slightly. She opened the white porcelain box and beautiful piano music began.

"It sounds like Charlotte is playing for me."

"If I recall right," Montgomery said, "that is one of your favorite songs."

"Yes. Thank you." Lillian looked down at her large stomach. "Oh," she said, "the baby kicked me. I will play it for the baby." She smiled at Zachariah, wide, generous, loving. "Though your singing is much better."

Zachariah's eyes brightened. He handed her a large, flat box. She tore open the paper and then her mouth dropped open. She carefully pulled out the red silk dress, running her fingers over the white lace collar. "It's lovely!" She stood up and held the dress up to her.

"Rachel will have to alter it, but I thought red would be a nice change from all your green dresses."

The whole table erupted in laughter.

Lillian grimaced. She set the dress back in the box and grabbed her stomach. Water gushed onto the floor.

*   *   *

"Looks like you're going to have that baby now," Bessie said.

Zachariah's eyes widened. His mouth became as dry as sand.

"Catherine, help her into bed," Bessie said.

"I'll boil some water," Dorothy called from the kitchen. "Martha, tear some sheets!"

Zachariah ran outside and hollered. "Caleb, go get the doctor! Lillian's having the baby."

Caleb ran into the barn and galloped out on Rambler.

Montgomery and Mr. Hildebrand joined Zachariah on the porch. Montgomery pulled his silver flask out of his coat pocket. "Drink?"

Zachariah shook his head. "No, thanks."

Mr. Hildebrand took the flask. "You might not need a drink, but I do. Reverend, it better be a boy. I don't know how many more women I can handle."

The doctor arrived in his buggy. He took his medical bag and rushed into the house.

Caleb busied himself taking care of the doctor's horse.

Jake, Rachel, Ivy, Francis and Martha walked outside. "Dey say too many folks in de house," Rachel explained.

Zachariah nodded.

All of them watched the sun sink lower on the horizon. The sky darkened into various shades of purple. Shadows slowly lengthened sprawling across the ground. Zachariah pulled out his gold pocket watch and checked it for the hundredth time. "What is taking so long?" he asked. "It has been hours."

"Sometimes it takes hours, Master Degan," Martha said. "Try not to worry."

Zachariah rubbed his sweaty hands on his knees. That was easy for her to say.

"Is there anything I can get you, Reverend?" Jake asked.

Zachariah shook his head. He jumped up and started pacing and pondering and praying.

Rachel walked beside him.

Finally, the door opened. Catherine walked outside, grinning. "You huv a boy, Massa Degan! Doctor's cleaning him up."

Mr. Hildebrand yelled and threw his top hat in the air.

Zachariah rushed through the house and into the bedroom where Lillian lay smiling. Zachariah kneeled beside the bed.

"Jordan Amos this is your Pa," she explained.

"Jordan? I thought we were naming him Joseph. Joseph is really important to me. It is a good biblical name too."

"Jordan is a biblical name like the Jordan River."

"Yes, but Joseph was my pa's name."

Lillian's eyes narrowed.

Zachariah swallowed hard. *She knows I'm lying. She knows I don't know my pa.* He looked down at the baby to break her stare.

"You don't know what I went through giving birth to this boy. I think I should have the right to name him."

Zachariah looked over at Mrs. Hildebrand.

"It was a difficult birth, Reverend. Quite long. I think you should name him Jordan."

Zachariah nodded with a yielding sigh. The baby looked at him with sleepy hazel eyes. He gently kissed Lillian's forehead and then Jordan's forehead.

"Welcome into the world," Zachariah whispered. "I never thought you would get here."

"Me neither." Lillian yawned.

Zachariah picked up his swaddled son. "You are much bigger than Dinah was," he said. The baby let out a piercing cry. "That is good. That means you're healthy." Zachariah rocked him in his arms. "Shhh." Joy put a bounce in his step. He carried Jordan outside to meet the rest of his family.

*   *   *

After Jordan had nursed, Zachariah climbed into bed and snuggled next to Lillian. He gently stroked Jordan's head, rocking him in his arms Jordan's large eyes studying him. "He knows I am his pa."

"Of course he does," Lillian said.

Once Jordan went to sleep Zachariah carried him into the nursery and laid him in the cradle. He returned and climbed into bed with Lillian. "Do you have something to tell me?" he asked, being hopeful.

Lillian opened her eyes and gave him a kiss. "I love you."

Zachariah smiled though a deep frown creased his heart. Weariness deflated his lips. He didn't have the energy to keep up the charade of contentment.

Lillian rolled over and went to sleep.

"Love," Zachariah said, caressing her hair. Did she really?

Now that he was a pa, did it matter?

Chapter 23

Park Hill, Cherokee Reservation
September 21, 1843

ZACHARIAH AND LILLIAN SAT outside their cabin on a blanket. Little Ivy held a parasol over Lillian to protect her from the sun. Lillian rested her right hand on Zachariah's knee listening to him read from *The Pioneers*.

Zachariah paused. "I did not realize James Fennimore Cooper wrote other stories about Leatherstocking. This was the best birthday present. But I like *The Last of the Mohicans* better."

"Me too," Lillian said, she leaned over close until they were sharing air and then a kiss.

Ivy giggled.

Zachariah continued reading until Catherine walked outside holding Jordan. The baby wailed at the top of his lungs.

Catherine shook her head, dark circles under her eyes. "Shh Massa Jordan. Shh. He's hungry, Misress."

Lillian got to her feet, took Jordan, and headed for the house.

Catherine yawned. "I's almost too old for dis."

Zachariah shot his ma a concerned look.

Catherine laughed accentuating her weary wrinkles. "I ain't really. It will get bedda."

A half hour later, Lillian returned carrying Jordan and a diaper. Catherine sighed.

"I can change him," Zachariah said. "Go take a nap, Catherine."

"Bless you, Reverend." She nodded to Lillian and then headed for the slave quarters.

Lillian laid Jordan down on the blanket.

Zachariah cleaned the squirming baby and then tied another cloth diaper on him. Jordan was just starting to get black peach fuzz on the top of his head.

"He's going to have your hair."

"I was hoping he'd have your blue eyes."

"An Indian with blue eyes?"

"Chief Ross has blue eyes."

Zachariah bit his tongue to stop his laughter. "Yes, I know."

He looked behind him when he heard a clucking noise. One of the hens a church member had given him, stood next to Ivy. "I think that hen likes you, Ivy."

The negro girl reached down at petted the bird. "Dey all like me cause I gather deir eggs. And dey don't hide dem much either."

Rachel walked out of the house. She blinked at the bright sun then shielded her eyes. She held white cloth in her arms.

"I's made Massa Jordan mo diapas," she said.

Lillian laughed softly. "Master Jordan appreciates them I'm sure."

"I do de washin' tomorrow, ma'am. Massa Jordan sure dirties his dresses."

"Catherine should give him a washing too." Her eyes brightened and she looked at Zachariah. "It is a pleasant afternoon. We can have a picnic."

"A picnic right here?" Zachariah couldn't believe it. It seemed like a lot of work for no reason.

"Of course!" Lillian said. "Rachel, go tell Dorothy we are having our meal outside."

Rachel nodded. "Yes, Misress."

Lillian sat back down. She gave Jordan her finger and he grasped it tightly, grinning.

"He really is a happy baby," Zachariah said.

"I hope he can sing like you."

Zachariah's eyes twinkled. Taking that as a cue, he began a hymn. When he finished, Lillian clapped and Jordan made a gurgling noise.

Zachariah looked up at Ivy. The little girl was smiling.

He picked his son up and sat him in his lap. They watched Andrew silently hoe the garden. Half of the expansive garden was towering cornstalks; the rest: pole beans, cabbage, carrots, onions, turnips and potatoes. Behind the house three apple tree saplings grew. They were really unnecessary except for shade. Mrs. Hildebrand kept Lillian and Bessie supplied with apples.

The stocky negro man stopped hoeing. He rose up, took off his straw hat, ran his fingers through his hair then wiped the sweat off his forehead. He glanced nervously at them.

"Andrew," Zachariah said.

The negro man's Adam's apple bobbed. He walked over to him, his hat in his hands. "Yes, Massa?"

"Take a break."

Andrew's eyes widened. "I-I thought I is."

Zachariah shook his head. "Go sit in the shade. You've been at that all morning. Wait till the sun passes over the garden."

Andrew's eyes moistened. "Thank you Massa. Ever since I's a boy I's just been told to work and work fasta."

"This isn't the cotton fields."

"I know, Massa. I know." Andrew sat down and rested his head against the back of his slave cabin.

Zachariah smiled with his eyes, inwardly pleased. The least he could do was give the help a good life. Perhaps later, freedom would come for all of them.

"Ivy," Lillian said, "leave us for a few minutes."

The girl set down the parasol and ran out to the garden where her brother Francis was pulling weeds with one hand and eating an apple with the other. Francis shared his apple with her, then the two played tag.

"They have a nice life here," Lillian whispered to her husband. "You do no have to give hem extra favors. Goodness sakes, Zachary. I had to bite my tongue when you gave them the rest of my birthday cake."

"What is wrong with that?"

"Wrong," Lillian said in an exasperated whisper. Didn't he understand the danger posed by their marriage? Her intense glare, made her head throb, her eyes attempting to pierce his heart. "You are treating them like equals."

"I am their equal."

"Equal in class, yes," she said, "but not in manners or learning or looks."

Zachariah's eyes narrowed. "Do not try to flatter me. You own me, remember?"

*

Lillian looked off towards the slave cabins, she swiveled her shoulders so one was pointing at him. A long moment of silence followed. She loved him, but she couldn't tell him the truth. The truth might ruin her independence, ruin his character, ruin their relationship.

"I know," she said finally, "but Andrew is very happy hoeing our garden. They are all happy."

"One cannot really be happy until they are free and working for themselves. I know how much work it is tending a garden. I know what it feels like to have my neck and hands sunburned."

"Andrew is happy," Lillian repeated. "You have to act more like a master. You have to separate yourself from them."

Zachary gritted his teeth and didn't respond.

"People are talking behind your back—about how you spoil your slaves. Ma hears it and tells me. You are reflecting poorly on my family."

"Many people favor their slaves."

"Yes one or two—not all they own. We can't have them talking. You understand? Do it for my sake and for our children. We don't want anyone to get suspicious."

"I don't think being known as generous is bad."

"All I have to do is write a letter and you'll never see your children again. You'll be begging Henry—"

"I will do it for my family," Zachary said, quickly, his words rushed together. "I'll start being stricter with the help."

"Good. Now there's something else I want to talk to you about."

*

Of course there was. "What?" Zachariah groaned.

"Well, I am not going to tell you until you are in better humor."

Dorothy walked outside carrying a basket of fried chicken. Martha followed her with a bowl of green beans in one hand, and a plate of rolls in the other. Jake carried out the plates and silver in his right hand and mashed potatoes in his left. Rachel brought up the rear carrying two glasses of buttermilk. She handed a glass to Lillian and then one to Zachariah.

"I will go get the butter," she said, heading back into the house.

"Ivy," Lillian called.

The little girl stopped playing and returned to holding the parasol. Looking at the feast she whined. "I's hungry and my arms hurt."

Martha shot her a dirty look.

Ivy bit her lip.

Jake took the parasol out of his daughter's hands.

Zachariah gnawed his tongue. Watching Jake take care of Ivy and Francis churned up all sorts of feelings. He witnessed it everyday. Even when Jake smiled at the children it brought him turmoil over not knowing his pa.

"Ivy, you may go inside and practice your sewing with Rachel," Lillian said.

The little girl rolled her eyes.

Martha boxed her ears.

"Ma!" Ivy said.

"You go inside now. You mind what Rachel says real good. You hear?" Martha said sharply.

Ivy pressed her lips together. "Yes'm."

Zachariah bowed his head and Lillian followed. "Lord, bless this food we are about to eat that it may keep us strong and healthy. Thank you for watching over my family. Amen."

The two then ate in silence for a while. "Have you considered running for council?" Lillian asked.

*   *   *

Zachariah stopped chewing his chicken. The birds in the trees above him stopped chirping. He looked at Lillian blankly. Finally, he swallowed with great effort. "No."

"I think you should."

Zachariah's eyes widened. "Why?"

"Because everyone has grown to like you. You're a good public speaker and writer and it is an honor to be on the council."

"Then why doesn't Montgomery do it?"

"He's too busy going back and forth between here and checking on the *Princess*."

"I really do not want to be on the council."

"The Cherokee Nation is still recovering. You could help them by writing laws. Don't you want to help them? Don't you want to at least try to get elected? My Pa's on the council. It is a great honor."

Zachariah pressed his lips together and locked eyes with her, searching for a reaction.

Don't you mean it would be a great honor for you? He swallowed hard forcing the words back down his throat. Didn't he put in enough time in front of members of the Nation preaching every Sunday?

He shook his head. "I do not want to run for council, Lillian." He paused as an idea formulated. "Why are you just asking me this now? You have to have a reason."

Lillian huffed. "There's talk that the council will try again to pass legislation prohibiting Cherokee from marrying white men. If I have a daughter—we have a daughter I mean—I want her to have that option."

Zachariah tilted his head to the side and looked into her eyes. He couldn't believe that her motives were that pure.

"And we need to get a female seminary built. Likely that will take a few years, but the council members need to value education. I know you value education."

Zachariah licked his bottom lip.

"You might not even get in," Lillian said, breaking the silence. "But can't you at least try?" Lillian leaned close to him and batted her long eyelashes. "Please," she dragged out the word.

Old instincts to obey tensed his gut. Zachariah looked down at the white blanket beneath him. "I guess I can try," he whispered.

Lillian squeezed his hand. "I love you."

Zachariah forced a grin, inwardly irritated at himself for letting her control him. Would he ever be able to stand up for himself? Not as long as she owned him, and she owned him in more ways than one.

*   *   *

Jake hurriedly helped Zachariah dress and shave while Catherine tied Lillian's corset.

"The Hildebrands ain't here yet," Jake said.

Zachariah nodded.

He had forgotten about the family breakfast. He looked down at his black coat. A distinct wrinkle ran under his left arm.

"Martha didn't iron this well," he mumbled.

Jake pressed his lips together. "Yes, sir. My wife will do better."

Zachariah folded his right hand into a fist. He couldn't believe he had just said that. He was starting to sound like a white master. Dammit.

He hurried into the parlor. He stopped, took a few deep breaths, let his heart beat slow to normal. Lillian joined them. A moment later, Isaiah drove Montgomery and Bessie to the front door.

Rachel took Dinah out of Bessie's arms and carried her into the nursery to be with Jordan. A few minutes later, Mr. and Mrs. Hildebrand arrived.

Caleb saw to their horses while Andrew watered the horses in the corral. The family sat down at the table and Caleb walked in with a pail of fresh cow's milk. Isaiah, Martha and Jake stayed in the room to wait on everyone.

Zachariah looked at his plate of biscuits and gravy and eggs. Then he smiled at Mr. and Mrs. Hildebrand, pleasant, thoughtful. He had long since gotten used to the Barlows and the Hildebrands. He couldn't wait until Jordan was old enough to eat with them. His son would be surrounded by family his entire life. His son would never have to face the hardships he had.

Zachariah bowed his head.

Lillian reached over and grabbed his hand under the table and bowed her head.

"Lord, bless this food that it may nourish our bodies. Thank you for this time to be with family. Amen," Zachariah said.

Lillian let go of his hand and began eating.

"Reverend, Lillian told me you were thinking about running for council," Mr. Hildebrand said.

Zachariah shot a look at Lillian. He hadn't even agreed to it till yesterday. "Yes, sir. Do you think it is a good idea?"

Mr. Hildebrand rubbed his chin. "You might not get elected the first time. But it will be good to let people know you care to be more involved with the Cherokee Nation. Have you thought about learning the Cherokee language?"

"I have heard some of the old people talking. It sounds complicated."

"Don't worry. It is not as bad as it sounds, Mr. Hildebrand said. I will teach you. Then once you can speak it, I will help you to read and write it."

"Thank you. I know Lillian doesn't speak it. Bessie, do you know Cherokee?"

"No. We are supposed to be a civilized people. I did not feel I needed to learn. Ma can speak it some."

Mr. Hildebrand rolled his eyes at his daughter. "Chief Ross doesn't know it very well either so I guess I shouldn't be too disappointed," he muttered.

"I could learn with Zachary," Lillian chimed in.

"Would you?" Mr. Hildebrand said, his eyes and voice pleading. "It is our heritage. We can't forget our heritage."

"I will learn. It will help him if we can speak it together."

Mr. Hildebrand sat up straighter, prouder, as if a weight had been lifted off his shoulders. He sat up straighter, prouder.

"What do you think Bessie?" Mrs. Hildebrand asked. "Don't you think you should learn it some so that Dinah will at least know a few words?"

"I want Dinah to be raised as white as possible," Bessie replied. "And Montgomery can make sure that happens."

"I know you are worried, dear, about the United States government, with the broken treaties and promises, but 'becoming white' will not protect you. Your Ma and I are both half white. You are too, but the United States government sees you as Cherokee, *not* white."

Bessie frowned, and her slumped, her eyes moist. She didn't say a word.

"I will take care of Bessie and Dinah," Montgomery said, putting a comforting hand on his wife's back.

"It is illegal for you two to be married in several southern states," Mr. Hildebrand pointed out.

"True. Though no one has yet to bring that up. Money has a way of making most people look the other way and Bessie is far from a squaw."

Bessie laughed then covered her mouth with her napkin.

Zachariah looked at Lillian and saw she had her right hand on her stomach, her face a grayish-green. She rose from her seat and hurried outside.

Bessie quickly followed.

Through the open door Zachariah heard the women vomiting.

Dorothy bit her lip. She looked at the food on the table. "Is something wrong wid the meal?"

Montgomery shook his head. "No. It tastes delicious."

Dorothy nodded, her eyes still filled with concern.

Lillian and Bessie returned to the table. "I have an announcement to make."

"Me too," Bessie said.

Lillian winked at her sister. "We can make it together."

A beat of silence followed and they said in unison, "We are both in the family way." Montgomery and Zachariah looked at each other and then at the women. A grin stretched across both of their faces.

Zachariah's heart danced.

"More grandchildren." Mrs. Hildebrand's voice rose with excitement.

"Congratulations," Isaiah said.

After breakfast, Catherine carried Dinah out into the dining room. The girl, thirteen months, wore a long pink dress. "Ma," Dinah said, her arms stretched outward.

Bessie took her. She gave her a kiss on the cheek. "I love you."

Rachel carried Jordan out and handed him to Zachariah.

"Bessie and I are both in the family way again," Lillian said to Catherine and Rachel.

Rachel's eyes brightened and joy filled her voice. "Wonderful!"

Catherine sighed. "More chillun."

Mrs. Hildebrand held Jordan. "What a pretty dress he's wearing. And look at all that black hair," she said. "And you've got John's eyes."

Then she handed the boy to her husband.

The man grinned at the baby. "Finally, a boy," he said. "Jordan, you are getting big. You and I are going to have lots of fun when you are older."

After nightly devotional, Catherine carried Jordan to his cradle. The other slaves retired to their cabins. Catherine slept on a rug on the nursery floor so she'd be close to Jordan at all times.

*   *   *

Zachariah cuddled with Lillian in bed. "What do you want to name our little one?" he asked.

Lillian yawned. "I do not know. It would depend on if the baby was a boy or a girl."

Zachariah laughed. "Naturally."

Lillian placed her arm across his chest. "If we have another son, I was thinking of naming him John Zachary. That way he'd have my pa's name and your name."

Zachariah forced a small smile, unconvinced. He appreciated her gesture, but it wasn't what he wanted. "That sounds like a good name, but I still want a son named Joseph."

Lillian sighed. "I've never liked the name Joseph or Joe."

"It was the name of Jesus' pa. You can't get any better than that."

"I know. I just don't like it."

Zachariah pressed his lips together. He ran his fingers through Lillian's long black hair. She looked so peaceful when she was sleepy. He gently kissed her cheek.

"If we have a girl, I want to name her Catherine," he said.

Lillian's eyes widened. "We can't name our daughter after one of our slaves!"

"There are other women named Catherine. I have already told people my ma's name was Catherine. I do not think it would cause a stir." Lillian didn't reply. There was a long moment of silence. "So what name were you thinking of if we have a daughter?"

"Suzanna. We can call her Suzy. Bessie's name is really Elizabeth, but she's never been called by her whole name."

Zachariah nodded. "Suzy," he said. He thought about how that sounded. "What about Catherine Suzanna?"

"That sounds horrible!"

"It is a rather long name," Zachariah said. He hugged Lillian tighter. "I guess we do not have to decide on names now."

"True." Lillian kissed his lips, short, teasing. "We have several months to think about it, though I do not plan on changing my mind."

"We can wait till he or she is born. Perhaps after seeing the baby we will know what name fits. Perhaps it won't be John, Joseph, Catherine or Suzanna. Perhaps our baby will look more like a Bill or a Jane."

She kissed Zachariah again. "If we have a baby that looks like a Bill or Jane, then you would not be their pa. Bill and Jane are plain, undignified names. You are handsome, intelligent and caring."

Zachariah smiled to put her at ease. He wasn't taken in by her flattery. After living with her for so long, he knew that she was just trying to butter him up to get her way. He wasn't going to let that happen again, he vowed. Not on something as important to him as the name of their child, even if it meant a heated argument with Lillian.

Chapter 24

Park Hill, Cherokee Reservation
March 10, 1844

LILLIAN CLOSED HER eyes, hoping her humming would calm the baby inside her. The baby felt like it was trying to kick its way out of her stomach.

"Can I get you anything, ma'am?" Martha asked.

Lillian rolled over in bed. She spoke is a sleepy mumble. "Where's Catherine?"

"She's feeding Master Jordan. He's gotten used to cow's milk."

The Indian woman groaned. "I want to get out of this bed."

"Doctor says you been havin' too many pains. Only a few mo' weeks till the baby's born. We don't want the baby borned yet."

"Dinah was born early and she was healthy."

"Dinah was a miracle. Doctor say so."

"Zachary's a reverend. Aren't I entitled to a miracle too?"

Martha made a clicking noise and shook her head. "You don't want to test the Lord, ma'am. Are you hungry? You need to eat for the baby."

"Go away."

Martha opened her mouth to protest. Lillian's glare made her stop. "Yes'm."

Being almost a year old, Jordan slowly walked in, holding Catherine's hand. His chubby legs shaking with the effort, but his face determined. Without any help, he climbed up on the bed to be with his ma.

"I have missed you," Lillian said.

Jordan smiled and lay down next to her.

She ran her fingers through his hair. "You will be a big brother soon."

"Can he sleep wid you, Miss?" Catherine asked.

Lillian caressed Jordan's cheek. "Yes." Her son snuggled close. "You are a lot like your pa. You know that?"

"Massa Jordan shore is," Catherine said. "I remember taking cur of Zachary when he's dat lil."

Martha and Catherine left.

Lillian kissed Jordan's forehead and tried to go back to sleep, bur resigned herself to resting with her eyes closed.

A few hours later, Zachary and Montgomery walked in.

"How is my beautiful sister-in-law?" Montgomery asked.

Lillian glared at him.

"Don't be like that," Montgomery said. "Children are blessings. And Bessie's been confined to bed a lot longer than you have."

"That does not make me feel any better, Montgomery Vincent Barlow. I would like to know why God didn't make men bare children."

Zachariah laughed softly.

Lillian switched to glaring at him.

"I am sorry," he said unable to suppress his growing laughter.

"If I could get out of this bed, I would hit you, Zachary. Don't you have any respect for my suffering?"

*

Zachariah grabbed his stomach with one hand and pressed hard forcing his laughter to stop. His smile reversed, the corners of his mouth pulled down, fast and sharp.

Her suffering? What about his suffering? What about the suffering of all their slaves?

"How is Bessie doing? I do not remember the last time I got to see her," Lillian said.

"She is well and in worse humor than you are," Montgomery replied. "I sure hope you two don't go into labor at the same time."

"That is unlikely to happen," Zachariah said.

"We have done just about everything the same these past eight months," Lillian said.

Montgomery nodded. "Well, I need to get back to her and Dinah. Your parents should be coming over soon."

"You have to go?" Lillian asked, pleading for more attention. "Visiting is what keeps me sane."

Zachariah walked out with Montgomery dreading returning to the house. He stayed and talked with Andrew a few minutes. He felt comfortable talking to the negro man. Andrew didn't act educated. He reminded Zachariah of his roots—of who he used to be. Lillian would not approve of their relaxed conversation, but she didn't have to know about every minute of his life.

Finally, he returned to her room, sat on the bed and took off his shoes.

"I told you to wear your light blue shirt this morning. Why aren't you?"

Zachariah held back a biting reply. "I know. I know it matches my eyes. But I like white. Preacher Simon always wore a white shirt to church."

"You are not Preacher Simon. Next week you better wear the blue one."

Zachariah sighed and rolled his eyes then climbed into bed with her and Jordan. "Yes, ma'am."

"I love you," Lillian breathed in his ear.

Zachariah rolled over on his side and kissed her, breathing in her scent, feeling her swollen stomach against his body. He pulled back and blinked. "I felt the baby kick."

"The baby's happy that we're happy."

Zachariah leaned closer, his lips lingering above hers.

Jordan woke. "Pa!"

Lillian closed her eyes. So much for that moment, Zachariah thought.

Jordan crawled up and threw his arms around Zachariah's neck. "Sing!"

The Reverend shook his head. "No. After church, I do not have much of a voice. I will sing later." Jordan frowned. "How about I tell you a story?"

Jordan lay back down and looked at Zachariah expectantly.

Zachariah let out a tired breath. He knew his love for the children would keep him under her thumb.

But he wasn't going to force them to grow up without a pa, like he had. He had to find a way to get his freedom.

*　　*　　*

Zachariah sprung awake, energy and excitement quickening his movements. Since Lillian wasn't allowed to leave the bed, he had the power to move freely around the house without his every movement being scrutinized and disparaged.

He kissed Lillian on the cheek. "Martha will carry in breakfast soon."

Lillian murmured, still half asleep.

Zachariah dressed and strode into his office. Somewhere in this house it was hiding. The key to his dreams. Right under his nose. *Where? Think, think, think.*

She wasn't going to be able to tear his children from him. He had to take away that power.

Think, think, think.

His eyes bulged. He got down on his hands and knees and felt for the loose floorboard. His heart raced, he moved the board, reached his hand down. Nothing. Where else would it be hiding? She had to keep the ownership papers somewhere.

He got up and headed into the dining room. Lillian continually admired the silver. Perhaps the drawer had a false bottom. He pulled out the drawer and moved the knives, forks and spoons to one side. He felt the bottom. He couldn't get it to budge. He quickly put the silverware back into place.

"What you doin'?" Catherine chided, with a smile. "Now I's got to clean dem all ovah again."

"Sorry, Catherine," Zachariah said. He looked around the room. The fireplace. He walked over to the fireplace and felt the bricks. His fingernails dug into the motor looking for a loose one. He sighed through gritted his teeth when none of them broke free.

"What is you looking for?" Catherine asked.

Zachariah shook his head, dismissing the question. "Dorothy," he said, his voice a grating grumble. "Why isn't breakfast on the table?" He frowned inwardly, disappointed. He hated that he had been corrupted by Lillian into a surly gentleman.

Corrupted him into a demanding master. Corrupted him into the type of person he had hated since childhood.

*　　*　　*

Two weeks later, Lillian rustled about in bed. Unable to enjoy the Bible passage Zachariah read aloud.

"Hey, you kicked me," Zachariah said.

"You deserve a little discomfort."

Jordan began crying. Lillian sat up.

"Catherine and Rachel will take care of him," Zachariah assured her.

"Then why is he still crying?"

"Don't worry. I will go to him." He placed the Bible open on the bed to save his place and stood up.

"He needs me," Lillian said. "And I *need* to get out of this bed."

Zachariah pressed his lips together. His muscles bunched. His body temporarily frozen, his mind raced. The doctor had snapped at her for walking around the bedroom. She couldn't walk that far. It would put the baby in jeopardy. Fear sharpened his voice. "No, you don't. You need to stay here. I will take care of him."

Lillian climbed out of bed and slowly walked to the door.

"Dorothy will be bringing supper soon. You need to get back to bed. You need to take care of yourself for the baby," Zachariah said, desperate, pleading.

"I need to take care of Jordan," Lillian said. "I am perfectly fine."

Zachariah grabbed her by the arm. "The doctor knows best."

"Let go of me," Lillian said, glaring at him. "Have you forgotten that my family and I take care of you?"

Zachariah let go of her arm. Concern rippled his forehead. He followed her down the hallway into the nursery.

She bent over the bed and screamed. Lillian stood in a puddle of water.

Catherine ran into the room. "Lawdy, Miss!" Her high-pitched voice echoed throughout the house. She wrapped an arm around Lillian's back and slowly helped her back to her room.

Zachariah ran into the kitchen. "Dorothy, Lillian's having the baby," he said so fast the words ran together.

He ran outside. "Andrew, go get the doctor! Caleb, go tell the family it is time for the baby!"

The negro men ran to the barn, saddled two horses and galloped down the road. Soon the doctor rode back in a buggy, Andrew accompanying him. A few minutes later, Mr. and Mrs. Hildebrand arrived. Caleb rode beside them.

Zachariah sat on the porch outside, holding a fussy Jordan. Rachel stood next to him. "You do not need to go inside, Mrs. Hildebrand. The doctor said it would be a while." He held up Jordan, "Would you like to hold him? I think he needs a woman's touch."

Mrs. Hildebrand ignored him and charged into the house. "I have witnessed the births of all my grandchildren," she said. The door slammed behind her.

Rachel bent down and took Jordan, rocking him back and forth.

"How'd it happen?" Mr. Hildebrand asked.

Zachariah took a deep breath. "Lillian heard Jordan crying, got out of bed and went into the nursery to check on him."

Mr. Hildebrand's forehead wrinkled and his eyes sharpened. "Why didn't you stop her?" he snapped.

*　　*　　*

Zachariah pressed his lips together and stared at his lap. He could not hide his guilt and shame. His cheeks warmed and the flush spread all the way down his neck. Still, he had to try to explain. In an even-keeled voice with a hint of desperation he said, "I tried, but she wouldn't listen to me."

Mr. Hildebrand shook his head. "I know Lillian is headstrong, but she does not always know best. She is like her Ma. She thinks with her heart and not her head. I guess women, being more emotional creatures, tend to do that. It is your job to protect her. God made man to be the head of the family.

"I know the scripture."

"You know the Bible well, Reverend, but you're letting Lillian run the household."

"I don't know how I can act like the head of my family when Lillian won't let me."

"Perhaps because I've had more experience … you have to assert yourself, Reverend. You have to be kind but forceful with her."

Zachariah nodded. Mr. Hildebrand was right. He had to take care of his family no matter the consequences. Lillian's threats were much less painful than Henry's actions. He could brave the storm. Things were going to change.

Andrew and Caleb finished tending to the horses and joined them. Jake and Martha walked outside a little later, Francis and Ivy in tow. Martha took Jordan out of Rachel's arms and wrapped him in another blanket.

Zachariah watched the fireflies lighting up the dark sky. Wrapping his arms around his chest for warmth, he wished the glowing moon provided heat like the sun.

Jake went into the house and returned with a thicker coat for him to wear. During the day it still felt like summer, but at night it turned as cold as autumn.

"Thank you," Zachariah said, putting on the coat.

"Another boy would make me very happy," Mr. Hildebrand said.

"Lillian wants a girl and, though I keep saying I don't care, I'd like a daughter too."

A few hours later, the doctor walked outside a cup of coffee in his hands. The darkness hid his expression.

Zachariah jumped up. He didn't hear any crying. When Jordan was born, he had heard his shrill cry.

"Mr. Degan," the doctor said slow, tentative, "you have a baby girl."

Fear shot through Zachariah's heart, burning a path through its chambers. His lungs seized. Breath did not enter or exit his lungs. The doctor did not say a healthy girl. His daughter had to be healthy. Or he would never forgive himself.

"Can I see her?" Zachariah asked, though what he really wanted to know was whether she was alive. He didn't hear any crying.

The doctor nodded. "She's having trouble breathing. I had to revive her. She needs to be kept calm." He put a hand on his forehead and winced. "You better pray, Reverend. It is God's will if she will live through the night."

*　*　*

The doctor's words resounded through Zachariah mind. Fear snagged on his heartstrings. He had to see her, hold her. He had to comfort Lillian.

He turned around to walk into the house when a galloping horse made him stop. He turned around and saw Isaiah racing towards him. "Doctor! Missus Barlow's in labor."

The old man looked down at the cup of coffee he hadn't even sipped. He yawned and went back in the cabin to get his medical bag.

Caleb hurriedly hitched the doctor's horse to his buggy.

"Jake," Zachariah said, "Ride back with Isaiah. Tell the Barlows about our little girl. Stay there till Bessie's baby's born so you can tell us."

Jake nodded. He walked to the barn, saddled Rambler and rode alongside Isaiah. The two negro men talked excitedly as they rode away.

Mr. Hildebrand went inside with Zachariah. He joined his wife by Lillian's bedside smiling at the dark brown-haired girl, squirming next to her ma. He put his hand on his wife's shoulder.

"Bessie's in labor now. We should get over there soon."

"We will see you in the morning, dear. Rest," Mrs. Hildebrand said in an unsteady voice. "You will have to tell us what this little angel's name is."

*   *   *

"Lillian, she has your eyes," Zachariah whispered. "I guess the line continues."

"I would not want to be the one to break it." Lillian kissed the top of the little girl's head. "I wish she would hold still. The doctor said she was born weak."

"She has your fiery strength. She'll live." His voice came out strong, but doubt twisted his stomach and bunched his chest. His eyes twinkled as he looked at the baby swaddled in a yellow blanket. "What are we going to name her?"

"She looks like a Suzanna to me," Lillian said, smiling, wide and persuasive.

Zachariah shook his head. He wouldn't give in that easy. "I think she looks like a Catherine."

Catherine's eyes widened. She tapped her fingers on her lips.

"Suzanna can be shortened to Suzy. Suzy is cute and endearing. Catherine cannot be shortened."

"It can be shortened to Cat."

"I am not going to have my daughter called by the name of animal!"

Catherine looked at the ground.

Zachariah's eyes narrowed. "When you say 'animal' do you mean a cat or a slave?"

"I can't believe you said that Zachary Degan! I mean cat. The kind with a long, fluffy tail."

"I need to have a say in this matter. You should treat me like an equal. I am your husband."

*

Lillian's face burned as hot as a blacksmith's kiln. Oh he could be infuriating! "I have always treated you like my husband. Where is this coming from?"

"I do not feel like I get a say in anything. You smile and bat your eyelashes and you get everything you want from me and Montgomery. Well, it is stopping this instant. We are naming our baby girl Catherine. Catherine Suzanna if you wish. You can still call her Suzy."

"Why can't we name her Suzanna Catherine? If we do that, no one will ever call her Cat. Cat is degrading."

An unsettling silence followed. Zachary shifted in his seat.

Lillian's rigid face relaxed. "I'm sorry, Zachary." Tears flooded her eyes, blurring her sight. "I know I can be stubborn," she choked out the words, sobbing. "I, I did not realize I was doing that. I did not realize you felt that way. I want you to have a voice. I want you to be happy." Her chin trembled, her heart twisted inside his chest like a wrung out rag. "But our daughter might not even live and I am so upset…"

She gasped for a long breath. Her lungs working overtime to intake air. This couldn't be happening. Zachary upset with her. Her daughter ill.

The walls of her family were crumbling down.

*

Zachariah bit his cheek. Seeing her in such an emotional, vulnerable state made him feel guilty. Considering the fragile health of their daughter it wasn't the right time for him to pick this battle.

He brushed away the stray tear clinging to her cheek. "Thank you." He kissed her warm and gentle. "But I think she looks more like Suzanna. Suzanna Catherine."

"Really?" Lillian sniffled.

Zachariah nodded. "Really."

Catherine stood back against the wall. Moonlight, coming through the window, streaked across her face. Out of the corner of his eye, Zachariah saw her grinning.

Catherine excused herself to take care of Jordan.

Zachariah watched Suzanna nurse. Life was close to perfect. He reached over and brushed a strand of hair out of Lillian's face and tucked it behind her left ear. All his family's needs were taken care of.

Except his freedom. And the freedom of his ma and sister. The desire, the need for freedom kept calling to him, haunting him, plaguing him.

After Suzanna finished, Lillian handed her to Zachariah. He held his daughter carefully, afraid he'd hurt her. He figured girl babies were more fragile than boys. She looked up at him with big green eyes. He ran his hand over her dark brown hair.

"You are a beautiful little girl." He looked at her tiny hand, so much smaller than one of his fingers. "You're even fairer than your brother."

"She must have gotten more of your blood," Lillian said.

"My blood making her white?" He pinched his eyelids with his thumb and forefinger.

All he could think about was his little girl. His baby fighting for each breath.

The sound of hoofbeats grew near. Late into the night, a horse and rider approached the house. Lillian sleeping soundly. Zachariah carried Suzanna into the parlor and showed her to Martha, Rachel, Dorothy, Ivy and Francis.

"Where are Caleb and Andrew?"

"The men went to bed," Dorothy said.

Zachariah looked down at his daughter. His beautiful daughter. "They can meet Miss Suzanna tomorrow." He choked back tears. Hopefully, they could meet her tomorrow.

"What a lovely name," Rachel said.

"Her name is Suzanna Catherine Degan, but we will call her Suzy."

Jake walked into the house with a tired grin, that didn't show in his eyes. "Miss Bessie, she have a healthy boy," he said. "Master Thomas James Barlow."

"They will all grow up together," Dorothy said.

Zachariah nodded. His mind reeling, lungs threatening to shut down. If Suzanna lives.

He carried Suzanna into the nursery and placed her in the cradle and prayed.

*   *   *

"I have a present for you, Catherine," Zachariah said.

"A present? You done give me a present wid naming Miss Suzy."

"That is not enough. I owe you so much." He pulled a small box out of his coat pocket and handed it to his ma.

Catherine cradled the box like it would break any moment. She lifted the lid and her jawed dropped. Inside rested a silver necklace with a cross charm.

"You helped make me the preacher I am. I want you to wear this always."

Ma smiled happy, prideful, shocked. "Thank you suh, thank you. I will!" She pulled the necklace out of the box and Zachariah clasped it around her neck.

"You huv everything you done want, Massa Degan," Catherine said, then yawned.

Zachariah cringed inwardly at hearing his ma call him master.

If he found his ownership papers, he could forge Lillian's signature on them. If he had to, he could forge her signature on Catherine's and Rachel's papers too. He closed his eyes tightly. The dreadful thought washed a wave of anxiety over him.

He hoped it wouldn't come to that.

Chapter 25

Park Hill, Cherokee Reservation
June 17, 1847

ZACHARIAH TOOK A deep breath. Many things had changed in the last years and yet many things had stayed the same. They were going to another party tonight. Living with Lillian had many advantages.

But it was getting harder to stomach the disadvantages. He still desired his freedom.

Isaiah stopped Mr. Barlow's carriage in front of the Degan's cabin. Jordan and Suzy raced out the front door to greet them; Rachel and their dog, Ace, chased after them barking. Lillian shook her head.

"When Catherine's sleeping, they turn into wild horses."

"I rather enjoy it," Zachariah said, his eyes smiling.

Lillian rolled her eyes. "I miss them as babies." The weary honesty in her voice unmistakable.

Zachariah smiled at her with a playful twinkle in his eye. "We could always have another baby."

Lillian laughed softly. "I do not know if I am ready for that."

Montgomery helped Bessie out.

Dinah and Thomas ran to play with their cousins.

Lillian hugged her sister. "You look beautiful in pink, Bessie."

"Thank you. I do not think I will ever get my figure back."

"You are just as lovely as when I married you," Montgomery said.

Lillian looked down at the plain yellow dress she was wearing, a light flush rose in her cheeks. "I have not changed for the party yet."

Montgomery watched the children play with Ace. The puppy rolled on his back and let them rub his stomach. His ears perked up. He stood and went to investigate some squirrels. The four children proceeded to join hands and walk around in a circle.

"I cannot believe Dinah's five. My little girl," he said.

Zachariah nodded. "Jordan's four and Suzy and Thomas are three."

"Ma, Pa, come play with us." Jordan said, eager, excited.

"Come on," Thomas said.

Zachariah, Lillian, Montgomery and Bessie joined the children turning the square into a circle.

"Sing, Pa," Jordan said.

"Remember your manners," Lillian said.

Jordan frowned, staring at the grass. "Please sing, Pa."

"Since you asked so nicely," Zachariah said and began the child's verse:

Ring a ring a Rosie,
A pocket full o' posies,
Hush! Hush! Hush! Hush!
We're all tumbled down.

At hearing, 'tumbled down,' all the boys bowed and the girls curtsied. Suzy giggled.

Thomas clapped. "Play again," he said.

"No," Montgomery said. "The grown-ups have to talk. You can keep playing. Dinah, Thomas mind Rachel and Isaiah."

"Yes, Pa," Dinah said. "Can Ivy and Francis play with us?"

Hearing their names, the two colored youths quit picking apples.

"Go on," Zachariah said.

Ivy and Francis left their buckets of apples under the tree and went to play.

Isaiah began talking with Rachel. Out of the corner of his eye, Zachariah thought he saw them holding hands. Later, he heard them laughing.

"A break," Lillian said with a sigh and walked in the house. "I enjoy parties more now just for that reason."

"I know what you mean," Bessie said. "We better hurry and get ready or we will be late."

"You know we're likely the only ones who trust our slaves enough to leave them," Montgomery said.

Zachariah examined his fingernails. "Every week you hear of slaves escaping around here. Seems the threat of being sold isn't as threatening as it used to be."

"Yes," Bessie said, "but with so many negroes, slave and free, being kidnapped and dragged off the reservation to be sold in the Deep South it isn't as safe for them as it used to be for them to stay here."

"You might want to think about learning to use a gun, Reverend. To protect your family and your property," Montgomery said. "Mr. Beard had two slaves stolen a few days ago."

Zachariah shook his head. "I don't see how guns and preaching mix. The Lord provides protection."

Lillian returned wearing the red dress Zachariah had given her for her birthday four years ago.

"That still looks brand new," Bessie said.

"I only wear it on special occasions."

Zachariah put on his top hat and white gloves then helped his wife into their carriage. He followed Montgomery and Bessie to his in-laws' house. When he brought the carriage to a stop, he whistled. There were horses, carriages and buggies everywhere.

Even after attending several parties he still couldn't believe he was accepted by the elite. His heart palpitated and sweat beaded his forehead. Would they discover the truth about him and send him to the pits of hell for his fakery?

If they did, would God rescue him and allow him to spend eternity in heaven for preaching the gospel?

*   *   *

They walked inside and the doorman took their hats and coats. Zachariah heard the sounds of people talking and the slow chords of fiddles.

"May I have this dance?" Lillian asked.

Zachariah lips struggled to find a comfortable grin. He nodded again letting her take charge of the occasion despite proper decorum.

As they waltzed he remembered how scared he had been when she first taught him to dance. Now his heart filled with joy each time he danced with his Indian maiden. He smiled, locked in her dreamy gaze. Those dreamy eyes cast a spell upon him. He gave her a kiss. Her lips, warm and gentle on his, sent a tingling flutter through his body.

After the song ended, Zachariah escorted her off the floor. Mr. and Mrs. Hildebrand found them.

"Welcome," Mr. Hildebrand said, shaking Zachariah's hand. "I just knew you'd be in that red dress, Lillian."

"I was thinking of having another one made just like it. I am sure Rachel could manage."

"But the styles are changing," Mrs. Hildebrand said.

"Love doesn't care about the latest fashion."

Love. She threw around that word so often—she must mean it. He should be able to use her love to obtain his freedom. Their children gave him leverage. His throat tightened at the thought. How could he bring it up?

"Zachary, come with me and get a glass of punch," Mr. Hildebrand said before his wife could reply. "There are several people I want you to talk to."

The festivities finally ended well into the night. Zachariah helped Lillian into the carriage. His feet ached, but the adrenaline from dancing kept him wide awake. The last tune of the night kept playing in his head. He broke into song:

What is louder than a horn?
Sing ninety-nine and ninety;
And what is sharper than a thorn?
And you are the weaver's bonny.

Lillian yawned. Zachariah looked at her with hopeful eyes. She relented and gave the response:

> *Thunder's louder than a horn,*
> *Sing ninety-nine and ninety;*
> *Death is sharper than a thorn,*
> *And I am the weaver's bonny.*

"You have a beautiful voice. I don't know why you do not sing more often. The only time I hear you sing is in church."

Lillian blushed. "I think you do enough singing for the both of us."

Zachariah finished the song:

> *You have answered my questions nine,*
> *Sing ninety-nine and ninety;*
> *So you are God's, you are none of mine,*
> *And you...*

He stopped singing. An officer stood outside his house. The tall Indian was talking with Isaiah and Catherine. Ace, chained to a tree, growled at the officer, barring his teeth.

Zachariah jerked back on the reins, sending Lillian forward. Zachariah stuck out his arm to catch her, his heart hammering his chest. He jumped out of the carriage and ran towards them. *Please let the children be safe, Lord.*

"Whose pocket watch is that?" the officer asked Isaiah.

Isaiah was stone-faced though the weight on his left foot and neck tilted to left showed his agitation. "How many times are you going to ask me that? Once a week?"

The full-blood Cherokee slapped Isaiah's face. "I am an officer. I have the right to question you. Not that I need the right to question a nigger."

Isaiah took a deep breath. "As I have told you before, the pocket watch belongs to Master Barlow."

"Then you stole it."

"No, sir. He gave it to me. I have to be able to know the time in order to perform my duties. Right now I need to keep track of the time to be sure to get Miss Dinah and Master Thomas in bed at the proper hour."

The officer glared at Isaiah for a tense minute then switched his attention to Catherine. He reached over and fingered the cross charm she was wearing. "Whose necklace is that?"

"It's mine, sir."

Isaiah cringed.

"Slaves are not allowed to own any property. Your necklace will be sold and according to law you will be given the money from the sale."

Catherine's eyes widened and her voice trembled. "I do not want money, sir. I want my necklace."

The Indian pulled on the chain breaking it off her neck. He held the chain and cross charm in his hand.

"What is going on here?" Zachariah demanded in a breathy rush, blood rushing in his ears.

"This wench said she owned this necklace," the officer said. "Property is not allowed to own property. Of course you should be familiar with all the laws, Reverend Degan, since you are on the council now."

Zachariah's eyes shrunk into hard beads. "That law was intended to keep slaves from owning other slaves or livestock not from small items like a necklace. I suppose you want to take their clothes away from them too."

The officer shook his head. "No one expects all the niggers to walk around naked."

"According to law, the necklace has to be sold. I will buy it. It is a cross for goodness sakes."

The officer's lips shifted into a smile, grudging, mean, sly. He puffed out his chest to display his strength and power and shook his head. "I'm not showing you any special treatment, Reverend. I will dispose of the necklace according to the rules." The officer mounted his bay, a sinister smirk on his face, and rode away.

Zachariah ground his teeth and glared at the man's back, shooting a look cold enough to freeze the officer's tiny heart. His image blurred and Zachariah felt tears in his eyes. He pressed his palm against his eyelids. "Where are the children?"

"Inside with Rachel, sir," Isaiah replied. "Mr. Gann, he's always been after me. He does not like colored folks looking richer than him."

The reverend nodded. He looked at Catherine. She wiped tears out of her eyes.

"What happened?" Lillian asked.

"Mr. Gann just took Catherine's necklace," Zachariah said.

"We will get you another one," Lillian assured her.

Zachariah pressed his lips together. "Montgomery and Bessie are still visiting. Isaiah, please use our carriage and take Dinah and Thomas home. You may return it in the morning."

"Yes, sir." Isaiah walked inside the house and carried out a sleepy Thomas. Dinah, yawning, followed behind him.

"I's go to the nursery," Catherine said. "Rachel needs to get to bed. We's the only ones left awake."

Zachariah nodded. "If they are asleep, you may go to the quarters with Rachel. Jordan and Suzy are old enough to sleep in there alone."

"Yes, sir."

This was the last straw. He had something to settle. He'd settle with her right now.

*   *   *

Zachariah waited till Isaiah drove the carriage out of earshot. Then he turned to Lillian his face somber, eyes serious. "We have to talk."

She followed him into their bedroom then shut the door.

"We can't get Catherine another necklace because Mr. Gann can take that one too. Catherine can't own the necklace because she's property. Because she's a slave. Can you imagine how painful it is to have your ma and sister be slaves?"

Lillian pursed her lips together and didn't respond.

"They are my family and you've owned them for over four years. Please, set them free."

The silence pushed them apart. Zachariah hands turned clammy. He ran his tongue around his mouth as he continued to endure his wife's disgusted glare.

Finally, Lillian looked away. "I suppose Catherine and Rachel will not leave us," she said. "They will want to be close to you and the children."

"I promise they will stay. But we will have to start paying them for their work. I hope someday they can get their own house."

"I understand but—"

"If you love me, you will free them. Your family is free. Mine should be too."

"You still can't acknowledge them as your family."

"I know that. But at least they will not be slaves. I cannot be master to my ma and sister any longer."

"I will take care of it in the morning."

Zachariah nodded with the glimmer of a smile.

Lillian cocked her head and gave him an inquiring look. "What else is on your mind?"

"You need to free me too."

*

Lillian felt her whole face burning with shame. She looked away sheepishly. How could she have done this to him? After a moment of silence, she sighed and shook her head. "No I don't need to sign your paper," she whispered.

Zachary grabbed her arm and spun her around making her face him. "What do you mean?"

Lillian pressed her lips together. Zachary's eyes demanded an answer. She struggled to form the words, to unbury the truth. The truth that could derail her dreams.

Her lungs constricted sending her heart rate soaring. She ran her tongue across the roof her mouth. Her throat was so dry, so tight, so sore she doubted she could speak.

But she had to. She couldn't keep this from him any longer.

With a push she forced the words out. They sounded the opposite of her usual speech—thin, wispy, delicate. "Mr. Travers signed your manumission paper before he handed you over to me. You couldn't read then and once you could read I hid them because I didn't want you to know."

Her Adam's apple climbed higher in her throat and then slid back to its usual place. She tensed waiting for the information to sink in, bracing herself for Zachary's reaction.

"What?" Zachary's voice exploded with force; it was so loud it hurt her ears. He gripped both of Lillian's shoulders, digging his fingers into her flesh.

She winced and hung her head.

He squeezed harder. "Look at me." His voice, a gruff growl, brought more tears.

She raised her head and looked into his eyes.

"Are you keeping any more secrets from me?"

"N-n-no," she choked out. "I swear it. All of my important papers are sealed behind the painting of the *Princess* in our room. Look for yourself."

Zachary did not let Lillian go. "Why did you lie to me?"

*   *   *

Lillian bowed her head, staring at her shoes. Her heart ached as if it had been trampled by a horse. The pain radiated to her stomach, limbs, neck. She opened her mouth and said in a small cracked voice. "I'm sorry."

It wasn't enough. But she didn't know what else to say.

A tear pushed out of her eyes and ran down her cheek. She restrained from sobbing like a baby. Hildebrand women were strong and confident and determined. She swallowed, pushing down her sorrow, pain, regret. "I was afraid that if you knew, you would leave me," she said slowly.

Zachary stared at her, forehead grooved, lips tight, he seemed to be searching for words. "We are married. Why would I leave you?" His voice was forcefully calm.

"Lots of Cherokee families have broken up ever since we moved to the reservation. I loved you so much…" She sobbed. "I was afraid you might grow out of love with me…"

"There is more to it than that," Zachary said, gruff and demanding. "I want the truth. The whole truth."

Lillian rubbed her tongue across the back of her teeth. The smooth roughness comforted her. "In a traditional marriage the woman is subservient to her husband. I-I couldn't do that. I've always been afraid of having a violent man in charge of me and I didn't want to give up my identity."

"So you made me give up mine," he bellowed, anger dripping off each syllable.

"No. I didn't see it that way." Lillian turned her head to the side. "I figured since you were born a slave you were gaining an identity not losing one."

"I have fought all my life to gain my voice. Thinking you owned me, reminding me that you owned me, holding the fact you owned me to my head like a cocked musket has made me hold my tongue. How could you do that to me? I have hated you for that."

"Don't say that." Lillian's shoulders shook with the force of each tear, with the force of her grief.

"Being your slave and your husband was a fine line. I never knew what role you wanted me to play. Though you always let me know when I chose the wrong one."

Lillian's sobbing grew louder and she choked on her tears.

Zachary took a deep breath and let her go.

Lillian saw some of the tenseness disappear from his face. His eyes remained sharp and irritated and confused.

Her insides remained tangled. "I know you are angry with me and you have every right to be, but please do not leave me."

"Yes, I'm angry," Zachary admitted. Then he took a deep breath and lowered his voice. "But I would not have done anything differently had I known."

"You mean you are going to stay?" she asked in a wavering tone.

"Yes. I'm going to stay. Before we left the *Princess* you gave me a choice. I have questioned, but never regretted my decision."

Lillian leaned in to kiss Zachary's lips.

Zachary pulled away leaving her puckering at air. "But what you have done will take time for me to forgive. I have lost my trust in you. I have lost my respect for you. But I have not lost my love for you."

Lillian frowned, her eyes and the corners of her mouth sagging. Her voice came airy, thin. "I am sorry, Zachary. I hope in time," she paused and swallowed hard, "you will learn to trust me again."

Zachary didn't say anything.

"I feel now that this is out, our love will be stronger than ever. Now we are truly equals."

Lillian walked over, took his hand, and squeezed it. Feeling his palm against hers, their fingers entwined gave her cautious hope. "We will get through this, won't we?" she asked, a nervous tone in her voice.

*

Zachariah looked blankly at the wall. Unfortunately, it didn't help him sort out his mixed emotions—love, hate, distrust, relief. His pain gave way to numbness. Sudden exhaustion made his head feel heavy, his muscles weak. He sat down on the bed before all his strength disappeared.

Lillian's face, riddled with concern, begged for a response.

Zachariah held his face in his hands, a throbbing headache rattling his brain. "I do not know. I do not know what to think of you any more. I do not know if I can trust that you have my best interest in mind, instead of only your own."

She hesitated, then walked over and put a hand on his shoulder.

Zachariah closed his eyes but did not pull away. He didn't want to let her know, but he still craved her touch.

He always would.

Chapter 26

Park Hill, Cherokee Reservation
June 25, 1847

ZACHARIAH SLAMMED HIS fist on the desk. Could he do anything without Lillian's help? He had been in his office all morning, but he hadn't written a single word on paper.

"I told her I could write this sermon on my own," he whispered to himself. "I insisted on it. I have to take control of my life." He hung his head. He had exhausted all the sermons he could remember from listening to Reverend Simon and Lillian was out visiting friends. He stared at the black cover of his Bible.

None of those sermons he had given over the years had been his words. Being Reverend Degan was an act following a carefully crafted script Lillian had laid out for him. He had gotten really good at it. He had everyone convinced but himself. He rubbed his forehead.

"What exactly are my thoughts on religion?" he asked out loud.

A moment of silence followed. God didn't give him an answer.

Sighing, he picked up his pen and wrote on the top of his paper "Slaves and Masters" then he opened to the first page of the Bible. He'd read it cover to cover to get the truth. He'd finally search for the answers. Answers to the questions he had had all his life.

He swallowed his anxiety with one gulp and began the first passage in Genesis. In the back of his mind he feared the answer. But he knew in his heart that all people, regardless of skin color, were created equal. Surely, since they were all children of God and all believers had a home in heaven, the Bible would say so. Or at the least, say something that he could use to better the treatment of slaves.

His eyes burned after hours of reading. The words began to blur together. He had yet to find anything. He looked up hearing a knock. "Who is it?" he asked agitation in his voice.

"Just Catherine, Reverend."

Zachariah pushed his chair back from the desk. "Come in."

Ma slowly opened the door and smiled, soft and caring. "You'se been in here all day. Doan you think you needs to spend time wid de chillun?"

"I'm working."

Ma looked down at the blank piece of paper on his desk then she gave him a long look. "Church is in two days and you ain't done nothing."

"I am reading the Bible," he said, agitated. "I'm working on something important."

Ma pressed her lips together. "Sure you is, sir. Playing with Jordan and Suzy is important too."

Embarrassment flooded his face. He shouldn't have snapped. He rubbed his forehead unable to wipe away the warmness. "I'm sorry I was cross with you. I do need to take a break."

He followed Ma out of the office. Outside, Jordan and Suzy left Rachel and ran up to him. Ace ran ahead, and sat at Zachariah's feet, his tail thumping the ground.

What's your sermon about?" Ma asked.

"Relationships," Zachariah said, picking up Suzy. "I think you will really like this one."

*   *   *

Zachariah's hand ached threatening to cramp from writing for hours. Draft, after draft, after draft.

He continued to work on his sermon while Jake drove the carriage to the church. He bit his lip and kept writing feverishly. It had to be perfect.

Bible in hand, he climbed out of the carriage. He had so much on his mind that he headed straight through the doors without helping Lillian down. He felt her glaring at the back of his head. He didn't care.

His heart pounded relentlessly as he approached the pulpit. His legs felt like dough. He gripped the sides of the stand trying to compose himself, and regain his strength. The Lord's word was more important than Lillian's feelings.

Zachariah looked out at his congregation. He swallowed hard, but the lump in his throat remained. He looked down at his notes then over at Ma and Rachel. He took a deep breath and began his sermon. "It has come to my attention that in all my sermons I have neglected to speak on one subject—the treatment of slaves."

Members of the congregation started whispering and murmuring.

Zachariah hit the top of the pulpit to get their attention. "I do not wish to give you my opinion, but quote straight from the Bible. If you wish to read this passage, turn to Ephesians 6.

"Verses 5-9 deal with the relationship between master and slave. 'Slaves, obey your earthly masters with respect and fear, and with sincerity of heart, just as you would obey Christ. Obey them not only to win their favor when their eye is on you, but like slaves of Christ, doing the will of God from your heart.' I should hope you all agree with this. The duty of a slave is to be a good Christian and serve the Lord. Because of their standing in life, they serve the Lord by serving their masters faithfully.

Members of the congregation nodded. They had pleasant expressions, but sat erect on the edge of their seats. He had never captured their attention so fully. Zachariah knew that what he had to say next was controversial.

"The next verse speaks to masters. 'And you, masters, do the same things to them, giving up threatening, knowing that your own

Master also is in heaven, and there is no partiality with Him.' This means that God does not see a difference between slave, free negro, white man and Indian. If we believe in God, we will all dwell in heaven together. God tells masters to not threaten your slaves. We should all have the fear of God in us when we order our slaves about, see to their needs and discipline them. We should ask ourselves, would God approve? Masters are also religious leaders for their slaves. Masters should be asking themselves, am I being the best Christian leader I can be?"

Zachariah stopped and took a drink of water. He glanced at the congregation and saw what he expected—angry faces and others with blank stares. The corners of his mouth turned upward slightly. Lillian even looked shocked. He had not revealed to her the subject of today's sermon. He had written it all on his own and he wasn't going to be persuaded from his stance, especially when he found the verses to back up what he knew in his heart was true. God cared for the treatment of slaves. God protected their souls.

"I did not know the Cherokee Nation before you moved to the reservation. However, I have heard many tell about how happy both the Cherokee people and their slaves were then. I have been told that few slaves ran away at that time. Now slaves often run away from their masters. I read advertisements offering rewards for their return in the *Advocate*. When slaves run away from their masters, they become lost sheep. They have left the protection of their shepherd. They have also turned their back on God, because God has commanded slaves to serve their masters faithfully as they would serve the Lord.

"The question that comes to mind is why are slaves escaping now? The Nation needs to band together. The Nation needs to pledge to treat slaves christianly so that they will not wish to flee. Remember the years in Georgia when you were happy? You didn't want to leave your land. If slaves are happy, if they are well provided for, they will not want to leave the reservation and they will serve their masters faithfully.

"Why are negro traders coming into the Nation and stealing slaves and free negroes to be sold on some southern auction block? Negro dealers and other malicious white men are like serpents among us. We need to be watchful of what they say and do. We need to protect our slaves and colored brethren from the hungry jaws of the wolves."

Zachariah finished his sermon. The room became dead silent. He sucked in his breath. An eerie feeling quickening his pulse. He shifted upon the balls of his feet. Everyone stared at him. Finally, he let out his breath and walked outside. He waited and no one joined him. He peeked around the corner, through the open door he heard the congregation talking amongst themselves in a muffled clamor.

Despite his uneasy situation, his heart felt lighter than had it in years. Those words completely renewed his faith. He knew there was going to be consequences for what he said. Consequences he was willing to face.

*　*　*

Mr. Hildebrand walked outside. Zachariah curved his lips into the imitation of a smile. He was too nervous and too weary to be convincing. He took a deep breath, relieved his father-in-law was the first to join him. Mr. Hildebrand looked disgruntled though not angry.

"That wasn't one of your typical sermons."

"No, sir."

"I know what you were getting at, and perhaps you are right, but the wealthy of the Nation are not ready to hear it. And I know that wealthy white men would not receive that sermon well either."

An awkward moment of silence followed. Zachariah didn't know what to say. "Those verses are in the Bible. They deserved my attention."

"I am afraid you are going to get a lot of unwanted attention after that."

"Yes, sir."

Zachariah helped Lillian into the carriage. She took his hand, stone-faced. He clicked his teeth and the horses started forward. His team was better company than his wife. Lillian did not say one word to him all the way home.

Zachariah tensed, all his muscles on high alert. This was the calm before the storm. He didn't know that she would take it so hard. They were already doing their Christian duty by treating their slaves well.

"Ma's mad," Suzy said. Lillian strode past them and into the house.

Zachariah picked up his little girl. "I know. We have to always tell the truth and sometimes people don't want to hear the truth, so they get mad."

Hearing the heavy tread of feet and quiet talking, he looked up. His slaves were returning. He watched proudly noting to himself that each of them had a good pair of shoes. Ma and Rachel led the column, grinning.

"Can I play with Thomas?" Jordan asked.

He looked into his son's hazel eyes. He was getting so tall. "Yes. You may go play with Thomas. Suzy, do you want to go play with Thomas and Dinah?"

She nodded.

"Catherine, drive the children to Montgomery's."

"Yes, sir." Ma helped the children into the carriage. The horses still hitched.

Rachel went into the house, retrieved her needle and thread and walked back outside. She sat on the porch and began mending a pair of socks.

Zachariah sighed, only voicing half the sorrow in his heart. Rachel and Ma were free now, but they didn't have a dime to their name. Lillian hadn't said it, but he knew that she wanted them to work for her for the rest of their lives. If they did that, they were little better than slaves.

*　　*　　*

A negro man, in holey clothes, rode up to his cabin on a white horse. Ace started barking loudly and ran up to the stranger.

"Quiet, Ace," Zachariah ordered. He looked up at the negro man. "State your business."

"Reverend," the man panted. "Ol' Bill, he's doing poorly."

"Then you should get the doctor."

"Doctor say dat he can do nothin' for him. Bill, he wants to talk to you 'fore he dies. Hurry, please suh."

"Caleb, saddle Rambler."

The young man ran into the barn and lead out the mare.

Zachariah mounted and followed the raggedly clothed slave to the quarters at the Carter place. They both dismounted. The negro held Rambler's reins. Zachariah hesitated a moment. He had never watched someone die. He didn't know what to say. He glanced up at the sky. God would help him. God loved the colored man too.

His heart sped a few beats. He opened the door and entered the framework house and saw a lone slave. The gray-haired negro lay on his back on the dirt floor, a wadded up blanket for a pillow. "Bill?"

The man smiled weakly. Zachariah's heart pulled him closer, a deep, dull ache in his chest. The wrinkles around Bill's eyes and mouth reminded him of Joe. "Reverend, I doan know you come."

Zachariah kneeled beside him. "Is there anything I can do to help you?"

The old man closed his eyes. "Tell me 'bout heab'n."

"Heaven's paved with gold. There's plenty to eat. You imagine something and it appears in your hand. You will never be thirsty either. There are plenty of streams with fresh, cool water. There is no pain in heaven of any kind and you will never be cold. You will be reunited with your family and friends."

"An' I be free in heab'n?" Bill whispered.

Zachariah fought back tears. He must remain strong. His voice carried the power of assurance. "Yes. You will be free."

Bill stopped breathing, a peaceful smile on his lips, like a child who had just finished a peppermint stick. Zachariah placed the man's limp arms across his chest. Then he bowed his head.

"Lord, Bill lived a good long life. Please welcome him into heaven. I hope everything I told him was true. I know he wasn't happy in this life. Reward him for his toil and for being a good Christian. Amen."

Zachariah stood up, solemnly walked outside and mounted Rambler.

"Bill's gone?" the slave asked.

"His soul's in heaven."

The slave frowned and nodded. "I best get a shovel an bury him den. Thank you, Reverend."

Mr. Carter walked towards them with determined steps, his gray eyes shooting daggers. "What are you doing on my property, Reverend?" The man's words were loud and lifted at the end.

Recognizing the threat, Zachariah's eyes widened. Mr. Carter was a large man with more white blood than Cherokee. "I was comforting Bill before he died."

"I did not send for you."

"I did, Massa," the slave whispered.

Mr. Carter grabbed the man's arm, spun him around and gave him a push. "I'll see to you later."

"He did nothing wrong," Zachariah said.

"He left the property without permission."

Zachariah met Mr. Carter's stony glare. He walked over to the slave the man had pushed. "This man is a Christian. Any Christian master would want their slaves comforted before they died. You should be happy that I came. And if a reverend wasn't able to come then someone should have been with Bill. You could have been with him. Or did he mean nothing to you?"

Mr. Carter did not respond. His eyes narrowed into a glare that dropped the temperature ten degrees.

Zachariah gritted his teeth. "No one should have to die alone."

"You are trespassing," Mr. Carter said, he voice deep and rough. The man's face darkened into a deeper red, his hands trembling. "Get off my land, Mr. Degan. I wouldn't be surprised if you were one of those malicious white men you talked about in church. You could be stealing our slaves and sneaking them out with Montgomery's help. Get off my land now!"

"Yes, sir," Zachariah said quickly. He spurred Rambler into a gallop and headed back home.

When he walked inside, he found Lillian sitting at the dining room table waiting for him. "Caleb told me where you went," she said, standing.

"I did not have time to tell you."

"They are all talking about you. About what you preached at church."

She walked closer until he smelled the faint remnant of perfume on her neck. She reached up and brushed her fingers across his cheek. "I'm going to write your next sermon."

"No." He took a step back, knowing her body was very persuasive. "But I will let you help me. This will pass."

"But…"

"I am not apologizing or taking back anything in my sermon. I meant every word."

"I know you did. While you were gone," Lillian continued, "I was thinking about what you said in church. You could have said it much worse. You didn't advocate freedom."

"You are not angry with me?"

"No." Lillian threw her arms around his neck. "I love you, Zachary. I knew moving to the reservation wouldn't be easy for you. But you did it for me. I realized the least I can do is support you."

Zachariah blinked, shocked by her abrupt change. He had wanted her to say those words for years. Still, they didn't ring true. Just more of her manipulation, more of her lies, more of her deceit. He looked into her emerald eyes searching for a granule of truth— and took a deep breath. Perhaps he would believe those words in the future.

"I tried to make my point as nicely as possible. I did not tell them to stop owning slaves. Though that's what I wish would happen. I have no right, no power to tell them that."

*

"Don't worry. I will help you get back into their good graces." Lillian batted her eyelashes, her mischievous grin failing to melt his serious demeanor. "I might have to use my womanly charm. Eventually they'll forget. Or maybe we can actually get them to see the truth in your words and the spirit in which they were intended."

She doubted it. Her feminine wiles alone would not smooth this situation. He'd created an uproar rivaled only by the government forcing them onto the reservation.

"Good luck. Mr. Carter ran me off his land."

Lillian bit her lip. "I will go visiting tomorrow and next month we will host a party. Music, good food and dancing always put everyone in a good mood. Somehow we'll fix this together."

An uneasy smile worked its way onto Zachary's lips. "I love you, Lillian. You will always have my heart."

"In time, I will free the others. I promise." Her voice came out in a squeak and she fought to control her emotions, hold back tears. She paused and looked away sheepishly.

"Deep down I knew slavery was wrong, but until I married you, I never realized how wrong. African blood stains one's skin only. Their heart, mind and soul remain pure." She looked into Zachary's blue eyes. "I could have never had the courage to free them, to go against my family without your strength."

"Why can't you free all of them now?"

Lillian sighed. "There is enough uproar at the moment. I will free the rest one at a time—starting with Dorothy because she's the oldest. We are making good money off our horses now. I will pay Dorothy and her family well if they decide to stay and work for us. I hope they all decide to stay. I do care about them."

"I know. But whether they stay will be up to them. Thank you for doing this for me, for them."

Zachary took her hand in his and squeezed. God had answered his prayers. He had changed Lillian's heart, made her see the error of her ways.

Once he was no longer master to the help their relationship could blossom further.

Chapter 27

Park Hill, Cherokee Reservation
September 15, 1847

"I'M GOING TO talk to Ned and Agnes about their wedding," Zachariah said, and walked out the door, not waiting for Lillian to reply.

Jordan rode on his shoulders. He held tightly to the boy's legs as he walked briskly around the lawn neighing. Jordan laughed loudly. Zachariah laughed too. He tilted his head back and looked into his son's twinkling eyes. It was hard to believe he was four years old. Wavy black hair almost reached his shoulders.

Catherine watched them, smiling. Rachel sat under an apple tree, Suzy in her lap. The little girl tugged on Rachel's long dark brown hair as the young woman told her a story. Zachariah set Jordan on the ground.

"You can go play with Catherine or listen to Rachel's story with your sister."

"I play with you, Pa."

"I know. I want to play with you too, but I have work to do. We can play when I get back."

"Can I ride Rambler? I'm big enough."

"You are big enough, are you? Rambler is a big horse."

"Please," he said, dragging out the word. "Please, Pa. When you come back."

Zachariah nodded. "All right." He couldn't resist his son's charms any more than he could resist Lillian's.

Jordan grinned and walked over to Catherine.

Francis threw down his hoe and ran to help Caleb saddle Rambler.

Zachariah considered scolding the youth for leaving the garden but held his tongue. He couldn't help but laugh at the boy's eagerness. He remembered how excited he had been to take care of Master Norton's horse.

He sighed. He hadn't thought of Michael, Ellen or any of the slaves at Hickory Rail Inn for a long time. He vowed to remember them in his prayers tonight. He hoped some day they'd all get a chance to live the good life.

Francis led Rambler out of the barn. The bay mare's coat shone in the sun. Zachariah rubbed his forehead and realized he forgot to put on his hat. He took the reins.

"Run inside and get my hat."

Francis nodded and took off.

Zachariah whistled a hymn while he waited. He finished his song and still no Francis. He looked back at the house. "It takes that boy forever to do anything," he muttered under his breath.

He watched Ma playing catch with Jordan and a wave of contentment flowed through his body. The little boy's eyes widened each time the rag ball flew to him. Suzy left Rachel and joined the game. Zachariah wanted to join too, but he had put off discussing the wedding ceremony with Ned and Agnes long enough. He'd play with Jordan and Suzy when he got back.

Rachel got up, brought out a kettle of water and start washing clothes. She seemed to do her chores faster these days to spend time with Isaiah.

"So you got yourself an Indian master," a familiar rough voice said.

Zachariah's gut clenched. Goose pimples popped up on his skin. His imagination was getting the best of him. *It couldn't be.*

He turned around and was face to face with Henry. Blood drained from his face and strength drained from his body. He struggled to breathe. He opened his mouth. "I-I-I," was all Zachariah could get out.

Henry smirked. "Lived with the savages so long you forgot how to talk," he said, then laughed. "Maybe I will buy you back. Pa would like that. I am in business for myself now."

"So why did you come here?" he asked, quiet, slow, unsteady.

"Business opportunity. I've been told slaves are cheap on the reservation."

Francis burst out of the house and ran into the yard, waving Zachariah's hat. "Here, Massa Degan, here," he panted.

Henry looked at Francis then at Zachariah. "You are a slave-owner now," he said more as a question. "I never thought you'd have that in you. You really have moved up in the world."

Zachariah looked down at the boy. "Francis, go back to the house." Zachariah's mind stumbled its way through the darkness of worry finally arriving at a solution. He hated it, but Henry was a stalking mountain lion. He had to be fed or he'd attack.

The minute Francis was inside Zachariah said, "I-I have some s-slaves I could s-sell you if you're interested."

Henry glared at him. "Just because you are free, you think you can look me in the eye. You still have African blood in you. Or have you forgotten that, yellow man?"

Zachariah bowed his head. "I have not forgotten, sir," he whispered. "The marks on my back will not let me forget."

Henry nodded once. "Good. As far as buying slaves from you…" he paused and scanned the property. His eyes settled on Rachel. Her slender frame bent over the steaming kettle. He sucked in his breath. "How much for that wench?" he said, pointing to her. He flashed a devilish grin. "She has just enough copper in her skin to make her exotic."

"Rachel is free. She just works for me," Zachariah replied unable to keep anger out of his voice.

Henry grunted. "Figures." He continued gawking at Rachel.

No doubt, undressing her with his eyes, Zachariah stewed. Why her? He had never taken advantage of any of the negresses at the inn. Of course, now that his pa wasn't around…

Zachariah gulped and forced the air down his throat.

Henry licked his lips slowly. "I will come back around in a few days and see what you have to sell. I'm headed over to see Mr. Carter now."

"Yes, sir."

Lillian stiffened as she walked out to them, recognition registering in every muscle of her face. Still, she offered a cordial smile. "Zachary, are you going to introduce me to your friend?"

*

Henry looked Lillian over not trying to hide his vulgar smile. Her amber skin was both enticing and repulsive.

Zachariah's right hand folded into a fist then he straightened his fingers. "This is my wife, Lillian. Lillian this is Henry Galloway. He's a negro dealer."

"It is a pleasure to meet you, sir," Lillian said in a formal monotone that indicated she was not pleased. "Seems I stayed at your inn a while back."

The veins on Henry's neck pulsed. A savage sleeping at the inn. Under the same roof as him and his distraught ma. How could he not have known? Pa was right. He had been in the bottle for far too long. His eyes pierced Lillian with the force of a dagger. They shifted from her to Rachel.

Henry smirked, his pulse picking up speed. The alcohol haze gone, he had one thing on his mind. The Pink Palace didn't cut it any more.

*

Henry's lewd expression made Lillian's heart hide deeper in her chest. Her hands became clammy. She looked down and straightened the wrinkles in her dress, rubbing off the sweat as daintily as possible.

The man looked different with longer hair and a full beard, but she knew that name, those eyes. By Zachary's demeanor it was the same man. Her heart beat in an erratic skip, jog, run rhythm. She reached for Zachary's hand to steady herself. He intertwined his fingers in hers, locking them together.

The small action of security and possession allowed her breathing to return to a normal pace. She raised her head determined not to be scared off by the likes of him. If this had been under different circumstances, she would have asked Zachary to have his way with her.

She offered Henry a smile, masking her displeasure.

"Mrs. Degan," Henry said, taking off his hat. "I have more business to attend to. Please excuse me."

Henry mounted his black stallion and rode away, his eyes focused on the road.

Lillian shuddered. A shock went through her as she realized Henry was just like Bill Harris. A womanizer.

*

Zachariah's ears burned. He bit his tongue to hold back curses. Glaring at Henry's back, he hoped the man did not sense his fiery anger, but he'd hard a hard time restraining the flames in his eyes.

Once the bastard was out of sight Lillian whispered, "What are we going to do?"

Zachariah remained silent for a long time before saying, "Nothing. There is nothing we can do. Perhaps Henry doesn't know our marriage is illegal. Pray he does not know."

He gently brushed away Lillian's tears. She laid her head on his shoulder and sobbed. He stroked her hair, desperate to comfort her. Her sobbing increased until her whole body trembled.

He didn't know what to say.

His insides knotted so tight, air barely pushed into his lungs, but he felt like a whole man for the first time—their marriage was solid. He was reassured that Lillian loved him. And she needed him.

He needed to be strong for her.

He gently lifted her head off his shoulder and gave her a tight hug. "I love you," he said with all his heart, with so much feeling it hurt. "Lillian, I have not said it often, but I really do love you."

*

"Do not leave me," Lillian said, shrill, pleading. "I need you. The children need you…" She took a deep breath and regained her normal tone. "If Henry does bring charges against us…" Her face became as white as the sheets on the bed. Her whole body shuddered at the thought of the sentence passed against them, at the thought of the humiliation brought upon her family, at the thought of their forced separation.

Zachary kissed her on the cheek. "I won't leave. I'll stay right here."

"In the house," she rushed the words together as if impending danger was near. "Perhaps if he doesn't see you he won't be tempted to…" She couldn't bring herself to say the words.

"I do not have to leave the house till Sunday. I can even spread word I am ill."

Lillian took a deep breath, calmed by his sensible reply. "All right. That will give us some time to plan to run away."

*

Late the following afternoon, Zachariah fluffed his pillow, sat up and looked out the window. Blinding sun filtered through. It was a perfect day to play outside with the children. He moved his legs restlessly under the covers. Lillian walked in carrying a bowl of soup. He stared at his supper. The broth did not appeal to him.

After three days, he didn't want to play sick much longer.

"Are you feeling better?" Lillian asked, shutting the door. She set the soup on the table and then sat next to him on the bed.

Zachariah shot her an inquisitive look.

She shook her head and sighed. "Bessie said Henry's still in the Nation. Montgomery wants to help. He wrote an anonymous article in the *Advocate* protesting negro dealers invading the Nation and inciting the slaves to escape."

"I do not know how much more of this I can stand."

"The waiting or being cooped up?"

"Both. Being helpless. I do have cabin fever but…" He put his arms around her waist and kissed her lips. "I have you and Jordan and Suzy."

"And one on the way," she said, her eyes twinkling.

"You are?"

Lillian's eyes welled with tears and she gave a short nod.

"It will be all right." Zachariah silently held her for several minutes. He pushed up her chin and kissed her again.

"I love you," Lillian whispered, she gave his thin frame a tight squeeze.

"I love you too. Bring the children in to see me after their nap."

"Of course."

"And when you go, tell Rachel I want to see her."

Lillian nodded. "If I did not know she was your sister, I would be jealous," she said, then winked. She massaged the nape of her neck and her forehead wrinkled. "You have been spending so much time with her lately. Is there something you're not telling me?"

Zachariah pressed his lips together and covered his eyes with his palm. "I got scared. I didn't know what to say. I told Henry I'd sell him some of our slaves. He's supposed to come back to do business with me."

Lillian's face became sober. "Anything else?"

"No."

Lillian sighed, her shoulder sagging. "Maybe if you sell him enough slaves he'll leave you alone. Our safety and future is on the line."

Zachariah bared his teeth. Henry had backed him into a corner. One snide comment from that bastard and his moral fiber had broken as if cut by a knife. How could he offer to sell any of Lillian's slaves? He cared about all of them. He knew the kind of life came with being one of Henry's slaves.

He didn't want them to suffer with Henry. But did he have a choice?

"There is a sun after every storm. We will have enough money to build a white frame house. The cabin is getting crowded."

"I do not care about a damn house," he said. The edge in his voice surprised him. "How can you say that? Don't you have feelings for them?"

Lillian's forehead wrinkled. "I know how that sounded, but I was just trying to cheer you up. I do care about them, but I care about having the skin on my back even more."

Zachariah licked his lips and shook his head. He feared Henry would not be easily satisfied with acquiring a few slaves.

A sickening feeling rose from his toes. He couldn't help but think Henry was out for blood.

His blood.

*　　*　　*

Rachel walked in and curtsied. "You wanted to see me, Reverend Degan?"

Zachariah pressed his lips together. His sister shouldn't curtsy to him. "Shut the door Rachel and then have a seat by the bed."

He smiled warmly at his sister. She sat in the chair, struggling to maintain the necessary distance between them. He didn't realize until now that she had grown into a handsome woman. The feeling he hadn't been doing right by her, or his ma for that matter, plagued him. He had to get it off his mind, his conscious.

In an uncertain voice he asked, "Do you like it here?"

"That's a silly question. I'm with you and Ma, and we's all free."

He nodded. Her English was near perfect now. "But without money you might as well still be slaves."

Rachel laughed, sounding like a lark scolding him for such thoughts. "Money ain't important. It's the fact we can't be bought and sold and we can choose our own boss. We choose you."

"You don't think that's wrong?"

Rachel shook her head. "I remember you telling me and Ma about your dream to buy us all free and be able to take care of us. You's done that, Zachary, and we's grateful. Even if we can't acknowledge you's our relation. You's in love and you's done start your own family. That's important too. And we's glad we get to see that, see your happiness, your children."

"Don't you want to have children?"

Rachel's eyes narrowed. "Is you saying I's already becoming an old maid?" she said, a playful sharpness in her voice.

"No. No. That's not what I meant."

"I know," she said, barely smiling. There was a moment of silence before she said, "There is several free negro men here. I's find a husband when the time is right."

"I just want you and Ma to be happy."

Rachel reached out and held his hand. "This shore has been weighing on your mind lately. I doan know how many times I can assure you that we is happy."

Zachariah gave his sister a peck on the cheek. "I won't ask again. I promise. Take care, Rachel."

She nodded. "I do enjoy talking with you, Reverend."

Zachariah sighed, a bad feeling rotting the pit of his stomach. The same feeling he had every day he worked at Hickory Rail Inn. Every day he tiptoed around Henry, fearing the next blow. He closed his eyes.

When would the next blow come this time?

"Lord, please protect Rachel and Ma and all my slaves from Henry's evil grasp. I trust that my family will be taken care of. You have always provided for and watched over me, even after I denounced your existence. No matter what happens, my faith will not be shaken again. I have learned that good can come from the world's evil. I pray that I may do your will as I am your humble servant. Amen."

*   *   *

Jordan and Suzy came into the bedroom with Ace at their heels. The black pup wagged his tail. Jordan and Suzy climbed on the bed to be with him. Minutes later, Ace joined, sitting on the mattress proudly.

Zachariah shook his head, but couldn't order Ace off the bed.

Jordan and Suzy petted him and his pink tongue hung out of his mouth sideways.

"What have you been doing today?" Zachariah asked.

"Playing with Ace," Suzanna said.

Jordan pulled one of Ace's ears. "He chases us."

"I'm glad you have a friend. We need many friends of all shapes and sizes." He wanted to say colors too, but he kept that to himself.

"You better, Pa?" Jordan asked.

Suzanna looked at him concerned.

Zachariah ran his fingers through her long brown hair. "Seeing you two always makes me feel better." He patted Ace's side. The dog licked his face. He pushed Ace's head away. "And a playful pup helps too," he said.

Jordan rested against his Pa. "Can you tell us story?"

"I guess so." He took delight in every minute with his children. He told a funny story and their giggles were music to his ears.

*   *   *

Zachariah drifted into a restless sleep. He heard a horse galloping in the distance. Then a thud, like an ax cutting into a log. He looked at the bedroom door. It was still closed. He felt Lillian lying beside him, her stomach pressed against his back. Another thud. Zachariah's heart raced and raced and raced.

He sat bolt upright and peered into the darkness of the room struggling to figure out where it came from. Ace started barking, but the pup barked at everything from his shadow to the wind. Zachariah was about to lay back down when muffled voices caught his ears, too quiet for him to make out any words. The voices grew louder.

"Zachary!" a woman shrieked. "Zachary, help me!"

He jumped out of bed wide awake. For a minute he looked around to gain his bearings.

Lillian yawned. "Is something wrong?" she asked groggily.

Holding the lantern, he ran to the window. His heart pounded in his ears. He saw Rachel galloping off on a black stallion slumped over, her hands bound to the saddle horn. Henry sat behind her pointing a gun at her back. Zachariah ran outside in his nightclothes.

"Rachel!" He shouted, desperate, squeaky. "Rachel!" the words drifted helplessly into the night.

Lillian threw on a robe and ran to him. "He took Rachel," Zachariah said, his voice cracking. "He wanted to buy her and I said she was free so he just took her. I could not protect her." Tears stained his cheeks, chin, neck.

Lillian grabbed him by the shoulders and shook him. "We will get her back."

Ma ran towards them holding a boy's limp body in her arms.

Lillian gasped when she saw Francis, the back of his head bleeding profusely, his breathing labored.

"A white man busted into our cabin. Francis done not go with them so he struck him on the head with his pistol. Afterwards he tell Rachel that if she doan go with them peacefully he start shooting. Then he pointed the gun at my head." Ma finished talking and collapsed to the ground, bawling.

Zachariah helped her to her feet.

"Montgomery will get men together. They will track Henry all through the Nation and into the neighboring states if need be. We'll get her back," Lillian said. "If we have to offer the biggest reward ever seen in the *Advocate*, we will do that too. We'll get her back. I promise."

"You can't promise that," Zachariah said. "There have been scores of negro kidnappings in the Nation over the last few years. They weren't all recovered and even if she is brought back, Henry will have his way with her."

Ma bawled even louder. "I doan want her to go through the horror I did," she muttered, "Not my lil girl. Lawd no!"

"Henry has plans for debauchery. That is for sure," Zachariah said.

"It will not do any good to talk like that Zachary Degan." Lillian's voice snapped with such force it made him flinch. "Go inside and start praying."

Zachariah held out his arms and Ma gently handed him the unconscious boy. Then she tore off part of her petticoat and wrapped the cloth around Francis' head.

"Jake! Caleb!" Zachariah kept repeating their names until the two were at his side.

"Francis," Jake said. He put his hand on his son's cheek.

Lillian locked eyes with Jake. "Doctor. Get the doctor."

Jake ran out the door and into the barn.

"Caleb, Rachel's been kidnapped," Zachariah choked out. "Go tell Montgomery. Tell him to get men together to get her back. Hurry!"

Caleb ran towards the corral.

"Tell them to check all the whore houses!" he hollered.

Caleb jumped on a chestnut bareback and galloped towards Mr. Barlow's house. It wouldn't take him long. Caleb knew the way by heart.

Zachariah carried Francis into the house.

Ma and Lillian followed.

Zachariah slowly lowered to his knees.

He closed his eyes. "Lord, I know I have not had any training to be a real reverend, but I try to do your work," he whispered. "Please give my hands the power to keep this poor boy alive. He has not harmed a soul in his short life. Let the doctor save him. I pray that Montgomery and the others may rescue Rachel quickly. Heavenly Father, give her strength and keep her safe. Bring Henry to justice. He is doing Lucifer's work and needs to be judged. Amen."

Tears escaped Zachariah's tightly closed lids and dropped onto Francis's white shirt. His heart was broken into so many small pieces it hurt to breathe, as if the shards had pierced his lungs. Why didn't Henry take him instead? Didn't he want to make amends with his pa? He could run the hotel and restaurant again. He'd even gladly wash dishes if it meant Rachel would be returned safely.

Time seemed to stand still. Yet when he looked up at the clock hanging in the hallway, he saw that several minutes had passed. What was taking the men so long? They needed to pursue Henry now before he got too far ahead of them. He looked down at Francis. The boy's pulse was getting weaker. The cloth around his head soaked with blood, forming a puddle on the floor. What was taking the doctor so long? Didn't everyone know that this was an emergency?

Francis took a long, ragged breath and then went limp.

Zachariah felt the boy's neck. No heartbeat. He looked at Lillian and Ma, horror-stricken.

"Rachel," he said, tears burning a path to his neck. "Lord, do not let her share his fate."

Chapter 28

Park Hill, Cherokee Reservation
September 26, 1847

LILLIAN PACED THE parlor floor for the thousandth time. *Zachary! Why did he have to chase after a madman?* There were dark circles under her half-open eyes. Her hands remained balled in the pockets of her dress, like they had been for hours. They ached, but she could not unclench them.

"Henry's no good," Lillian muttered. "He just wants to make Zachary's life miserable."

"This ain't pers'nal," Catherine said.

Lillian swallowed hard and looked at her blankly. Zachary had refused to burden his ma about his past and Lillian wasn't going to betray his trust. Catharine didn't need to know about Henry.

Sadness was engrained in Catherine's face along with several new wrinkles. She looked thinner—her stress manifested in her appetite. She ate only enough to keep herself alive.

It had been eight days. Eight days without Zachary by her side. Lillian couldn't believe he had defied her wishes and galloped off with the posse—probably to get himself killed. No, she couldn't lose him. Her vision blurred with tears.

Isaiah walked over and put a gentle hand on her shoulder. It was his turn to stand vigil. Lillian sat down and sipped a cup of coffee. She wanted Zachary to rescue Rachel, she was a lovely girl, but fear for her husband kept her on edge.

*

The posse had only slept for a few hours before resuming the pursuit. After a restless night on the cold, hard ground Zachariah's head and heart ached. Still, he rode at the head of the column, eyes constantly scanning. He wanted to be the first to find Rachel, and then hold her in his arms and brush away her tears.

When he spied Henry's horse his chest burned, the pain radiating up his throat and down into his stomach. Montgomery rode up beside him. "Let us take care of Henry. Lillian would never forgive me if you got hurt."

"No," Zachariah said. "I need to finish this."

Montgomery nodded and waved for the men around him to move into position. The posse circled around the grove where Henry was sleeping. Rachel lay beside him, a gag in her mouth, her hands and feet bound with rope. She locked eyes with Zachariah and they brightened a little, silently pleading for help.

Zachariah dismounted and ran to her, knife in hand to cut her free. Henry awoke and attacked him from behind.

Gag gone, Rachel screamed.

Zachariah swung his knife and slashed Henry's shoulder. "Why you nigger," Henry growled, "I'm going to kill you for that."

Zachariah dodged several blows from Henry's large fists, and he lanced Henry's cheek with his blade. Adrenaline raced through his blood making him blind to the danger.

Henry grabbed Zachariah's wrist and tried to force him to drop the knife. Zachariah bit back the cry of pain and lunged, punching Henry's gut with his other arm. Henry staggered back, letting go of Zachariah's wrist.

It felt like he was fighting the man for hours, but it was mere minutes. Zachariah stabbed Henry in the stomach and the man dropped to his knees. His heart about to explode out of his chest, Zachariah held the blade to Henry's throat.

Seconds later, the posse had their rifles trained on Henry, and Henry surrendered.

Breathing heavily, Zachariah thanked God that Henry hadn't reached for the pistol nestled in his bedroll.

Zachariah finished freeing Rachel and ran a hand through her tangled hair. She sobbed unable to speak. Her dress torn. Her breasts and legs exposed. Her arms and face covered in bluish-purple splotches. Bruises Henry had inflicted. Inflicted to force her to his will, to violate her.

Zachariah took off his coat and wrapped it around her trembling shoulders. "You're safe now. I will take you home."

The posse bandaged Henry's minor wounds, had him on his horse, his hands tied, and under heavy guard. Henry hunched over in the saddle, but the wildness in his eyes had not dimmed. "Zach here has been living a lie," he said. "That man is a slave."

*

Ace barked with viscous excitement. It sent shivers down Lillian's arms. She leaped to his feet and ran outside. Catherine and Isaiah followed. They squinted and saw horses in the distance kicking up a cloud of dust.

As the horses drew closer Lillian's heart galloped with them. She saw Henry's black stallion. On one side Montgomery rode beside him, his pistol drawn. Zachary flanked him on the other. Mixed in with all the other men on horseback was Rachel riding a mule.

Relieved to see Zachary and Rachel alive, Lillian sent silent thanks to heaven, even as her heart clenched to see Henry once again.

All the riders stopped in front of his house. Rachel got off and dropped to her knees, tears flooding her cheeks. Catherine rushed forward and helped Rachel to her feet. "Po' baby, po' baby, po' baby," she cried.

"Thank you all," Zachary said, his voice cracked. "It is a great christianly act to come to the aid of a black woman."

Lillian sensed that there was something very wrong. Zachary remained tense, his face somber.

Montgomery looked at Lillian with furrowed brows and pursed lips. "Mr. Galloway claims that Reverend Degan is a negro and that he has proof to back up his accusation."

Lillian's eyes flared. "That is ridiculous!"

Isaiah gasped and Catherine bit her lip.

Zachary slid off Rambler, but remained at the horse's side, an arm around the mare's neck. Henry sat in the saddle, his hands bound and his head slightly bowed, looking at him smugly as if searching for a reaction.

Lillian held her breath, and felt twinges above her eyes. "Ridiculous as it may be," Montgomery said, "the officers have agreed to press amalgamation charges against you and Lillian. You will have your day in court. As will Henry."

*

Zachariah exhaled through his nose, hoping his discomfort wasn't visible. Somehow Montgomery had managed to avoid using an I-told-you-so voice. But his gut tightened just the same. Zachariah swallowed, clearing the jitters out of his throat. He must sound strong and unaffected. "I understand. Are you arresting us?"

"No," one of the officers said, shaking his head. "We trust you will remain at your house and appear in court."

As soon as they left, Zachariah took Rachel's hand and looked into her brown eyes full of terror, shame, worry. He didn't know what to say. She looked like a wild animal that the slightest movement would scare away.

"I never thought I would see you again," Rachel said in a raspy whisper.

"The Lord brought you back to us."

Rachel brushed tears out of her eyes, her body shaking.

"He had his way with me repeatedly. Said the more we did it, the more I'd like it. He said once we got to Texas…" she choked out.

Zachariah pushed up his sister's chin. "What was going to happen in Texas?" he breathed.

"After he was through, he was going to sell me at auction there."

Zachariah gritted his teeth. "You're safe now." The words rang empty, hollow but he needed to say them for his own good. He wasn't going to let Henry ruin his joy. He steadied his breathing and his heart returned to a normal pace.

"Are you hungry?"

Rachel nodded.

"Take care of her, Isaiah. See that she has everything she wants."

"Yes, sir," Isaiah said. He took Rachel's hand and escorted her into the house.

Catherine went with them. "I's take care of you. After you eat, I will clean and patch you up."

"Lillian," Zachariah said, his hand out stretched to her.

She walked into his embrace, sniffling. "I feared this day."

"Don't."

"I've ruined both of our lives." Her tears soaked his shoulder.

He reached up and caressed her head. "Shh, shh, shh. Henry coming here, that was not your doing. He would have came here anyway. He came here because the colored people are so easy to kidnap. He lives outside the law."

Lillian took a deep breath. "We have been living outside the law too," she said under her breath.

"I have learned something Reverend Simon didn't tell his congregation. There are different kinds of sin. I think God would approve of our loving lies."

Lillian shook her head. "The Nation will not see it that way."

"Since when did you care what the Nation thought?"

"Since they have the power to…"

Zachariah kissed her on the cheek. "Let's go to the children. We can take comfort from them."

*   *   *

Zachariah escorted Lillian into the nursery. He let go of her hand and kneeled next to Suzy and Jordan's beds where they were taking their midday nap. "I love you," he whispered to the sleeping children. He softly kissed their foreheads. Suzy rolled over on her side, but Jordan didn't stir.

Zachariah fingered Jordan's black wavy hair. He smiled, looking at their faces—his own little angels. Suzy's arms were wrapped around the blond-haired baby doll he had given her. Zachariah began whispering Suzy's favorite song.

> *Come, little children, come*
> *And seek your savior's face;*
> *In all your ways acknowledge him,*
> *And trust upon his grace.*

Lillian's hand on his shoulder made him stop. "I know you are trying to ignore the charges brought against us, but you can't," Lillian said. "They're not going away."

"I am not trying to ignore them. I want to spend time with my son and daughter."

Lillian shifted her weight and kept looking at the door. The desperation in her emerald eyes both frightened and thrilled him.

"What are we going to do?" she said, her voice hushed.

Zachariah took a deep breath. "You are not going to do anything. I will take care of this. My family comes first. I will handle this in the best way I know how."

Zachariah expected Lillian to argue with him, but instead she merely asked, "What are you going to do?"

"They are not going to harm you. I will make sure of that." He caressed her warm cheek.

Her voice trembled. "Henry has proof. We have to make up a story. We have to get the court to think Henry is lying—"

"Lillian," Zachariah interrupted. "I know you are frightened, but that will not work."

Panic flashed in her eyes. Her voice grew louder and threatened to crack. "We have to do some—"

Zachariah put a finger to her lips. "Don't wake the children," he said. "I have another plan." He looked into her eyes. "Trust me."

"I trust you but—"

"I do not want you to worry about what is going to happen," he said in a soothing tone. "I just want you to focus on our love for each other and our children. I will do the same."

Lillian rested her head on his shoulder.

Zachariah brushed away her tears and stroked her black tresses. He breathed into her ear, "I will take care of everything. I promise."

He had two families to protect now. He had to protect Lillian and the children. He had to protect Ma and Rachel.

Realizing the welfare of everyone he loved rested on his narrow shoulders made his chest heavy and breaths short.

He stood there for several minutes taking in Lillian's touch, straightening his thoughts with every pound of her heart.

He ran his hand across Lillian's cheek.

He was ready.

Chapter 29

Courthouse
October 1, 1847

"THE DEFENDANT WILL rise," the judge said.

Henry stood.

"Henry Galloway, I will now pass judgment on you. In all the days you spent in the Nation you did not buy one slave. I therefore look at you as an intruder. Since your visit, fifteen slaves have run away. I find you guilty of inciting slaves to leave their masters. On the charge of attempted kidnapping and murder of the slave boy Francis belonging to Lillian Degan, I find you guilty. On the charge of kidnapping of the free colored woman Rachel, I find you guilty. I hereby sentence you to be hung by the neck until dead."

Many people in the courtroom clapped and cheered.

An Indian man shouted. "You bastard."

"You're getting what you deserve!" another said.

"I will have order in my courtroom," the judge said loudly. He waited for everyone to sit down. The room fell silent again. "Mr. Galloway, since you are the plaintiff and witness in the next case I will have you stay in the courtroom. The next case is Zachary and Lillian Degan vs. the Nation."

An officer escorted Henry to the back of the courtroom.

Zachariah and Lillian walked forward to the defendant's chairs. As soon as they were seated Zachariah gave Lillian a quick kiss. "Remember let me do all the talking," he whispered. "No matter what happens remain silent."

Lillian nodded, jaw tense, worry in her eyes.

"Will the defendants rise," the judge said. "Reverend Zachary Degan and Lillian Degan, you are both charged with amalgamation. How do you plead?"

Zachariah took a quick glance at Henry. "I plead guilty your honor," he said.

Lillian's mouth opened, but no sound came. She slumped back into her chair.

*　　*　　*

The judge's voice rose and he spoke slowly as if trying to comprehend it. "You plead guilty? A negro man in violation of the amalgamation law receives one hundred lashes on the bare back. And the Cherokee woman fifty lashes you—"

"Forgive me for interrupting, Judge," Zachariah said, "But Lillian did not know I was a negro since I am very light skinned. When we met I had on gentleman's clothes, spoke perfect English and introduced myself as a white man. We fell in love and got married and for all these years I've kept my ugly secret to myself."

The confession elicited a collective gasp from the courtroom. "You are so white," a woman said.

"And you are a learned man," another chimed in.

The judge looked at Lillian who was pale and appeared frozen in place. "Doctor, see to Mrs. Degan. She's in shock." Then he looked at Zachariah again. "How does Mr. Galloway know you?"

Zachariah's skin tightened and turned numb. With great effort, he pressed out the words. "His pa used to own me, sir."

The judge stared at him.

The tension in the room was like invisible hands strangling his throat, pressing tighter and tighter and tighter forcing breath out of his lungs. Zachariah gasped for breath.

"Were you freed or did you escape?" the judge asked finally.

"I was freed, sir, and I have proof."

He took his manumission paper out of his coat pocket and unfolded it. One of the officers took it out of his hands and handed it to the judge.

The room felt as cold as a coffin already six feet under. The judge looked over the paper, blankly as if all he was reading was a list of supplies.

"According to the manumission paper, Alexander Galloway gifted you to Jasper Travers on April 24, 1842, and Mr. Travers freed you five days later."

Out of the corner of his eye, Zachariah saw Henry frown, his fun smothered.

"Do you acknowledge this, Mr. Degan?"

Zachariah stood there solemn, his muscles tense. The courtroom gawked at him while he searched for the words. The dreaded confirmation. The two words he knew would end his marriage, possibly his life.

His heart pounded in his ears drowning his thoughts. He rubbed and rubbed and rubbed his clammy hands on the front of his pants. Sweat dampened his hair, plastering it to his forehead.

The words stuck in his throat. He swallowed. He couldn't sound weak, afraid, ashamed.

He took a deep breath and said clearly, "Yes, sir." The voice didn't sound like his. He closed his eyes, pressed his lips together, and hung his head to hide his burning, red complexion. Having the truth out in the open flooded him with strange relief.

He glanced at Lillian. He'd taken this on himself—for her. He would do anything to protect her and the children.

The judge slammed his gavel on the desk.

Zachariah flinched.

"Since you were not freed by a Cherokee, you will not be allowed to stay in the Nation after the sentence. You will immediately be escorted out of the reservation as an intruder."

Lillian shrieked, tears flooded her cheeks and stained her green dress.

Zachariah looked at her, his heart breaking like a dropped looking glass. Silent tears filled his eyes. He wanted to comfort her, but he could not. He looked at the negro section in the back of the room where Ma and Rachel sat. He wished he could see Jordan and Suzy, but they stayed at home. Dorothy, Martha and Jake were watching them, along with Thomas and Dinah.

"I will now pass sentence," the judge said. "Based on Mr. Degan's testimony, I find that it was only due to deception that Lillian Degan broke the amalgamation law. I, therefore, find her innocent.

"Zachariah Degan, I find you guilty of amalgamation and sentence you to one hundred lashes on the bare back. Since they were married under false pretenses, I also hereby grant Lillian Degan a divorce from the negro man Zachariah. Officers you may escort the prisoners out."

*

Grief paralyzed Lillian's muscles like a strong drug. A little more of the drug and her heart would stop.

Montgomery and Bessie hurried over to her and helped her to her feet. Distraught, she leaned heavily on Montgomery, barely having the strength to walk. Together they escorted her out of the courthouse. Montgomery extended his hand to help her into his carriage, but she bit her lip and shook her head.

"You can't watch what is going to happen," Montgomery said firmly, "especially now that you're in the family way." Lillian didn't move. "I am going to take you home," Montgomery ordered.

This time when he extended his hand, she accepted his assistance into the carriage. Next, Bessie did. She held her sister's hands tightly, crying with her. Blurry images passed before Lillian's eyes.

Henry was astride a gray horse, his hands tied behind his back. One of the officers took the reins and led him over to a tree.

Another officer stood beside Zachary. Still in his black reverend clothes, he bowed his head and silently prayed.

"I don't know why they're doing this so quickly," Montgomery muttered.

Catherine shielded Rachel's eyes.

Montgomery put one hand over Bessie's eyes and one hand over Lillian's. The order was given.

Henry's lifeless body dangled from the oak tree. The corpse was taken down, placed in a coffin, nailed shut and loaded onto a wagon.

*

The officer beside Zachariah gave him a push. "All right, Mr. Degan," he said in a mocking sing-song voice, "it's your turn in the spotlight."

Zachariah shed his clothes unable to take pleasure in his tormenter's death knowing the suffering to come. He was tied by the hands from the same tree used to hang Henry. Did that make the colored and the white man equal in the eyes of the law?

The whip flailed against Zachariah's shoulders. He cried out. The blood trickled down his back, down his thighs, down his legs.

His wrists burned from trying to break free from the rope binding. His flesh shivered, anticipating the next blow. Tears flooded his eyes, not from the pain, but from the thought of never seeing Lillian again. Never seeing Jordan and Suzanna again.

Never seeing his unborn child ever. He gritted his teeth. *Why did I let Lillian talk me into this life? Why had I wanted this life so badly after my first taste of it? Why hadn't I seen this day coming?* Why did he have to be imitation white?

Ma wailed, "Oh Lawd! Oh Lawd!" over and over.

Rachel sunk to her knees, her red dress soaked with tears.

The whip moved down to his upper then middle back. His throat, already raw from shouting, began to swell. The flogger counted out the lashes, but Zachariah did not hear him. The only thing that echoed through his head was Lillian crying as Montgomery drove her away.

Zachariah's heart raced and he took deep breaths trying to calm himself. The whip tore his skin with each infliction. His shouting now reduced to soft cries. The flogger stopped.

The doctor walked up to him, his face pale.

Zachariah looked at him through red, puffy, moist eyes.

"I am sorry, Reverend," his whisper barely audible. He reached up and felt Zachariah's neck. Then he walked back and rejoined the crowd. "He can stand the whole," he said.

Zachariah's heart faltered and threatened to stop. The whip now struck his lower back. Every inch of his backside would feel the whip's angry bite. His face withered with pain. His moans became softer until he was silent. Still, the lashes continued and continued and continued.

Zachariah felt the blood puddle around his feet.

The flogger shouted, "Ninety-five!"

Zachariah's legs trembled. All of his strength gone. He looked at the courthouse in front of him. The building became blurry and darker. Did the sun go behind a cloud? He barely heard the voices around him. Were they whispering?

*

Hot tears threatened to pour from Lillian's eyes. She bit her tongue to keep her emotions under control.

Lillian heard the whip crack. Zachary moaned. Her heart pained her something fierce and she gripped her chest. Zachary let out a piteous yell. She tasted bitter blood in her mouth. She had bit her tongue.

One hundred lashes. She shut her eyes tightly trying hard not to picture his bloody, lacerated flesh. But trying not to picture it made it come into her mind even faster and more vividly. A shiver made her twitch. A revolting taste rose in her throat.

Dark thoughts raced through her head. *They will kill him. He can't stand one hundred lashes. I will never see him again and it's all my fault. I forced him into this situation. Montgomery was right. I should have thought with my head not my heart.*

Montgomery climbed into the driver's seat and slapped the reins. He had the horses going at a near gallop.

Lillian gripped the side of the carriage. She knew when she got home she couldn't put on a black mourning dress. She'd have to settle for a dreary gray.

How was she supposed to hate her husband? Hate the father of her children for supposedly deceiving her? Hate the man she loved because he had some African blood in him, so little it showed only in the wave of his hair. That was impossible.

She brushed away her tears. She wanted him to be a white man, but she couldn't erase his past. Even his good standing in the Nation didn't help. She wanted to be with him worse than before. He had protected her. He truly loved her.

*

A bucket of water thrown in his face brought Zachariah to his senses. He felt a gentle hand on his cheek.

"Lillian," he whispered.

"No, son," Ma said.

He blinked. Ma and Rachel sat beside him. The wagon stopped and Ma and Rachel helped him out. Zachariah's legs gave out and he dropped to the ground. The wagon turned around.

"If we catch you in the Nation again, you could catch some lead," the driver threatened and he headed back into the reservation.

Ma and Rachel wiped tears from their inflamed eyes. "We's not leaving you," Rachel said.

"You were freed by Lillian. She's Cherokee. You can stay here. I want you to watch over my children," Zachariah whispered.

Ma shook her head. "Lillian, Montgomery and the rest of her family will take good care of the children. We needs to take care of you." Zachariah didn't say a word. "I got to stop the bleeding, son. Some of those cuts is so deep I's have to sew them."

"You're good at sewing, Ma," Zachariah replied. He bit his tongue when the needle penetrated his flesh. The ground began spinning and he closed his eyes.

"Stay with us, Zachariah," Rachel's voice a forceful plea. "Stay strong. We need you. Your family needs you."

Some time later, smelling salts awoke him. He saw a man's black boots in front of him. His forehead creased. The doctor wore brown shoes.

"I am going to help you," Montgomery said, brown bag in hand. "I have come to like you, Zachariah."

The young man spoke is a raspy whisper. "Thank you, sir."

"We have to prevent infection. Salt him down, Catherine."

Ma shook her head, tears making trails on her cheeks. "I can't hurt him. I can't hurt my boy."

"You sewed him up."

"I can't do it, Mistah Barlow," Ma said.

Montgomery bit his lip and dropped to his knees. He reached into the small brown bag, pulled out a handful of salt and rubbed it on Zachariah's shoulders.

The yellow man grimaced.

"Pain is good," Montgomery said. "It is dangerous when you lose consciousness."

Zachariah didn't reply. Half his cuts salted, Montgomery's voice became garbled. Suddenly his face stung.

Montgomery struck his cheek again. "Keep talking," he ordered.

"Yes, sir," Zachariah whispered.

Montgomery pressed clean rags onto his cuts. This made the salt go even deeper, but it also stopped the blood.

Zachariah moaned and bit his lip till it bled.

When Montgomery finished, he handed Ma a stick with a blanket tied to it. "Inside is food, canteens of water and money," Montgomery explained. He mounted his horse.

"Thank you, Montgomery," Zachariah choked out, his tears watering the ground. "Watch over my children and Lillian. I'm never going to see them again. I don't see why I should keep living."

"Don't say that," Rachel said, her voice high-pitched, pleading. "We're yo' family too."

Ma frowned, sadness carved deep in her face. "Rachel," she whispered, "He got a family of his own now. You's not married. You don't understand the pain of leaving them. I remember when yo' pa was sold away…" her voice trailed off.

Montgomery took a deep breath. Zachariah felt the man's eyes on him, examining his helpless body. He lay at the side of the road. It would take days before he could walk anywhere.

"I know you love them," Montgomery said. "And you have been good to them." He silently studied Zachariah. "Would you do anything you could to still be able to see them?"

Zachariah's eyes widened. He raised his head as high as he could. "Yes," he said loudly.

Another moment of silence followed. "Even if that meant becoming a slave again?"

Rachel gasped.

"No," Ma said, her voice shaky.

"Yes, sir," Zachariah said quickly, without a second thought. "I will die if I never see them."

Montgomery nodded. "I can draw up papers. You can sell yourself back into slavery to me. How much do you think you're worth?"

Zachariah saw Ma and Rachel's mortified faces. He reached out, held Rachel's hand and squeezed it. "I need enough money for my ma and sister to make a good life for themselves. They need to buy a house and some property. I expect my sister to start a family of her own soon. I will work hard for you my entire life, sir."

"Please don't do it," Rachel said. "We do not need no house we need you. I spent enough years without you."

Zachariah turned his head back to Montgomery to avoid her pleading eyes.

Montgomery's face tense, business-like, iced the hurt in Zachariah's heart.

"Two thousand dollars," he said. "And that is a generous offer."

"I will take it."

Ma and Rachel burst into tears. Their cheeks stained afresh. "No, no, no," Ma kept saying.

"Does that mean I can live on the reservation?" Zachariah asked eagerly.

Montgomery shook his head. "The Nation would not like that and it would be dangerous for Lillian. If you two were seen together intimately, they would press charges against both of you again. I will have you work on the *Princess*. Lillian and the children will visit you periodically."

"How often is periodically?" Zachariah remembered the last time Isaiah saw his parents and sisters was three years ago.

"Does it matter?"

Zachariah's heart turned inside out. "No. I will be grateful to see them any time, Montgomery."

Montgomery nodded. "You will refer to me as master or sir from this point on."

"Yes, master," Zachariah replied. "What will I be doing on the *Princess*?"

"Whatever I or Arthur says," Montgomery replied curtly. "You don't have a voice, Zachariah. And if you don't please me I can sell you. Do you still want to do this?"

Zachariah frowned, for a moment his mind riddled with doubt. His pulse skidded out of control. His mouth felt dry, his face warm with indecision.

He had to do this for both his families.

He had a voice now. He had his had his own will, desires, dreams. He had the courage to do what he wanted. What he wanted was to give all that up. In a small, but firm voice he said, "Yes, sir."

Montgomery nodded. He turned his horse around. "I will be back shortly with the papers and the money."

Zachariah, Ma and Rachel watched him ride back into the reservation. "Why'd you do it, son?" Ma said. Zachariah did not reply.

"You have not signed the papers yet. There is still time for you to change your mind," Rachel said. "Nothing good can come from you bein' a slave. Mr. Barlow can still keep Lillian and your children from you."

Zachariah glared at a rock in front of him. "No." His words carried force, he spoke slowly to add more power. "Mr. Barlow is an honest man. He would not do that." He enunciated his words to drive home his point. "He will let me see my family. And now I can finally take care of you and Ma the way I have always wanted. You can make a good life for yourselves with 2,000 dollars."

"Us make a good life?" Ma said. "What about you? What life is you making for yourself?"

Chapter 30

Park Hill, Cherokee Reservation
October 15, 1847

LILLIAN REFUSED TO come out of her room. She looked into the mirror. The dreary gray dress she wore added several years to her appearance; dreary like her mood and dreary like her soul.

Zachary. She needed him. She needed him more than she ever knew. Isn't that how it was? You didn't miss something until it was gone?

There was a heavy knock on her door. She groaned. With Montgomery and Isaiah gone, she knew it was her pa.

"Two weeks is quite enough of this," Mr. Hildebrand said in a stern tone.

"I have no reason to enjoy life."

Mr. Hildebrand grunted. "You have two children. They miss you."

Lillian rolled her eyes. She did not want to answer their questions about where their pa had gone. Montgomery had said to tell them that Zachary had died. She couldn't do that. She'd been living lies for far too long. She needed to start living the truth.

She pulled a piece of paper out of her desk drawer, a bottle of ink and a pen.

"Lillian," her pa said again.

"Go away. Give me time to work things out." She grabbed the arm of her chair as she sunk to her seat.

"How much time do you need? Mr. Harris has graciously agreed to marry you. He wants to make an honest woman of you and raise your children."

Make an honest woman of her? What did her pa think she was? A whore? She knew that considering the circumstances, her pa wouldn't let her back out of the marriage this time. Maybe the servitude that came with this coupling was what she deserved.

"Fine," she called back, her voice flat. "I'll marry Mr. Harris. My children need a pa."

"That is right. They do. I am glad you're thinking clearly about your future and theirs."

Lillian did not reply. She waited for her pa to say more. He didn't.

She looked down at the piece of paper, the whiteness glaring at her. Black ink was exactly what it needed. Too white, too black, too red was a bad thing.

She dipped her pen in the ink and began writing her thoughts.

If I were given another opportunity, I would unselfishly give you my future.

If I were given another opportunity, the chance to consider my decisions with a sharp mind and unwavering heart, I would unselfishly give you my future.

If I were given another opportunity, knowing my actions would tear my family apart, I would unselfishly give you my future.

If I were given another opportunity, I would not remain consumed by worry or fear, I would unselfishly give you my future.

If I were given another opportunity, I would embrace the chance with open arms, I wouldn't look back, I would unselfishly give you my future.

As she read the words that had spilled forth from her heart, an idea began to claw at the back of her mind. She could form her own destiny. She could have another opportunity. She could give him her future. She just needed a little help.

*   *   *

Lillian stood up, folded the paper and stuck it against her breast. No one would find it there. She walked to the door with depressed but determined steps. Opening the door, she peered out. No one was around. She heard the voices of her parents. They were last people she wanted to talk to. She pressed her lips together. Why had Montgomery insisted that she move back in with them?

"Jake," she called softly. Her heart beat so loudly it drowned her voice. Dread rested heavy in her stomach. She didn't want to repeat his name. She didn't want to draw attention to herself. She stood there and waited.

Jake walked down the hallway and Lillian exhaled.

"Yes'm?" Jake said.

Lillian waved him inside her room and quickly shut the door.

Jake's concerned face and demeanor grated on Lillian's already frayed nerves. She motioned for him to sit at the desk.

"I have a bargain to pose to you."

"If you want me to do something, Miss, I will do it."

"I know you would, Jake. But this is different."

Jake sat up straighter.

"I need to get to the *Princess*."

Jake tensed but remained silent.

"Zachary is headed to the *Princess*. I need to get there with my children. We will have to leave the reservation under false pretenses. In exchange I will free your entire family."

Jake licked his bottom lip repeatedly.

"Can you do it?"

"Yes'm," Jake said quickly. "I can do it."

Lillian flashed a worried smile, the corners of her lips weighted by what lie ahead. "We need to plan."

*   *   *

Jake left and called Catherine into the room.

Lillian put her hand on the somber woman's shoulder. "I am going to be with Zachary again soon and you are too."

Catherine's mouth parted, but she did not speak.

Lillian opened her wardrobe and pulled out her emerald dress. "Help me dress. I have to look becoming for Mr. Harris."

The confusion written on her face made Lillian grab both of Catherine's hands. She squeezed them tightly. "Trust me."

Catherine nodded and began unbuttoning the back of Lillian's gray dress. After what seemed like a whole day of getting ready, Lillian finally walked into the parlor.

Mrs. Hildebrand stood and walked over to her. "My dear, you look lovely," she said.

Lillian felt the blush rise in her cheeks. "Thank you."

She gazed across the room and saw Mr. Harris sitting on the sofa. He was a bear of a man with thick arms and large hands.

A bitter taste soured her mouth, soured her thoughts, soured her feelings. She wanted to run, but couldn't. She had the urge to call him every dirty word she'd learned from the roustabouts, but couldn't. She dreamed of spitting in his face, but couldn't.

She was tied by her situation and station in life.

She curtsied. "Mr. Harris."

He approached her, invaded her space. His eyes migrated to her breasts. She bit her cheek. She was never going to be tamed into a meek, modest maiden. She stood her ground.

It was tough to swallow her spite, but she managed.

He took her hand and kissed it. "Finally, we are going to wed."

Where his lips touched, her flesh turned cold.

Her eyes locked with Mr. Harris'. She had to force the words out of her tight throat. Being around him was like a severe allergy. "I'm looking forward to it," her voice grating.

"I was discussing our wedding with your pa. I hope the same plans we had before are agreeable to you."

Lillian nodded. "Yes of course," her voice squeaky, unnatural.

She looked down at her gown. "I do need another wedding dress. Everything in my wardrobe reminds me of well, you know."

An eerie, self-satisfied smile spread across Mr. Harris' lips. His look reminded Lillian of a rapist after finishing his dirty work. "I understand. You shall have the gown of your dreams," he said, his voice calm and smooth.

Lillian let him lead her over to the sofa and sat through a lengthy conversation of the happy life she was going to have with him. Lies. All lies. Lillian licked her lips and shifted her weight. "It has been a while since we have talked. I hope you will tell me about yourself."

Every word out of his mouth was a lie.

He talked about his political ambitions, elaborating on what he wanted out of life. Mr. Harris grew increasingly uncomfortable. He crossed and then uncrossed his ankles, his shoulders slumped slightly forward.

They talked for hours and then Mr. Harris dined with the family and they talked some more. Whenever the children were mentioned or Lillian's expectations for their marriage, Mr. Harris tapped his boot on the hardwood floor.

The noise tightened Lillian's stomach, rang in her ears as a falsehood. When Mr. Harris answered her questions about their future his tapping became faster.

It was the worst rushed courtship Lillian had ever seen. Pa's doing, she knew. Pa wanted her to be accepted in the Nation, not mocked and ridiculed and disgraced.

She restrained a yawn and glanced at clock above the fireplace. If he was planning on staying over at their house, she would sleep with a knife under her pillow.

She took a deep breath. Her pa wouldn't allow that. It would reflect poorly upon the family. Engaged wasn't the same as married. *Thank God.*

At the end of the night, the date of their wedding was set. Four months away. That gave Lillian time to make the long journey off the reservation to find her perfect wedding dress.

It was three a.m when Mr. Harris got up to leave. Lillian walked him to the end of the yard. He wrapped a hand around her waist and pulled her close. She recoiled, but his strength kept her standing. He leaned his head down and kissed her lightly. She did not reciprocate the kiss. Anger flashed in his eyes quick as a streak of lightening. He kissed her again forcefully, leaving Lillian's body limp and weak. It had taken every ounce of strength to endure his eyes, his smile, his touch.

He mounted his white horse, looked over his shoulder at her and nodded then rode off into the shadows.

When she returned to the house, she saw her parents discussing her wedding over cups of tea. Lillian rubbed her forehead and yawned. "It has been a long day. I am going to bed."

"Certainly," Mrs. Hildebrand said, standing. "When are you planning to go to the city, dear? You have kept Mr. Harris waiting all these years. It is only right that you marry him as soon as possible."

Lillian nodded hoping her gritted teeth did not show. She'd rather marry a mountain lion. The only way she'd marry Mr. Harris would be at gunpoint. "Give me a week to pack. I am going to catch the *Princess* and go shopping in New Orleans. They have the newest fashions there."

*   *   *

Good thing she wasn't accustomed to traveling light, Lillian thought. She looked over her shoulder and surveyed all the trunks stuffed in the back of the carriage. Her parents, sister and Mr. Harris had gathered to see her off.

"All right, Jake," Lillian said.

The man nodded and slapped the reins. The carriage rolled forward. Lillian leaned out the window and waved. Her heart flipped, but jitters wormed into his stomach. They didn't suspect a thing.

The heat from Catherine and Rachel's bodies made the carriage feel small. Suzanna sat on Lillian's lap and Jordan on Catherine's.

The long journey to the *Princess* was a hot, uncomfortable sacrifice. Just catching it wasn't going to be the end of Lillian's problems. She doubted Montgomery would allow her on board. She'd have to find a reason for Montgomery to send Zachary off the ship.

"Catherine, did you pack Zachary's reverend clothes?"

"Yes, ma'am."

"Are you sure?"

Catherine nodded. "I want my son to have the family he's always dreamed of. It was one of the first things I packed."

Lillian exhaled.

"We are going to see Pa?" Suzanna asked.

Lillian kissed her cheek. "Try to go to sleep. It is a long trip."

Suzanna stretched out and laid her head on Rachel's lap. "Will you wake me up when we get to Pa?"

Lillian smiled trying to be comforting and confident, but faltered. "Yes." She brushed her fingers through Suzanna's hair. "But it will take a few days."

Her plan went terribly wrong once. If it went terribly wrong again, she'd have no family to fall back on. She was on her own now.

Her future was intertwined with Zachariah's.

Chapter 31

Arkansas City, Arkansas
October 22, 1847

ARTHUR AND THE young man, Patrick, walked out to meet Montgomery. Zachariah's face flushed when he was ignored.

Isaiah climbed out, ran up to his pa and gave him a quick hug.

Arthur's eyes twinkled, though he maintained a sober face. He walked to the back of the carriage and picked up Montgomery's trunk.

"Patrick, take the carriage to the livery. I will not be getting off the boat on this trip."

"Yes, Master," Patrick said, climbing into the driver's seat.

"Welcome back, Mr. Barlow," Arthur said.

Zachariah ran his tongue across his teeth. Of course Arthur would no longer give him a warm greeting.

He stared at his black dress pants, white shirt and white coat. He sighed. He'd spend the rest of his life as a waiter.

"You look like an undertaker dressed in all black, sir," Arthur said.

Montgomery's body became rigid, his face somber. "Mr. Degan died a month ago. I will be dressed like this for a year to mourn his passing. Lillian has taken his death hard."

Zachariah stood stone-faced, heart racing, hands clammy, a sinking feeling in his gut.

He'd gone from a slave to a husband and now he was only a ghost. A working ghost.

How many more times would he have to listen to his supposed death?

He looked at the ship. The gangplank was down, but none of the roustabouts were working.

Montgomery noticed it too. The *Princess* was the only steamboat not in the process of loading or unloading. "What are the boys doing? Sleeping?" he asked, a little disgruntled.

"No, sir," Arthur said, grinning. "The *Princess* is ahead of schedule. We were waiting for you."

"Ahead of schedule?" Montgomery's pitch inched a little higher. "During the cotton season?"

"Yes, sir."

"Looks like I should raise your allowance then," Montgomery replied as he walked up the gangplank.

"Speaking of my allowance," Arthur said, then hesitated once he had Mr. Barlow's full attention. He flicked a glance sideways. "Charlotte and I have been saving our money the past several years, sir. We would like to buy Isaiah's freedom."

Montgomery blinked at Arthur. "I said I would free you and your family and I will in a few years. I have been looking for someone else to run the ship."

Arthur looked Montgomery in the eye, not threatening, but not backing away. "We want Isaiah with us, sir. You have been saying that for a while now. I believe you, but I think it will be a long time before you find someone else to be the steward on the *Princess*. I was doing it for your father when you were little. If you free me and my family, I would be willing to continue to work on the *Princess* for you."

Montgomery looked at Isaiah and then back to Arthur.

The negro man bowed his head slightly.

Zachariah sucked in his breath. Arthur was always polite to his master, but he had never shown any sign of deference. The tension was two sparing swords, a duel between equal foes.

"If you sign a contract agreeing to work for me for the next eight years, I will free all of you. I can take Gideon back to the reservation with me in Isaiah's place. I don't need an extra waiter on the ship."

Arthur and Isaiah both beamed as if all their hopes and dreams and desires had come true. "Yes, sir," Arthur said. "You draw up the papers. I'll sign."

"Thank you, Mr. Barlow," Isaiah said.

Montgomery nodded and they all walked onto the ship in silence.

"I will take your trunk to your room, sir," Arthur said. He whistled as he climbed the stairs.

"Is there anything I can do for you, Mr. Barlow?" Isaiah asked.

"No. You may go see your sisters."

Isaiah headed towards the galley.

"They are so happy, but Arthur's still going to be tied to this ship. Eight years is a long time. Arthur will be in his fifties," Zachariah said.

"And with him on the ship, I doubt Charlotte will leave, which is good because I haven't even started looking for another piano player. Finding a beautiful, musically talented negress will take a while too." He looked at the water and appeared lost in thought. "Arthur's in good health. He'll get to enjoy his freedom and the money I give him. Follow me, Zachariah."

"Yes, Master."

He smelled the food—steak, catfish, pork chops and biscuits— as they walked towards the galley. Zachariah inhaled it deeply, the smell filling his lungs making his stomach beg. He licked his lips. People talking became a constant mumbling buzz.

Montgomery opened the door and Zachariah followed him into the small crowded kitchen. The room instantly went silent.

Several black faces, predominately male, looked at both of them curiously. Isaiah walked over to them. "Do you want me, sir?"

Montgomery shook his head. "Gideon."

A thin man with a white apron turned red. Slowly he walked over to them. "Yes, Master?"

"Zachariah is the new Texas tender. Give him your apron."

A deep frown creased Gideon's face. He obeyed, eyes downcast. "Am I to see Arthur or are you going to sell me, Master?" he asked, his voice reedy.

"No. I am taking you back to the reservation with me as a manservant."

Gideon's eyes widened. "Thank you, Master! Thank you."

"Isaiah will tell you what your new duties will be." Montgomery turned to leave. "Zachariah, come with me."

* * *

Zachariah nodded. He followed Mr. Barlow out of the galley. They climbed the stairs to the boiler deck. Zachariah expected to wait tables in the parlor, but instead of heading there they climbed to the hurricane deck.

"As you know this is the officers' deck," Montgomery said. "You will be waiting on the officers taking refreshments to the pilot house and delivering food to their rooms. Arthur will likely have you running errands too, since the cabins boys are kept busy all day waiting on passengers."

"Yes, Master."

They walked into the pilot house. Mr. Barnaby nodded to them and left the room. The captain sat on the sofa and across from him on the leather cushioned bench, sat a blond-haired man Zachariah did not recognize.

"Welcome Mr. Barlow, Reverend Degan," the pilot said, offering a good-natured smile.

Montgomery's face turned grave, his eyes narrowed. He looked at the captain then the pilot and the other man in the room. "Reverend Degan died tragically a month ago. The whole family is in mourning."

"He's not—"

"Do you want to keep your job?" Montgomery said, cutting him off, his voice sharp. "I can easily get another pilot."

The pilot sat back in his seat, blinked several times before answering. "I won't say another word, Boss."

Montgomery nodded. "This is Zachariah," he said emphasizing the end of the word. "He is the new Texas tender. He's had training as a waiter and he's generally polite, but if he forgets his place or gives you trouble send him to Arthur."

"Yes, sir," the captain said.

Zachariah stared at his shoes, his face flushed. The moment of awkward silence mocked him, the universe laughing at the irony.

Finally, Montgomery spoke. "Zachariah, it's a hot day. I would like a glass of lemonade."

All the officers agreed.

Zachariah didn't move or speak.

Montgomery glared at him with surprising coldness. "You know where the galley is, boy, make haste."

"Yes, Master."

Zachariah left the pilot house, climbed down the stairs to the main deck and walked into the galley.

"Zachariah, this is my oldest sister Lacey," Isaiah said. "Lacey this is Zachariah."

Lacey, a handsome slender woman with straight black hair, was a spitting image of her mother. "Glad to be working with you."

Isaiah tapped the taller woman, bent over the stove, on the shoulder. She looked up.

"This is my other sister Savannah. Savannah this is the new Texas tender, Zachariah."

Savannah had homely beauty with a pronounced nose and large lips. She looked more like her father. A few strands of curly black hair peeked out from under her red bandanna. "Nice to meet you," she said, her lips tight, eyes dull. She quickly returned to cooking.

Zachariah didn't reply. He stood there looking at the cooks, waiters, washers and dryers. This seemed a strange nightmare, a product of his active imagination. It had been a long journey to the steamboat, but with every mile he kept expecting to see Lillian around the next corner.

"Did you need something?" Isaiah asked.

"Uh? Oh. Four glasses of lemonade."

Lacey handed him a tray, poured four glasses of lemonade and placed them on the tray. Zachariah carefully carried the glasses up the stairs to the hurricane deck and into the pilot house.

"What took you so long?" Montgomery said, taking his lemonade.

His short, irritated tone took Zachariah by surprise. He bit his lip. "I am sorry, Master."

The officers each took a glass.

Mr. Barlow glared at him, cold unfeeling. "Go see Arthur," he ordered.

"He was not that late," the pilot said.

"Are you sure you do not want to find another job, Mr. Coburn?"

"I am sorry, sir. It was not any of my business."

"That is right. Kindly stick with driving the ship," he said loud and gruff. Montgomery went back to looking at Zachariah. "Are you weak-minded, boy? I said go see Arthur."

Zachariah swallowed hard. "Yes, Master." He slowly headed down the stairs and into the parlor, carrying the empty tray. He found Arthur listening to his wife play the piano. "Master told me to see you."

Arthur scratched his head. "You know how to get to the ship's hold?"

"No."

"No, sir," Arthur corrected then sighed. "Come with me."

The negro man led him down into dark, dusty hold nearly full of cotton bales. He squeezed through the path just big enough for one person. Zachariah's mouth parted. Against the far wall was a roustabout tied in a ball, tears running down his face, his knees drawn up, his arms around his knees. A large stick stuck out between the man's elbow and knee joints, so he could not move. A stick tied in his mouth served as a gag.

Arthur pulled out his gold pocket watch and checked the time and walked over and untied the stick from the man's mouth. The man moaned loudly.

"Do huv mercy, Arthur," he pleaded. "I's real sorry. I's be real respec'ful now on."

Arthur gave the roustabout a hard look. "Next time you back talk to one of the mates I'll give you a good flogging," he said sternly.

"Yessuh. I understand, suh."

Arthur untied him. The roustabout stretched his long limbs, moaning. He grimaced as he massaged his legs.

"Go up on the main deck when you're able," Arthur said, gruff, unfeeling. Then he turned his attention to Zachariah. "What did you do?"

Zachariah blinked. He didn't say anything.

Arthur's eyes narrowed into slits. "You're not going to get any special treatment, Zachariah. And in case you are wondering about lying, I always find out the truth and you will quickly regret it."

Zachariah sucked in his breath, taken aback by his sharpness. "I do no expect special treatment, sir. Master said I worked too slow."

Arthur took a deep breath, his face blank. Something in his eyes worried Zachariah. It was as if Arthur knew more than he could say.

"I expect he just wanted you to see Dave," Arthur said, motioning with his head to the roustabout.

"I am not in trouble?"

"I did not say that. I'm taking away your supper. Now get back to work."

"Yes, Arthur."

He followed the negro man out of the hold. "When you said you were in charge of all the slaves, I did not know you meant discipline."

Arthur grunted.

"What was for supper?" Zachariah asked.

"Leftovers from the cabin passengers."

When Zachariah walked back into the galley, it became silent. The hair on the back of his neck stood on end. An uneasy, fluttering feeling began in his stomach. He shot a look and Lacey and Savannah. The two women wouldn't meet his gaze. He bit his lip. He suspected they'd all been talking about him.

*   *   *

Zachariah slowly got used to his new life. He got used to eating leftovers on the right side of the main deck. The left side reserved for the Irish deckhands. He got used to sleeping on the parlor floor with the other cabin slaves and being roused at odd hours to perform tasks. He quickly learned the names of the slaves in the galley and the other waiters on the ship. It took him longer to learn the names of the roustabouts, white mates, and Irish deckhands.

He paused and looked out at the Mississippi from the boiler deck. They were getting close to New Orleans. His heart ached with the intensity of a broken bone, throbbing sharply with every movement. He remembered his first time in the big city, a shopping trip with Lillian. He wished he could have kept *The Last of the Mohicans* or the gold watch she had given him. Of course anything tying him to his lie-filled life had been stripped away.

Every luxury, every tintype, everything but his memories.

Memories he clung to stronger than life. Memories of Lillian. Memories of the children. Memories of happiness, of family, of love.

* * *

A hand gripped Zachariah's shoulder and he jumped. "Are you all right?" Montgomery asked.

Zachariah blinked at his master. He hadn't said a kind word to him since they had started their journey to the *Princess*.

"Come with me."

Zachariah swallowed and obediently followed his master, choking back tears with each step. Mr. Barlow led him to his stateroom.

"Have a seat," Montgomery said, motioning to the chair by the table. He shut the door and sat on the bed. "You already knew what a slave's life holds for you, that a slave's life is not envied by anyone."

Zachariah wiped the tear off his cheek as if it was a pesky fly. He needed to stop wallowing in self-pity and bravely lie in the lack of bed he had made for himself. Still, anxiety sat on his chest, crushing him like a cotton bale.

"I can see I will have a decent life here, but my heart pains me something awful. I miss Lillian and Jordan and Suzy."

"Next to laying down your life for your family, relinquishing your freedom is the noblest sacrifice you could make. You will see them after the baby is born and old enough to travel. I give you my word."

Zachariah took shallow breaths, struggled for a sense of control. He regained his composure and nodded. That was a long time from now. A long, long time.

He knew it had to be that way.

But if he had to, he'd wait for Lillian for eternity.

"You can write her letters and she can send you letters. Address the letters to me. Arthur will mail them."

"Thank you, Master," he said. He smiled meek and cautious the same as he had dared around Henry. "That is very kind."

Silence drove a wall further between him and Montgomery. A wall he doubted would ever be broken. Zachariah buried his head in his lap.

Montgomery walked over and placed a caring hand on his back. His touch sent competing jolts of uneasiness and comfort through Zachariah's body. Uneasiness won out and landed with force in his gut.

"I want you to have a good life, Zachariah. I am sorry I was cold earlier, but I had to get you readjusted to being a slave. Once you have been on the boat a while, I will give Arthur permission to take you ashore with him and his family."

"Thank you, sir." His question temporarily caught in his throat, but found its way out. "Arthur is far from friendly. Did you—"

"I have instructed Arthur not to be friendly," Montgomery interrupted in a matter-of-fact monotone.

Zachariah wrung his hands in his lap. "Master, did you tell the other slaves not to be friendly too?"

"No." Montgomery paused before explaining, "They will warm up to you in time. It will help when they realize you are going to be treated the same as them. In case you have not noticed, everyone knows that you're Lillian's husband."

Zachariah's ears started to burn, embarrassment spreading the hot flush to his limbs. He wiped his forehead, hoping his touch would ease his ribcage rattling heart. "If only I was not separated from my family this close to Christmas."

"There is quite a celebration on the *Princess* at the holidays. I hope that helps some. Try to think of happier things. I will send you a letter as soon as the baby is born. Do you want a boy or a girl?"

Silent tears Zachariah had tried hard to imprison, broke free and trickled down his cheeks. "I want a boy and I'd like to name him Joseph after the old negro man who befriended me at Hickory Rail Inn. He was like my grandpa. But if it's a girl I'd like to name her Rachel."

"After what you did for her, I am sure Lillian will oblige."

Chapter 32

Natchez, Mississippi
November 6, 1847

ZACHARIAH CARRIED THE captain's breakfast into his room. As usual, the spindly brown-haired man was sitting at his table writing in a journal. He stroked his manicured beard.

"Good morning, sir. Steak, eggs, toast, and coffee," Zachariah announced cheerfully.

The captain shut his journal and cleared the other papers off the desk.

Zachariah took a deep breath and headed out of the room with his empty tray. He didn't even get a thank you.

Isaiah offered an encouraging smile. "Pa has something for you to do."

"Yes, sir."

Isaiah gave him a funny look. "You do not have to call me sir."

Zachariah pressed his lips together, a roar in his ears. He rocked on his heels. "You're free now. I feel like you're above me," he explained, "and since your pa's my boss it just comes naturally."

Isaiah nodded. "I am real sorry, Zachariah. This never should have happened."

"It was God's will. Excuse me, sir."

Zachariah walked into Arthur's room. The negro man was eating breakfast with his wife.

He looked up at the Texas tender a little surprised. "Remember to knock next time."

"Yes, sir. You have an errand for me?"

Arthur pulled a piece of paper and pen from his coat and handed them to Zachariah. "You know what to do."

Zachariah's eyes brightened by the prospect of one of the few pleasures he was allowed. "Yes, sir. Thank you."

He put the paper and pen in his vest pocket and left. He headed to the boiler room with quick, determined strides. The noisy roar of the engine nearly deafened him. Instantly he began to sweat. He looked down at the floor as he walked to make sure he didn't step in a puddle of grease or water. He flashed a smile at the small-framed negro man busy oiling machinery parts.

The white engineer, bent over him playing with the gears looked up and winked. "I do not see you," he said.

"Zachariah." The stoker shouted above the monstrous roar.

The negro man, wearing only dirty trousers, was soaked with sweat. His arm muscles rippled as he tossed more wood into the hungry furnace.

"Doc," Zachariah returned the friendly greeting.

The stoker tilted his head back. "De hammock's yo's."

Zachariah scrambled onto an improvised scaffold above the boiler. He wondered if calling the scaffold a hammock was a joke. Surely, Doc couldn't sleep here—the hottest part of the ship. Zachariah wiped his forehead and then shook off the moisture. He wished Arthur could find a better private spot for him, but this was one place passengers were guaranteed not to go. Zachariah took out the paper and pen and began his letter.

Dear Lillian,

I hope you and the children are well. Please take care of yourself. I wish I could be there with you, especially for the birth of our child. Know I love you with each breath.

Is Suzy still playing with the doll I gave her? Please give Rambler to Jordan when he is older. Keep giving them hugs from me.

I am doing fine. Doc is giving me his hammock so I can write you this letter. I know the other slaves will accept me in time. When he is not working, Jasper plays cards with me. I laugh every time I see the long knife he carries. He scared me half to death with it years ago, when delivering me into your arms.

I wish I was in your arms now. Please stay true to your word. Please free Dorothy and her family. They have been with you so long I doubt they would leave the reservation. Freedom is liberating, illuminating, life-altering. I felt it for a fleeting few years. Let Jake, Martha and Ivy feel the joyousness.

Maybe, some day, I will get an allowance like Arthur. Maybe, some day, I will get the privilege to go ashore in the major cities. Maybe, some day, I can use the learning you gave me.

The river is lonely, especially at night when all the passengers are sleeping. I go out on the deck and look at the stars. I remember what Ma told me when I was a boy. The same stars that are above you are also above me. God's watching over me, just as he's watching over you and our children.

I love you. You will always be my Indian maiden.

He folded the letter, put it in his vest pocket and sighed. There was so much more he wanted to write but he couldn't put it into words and didn't want the heat from the boiler to melt the flesh off his bones. His upper body shook but sweat hid the tears rolling down his cheeks.

"Lillian," he whispered.

Zachariah climbed to the ground and hurried out of the boiler room. He stood on the main deck a moment taking in the fishy smelling breeze, holding his arms out like a bird in flight, hoping to dry some of his sweat. It was useless. He walked back up the stairs and knocked on Arthur's door.

"Come in."

Zachariah entered. He handed Arthur the letter and pen then he picked up Arthur and Charlotte's dirty dishes and carried them back to the galley.

* * *

Once he no longer felt feverish, Zachariah ate his stew then returned to the parlor. He stood against the wall, listening to Charlotte playing the piano and watching the wealthy passengers dining and the men gambling, catching bits of their conversations. Jasper smiled at him. Arthur motioned for him to come near.

"Yes, sir?"

"It doesn't look good you just standing there. Go sing a song with Charlotte. There are many women passengers on this trip. I think they would enjoy it."

Zachariah managed a half-hearted smile and nodded. Singing with Charlotte was the best part of his job.

He walked over to the piano. "What would you like me to sing with you ma'am?"

Charlotte lightly brushed her fingers over the keys. "The Devil's Nine Questions," she said "That is a good duet. Sing loudly now. You have to command their attention."

Zachariah swallowed his jitters, waiting for the song to begin. He sang the question and Charlotte gave the response in an angelic soprano.

Zachariah began the next verse, his smile widened until all his teeth were revealed. He felt the attention of the room focus on him, felt the goodwill in their eyes, felt their pleasure.

After the song, Zachariah returned to the galley and poured himself a cup of coffee.

Another day on the boat, another day without Lillian and his family. He rubbed his eyes with his left hand. The passengers were already routine. The officers were already routine. The stops were already routine. The bells were already routine.

He began wishing for something, anything to break the monotony.

*

Lillian gripped the seat of the carriage. Jake had the horses at a gallop. Been at a gallop whenever they were on open road. Lillian held his manumission paper and his family's manumission papers hostage. Delivered when she was reunited with Zachary. The sooner they met up with the *Princess*, the better.

Jostled about, Lillian's face was permanently tense, panic in her eyes; but she did not utter one complaint. At this speed they felt every rut in the road but if the horses could have gone faster without tipping over the carriage, she would have willed them to. Jordan and Suzy were rocked to sleep with the roll of the wheels. Lillian smiled at them and shook her head. It was unbelievable how trusting children were. They trusted Jake to not crash and they trusted Lillian to see to their protection. The duty weighed down her shoulders.

Soon Zachary would help her raise the children, protect them, and see to their education. She put a hand on her stomach. And the next little one.

Chapter 33

Baton Rouge, Louisiana
November 7, 1847

THE BELL ECHOED through the crisp morning air clear and clamorous, indicating mid watch. Zachariah glanced at the docks looming in the distance. Slowly the boat maneuvered to shore.

Stiff and self-conscious, he carried a tray of tarts into the pilot house. Only the ship's officers were in the room. Not Montgomery. A shiver of relief eased his tension by a hairsbreadth allowing him to smile. He set the tray on the small table.

"Thank you," the captain said.

Zachariah nodded. "Is there anything else I can get you, sirs?"

"No," the pilot replied.

Zachariah turned to leave.

"Zachariah, you can stay here a few minutes if you'd like. We're taking on cotton."

"Thank you, sir."

He stood in the luxurious room looking out the window.

The pilot blew a loud whistle then rang a bell several times to summon the roustabouts to their labor. Slowly, he maneuvered the boat into the landing.

Cotton landings were always a show. He left the pilot house and stood on the hurricane deck, to watch. The steamboat pulled up next to a high bluff rising out of the river. He tilted his head back to see the building on the top of the bluff. The gangplank stretched out to the bank. The roustabouts scrambled ashore like a line of ants.

"Be quick about it you nigger swine," one of the mates said in a gruff, roar. The roustabouts sang as they ran:

> We hear de whistle blowin'
> We hear dat noisy bell
> Callin' us to our labors
> We doan eben get to rest a spell
>
> De Massa he's on board
> So watch what yuh do
> If we please him wid a show
> He might give us a dollar or two
>
> De Cap'n and de massa
> Deir pockets is full of money
> We do de work day and night
> We eben work on Sunday
>
> But do we get paid for our labor? No.
> At least give us brandy for our pains.
> De white man expect us to break our backs
> For deir pers'nal gains.

Zachariah watched in awe as the roustabouts guided cotton bales down the steep decent with a short cotton hook as they ran down the plank behind each bale. The bales slid quickly down the steep slide. Skilled roustabouts loaded one bale after another without any mishap. The mates directed them where to put the bales, while the Irish deckhands pulled the ropes of the capstan, the device that helped hoist cotton bales into place. The bales were stacked high over the railings.

There was a short pause in the loading. Zachariah left the pilot house to get a closer look. He shielded his eyes from the sun and looked to see the problem. His jaw dropped. He saw Dave jump on a bale and fasten the hook to the far side. One of the other roustabouts gave the bale a push over the bank. Dave rode it down all the way to the bottom. When he got off, many of the passengers clapped and cheered. Zachariah did too.

Dave grinned like a dancer asked for an encore. He gave a quick bow before returning to the top of the bluff. With everyone watching, Dave climbed aboard another cotton bale. Zachariah's eyes widened when he realized this time the bale wasn't sliding straight. It caught one of the cables supporting the gangplank and Dave was thrown headlong into the river. As soon as he climbed out of the water one of the mates punched him in the face knocking him back in. Dave swam to the other side and climbed aboard.

The mate who had struck him, marched over to him, his face red. He grabbed a piece of wood from the woodpile, struck Dave in the head, knocking him flat on the deck.

The negro man pushed himself to his feet and was beaten with the piece of wood five more times. Throughout the beating, the mate had a long, expletive-laced talk with him.

Afterward, the roustabout returned to his work and did not ride down any more cotton bales. Zachariah shook his head as the bales continued to be moved to every open space. The ship was large, but he didn't think it had enough room to accommodate the load. When they left the landing, there wasn't free space in the hold for another bale and cotton was stacked along the main deck.

"Dave, go see Arthur," a mate said, his voice strong and forceful, a smile in his eyes. "And I want to see your backside afterward."

Zachariah's stomach knotted. He envisioned Henry smiling smugly with mischievous eyes. Zachariah's lungs tightened, making him dizzy with dread. He put his hands over his face, took slow, shallow breaths, struggled for a sense of control.

*   *   *

"Are you feeling ill?" Isaiah's voice dripped with concern.

Zachariah lowered his hands. He blinked.

"I'll take you ashore in New Orleans. You're a pale shade of green."

"I am fine," Zachariah replied, confused.

Isaiah shook his head. "Don't argue with me. Go down to the hold and rest on a cotton bale. I will do your job for a few hours."

"Thank you."

Isaiah reached out and grabbed Zachariah's hand pressing a piece of paper into his palm. Out of the corner of his eye, Zachariah saw one of the mates watching.

"You are just not used to the life yet. It will grow on you," Isaiah said.

Zachariah grasped his hand tightly around the piece of paper and headed to the ship's hold. Only a small path between the stacks of cotton bales was left. He twisted his body sideways and shuffled along to the back of the hold. In the dark, shadowed by towering bales he unfolded the piece of paper. He strained his eyes, not waiting for them to adjust to the darkness. Squinting, he read the script.

I met Lillian in Vicksburg. She will meet you in New Orleans. I will take you there. She has the children and a plan to flee. No one is to know. Act sick.

Zachariah ripped the paper into mice bite shreds. Act sick. He faked being sick before to avoid seeing Henry but that had required merely staying in his room. This time he'd have to convince Montgomery. He gripped his stomach with both hands. Anxiety and fear and dread turned his stomach, drained the strength from his body. He closed his eyes and took slow, shallow breaths to tame his sudden dizziness.

Sick. He could act sick. This whole plan made him sick.

Chapter 34

New Orleans, Louisiana
November 8, 1847

ZACHARIAH HEARD FOOTSTEPS, light, and quiet. He didn't bother opening his eyes. Sleep offered him comfort. Reprieve from reality. A hand grabbed his shoulder.

"We docked," Isaiah said. "Time to go."

Zachariah sat up though it took great effort.

Isaiah rolled in his lips, his forehead wrinkled. "You really do look ill," his voice sympathetic and soft. "Are you all right?"

Zachariah nodded, not having the strength to speak.

Isaiah took Zachariah's hand and pulled him to his feet. After they made their way to the stairs, Zachariah leaned on him heavily with each step.

When they made it to the deck Zachariah shut his eyes, blocking out the blinding sun.

Isaiah dug his fingers into Zachariah's arm.

Zachariah winced. His eyes opened and he gave Isaiah a sideways glance.

"I am not leading a blind man," Isaiah said, an unusual gruffness to his voice.

Zachariah didn't reply but allowed Isaiah to lead him towards the gangplank. Montgomery stood there talking to one of the mates. Zachariah's pulse palpitated, breathing quickening as they walked closer and closer and closer.

"Mr. Barlow," Isaiah said loud enough to grab his attention. Montgomery stopped what he was saying and turned around. "Zachariah is ill. I would like to take him to a doctor."

Montgomery rubbed his forehead, examining Zachariah. "What's wrong?"

"My stomach pains me, sir," Zachariah said in a weak groan. "And I'm dizzy, no strength."

Montgomery nodded to Isaiah. "Go ahead. Take him ashore," his voice level without a hint of concern. "I'd hate to lose a $2,000 investment. I'll check in on him later and pay the doctor."

Zachariah licked his lips. His former brother-in-law saw him as nothing more than an investment, like a racehorse or a house.

"Yes, sir," Isaiah said.

"Thank you," Zachariah mumbled.

*   *   *

Isaiah assisted him down the gangplank, down the street, and around the corner. Once they were out of sight of the *Princess*, Isaiah stopped and shook Zachariah's shoulder. "I'm not carrying you any farther. You'll have to walk to the doctor's under your own power."

Zachariah stood up straighter, took a deep breath. He didn't know what to say but Isaiah's eyes anticipated words. In a squeaky tone he said, "I can make it." The words assured him.

"I can make it." The second time he believed it.

"You need strength for the journey ahead," Isaiah whispered.

Journey ahead with Lillian and his children. Zachariah's steps became purposeful, almost eager as he approached the doctor's office. Lillian waited for him.

Isaiah knocked on the door.

A gray-haired man answered, his glasses low on his nose. "What do you want?" His tone unfriendly.

"Zachariah is ill. Would you look at him?"

The doctor tilted his head to the left. "That depends. Are you going to pay me?"

"Yes, sir," Isaiah said. "His master will. He works on the *Princess*."

The doctor pushed his glasses up. "You work for Mr. Barlow, boy?"

Zachariah nodded.

The doctor licked his lips slowly the way old folks often do. "Come in."

"Does he know the plan?" Zachariah whispered into Isaiah's ear. His heart clenched and chest tightened. He sure didn't act like it.

Isaiah put a hand on Zachariah's shoulder, steadying his body and his confidence. "He knows. Lillian paid him good."

Zachariah sat on the doctor's table. He strained his ears to hear Lillian's voice or his children. The room was dead silent.

"Take your shirt off," the doctor said. "Let me examine your chest."

Zachariah peeled off his coat and shirt. The doctor's lukewarm hands pressed against his ribs firmly, like he was checking the fat on a heifer. "You feel solid to me. Strong heartbeat." He put his hand on Zachariah's forehead. "You do not have a fever." He stopped and glanced over at his medicine cabinet. "Maybe your clothes are infected. Best get you changed into something clean." He turned back to Zachariah and winked. "I need to go to the store to get some herbs. I'll be right back."

He left. Isaiah followed. The door shut behind them, loud enough to wake all the sleeping hounds.

Zachariah shifted his weight, tired of sitting on the table.

"Zachary Degan," a small, feminine voice called from the back room.

Zachariah's heart flipped. He stepped off the table and wondering if he had imagined it.

"Zachary," the voice called again a little louder this time.

Zachariah's pulse raced faster than his legs. He headed into the back room and found Lillian sitting in a wooden chair with both children crowded in her lap. He gave the three of them quick kisses knowing they didn't have time for a lengthy, tearful reunion.

Lillian pointed to a bundle at her feet. "Your reverend clothes. Change into them. Catherine and Rachel are waiting in the alley with the carriage."

In minutes, Zachariah was dressed in his familiar black outfit. The outfit that brought him instant respect.

"Where are we going?" Zachariah asked.

"We are going to start a new life in San Francisco. I have to buy tickets for the steamboat. Catherine and Rachel are coming with us. I have turned my back on my family to be with you. I do not want you to turn your back on yours."

*   *   *

Those words touched a button buried deep in his soul sending the widest, brightest, happiest grin across Zachariah's face. Family, both of his families together, free and safe.

Lillian stood and handed Suzy to him. She wrapped her chubby arms around his neck. Jordan took Lillian's hand and they headed towards the door.

She shrieked when the doctor walked in, Montgomery behind him.

Montgomery eyes darted from Zachariah to Lillian to the children. "Where the hell do you think you're going?" his gruff voice equal parts anger and confusion.

Zachariah jaw dropped and trembled. Many thoughts entered his head but all failed to reach his mouth.

"What does it look like?" Lillian fired back.

Montgomery's face tensed, his eyes hardened into an unfeeling glare. "It looks like I should have you arrested for stealing my property." His voice, usually restrained and business-like was now loud, harsh, menacing.

Zachariah set Suzy down and she clung to her mother's dress.

Montgomery looked around the room—searching. For what Zachariah didn't know. "Where is Isaiah?" His words barreled out in a growl.

Lillian took a deep breath and replied with eerie calm, "Isaiah went back to the ship. He did not know about this. He thought

Zachariah was ill. You did too or you would not have allowed him to go ashore."

Montgomery revealed his gritted teeth. "I hate being taken for a fool. You and your sister think you can do whatever you want with my money. Well, I'm not going to allow you to take Zachariah and live in sin for the rest of your life. I did you a favor by buying him. A 2,000 dollar favor. I did that out of love and I am also keeping you from this damn nigger out of love."

Montgomery lunged forward and grabbed Zachariah's arm. "You are coming back with me if I have to tote you there bound and gagged over my saddle."

Zachariah winced as Montgomery's fingers dug into his arm. He was held captive not by a reserved ship owner but by a beast.

"Stop hurting him!" Lillian said in a loud whine, trying to pry off Montgomery's grip. "I expected to compensate you for your loss."

"Uncle Montgomery," Jordan said, "let Pa go," he said in a childish squeal.

Suzy screamed. "You're hurting him!"

Montgomery's face softened slightly. He let go of Zachariah's arm but held the back of his coat collar to keep him still. "Compensate me how?"

"Andrew. I'll give you Andrew."

"Andrew," Montgomery spit out his name like it was an unripe peach. "That clumsy ox. He's fit to be a roustabout or fireman and nothing else. I need a Texas tender."

"Andrew is strong. You can sell him. Get your money back and buy a more refined slave to wait on you and your damn officers."

*

Lillian's stomach tightened into more knots than she could count. If Montgomery was going to make this a battle, she was ready.

"Doctor, please leave us," Montgomery said, low, forceful, in a tone meant to be obeyed immediately.

The doctor nodded and walked outside.

Montgomery shifted an ear towards the door. Satisfied, he straightened and glared at his sister-in-law. "Running off with Zachary is a bad idea, Lillian. A very bad idea."

"Zachary is a good reverend. You said so yourself. It worked once, it will work again. There isn't as much racism in San Francisco."

"Not as much racism against negroes, but there sure as hell is racism against Indians."

Lillian puffed out her chest, her shoulders back in a conscious display of strength and defiance. "I can handle it. Zachariah and I can handle it."

"You might think you can handle it now, until you are actually faced with it. It Is not too late to return home to the reservation. Marry Mr. Harris."

"I am already married. To Zachary. The Nation might have divorced us, but when I said my vows I meant them. God knows I meant them."

"If you do not marry Mr. Harris, you will be turning your back on your family."

"I know."

"Not just your parents, but Bessie too."

Lillian's lips pressed into a grim line. "If that is the way it has to be. My children need their pa."

Montgomery took a step forward dragging Zachary with him. He locked eyes with Lillian. "How are you going to survive? How are you going to support yourself? You'll have no horses, no garden, no house. Zachariah won't even have a congregation. He'll have to build a church."

"I have faith that God will provide for us. Faith in Zachariah's abilities."

Montgomery laughed, loud, mocking. "Do not be so sure. On the reservation he had people needing direction. He had you giving him credibility among the Nation. In San Francisco he's just going to be another black robe in a sea of preachers."

"I. Do. Not. Believe. That."

"Since you will not listen to reason," Montgomery said, "I am forced to take away the temptation." He opened the door, yanked

Zachary's arm behind his back, and held him with all his strength. "Move."

"Stop!" Lillian's voice an angry plea.

Jordan and Suzy screamed. They broke into tears and charged after their pa.

*

Zachariah headed down the street, grimacing, fearing Montgomery would break his bone. His arm wasn't meant to be contorted in this way.

His stomach tightened and tightened and tightened. His raging pulse rang in his ears like a loud warning bell.

Disaster.

He was headed for disaster.

Sweat soaked his clothes despite the winter chill.

Lillian shouted, her voice cracking. "Montgomery, stop."

Zachariah turned his head. She ran after him as fast as she could, holding Suzy and Jordan's hands. She might as well be a snail chasing a rabbit.

"I do not have time to put you up for auction," Montgomery said, his words rushed together. "I know who will buy you without any questions. Your paper's on the ship. He'll get that later. It will be legal. Too bad you have to stay in those clothes."

Zachariah wanted to speak, needed to speak. He licked his lips then choked out the words, "Who are you selling me to?" That's not what he wanted to say but gushing about his love for Lillian would just make the situation worse.

"I am selling you to someone to work his cotton plantation. Mr. Garrah takes all the hands he can get. Works them hard."

Hard? Zachariah's lungs twisted, making it difficult to breathe. Did that mean he worked them to death? He was not about to ask.

Zachariah prayed long, hard, earnest. Prayed that Lillian's love would melt Montgomery's money-hungry heart.

*   *   *

"Montgomery Vincent Barlow," Lillian's high-pitched voice echoed through the air, sharp, grating. "You sell Zachary and I will tell the authorities about all the cargo you have transported on your ship."

Montgomery stopped and turned around, still holding Zachariah prisoner.

His eyes bulged, glazed with panic, his mouth partly open. "What do you mean *all* the cargo?" he asked in an unsteady voice.

"Slaves are not the only people you've transported in chains," Lillian said in an innocent yet threatening tone.

Montgomery's face turned as white as the snow on the mountain tops.

"You could spend a good stint behind bars for breaking your cousin out of jail and helping him get to Canada."

"How, how did you know that?" Montgomery stammered.

"All your slaves have ears," Lillian replied, a sly, slippery smile on her lips.

"My cousin was innocent," Montgomery said. "He was framed. They were going to hang him."

"The court convicted him. He wasn't the only person wrongly persecuted."

Montgomery's lip quivered but he clamped them shut. With sharp, narrow eyes he looked at Lillian as if testing her resolve.

Zachariah's skin goose pimpled. Who would blink first? It seemed like hours though it was only minutes.

Montgomery dropped Zachariah's arm. "Fine. Take him."

Zachariah ran into Lillian's embrace.

"This still is not going to end well," Montgomery warned, his voice gentler than before. "But you have my back up against a wall. Don't come crying to me when San Francisco is not all that you expected."

Lillian kissed Zachariah long, warm and sensual. He felt the heat of her body against him, smelled her perfume. Their hearts were connected, their souls were connected.

Their lives were connected. That was all that mattered.

Their future was in their hands. They just had to grasp it.

Epilogue

San Francisco, California
January 12, 1867

DEAR MRS. BARLOW,

I take pen in hand to send you some very sad news. Lillian has cancer and the doctor says she only has a few months left to live. I pray that you take this time to rekindle your sisterly bond. I have given up on Mr. and Mrs. Hildebrand. They have returned every letter we have written unopened.

Is love such a grievous sin? Now that the Civil War is over and all the slaves freed does it still matter that I have a drop of negro blood in my veins? I am blessed that Lillian did not think so. She has been a loving wife and devoted mother all these years. It is hard to believe our children our grown. Jordan, Suzy, and Joseph are taking her illness better than I am. I take strength from them.

I must close now. I feel tears welling in my eyes. My children, family, faith and congregation are helping me through this difficult time. But as much as we try, I do not feel Lillian has found peace. She is taking laudanum to dull the pain, but in these final days her heart aches worse than the cancer destroying her body. She has made my family complete. She has made my dreams come true. She has filled our home with love.

She wishes to share this love with you, if only you will accept it. Sometimes in her drug-induced sleep she mumbles about the past on the reservation—about you and Montgomery and her parents. Please visit her before it is too late.

Your brother-in-law,
Zachary Degan

Connect with the Author

Dear Reader,

Thank you for reading *Living Half Free*. I hope you enjoyed Zachariah's journey to manhood, his struggle to find his voice, and realize his faith. Since I was a little girl, I have been fascinated with history, especially the 1800s. Mark Twain is my biggest inspiration. *The Adventures of Huckleberry Finn* is one of my favorite stories. I've always wanted to take a steamboat ride down the Mississippi. So what does an author do? Research, imagine it, and bring it to life!

I have a history B.A and a teaching endorsement. It has been my dream to write and share little known U.S history with the world. I was shocked to learn that many people did not know that some slaves had white skin just like their masters. That realization spurred a dream which became Zachariah's story.

This is my first novel. More novels are coming soon! Subscription to my newsletter and visits to my website, http://HaleyWhitehall.com, will give you access to freebies, outtakes, contests and all things history.

A good novel is the best way to experience history. Don't you think?

Sincerely, Haley

I love to hear from readers! You connect with me online:

Twitter: https://twitter.com/#!/HaleyWhitehall

Facebook: http://www.facebook.com/HaleyWhitehallAuthor

Fan Page: http://www.facebook.com/LightonHistory

Goodreads: http://www.goodreads.com/user/show/5752668-haley-whitehall

Weblog: http://haleywhitehall.com/

Grits and Glory

(Plantation Shadows Series, Book 1)

During the Civil War, Peter Warren, a disowned Southern gentleman spies for the Union army. Plagued by memories of his alcoholic father's brutality on their plantation, he has vivid flashbacks and nightmares which could betray his identity with a slip of the lip. He also fears being recognized as an Underground Railroad conductor since posters with his likeness blanket the South. To make his situation worse, his father has offered a large reward for his capture. As the war progresses, he is torn between fulfilling his duty, and saving his skin.